CHARLOTTE BINGHAM

'A perfect example ...

a t...

The Nightingale Sings
'A novel rich in dramatic surprises, with a large cast
of vivid characters whose antics will have you
frantically turning the pages'
Daily Mail

To Hear A Nightingale
'A story to make you laugh and cry'
Woman

The Business
'A compulsive, intriguing and perceptive read'
Sunday Express

In Sunshine Or In Shadow
'Superbly written . . . A romantic novel that is romantic
in the true sense of the word'
Daily Mail

Stardust
'A long, absorbing read, perfect for holidays'
Sunday Express

Change of Heart
'Her imagination is thoroughly original'
Daily Mail

Nanny
'Charlotte Bingham's spellbinding saga is required reading'
Cosmopolitan

Grand Affair
'Extremely popular . . . her books sell and sell'
Daily Mail

Debutantes
'A big, wallowy, delicious read'
The Times

The Kissing Garden

Charlotte Bingham

BANTAM BOOKS

LONDON · NEW YORK · TORONTO · SYDNEY · AUCKLAND

THE KISSING GARDEN
A BANTAM BOOK: 0553 507176

Simultaneously published in Great Britain by Doubleday,
a division of Transworld Publishers Ltd

PRINTING HISTORY
Doubleday edition published 1999
Bantam Books edition published 1999

Set in 11/13pt Palatino by
Phoenix Typesetting, Ilkley, West Yorkshire

Bantam Books are published by Transworld Publishers Ltd,
61-63 Uxbridge Road, London W5 5SA,
in Australia by Transworld Publishers,
c/o Random House Australia (Pty) Ltd,
20 Alfred Street, Milsons Point, NSW 2061,
in New Zealand by Transworld Publishers,
c/o Random House New Zealand,
18 Poland Road, Glenfield, Auckland,
in South Africa by Transworld Publishers,
c/o Random House (Pty) Ltd,
Endulini, 5a Jubilee Road, Parktown 2193.

Reproduced, printed and bound in Great Britain by
Mackays of Chatham plc, Chatham, Kent

For Terence
My inspiration
As always

Foreword

The idea for the Kissing Garden came to me when our house was being blessed, for it was then that I noticed that while every nook and cranny received a prayer, the garden is usually ignored. What spirits of the past danced and swayed beneath our ancient yews, I wondered? Whose were the initials on the old sundial? And so this book was born, perhaps influenced by some enchanted shade from long ago.

Hardway, 1998

Long Ago

It was hedged on four sides, walled by dense ever-
green in which robins nested and sweet-smelling
columbine grew. From the inside it would appear
there was no entrance to this most secret of places
until the eye was drawn to one corner which
seemed not to run perfectly true. Here in fact was
the only entrance, a gap set behind a step in the
growth like a small antechamber, wide enough
to admit only one person at a time. Beyond these
high green walls on three sides lay dense wood-
lands which in spring were carpeted with small
white and blue-belled flowers and in winter were
half buried in deep, enveloping snow. Beyond
the fourth wall, the hedge containing the hidden
entrance, a bank ran down to the edge of a lake
which was surrounded by a forest of trees, while
high in the skies above them larks sang and
occasionally a great hawk could be seen hung
suspended in motion.

It was here one misty autumn morning that
they brought his body to his final resting place.
They laid him to sleep below the ground on
which he had once stood dreaming of their future,
covering him with its rich earth. At that moment

the birds in the dark woods stopped their song and the creatures hidden in the shadows of the trees abandoned their hunting. Only one bird sang, a robin: perched on long thin legs and puffing his beacon-like breast, he sent forth a thread of silvery sound that echoed over the russet landscape and hung in the quiet misty air.

Minutes later they took to the boat once more and started to make their silent way back across the lake. Halfway across one of the men held up a gauntleted hand and his companions stopped rowing, as the man in the prow took up something from the bottom of the boat, a glittering silver object which caught the pale rays of a sun that was now breaking through the October mist. For a moment he held the object high, until with the sunlight still glinting sharply on its silvered surface he dropped it over the side, watching silently with the rest as it disappeared into the black waters to settle far below them in the darkness. And from that time, as the lake closed its waters over its hidden treasure, no hail or rain, nor any snow fell on that sacred place, nor was any winter wind allowed to trumpet its triumph.

Part One
1919

'When you are deluded and full of doubt,
even a thousand books of scripture
are not enough.'

Fen-Yang

One

He appeared out of the smoke as if from battle, standing to attention by the huge locomotive which had drawn the dozen teeming carriages into Midhurst station. Amelia felt her mother's hand under her elbow tighten, preparing to restrain her from running towards him, and making some unseemly display. But she need not have bothered, for it was clear that he was neither looking at Amelia nor indeed for her. He was simply standing, as if still on the battlefield, his gaze fixed far over their heads.

'George?'

Amelia heard Lady Dashwood call out suddenly from the group standing just ahead of her, then watched as she detached herself to hurry to her son's side.

'George, my dear, dear boy!' she cried. 'Home, home the warrior!'

With her own mother still holding her back, Amelia watched as Lady Dashwood stood on the tips of her toes to kiss her tall, handsome son on the cheek. She knew her mother was restraining her because it was not Amelia's place to be the first to welcome George home. They had discussed the

3

protocol on the journey to the railway station, much as if they were discussing the formalities of a social arrangement rather than the safe return from war of a man now loved by two families. And Amelia knew her mother's directions were right, for although George Dashwood and Amelia Dennison had long ago promised each other they would marry, and although this fact was well known to both their families, they were still not officially engaged.

Even so, it was almost more than Amelia could bear just to stand and watch as the Dashwood family surrounded the man with whom she had been so longing to be reunited that she had been unable to sleep properly since she had learned the date of his return. All who loved George had lived for this moment but perhaps none so much as the dark-haired young woman who for four long years had prayed every night for the safe return of the childhood friend who she fervently hoped would soon be her husband. At this moment all she wanted was to do what she had dreamed of doing at this time, to run to George, put her arms round his neck and tell him how much she had missed him and how agonizing had been their separation, but instead she had to remain dutifully where she was, a dozen or so paces from where the uniformed General Dashwood had now come forward to welcome his only son.

'Captain Dashwood,' General Dashwood said,

acknowledging his son as he might any of his junior officers.

'Sir,' George replied, raising his hand in salute.

'I know that's *correct*,' Clarence Dennison sighed to his wife and daughter, safely out of earshot. 'But hardly necessary, surely? After more than four years at the front? Could he not just shake hands? Hardly a court martial offence, I'd have thought, but then that's General Dashers all over.'

'Clarence,' his wife sighed, taking his arm. 'Not everyone is as demonstrative as you, my love. Particularly the military. And I think we're about to be summoned.'

She nodded ahead, where Lady Dashwood had turned to face them, indicating with the index finger of one gloved hand that the Dennisons could now join the welcoming party.

'Something's the matter,' Amelia whispered to her mother as they moved forward. 'You can see it from her face.'

But it was at George, not Lady Dashwood, Amelia was looking so anxiously as she approached, for he still seemed to be staring into the distance somewhere over Amelia's head, still not acknowledging her presence.

'George?' Lady Dashwood was saying, now with a definite note of anxiety in her voice, prompting Amelia to take a more measured look at the homecoming hero. 'George, dear? Amelia is here, George. Do you see? Amelia and her parents.'

Lady Dashwood turned and all but impercep-tibly shook her head at the Dennisons.

'I'm afraid it might be proving a little too much just at this moment,' she said with her back to George. 'But then he was often like this as a small boy, coming home from school.'

Amelia did her best to acknowledge a remark she knew to be an excuse before touching one of George's hands lightly with her own.

'George?' she said. 'It's me. Amelia.'

'Amelia?' George said, now looking down at her with a smile. 'Amelia – how wonderful to see you. Forgive me – I'm sorry I was a little distracted. Forgive me, won't you? It's just – it's just been a bit of a long journey.'

'Haven't found your shore legs yet, that's all,' his father remarked, brushing the edge of his white moustache upwards with the back of one index finger. 'Simply hasn't found his shore legs.'

'That's all right, George,' Amelia said, smiling up at him but noticing the faraway look that was still in his eyes. 'I'm so happy to see you. And so glad you're home safe, at long, long last, George.'

They were such silly little words. Words that covered days, and nights, months and hours of just one prayer. *Please, please God, help George to be all right*.

'And I'm so very happy to see you, Amelia,' he assured her, offering her his hand, which Amelia was not altogether sure whether she was meant to shake or to hold. 'You must understand – if you

6

can. This is all a bit – well. A bit overwhelming.'

'Of course.'

Given the number of people who appeared to be staring at them Amelia chose to shake George's hand, feeling more than slightly ridiculous, since all she really wanted to do was to put her arms about him and try to vanquish the memories of the last five nightmare years. However, she had no idea if that was what George wanted or not, because rather than continue talking to her, or even looking at her, he was again staring into the distance somewhere a long way past her.

Two

The two families travelled back from the station to Dashwood House in separate motor vehicles, the Dennisons' old pre-war Hillman 6 following the Dashwoods' brand new Lanchester, purchased by the general in celebration of the Peace, past Itchenor harbour with its gaily painted sailboats, its air of invitation to holiday. Out on the waters Amelia could see a small blue and white-painted dinghy, almost identical to the one in which George had taught Amelia to sail seven long summers ago, when she was a twelve-year-old and George was sixteen, and any talk of war had been vague, and confined to adult circles only.

The weather had been perfect, a long unbroken summer which the young had spent messing about in and around boats, swimming in the warm fresh seawater off the Sound and walking high on the Sussex Downs with their dogs, the Dennisons' cheerful fox terrier and the Dashwoods' pair of English setters.

Once, Amelia remembered, when the two of them were out alone, searching for fossils in the chalk high up on the Downs, George had teased her by saying that, since they were such good friends, perhaps one day they might marry? Amelia had thought the idea so hugely funny that she had exploded with laughter. Her laughter continued for such an age that she ended up being chased by George, wrestled to the ground and tickled.

'Stop it! Stop it! I'll promise you anything, if only you will stop!'

'I certainly don't want you to marry me!' George had retorted, refusing to ease up his tickling. 'I can't think of anything worse than being married to you, Amelia Dennison!'

Finally he had let her go, rolling full-length down the hill pursued by barking dogs while Amelia tried to compose herself, sitting on the summit and pulling the dried summer grass from her long brown hair, hoping she would always be this happy, hoping against hope that she and George would somehow escape growing up; or if they did have to grow up they would always be together as they were now, laughing and happy, and full of that childhood ease that is so companionable.

They had known each other for as long as either of them could remember, their two families having, it seemed to both George and Amelia, always been friends. Never mind that the Dashwoods were military and the Dennisons artistic, in Sussex, a county which embraced its poets and its painters, it seemed that no-one found this odd, and it was a common sight for General

Dashwood and Clarence Dennison to be seen strolling the Downs together rapt in conversation, or calling in at the Spread Eagle for a 'little something' on a stormy day after rain had 'stopped play'.

But, of a sudden, on Midhurst Station, it had seemed to Amelia that the past was no longer of any importance, and that far from being intimates of each other, the two families had stood apart from each other, all too aware that the Dashwoods were the *Dashwoods*, and the Dennisons merely *bohemic* as Amelia had often heard Lady Dashwood describing her parents.

Not that they had discouraged George's growing love for Amelia. They had neither discouraged it, nor encouraged it. And so when George came home on leave from the front in time to help celebrate Amelia's sixteenth birthday and had realized how much he was in love with the pretty, vivacious dark-haired girl whom, it seemed to him, he had known all his life, it had come as no surprise to either family when he made plain his intention to propose to Amelia as soon as was perfectly possible after the war was over, which just at first, they had all thought would be pretty soon.

That had been nearly four years ago now, and while they had all done nothing but hope and pray for the young handsome boy who had gone off so confidently to fight for his country, and who had, at first, written to Amelia that he would be back to marry her 'sooner than you can turn round' they had none of them thought that they would be greeting – a stranger.

Amelia frowned as she stared out of the window at the all too familiar fields and hills that they were passing, at the cows, at the leaves on the trees, each one of which seemed to be frowning back at her as she wrestled with the reality of the last hour. She had imagined a maimed George, a George without an arm, a George who might have been gassed, but not what she had just seen on the station, someone who had, in effect, gone missing.

Sensing her disquiet, Constance tapped her daughter sharply on the shoulder making Amelia jump.

'Uncross your ankles, darling – so common, you'll give Lady Dashers a blue fit if she sees you like that.'

Tea had already been set out on the lawn in the shade of the old beech trees. Trees which George had taught her to climb behind the backs of their parents, and up which they would both sit for what had seemed like hours on end being bored to tears by the conversation of the unsuspecting grown-ups below.

But now they were the 'grown-ups,' and George was sitting beneath the comforting shade of those same branches, as the shadows of the afternoon lengthened, but there were no children up the trees, just a uniformed officer below, silent, wordless, his hat and swagger stick on a chair beside him.

Everything about him was quite still, excepting one hand which gently stroked the heads of the family dogs, the sunlight catching the gold of his signet ring. Perhaps because of this almost statue-like stance he was largely ignored by his family and friends, who sat eating their cucumber sandwiches talking to each other, politely and decorously, as if the appalling calamity which had just befallen the world had been a single skirmish in a distant foreign field.

Now George had been welcomed home, it seemed that Clarence would return to his usual light banter as he sat alternatively sketching and sipping tea. That Constance would gossip to Lady Dashwood about the 'ghastly newness' of some house being built nearby. That everything would just resume, return to being what it had been two hours before the train came chugging merrily into the little Sussex station, and they had finally seen the reality of George, home at last. Even his father seemed reluctant to engage in any lengthy dialogue, although as Amelia suddenly determinedly moved her chair nearer to George, she did hear him say, 'Good about your decoration, George, makes one very proud. The first in the family, you know. Quite something that.'

'Thank you, Father.'

'Lucky fellow, you know. Seeing as much action as you did.'

'Quite.'

'Think what you'll have to tell your children,

12

and your grandchildren. First-hand accounts of the greatest war ever fought. First-hand accounts, quite something that, I should have thought.'

'So I shall, Father.'

'Better than fighting a war from behind a desk in Whitehall, I can tell you. They wouldn't send me back out, after Ypres, unfortunately.'

At that word 'unfortunately' George turned and stared at his father, or rather, it seemed to Amelia, that he stared through him. As if he was a ghost, or as if, Amelia suddenly thought, as if behind the General, beyond him on the lawn, George saw only ghosts.

'No, you can't fight a war from behind a desk, my boy.'

'No, sir. I think that became increasingly apparent.'

The General went on to say something, but seemed to think better of it, clearing his throat instead and drumming his fingers on one knee as he tried to form the words that were in his mind. 'It will all fit into place soon, George. Take my word for it. It always does after a war, take a bit of time. Now here is young Amelia, come to make you laugh, doubtless. The way she always did, eh?'

How Amelia wished that the General had not said that she was to make George 'laugh'. It made her feel so utterly lightweight, and more than faintly ridiculous. How could she make someone 'laugh' who had just lost all his friends in a terrible war?

Feeling more inadequate than she had ever felt, in desperation she plumped for those small and insignificant generalities which pass for conversation in polite society, remarking on the clemency of the weather for such a special day, the state of the Dashwoods' garden and the number of friends who were about to call on the Dashwoods to welcome him home. To her relief George seemed more than happy to hold their conversation at this level, so Amelia did her best to keep him entertained, until she finally felt brave enough to touch on what she had written to him in her letters, reminding him of the funny, silly sketches of home life she had drawn for him. After a quarter of an hour spent in this fashion, George seemed a great deal more relaxed, eventually beginning to ask questions of his own, and starting to smile and even to laugh at shared memories drawn now from childhood, now from her letters. Gradually it seemed as if they both relaxed, until for a long lovely moment as they sat in the warm summer sunshine Amelia felt as if George had hardly been away from her at all, let alone for five long and dreadful years.

'I had forgotten quite what a trout I was to your mayfly.' George smiled suddenly while gently pulling his dog's ears. 'And how skilful you were at casting.'

Amelia smiled back, also fondling the dog sitting between them.

'What's it like to be home, George?'

'What do you think?' George looked around him at the party in the lovely garden and at the fine stone house his grandfather had built for his family. 'What do you think, Amelia,' he repeated, but not as a question. 'After all this time away.'

They both fell silent, as George continued to stare without any apparent emotion at his surroundings, still rhythmically stroking his dog's fine head. After a long moment he sighed and closed his eyes, as if suddenly infinitely weary, sitting back with his arms folded across his chest.

'Would you rather not talk, George? You must be so dreadfully tired after your journey. And after – well. You must be most dreadfully tired.'

'On the contrary, I'd rather talk,' George said, without opening his eyes. 'Don't worry about me. Tell me all that's happening here. All the gossip about our friends.'

To indulge him Amelia related all the most frivolous gossip she could remember, and what she failed to remember she invented, keeping George entertained with the behaviour, supposed or otherwise, of all her girl friends, particularly her best friend Hermione – who, as both she and George knew, was just as struck on George as Amelia – until inevitably she arrived at the subject she most wished to discuss but was almost afraid to mention: the arrangements for her forthcoming birthday. As soon as she broached the matter George stopped smiling and fell into silence.

'Is something wrong, George?' Amelia began to

falter, aware of George's sudden mood change. 'I haven't said anything to upset you, have I?'

'Not a thing. I was just thinking, that's all.'

'Can I know what you were thinking? Or was it private?'

'If you must know, I was thinking that you might be a little short of dancing partners compared to – before the war, you know, when you used to have so many. That's how I used to think of you when I was out there, dancing round and round, and laughing up at some lucky young man.'

Not knowing how to reply lest she should say something utterly tactless, Amelia kept quiet, knowing that what George had observed was perfectly true. She and her mother had already encountered the greatest difficulty in trying to produce any sort of guest list.

'I'm afraid it's a shortage which is going to prove a national one,' George said after a silence. 'A shortage it isn't going to be easy to correct. Will you excuse me?'

As George stood up from his chair Amelia said in a low voice, 'I didn't mean to upset you.'

'You haven't. It's just that I'm a little tired, and perhaps I talked too much.'

'You mean I talked too much.'

'You were as delightful as always.' George smiled at her. 'I really am very tired. So will you excuse me?'

'Of course.'

Amelia got up as George left her and went to sit with her father, who was sketching in a pad on his knee in the shade of an old apple tree. She watched George disappear into the house before sitting herself down again.

'Everything all right, Amelia?' her father wondered, glancing in the direction in which he saw his daughter was looking.

'I think I tired him out with my prattle, Papa. I wasn't really thinking.'

'I'm quite sure you were, darling girl. You're not one to do things without thinking. Never have been.'

'What are you drawing?'

'People.'

'May I see?'

'I'm not sure you should.' He looked at her, sighed, and then turned his sketch book round to her. He had drawn the gathering of people they could both see before them, seated and dressed as they were, drinking their tea and eating their sandwiches, and he had drawn George as well, bang in the middle of them. But instead of wearing his best uniform he was dressed in battle fatigues, with a helmet instead of a cap and a pistol in his hand instead of a teacup, and he was standing in a trench, not sitting on a garden seat, with the bodies of his dead comrades at his feet.

Amelia stared at the drawing. She was used to her father's poetic and often abstract interpretation of life, but somehow, because this was about

17

George, and their friends who would never return, about the past which must be going to make for a very different and perhaps much more complicated future than they had ever anticipated, she was shocked. All the time he had seemed to be just passing the time of day, this was how he had been feeling.

'It's all right,' her father assured her. 'I'm not going to show it to anyone else. Least of all George.'

'I do hope he's all right,' Amelia said, looking back at the house into which George had taken himself. 'Although I am quite sure he is not.'

'I'm quite sure you're right, Amelia. But I'm quite sure he will be. Given time. The thing is not to press too hard.' Her father closed his sketch book and began to fill his briar pipe. 'The point is – try as we may, it doesn't make any difference, because people like us can have no real idea. Not about what George has been through. We can't have even the very slightest of ideas. So the thing is not to press too hard.'

He put his hand on hers and squeezed it. 'He will be all right, Amelia. Just give him time.'

'But now he's home, Papa—'

'Now that he's home, darling girl, he is going to find matters even *harder* to bear. What seems to you to be all behind him now will be in the front of his mind every hour of every day. And possibly every minute of his night, too. So just give it time.'

*   *   *

18

Anxious to hear what her mother might have to say on the matter of George's welfare, Amelia sought her out before dinner that night, finding her in her dressing room where she was trying on a newly fashionable amber necklace and earrings.

'You don't have to be actually shell-shocked to be shell-shocked, if you get my meaning,' Constance Dennison told her, leaning forward at her dressing table the better to examine her complexion. 'Not that we women are expected to understand the niceties of war, you realize. Even though we're the ones who actually give birth to soldiers. But then there you are. If men will make wars then it is the men who must fight them until one of them sees sense. Although why people want to fight each other the whole time is quite beyond me. Now I need reminding who we have coming to dinner this evening. Do you know who we've invited, Amelia darling?'

Amelia told her who their guests were that evening, and then while her mother continued to make herself ready she stared out of the bedroom window at the landscape beyond and recalled the walk she and George had taken up on the Downs during his last leave. A sudden summer storm had blown up and caught them unawares, driving them to shelter in an old shepherd's shed tucked in the cleft of a hill back on to the prevailing winds. They had stood there in silence at first, watching the changing patterns of light and shade as the rain swept in torrents across the landscape, but when the thunder began and the vivid lightning forked the brooding sky Amelia had become really frightened, as she so often was by storms. George had remembered this and given her his hand. She had often held his hand before, when she needed help over a stile or up a steep hill or climbing a tall tree, but this time the feeling was different, as electric as the lightning that was ripping the skies above them, so that when she had found herself looking up into George's deep blue eyes it came as no surprise to find that George was looking back at her, as if they had both snapped on the moment as they had so often snapped on the same playing card.

Amelia knew then, as George did, that only death could part them, but on that stormy summer's day, although the sky was full of thunder and the clouds had burst with rain, death was the most distant thing from both their minds, even though now as she remembered the moment it seemed the skies had been filled not with thunder but with the rumble of great and distant guns.

'I wonder if George will propose,' Amelia said, coming out of her reverie and picking up the dark red velvet gown her mother had decided to wear with her new jewellery.

'How on earth should I know, Amelia dear,' her mother replied, stepping out of her dressing robe and unfastening her hair. 'As your father always says, we all spend too much time in speculation and not enough in creation. I should *imagine* he will, of course. Why should he not? Unless of course he's fallen for some foreign floozie or other over there, but then that would hardly be George, would it?'

'Of course it wouldn't, Mama. At least I hope not.'

'Then you will just have to wait and see.'

'It's just that I don't want him to feel that he has to,' Amelia explained. 'Simply because of what he said on his last leave. Papa said he needed time to recover—'

'George is man enough to sort out his own worries, darling,' Constance interrupted. 'Now be a good girl and call Rose.'

'Rose *left*, Mama,' Amelia reminded her. 'After her brother was killed on the Somme.'

'Of course. How stupid of me. What's this new girl called?'

'Betty, Mama. You should know by now.'

'I know I should. It's just that Rose was with me for so long. Blasted war. Now be an angel and find me Betty or I shall be even later than usual. And do stop looking so *anxious*. The war is over, and George is home. Just think of all those other poor young women who aren't quite so fortunate.'

'Of course, Mama. I'm sorry.'

Duly chastened, Amelia went in search of her mother's maid before going herself to change for dinner. Her father was dressed and ready by the time Amelia finally came back downstairs, sitting at his desk in one window of the drawing room, writing in another of the specially bound marbled notebooks which he favoured for both his poetry and his sketches of people's dogs or horses – painting, and particularly animal portraits, being his other great gift.

It was this talent far more than his verses that had endeared him to Society – and this despite the fact that he was much in demand by local hostesses who loved him to stand up and declaim his latest poetic works. But although such recitals were received in courteous if not reverential silence, they were not appreciated to quite the same degree as his portraits of spaniels or retrievers waiting for their masters. These deliberately evocative and extremely well executed paintings, with titles such as *Are You Coming Walks?* or *Waiting for Mistress*, had brought to Clarence Dennison the kind of affection which only the English can bestow on a favoured painter. He himself settled his artistic conscience with the knowledge that without such a profitable sideline he would not be able to produce the poetry that was his true vocation.

This evening Clarence was writing rather than sketching and seeing his concentration Amelia knew better than to interrupt him, instead sitting down quietly by the open French windows to watch myriad small white butterflies fluttering around the pale blue night-scented stocks.

'Done,' he suddenly announced, putting his pen down and getting up from his desk. 'At least

I think it is. See what you think, Amelia.'

'I'm listening,' Amelia said, settling herself in her chair.

'It's only the first verse,' Clarence explained. 'Although maybe this is in fact only a one-verse poem anyway. See what you think:

Quiet now the guns their killing done
War's fodder buried piecemeal in the mud;
Unclaimed their shortened journeys run
To lie beneath a simple wooden cross
Asleep for ever in a grave they won
In battle for a yard of ground they lost
The month before – at fearful cost
To mothers who had borne their sons
To fall beneath these mighty guns
Silent now their killing done.'

'It's very good,' Amelia said, as her father closed his notebook. 'Though maybe not one to read out over dinner,' she added wryly.

'I know what you mean. But you like it, do you, Amelia?'

'I'm not sure it's possible to like something so tragic.'

'*Like* is the wrong word, of course. I suppose what I meant was – is it good? And that's not fair either. You're hardly going to tell me whether it's any good or not.'

'I have before, Papa.'

'Have you? When?'

'When you wrote that awful poem about blue-bells. It wasn't you at all.'

'I still like it.'

'No-one else does. Even so, I remember regretting telling you, because you sulked for a week.'

'Did I? *Did* I?' Clarence frowned and then suddenly laughed. 'Yes – yes I think I did, didn't I? Now – where's Grimes got himself to? A man could die of thirst in this household.' Clarence Dennison rang the bell by the fireplace to summon his butler. 'But this . . .' He tapped his notebook which he still had in his hand. 'I think this is more the stuff. The first line came to me after we'd finished talking this afternoon, and you'd gone to find Hermione. And I went on watching everyone making tea and exchanging small talk as if the last nightmare years had never happened. The first line then came to me.'

He snapped his fingers lightly, and perhaps by coincidence, but certainly on time, Grimes appeared as he always did, to pour the whisky.

'Would you have fought, Papa? If you'd been allowed?'

'If my health had permitted? Of course I would have fought. Bad enough to be here and not be able enough, but to be able, and not be there, that would have been intolerable. Conscience does indeed make cowards of us all, Amelia. Could not have lived with myself.'

'Yet your new poem is so dreadfully anti – it's practically *conshie!*' Amelia exclaimed, frowning.

'A great many poets fought,' her father replied abruptly, replacing the notebook on the desk. 'A great many poets died.'

George found himself awake, sitting up in his bed drenched in the sweat of a night terror, shaking uncontrollably, and awakened by his own terrible, primal noise, a sound born of utter despair.

Along the corridor, two rooms away from his own, his mother heard it too. The dreadful sound woke her from sleep. She sat up, and after a few seconds started to pull back the bedclothes and search for her slippers, determined on going to see her son, but the General's voice came across the room, commanding and stern.

'No, Louisa, leave him be. He'll come to his senses soon. We all do.'

In his room George stared into the darkness, remembering how, as a child, he had suffered endlessly from nightmares, the product of an over stimulated imagination, he was always being told. He remembered too how he had once or twice called out for his mother, but, eventually, since she had never seemed to hear him, had somehow composed himself for sleep again. In those far off, safe and distant days he had, in his imagination, counted the stars in the Sussex night sky. He had pretended to himself that he was among them, that he had a robe of darkest blue, and every inch of it was a star. More than that, he had pretended that he could look down upon their old tile-hung

Sussex farmhouse and thrown those same stars so that they fell to earth as his parents cheered. Now no such thoughts brought comfort. Only Amelia, her bright smile, her dark hair, her anxiety for him, that brought solace, until at last, he was asleep once more.

She was so busy making arrangements for her party that Amelia hardly saw George during the next fortnight. One of the rare occasions when they did find themselves enjoying each other's company was when in the midst of shopping one day in Midhurst she saw him coming out of Dr Minter's house in the High Street.

'George?' she called, hurrying after him since he had obviously not seen her. 'George?'

He stopped as soon as he heard her call, hesitated for a moment, then turned to wave at the pretty little figure hurrying along the pavement towards him.

'How are you, George?' Amelia asked breathlessly once she had caught him up. 'I've hardly seen you . . .'

'I've hardly seen you, Amelia. Dashing about the place like the White Rabbit.'

'I know, I know. But there's so much to do. And there's this awful shortage of staff. Are you all right?'

'What? Because I've just been to the doctor's, you mean?' George glanced over his shoulder at the front door of the white-painted Queen Anne house behind him as if to underline his point. 'I'm fine. I've been having the odd headache, that's all. Rather predictable and nothing to worry about, I assure you.'

'You're going to be well enough to come to my party, I hope.'

'I should come on a stretcher if I had to, Amelia, you know that. What are you doing in town?'

'Shopping with Hermione. She's buying some shoes at the moment and being a little too long.'

'How are you doing for young men? For your dance, I hasten to add.'

'We've rounded up a few more from here, and Hermione's importing some of her brother's friends from Haslemere. So we should be up to scratch. Trouble is they're all a bit on the young side. Mostly sixteen and seventeen-year-olds.'

'We'll keep them in order, don't worry. I'll borrow my father's uniform. Which way are you going? I have an appointment at the bank in a few minutes, so if you're walking that way?'

'Oh yes, of course. I have to dig Hermione out of Chapman's anyway.'

George offered her an arm as they turned back along the High Street, and so, Amelia happily locking her arm to his by linking her two hands together, they continued to discuss the arrangements for her party and dance.

'I've forgotten how old you're going to be,' George teased, widening his blue eyes. 'Remind me.'

'If you've forgotten that, George Dashwood, then you must have forgotten your own age.'

'Imagine you being twenty, Amelia. Did you ever think when you were small that you'd ever be that old?'

'Did you?'

'I thought sixteen was old. When I was a little boy, I could never think beyond that. I used to think in terms of *when I'm grown up* – but being grown up seemed to stop at sixteen.'

'Me too. Eighteen was old, and I mean twenty—'

'Twenty was ancient.'

'*Ancient.*'

George stopped them in front of a bookshop and looked in the window. 'Which reminds me, I must get you a present.'

'*How To Grow Old Gracefully*?'

'I prefer *How To Grow Old Disgracefully*. Won't be a minute.'

George smiled at her, gently unpicked her arm from his, and disappeared into the shop, leaving Amelia staring at the display in the window.

'Hello?' Hermione's voice said behind her. 'Didn't I just see George?'

'He's inside, buying me a birthday present,' Amelia replied.

'Beware. Men only buy girls books that *they* want to read.'

'Now you've spoiled the surprise. No shoes?'

'Not one pair I really liked. I mean honestly.' Hermione pulled a despairing face, then, taking

28

Amelia's arm, tugged her away from the book-shop window.

'Guess who I saw in Chapman's? Which was really the reason I was so long. Fiona Staveacre. And guess what?'

'What? *What?*'

'She's only called off the engagement.'

'To Martin?' Amelia asked in amazement. 'But they're like George and me. They've practically known each other since the cradle.'

'Martin's gone a bit funny, apparently,' Hermione went on, dropping her voice. 'He's only just got back, you know – like George. And spends the whole time babbling in French. And calling Fiona *Claudette.*'

'That's why she isn't going to go ahead and marry him? I mean, what a blow for Martin. If he's only just got back—' Amelia glanced into the bookshop behind her, as if thinking of George.

'It's not just that,' Hermione continued with a dramatic sigh. 'He's drinking fit to beat the band as well. He hasn't had his hand off a bottle since he got off the train, it seems. Or fell off, rather.'

'Yes, but surely given time—'

'I think she's mad, I agree.' Hermione shrugged. 'I mean Fiona is going to be lucky to catch anyone else. With that awful laugh of hers. Sssh – here's George.'

As always when she saw George Hermione smiled her best smile and opened her green eyes a little bit wider, but George it seemed barely noticed her, other than doffing his hat and nodding politely. He was swinging a brown paper parcel by its string in one hand and appeared to be in good spirits as he walked the two girls down the High Street before stopping outside his bank. Learning that his appointment promised to be a long one, Amelia wished him goodbye, standing on tiptoe to kiss him on one cheek while holding onto her hat against the gusting summer breeze. George smiled at her, doffed his hat once more to Hermione and was gone.

'He has to be positively the dishiest man ever born,' Hermione sighed. 'Whatever did you do to deserve him, Amelia Dennison?'

'I wish I knew. Sometimes I think it's all just too good to be true.'

'Supposing George doesn't propose to you at the party. What would you do?'

'What a funny thing to ask, Hermione. Why *shouldn't* George propose?'

'I was just thinking, that's all. Everyone I meet who fought – well. It's just that things aren't quite the same, now the war is over.'

'Oh, George is quite the same, quite his old self. George is quite what he was.'

'You think.'

'No, Hermione. I know.'

'How can you be so certain?'

'Because I know George. I have known George for most of my life. I know him better than I know myself.'

But Amelia knew that neither of them believed her which was probably why she suddenly fell silent.

Amelia had her own private worry about George and his intended proposal, for of course since the outbreak of the war, young as she was she had seen how foolish it was to take anything for granted. She knew that there was every possibility that George might change his mind at the last moment, and she also knew that if that was what he wished, she would not try to hold him to his word. She was just not that sort of person. She therefore put the matter out of her mind, and busied herself instead making ready for the party, which was to be held at her family house in the pretty little village of Passmore at the foot of the Downs. Originally the plan had been to hold just a small dinner dance for family and close friends, but now that it was generally assumed by those in the know – which included everyone of any note within the neighbourhood – that those gathered might be celebrating not only Amelia's birthday but the announcement of her engagement to one of their gallant young war heroes, the list of guests had grown from thirty to over one hundred and twenty, transforming the intended intimate party into practically a full scale ball. Normally Amelia enjoyed such social occasions to the full, both in anticipation and in reality, but now the closer she got to celebrating what she privately hoped would

31

be the most important birthday of her life she found herself becoming increasingly apprehensive. Luckily, however, the closer the great day came, the more numerous the distractions.

'I absolutely refuse – and I am quite sure that you do as well, Amelia,' her mother had announced on one of their earlier visits to their dressmaker, 'I simply refuse to wear the quite frightful sort of gown that Lady Dashwood favours – *and* expects everyone else to favour also. Those perfectly awful satin and lace things. With those dreadful bifurcated trains which make a woman look like an unmade bed. They really are extremely dull, and I'm quite sure – aren't you? – that after all this fighting and misery the very last thing we all want to look is dull. We should be celebrating what is after all our victory, I would have thought.'

'The trouble is there are still fabric shortages, Mama. I gathered from Mrs Fulton the other day, that we're to be rationed to four and a half yards of material per dress or coat.'

'What sheer nonsense. Wool is short, certainly, but we're not looking for wool. We want silk, and Papa's cousin assures me that there is no shortage of silk, not even in France. Lyon apparently is still making the very best quality silk in the latest designs, war or no war – and so silk it is to be. Particularly with what I have in mind for you. That oriental dinner gown in embroidered brocade I showed you? Remember?'

'The one worn over a pearl grey *charmeuse* under dress?'

'And a matching small turban. Very chic and quite, quite stunning. And I am also going to dress *un*-dull. A flesh-coloured satin bodice and a silver lace skirt strung with pearls, with a headband in the same-coloured satin as the bodice.'

Now as they stood in all their finished finery in the tiny backroom of Mrs James's town house, both Amelia and her mother were delighted with their dressmaker's handiwork. The end results were both refined and artistic.

'Excellent!' Constance exclaimed as she turned herself in front of the mirrors. 'Oh yes! The fight is over – the battle won! And the light of victory is well and truly in our eyes!'

'You don't think that perhaps this is a little too – well – bohemic?' Amelia wondered nervously, as she too examined her image in a looking-glass.

'My dear young lady,' Mrs James said through a mouthful of pins. 'Bohemic? This is Paris, France come to Sussex, England. *Bohemic* indeed. Whatever that may mean.'

'It means everyone else will be in conventional ball gowns with probably much, much more to them, Mrs James. While my mother and I—'

'Will be *les belles du bal*!' Mrs James assured her, adjusting the angle of Amelia's turban. 'Believe you me.'

'I look like something out of a play. This really is very theatrical.'

'And why not?' Constance demanded. 'The world *is* all a stage – it's true. And if so then we must decorate it as best we may. Would you not say, Mrs James?'

'I would say, Mrs Dennison, that lucky the man who chooses this beautiful girl. That's what I would say.'

On the return drive home, conducted at a snail's pace thanks to Grimes's morbid fear of speed, while her mother began reading her newly purchased copy of Lytton Strachey's *Eminent Victorians*, Amelia watched the summer clouds scudding high above the Downs and reflected on her present situation. She felt more than a little ashamed about her remark in the dressmaker's since she knew that whether she liked it or not she had once been just as *bohemic* as her parents, and was probably still more than a little so inclined. Being an only child meant that not only had she enjoyed the undivided attention of both her parents but she had been allowed to grow up without any of the more conventional social restraints. Not that she was spoilt – indeed, far from it. Her father might be a poet and a painter but his own family had been a military one and he had not altogether discarded the book of rules. Clarence Dennison had certainly not spoiled his only daughter, instilling in her a proper sense of both duty and honesty at the same time as allowing her much more mental freedom than that enjoyed by her friends from more orthodox families. By the same token her mother had dressed her in a variety of hand-embroidered smocks and loose, flowing dresses while at the same time letting her run about without any stockings in summer, things which were then still considered very avant-garde, although now after the end of a war which had changed the nature as well as the shape of the world they were becoming much more commonplace.

Even so, Amelia saw her remark about her possibly bohemic appearance as a sort of small treachery, since before she had actually realized she had fallen in love with George she had never *split ranks*, as her father called it. Now, worried in case George had for some reason changed his mind about proposing, Amelia wondered whether she might perhaps be trying to blame his change of heart on the difference between her parents' artistic background and his own rather more orthodox military one.

'I do hope that's not what it is,' she said, suddenly voicing her thoughts out loud. 'You don't think we aren't quite enough *them* for George's family? The Dashwoods are so military, and it seems always have been. While as a family we have always been – what is it Papa calls it? *So hopelessly artistic*.'

'If you're talking about us not being *them* enough for the wretched Dashers, then you're talking nonsense,' her mother replied, glancing up from her book. 'Think about it. The Dashers could well not be *them* enough for us.'

'Hardly, Mama. The Dashers are – well. They're *It*. You can't be much more It than the Dashwoods.'

'You're not getting cold feet, are you, Amelia darling? Not that I'd blame you? The thought of getting engaged often does that to people. And I can't say I blame them. Particularly marrying into a family as stuck-up as the Dashers.'

'The Dashers aren't stuck-up, Mama!' Amelia protested in some shock. 'A bit grand certainly, but hardly stuck-up.'

'Of course they're stuck-up, Amelia! Lady D in particular. I adore old General Whiskers but dear darling Louisa is sometimes too toffee-faced for words. *Comme toute la haute bourgeoisie.* Is that what's making you anxious? Because you don't think you're Them enough?' Constance laughed and took her daughter's hand. 'Do stop looking like Mopper before she has kittens. Artists have pedigrees too, you know. And yours is a long and illustrious one – so it's them who should be worrying about whether they're Them enough for you, darling girl.'

'I couldn't bear it if George doesn't want to marry me after all,' Amelia blurted out. 'Really, I don't think I could. I thought I could but now – I don't think I can.'

'You could bear it more than being married to a

36

man who didn't love you, darling girl,' Constance replied. 'Now stop being so childish and do stop fretting so – really you must. As it happens I am quite sure George will propose to you. He has said he will, and George being a gentleman is a man of his word.'

Constance squeezed her daughter's hand and returned to her book, while Amelia returned to staring out at the view, hoping the sun would come back out. But the clouds had now been joined by a host of others, the sky darkened, and it rained all the way home and non-stop for the next week.

Meanwhile George was having a set of second thoughts all of his own.

Three

'Come on along!' the young man called to everyone he passed in the corridor. 'Come on along – and listen to Alexander's Ragtime Band!'

Hermione caught Amelia going the other way and, taking hold of her arm, turned her round to drag her off in the direction of Clarence Dennison's study.

'I'm looking for George!' Amelia protested above the noise of the party. 'You haven't seen him, I suppose?'

'If I had, you'd be the last to know!' Hermione laughed, keeping a firm hold on Amelia.

'Seriously, Hermione! He's completely disappeared!'

'Probably down on his knees somewhere! Rehearsing his proposal in a corner! Come on!'

'Come on along!' the young man picked up, singing the words now rather than calling. 'Come on along – come on along – let me take you by the hand!'

'What is all this anyway?' Amelia wondered, watching the string of young people doing a conga down the passageway. 'Is that Ferdy making all the noise?'

'He's got some brand new record of some brand new band he's dying to play!' Hermione called back over her shoulder. 'Jazz!'

It was the talk of the party, nothing but jazz and the brand new dance steps that were being tried out all over Europe. Ferdy, the young man in question, had arrived with a phonograph recording made by the Original Dixieland Jazz Band as a birthday present for Amelia, and now while the majority of the guests were dancing to Strauss he was determined that the birthday girl and her friends should be treated to the music that was sweeping the Continent.

'This is the New Thing, Amelia!' Hermione called as they poured into the study where Clarence Dennison kept his precious phonograph. 'You will just go wild when you hear it!'

'I really should go and find George!'

'Nonsense! Let him come and find you! Much the best thing!'

'The tune you are about to hear,' Ferdy Fairfield announced as he wound up the gramophone, 'is a tune called "Tiger Rag". A man called La Rocca claims to have composed it but as it happens a friend of ours who's also a musician—'

'Just put the recording on, Ferdy!' Hermione barracked, pushing another cigarette in her long holder. 'Really, Ferdy – you're nothing but a walking old encyclopedia!'

'This friend of ours claims that at the beginning

of the century there were four versions of this particular number—'

'Put the record on, Ferdy!' everyone carolled in unison after Hermione. 'Put the record on!'

'One was an old French quadrille,' Ferdy continued, determined to finish his introduction, but he was soon shouted down, and he lost his record to Hermione who seized it and put it on the turntable.

'"Tiger Rag"!' she announced. 'Take your partners, everyone!'

In a moment the room was full of young men and women dancing wildly to the new rhythm, half of them trying to foxtrot to it as the more adventurous improvised steps, the less well behaved dancing up and over the armchairs and sofas as they did so. Halfway through the fourth account of the Rag, while two young men who were totally unknown to Amelia took it in turns to whirl her round the room and then backwards and forwards to each other, to Amelia's intense amusement, the study door opened and she caught a glimpse of George's face looking in.

'George!' she called, trying to disengage herself. 'George – wait! Don't go away!'

But he was gone, and by the time Amelia had got herself free he had vanished completely into the throng of people milling round her house.

After a five-minute search she finally ran him to ground in the library, which emptied almost immediately she came in as the orchestra struck up the next set of dances.

'I've been looking for you,' she said as he stood up to greet her. 'Where on earth have you been?'

'I went to get myself a drink.' George gave a boyish smile. 'That's all. I got rather hot and I just felt like a drink, that's all. You seem to be having fun.'

'I was. You should have come in. Ferdy gave me this terrific new record as a present. The Original Dixieland Jazz Band.'

'Sounded great.'

'You really should have come in.'

'As I said. I was rather hot – and wanted a drink.'

'I thought you went to get a drink some time ago.'

'I did. And then I went to get another one.'

'You're not a bit – a bit tiddly, are you?' Amelia leaned towards him, peering up into his eyes. 'Oh yes – yes those blue eyes are definitely a little bit bossed.'

'I am not the slightest bit tiddly,' George protested, pulling himself upright and raising his eyebrows. 'I do not like *getting tiddly*, as you put it.'

'Well – tight, then. Why do they call it that? Tight?'

'Because that's how you feel when you've had too much to drink. As if everything is very tight. As if your head's all tight. I can't say I like it much, which is why I try not to get it – to get tight.'

'I see.' Amelia smiled at him and tipped her head on one side. 'So when you drink, when you want a drink—'

'It's either because I'd like one, or because I need one. For courage.'

'You need courage now, George?'

'Yes.' George looked back at her, very steadily. 'Yes, Amelia, as a matter of fact I do.'

He held the look for a moment, then took his silver cigarette case from his inside pocket.

'And now you also want a cigarette?'

'Yes,' George replied, tapping the end of a cigarette against the case. 'Do you mind?'

Amelia shook her head and watched while George lit his smoke. She saw that his hand was a little unsteady, and at once lowered her head to hide her sudden smile. *George of all people*, she thought. *George who survived this awful war, George who was always being mentioned in despatches, George who finally won a VC, George her dashing wonderful hero going to pieces because he was about to propose? Or was it because he was not going to propose?*

Across the corridor from them some people hurried into the study, which to judge from the music pouring out as they opened the door was still very much in full swing. George looked up and listened, pulling an appreciative face at the music as he drew deeply on his cigarette.

'One of the men – one of my men – he had a

gramophone. Used to play it in the trenches, would you believe.'

'How intriguing.'

'Ralph. He was a fellow officer. A second lieutenant. You'll probably meet him one day. We became good friends.' George took a second pull on his cigarette and raised his eyebrows as he remembered. 'Ralph pinched this fellow's gramophone one night and took it out on a recce. He'd been sent out to spy where this machine-gun nest was. He couldn't find the nest but he found himself all of a sudden right on top of this German trench where there was just this one German on sentry duty. Heaven knows what inspired him to take the wretched gramophone when he could have been shot dead at any moment, but that's Ralph. Anyway – he found himself slap bang on top of this German, put the gramophone down in the trees just behind him, wound it up and put a record on. Frightened the life out of Fritz, I can tell you.'

'I can imagine.'

Amelia laughed.

'Yes,' George said thoughtfully, exhaling a plume of smoke. 'Frightened the life out of Fritz.'

George fell to silence while Amelia watched him, wondering how and when he was going to broach the subject. Obviously not immediately, judging from the way George was smoking his way right through his cigarette and then helping himself to a large whisky and soda from the tray

43

of drinks Grimes had just brought into the library. The longer she waited the less she could understand why it should be so difficult for a man of George's undoubted valour to propose marriage not only to someone he had known for most of his life, but to someone to whom he had already promised such a proposal. The more she thought the more she remembered the countless instances in novels she had read where similarly redoubtable men were reduced to either silence or gibbering idiocy when it came to the moments they had to ask if their loves would marry them, so she continued to wait patiently while George smoked another cigarette and drank most of his glass of whisky.

When they did speak it was both at the same time.

'I'm so sorry—' Amelia said, quickly.

'Not at all,' George insisted. 'It was my fault.'

'Sorry – what were you going to say?' Amelia wondered, after another but much shorter silence.

'What was I going to say?' George repeated with a frown, dropping the remains of his smoke on the log fire. 'Yes. Look – why don't you sit down here by the fire, Amelia, while I try and put what I want to say into words.'

Dutifully Amelia sat, suppressing the sigh of disappointment she felt welling up inside her. This was not at all how she had imagined it. In her imagination she had been dancing with George, who had then smiled at her before suddenly sweeping her with him out through the open French windows and onto the terrace where, taking her hands in his, he had made the most beautiful speech of proposal. In return Amelia had teased him a little before happily accepting the invitation, throwing her arms round George who had then kissed her – kissed her properly, in a way she had never been kissed before, in the way she and Hermione had so often dreamed of being kissed, with a kiss so magical it would bind her to George for the rest of her life.

Now, instead of a poetic proposal out on the terrace in the moonlight followed by a life-changing kiss, she found herself sitting looking up at a man who was standing nervously biting the back of one index finger while staring down at the fire in front of him.

'I don't know where to begin,' he said, finally straightening himself to look in the glass which hung above the fireplace. 'Or quite how to put this.'

'Is something the matter, George?' Amelia said, about to get up as she realized that whatever it was that was holding him back it was not the making of any marriage proposal.

'It's all right,' George assured her. 'If you'll just be patient I'll do my best to explain.'

Amelia frowned, then sat back in her chair and waited.

'Do you think I've changed, Amelia?' he asked, looking round at her.

Amelia thought long and carefully before she replied, beginning to suspect the cause of George's apparent anxiety.

'If you mean "changed" as in "different" then no I don't,' she told him. 'I think – from what I can tell – I think you're still the George I know, the George I grew up with, the George who—' She checked herself, not wishing to appear in the least forward, not out of propriety but in case she should frighten George off with her presumption. 'As far as I can tell, George, and as far as my own feelings go, you're not a different person. But you could well *be* different, in as much as what you've endured would change anybody's attitude, and the way they thought and felt about things – anyone that is who has any sensitivity at all, which my father assures me most people have. So yes – you are bound to have changed. Events change us all, and the events you have just been through must have affected you deeply.'

George looked at her long and hard, and then nodded several times more to himself than to her, before turning away to look back at his image in the glass, as if to check that physically at least he was the same person.

'I think that's very well put, Amelia,' he said, still looking at himself. 'Very well put indeed. I was afraid I might have changed entirely. Not towards you, I hasten to add.' He turned to her and half smiled. 'I haven't changed towards you one bit. Not my feelings. In fact the longer I was away from you, the more – the more I felt for you.' He gave a deep sigh and shook his head. 'It's just that since coming home, since being back here, I can't help it – I feel so very different. I feel as if I'm an entirely different person. Everywhere I go, where I walk, what I see – I keep trying to feel what I did before I went away. But I can't. I don't. I feel inside me – inside I feel as if I'm someone else. A stranger. An outsider. In fact there are times when it's as if I was standing outside of myself, as if I was completely detached. Watching myself as if I was another person. You don't think I'm going mad, do you?'

Suddenly to Amelia he looked like a little boy again, as frightened as he had been when they were both climbing the great apple tree in his garden and he had fallen from a high branch, landing so heavily on his back that he could not move for what seemed an age. *Have I broken it, Amelia?* he had wondered in a whisper when he found he could not move his legs. *Do you think I'm going to die?* Now he seemed as frightened, looking anxiously at Amelia while waiting for her verdict. *No, you're not going to die, George,* she had told him. *Look – you can move your toes, and your fingers.* Just as she told him now that she didn't think he was going mad.

'George,' she said, getting up and going to his side to take his hand. 'I can't imagine what this must be like for you. Coming back to this place, to your home, your family and your friends—'

'And to you.'

'To me as well,' Amelia nodded. 'I can have absolutely no idea what it must be like. None of us can, at least we women can't, and neither can those men who have never fought. Your father will understand – he has to. This sort of thing has been his entire life, so he must understand your feelings, although I have to say from what I gather that compared with all you have been through in this particular war—'

'I don't think my father understands,' George interrupted. 'Not any more. I think he's shut himself off from this sort of thing. Otherwise – otherwise he couldn't have gone on. It wouldn't have been possible.'

'What about you, George? What are you going to do?'

'That's the whole point. I don't think I'll be able to do what my father has done. I don't think I'm capable of it.'

'But why? You? I mean you're—'

'Yes?'

Amelia stopped and fell silent, afraid once more of saying the wrong thing.

'I'm a hero, you mean,' George said for her. 'A VC. I am Captain George Dashwood VC, the illustrious soldier son of an illustrious soldier father.'

'Give it time, George,' Amelia said, taking his hand in both of hers. 'Papa said you would need time.'

'You've been discussing this with your father?'

'Only because he sensed your pain on your return. My father may not have ever fought, not physically. But he has in his mind, over and over again.'

George considered what she had just said, closed his eyes and shook his head regretfully.

'I'm so sorry, Amelia. I've spoiled it all for you. I'm so terribly sorry. I shouldn't have talked about this now. Not on this day of all days.'

'Which day is that, George?'

'Your birthday.'

'Oh. Is that all it is?'

George opened his eyes wide. He stared at her in wonder.

'You surely don't—' he began, then stopped to start again. 'After all I've just said?'

'You haven't *said* anything, George. Other than you're finding it difficult being home.'

'I've changed, Amelia.'

'So? So have I. Every morning when we wake up, we're all different. Different from the way we were the day before. Otherwise there would have been no point in living the day before.'

'I think I've changed quite a lot, Amelia. A lot more than that.'

'So? If that's the case, then let's find out.'

'You mean—?'

'Yes, George. I do.'

'You mean you still want to marry me?'

'More than anything in the world.'

49

The next thing Amelia knew she was in his arms while he hugged her to him so tightly she thought he might asphyxiate her. She managed to raise one hand to reach up to him, touching the back of his head, stroking his thick dark hair gently and rhythmically, the way her mother used to stroke her own hair whenever she had cried as a child.

'It's all right, George,' she whispered. 'You're going to be fine. Really you are. I shall make sure. I shall look after you.'

A moment later George eased his hold on her, leaning back so that he could look into her eyes.

'Do you love me, Amelia? Do you love me as much as I love you?'

'I don't know the answer to that, George. I don't know how much you love me. But if it's as much as I love you, then yes – I must do.'

From the way he was looking at her surely now he would kiss her. Amelia, lost in the look he was giving her, feeling her heart starting to pound, felt sure that would be the outcome. She saw his face coming closer and closed her eyes, only to hear the library door open and the voice of Grimes informing them both that they were required at the family table.

Arm in arm they made their way dutifully to where both sets of parents awaited them, and judging from their universal expression it was clear they considered the two of them had enjoyed more than enough liberty to get the matter of the marriage proposal safely out of the way. The announcement that followed seemed merely a formality since George had already obtained Clarence Dennison's permission to ask his daughter to marry him on his last leave, so although the news was greeted with pleasure it really came as no great surprise. Even so, as soon as the engagement was formally announced the whole gathering greeted it with genuine delight, George and Amelia being seen as the ideal couple.

'Congratulations,' Hermione said, taking Amelia aside from the group of people crowding round George to congratulate him. 'You got him, then.'

'That isn't a very nice way of putting it. I did not set out to *get* George and you know it.'

'Sorry, darling. I'm just jealous. I mean, look. Look around you – not a decent free chap in sight. The only ones who are there for the taking have all got something dreadful wrong with them, thanks to the war, or had something dreadful wrong with them which prevented them from going to fight in it. You really don't know how lucky you are, Amelia Dennison.'

'Don't be so ridiculous, Hermione. Someone as pretty and as much fun as you will soon find someone.'

'Amelia – you don't know the score. Haven't you heard? Not only are there no young men, but the few who are still alive and in one piece are being snapped up by the war widows – the ones with money and estates they've been left by their dead husbands. So what chance have girls like me? My mother is trying to persuade Papa to give me a "dot", some sort of inheritance, now – and she means a decent one too – because otherwise she thinks I shall never be off their hands. And she's right.'

The leader of the orchestra was calling everyone onto the floor for the last waltz, so Amelia excused herself and went to rejoin George who she saw was looking round for her. When he gathered her up in his arms to dance Amelia suddenly felt that part of her dream was going to come true after all, for just as she had imagined George waltzed her out onto the deserted terrace and he led her to a corner out of sight of the dancers. For one heavenly and heart-stopping moment, as George took both her hands, Amelia thought at last she was to be kissed, but after looking very seriously at her George did nothing more than shake his head.

'Whatever is the matter now, George?' she asked, trying to keep the disappointment out of her voice.

'I want you to promise me something, Amelia. If you can.'

'You know I always hate it when you ask me that,' Amelia sighed.

'This isn't like that. It isn't like when we were children.'

'Even so, you're going to have to tell me what it

is you want me to promise before I'll promise it.'

'That means you don't trust me. Which is the whole point.'

'George? You just said this isn't like when we were children, remember?'

Amelia smiled as if to show she was half teasing, but she was not. More than anything she had wanted George to kiss her, just once. One kiss would have sufficed to make this moment a magical one, but instead George was determined to elicit the promise he was demanding from her.

'I just want you to promise me that you will always love me,' he said, still holding her hands.

'Just? Is that all? I thought it was going to be something *important*.'

'I'm serious, Amelia.' George tightened his grip on her hands.

'Ow!' Amelia protested. 'So I gather.'

George relaxed his grip but refused to let go. 'Well?'

'You want me to promise that I will love you for ever, George? Why else do you think I said I'll marry you?'

'That's not an answer, Amelia. At least not the one I want. I want you to promise me that you will always love me – whatever.'

'Whatever? I don't understand. Whatever what?'

'Whatever might happen.'

'Whatever could happen, George?'

'I don't know. I just know things can – and do.

And if they do, when they do – people can change.'

'I see. For a moment I thought perhaps you were going to ask me to love you whatever you do – the way some men ask their wives, or fiancées rather. So that they can go off and be unfaithful with a clear conscience.'

'That is *not* what I meant. I will never be unfaithful to you. Never.'

'Is that a promise?'

'Of course.'

'In that case I promise you I will always love you. Whatever happens.'

Amelia looked back at him, and seeing the obvious anguish in his eyes at once regretted her teasing.

'I love you, George,' she said again, squeezing both the hands which held hers. 'And I promise that I always will. Until death do us part.'

'And I shall always love you, Amelia,' George replied. 'I promise. Whatever you do, or I do, whatever happens to us both I shall always love you.'

And so at last he kissed her. He kissed her with the first of many thousands of kisses they would share in a lifetime, although perhaps no kiss after this was ever quite so special nor so sublime. He kissed her once, then he kissed her twice, then he put both his arms round her, hugged her tightly and slowly lifting her up off the ground kissed her again.

It was all just as Amelia had dreamed.

*   *   *

'So what was it like?' Hermione demanded when she entertained Amelia for tea the following day at her family's summer house in Bosham. 'I want to know exactly what you felt.'

'I can't tell you,' Amelia sighed. 'There aren't words to describe it.'

'You could try.'

'I couldn't. Even the word heavenly falls a long way short.'

'Lucky you.'

'Lucky me.' Amelia grinned and popped another tiny sandwich in her mouth.

'Pig.' It was Hermione's turn to sigh. 'Sometimes you are an utter and a complete pig.'

'I thought I would faint actually,' Amelia confessed. 'The one thing I can tell you is that for one moment I really couldn't see straight, and then I thought I would pass out.'

'As in *swoon*?' Hermione giggled. 'With the back of one hand to the forehead? And a cry for the *sal volatile*?'

'I'd have made quite sure to fall into his arms,' Amelia replied. 'Don't you worry.'

Hermione thought for a moment with half-closed eyes, while carefully nibbling on a piece of sponge cake.

'I wonder what it's going to be like when you're actually married?' she said.

'What *what's* going to be like?'

'It. What It's going to be like.'

'Oh,' Amelia said, before giving it some thought. 'Ravishing, I suppose. Or else we wouldn't have the word ravished. Would we?'

'Ravishing,' Hermione echoed. 'Always been one of my favourite words.'

'Except do you actually know what actually happens, Hermione?' Amelia wondered.

'Happens, Amelia? You mean as in *It*?'

'Yes. Exactly.'

'Yes, well of course,' Hermione said, as if the question need never be asked. 'Don't you?'

'Well yes of course,' Amelia lied. 'Who told you?'

'My mother, naturally,' Hermione replied. 'You?'

'Same here. Naturally.'

'Even so,' Hermione went on with her usual surface confidence. 'I don't think we should talk about it. *It* is not the sort of thing people like us discuss.'

'I think it's all right if you're just about to get married.'

'Probably.' Hermione gave an envious sigh and a sly smile. 'Anyway – you'll soon find out, won't you? Lucky you.'

Amelia fared no better with her mother when the subject came up, albeit by accident. They had been sitting out in the garden discussing marriage in general rather than in the particular, with Constance propounding her usual views on what constituted happiness in wedlock.

'That's the way it is, my darling girl. The way it is with marriage, anyway. People simply don't get to know each other until it's too late sometimes. I've often said as much to your father. You meet someone and you're attracted to them, you go to a church where they read this service over you – and abracadabra! You are now in marital bliss, expected to spend the rest of your lives together in happy – happy – whatever *is* the dratted word? The same as that thing in grammar – yes, *conjugation*! You're meant to happily conjugate for the rest of your life with the same person just because you both wanted to make love. I mean really!'

Constance closed her eyes the way she always did when a bad bout of laughter overtook her, tipping her head back and dissolving in mirth while Amelia, more than a little taken aback by the outburst, began to examine one of her fingernails in mock anxiety.

'Actually, while we're on the subject, Mama—' she began.

'What subject?' her mother wondered, stilling her laughter. 'I do sincerely hope you don't wish to discuss anything intimate, Amelia dear.'

'Yes, I do, as it happens,' Amelia replied, dropping her eyes and pretending now to look at the pictures in the magazine on her knee. 'As it so happens it's about what you were just talking about. Marriage. And – well. It. Conjugation, that is.'

'Oh lord,' Constance said, pulling a suddenly

over-concerned face. 'What is it you want to know? I mean there's nothing to be *afraid* of, if that's what you're afraid of.'

'No, I know. At least I hope there isn't.'

'Oh lord,' Constance sighed again, sitting back and rearranging her skirts. 'It really is so difficult, and for girls in particular. It's a wonder any of us ever survive the shock.'

'The shock?' Amelia wondered anxiously. 'What shock are you talking about?'

'The shock of our wedding night, of course. What else? Your grandmother – no, no I can't tell you that, not now,' Constance said, pulling herself up short. 'When you're older maybe, but certainly not now. No, no, no.'

'What, Mama? What can't you tell me about Grandmother?'

'When you're older, Amelia darling.'

Amelia frowned at her mother and fell silent, wondering what specific marital horror her mother was keeping from her. She had heard similar dark hints in conversations with her closest girl friends, Hermione in particular, but nothing had ever been specified other than vague intimations of pain and rumours of horrified surprise. But before she could press her mother further Constance suddenly leaned forward and took her hands in hers.

'Amelia darling,' she said with genuine concern. 'You are *au fait* with what matters, *n'est-ce pas*? Because if you are not, I am quite and utterly hopeless at explaining this sort of thing in any way. Besides, I don't really think it's for a mother to say. Not unless it's a sort of last gasp situation. Much better to learn it from one's girl friends, just as I did. Much, much better because then it is like to like, if you see what I mean. I'm quite sure you and Hermione must have discussed this sort of thing on countless occasions, just the way I did with my friend Agatha – who, I have to tell you, knew it *all* and taught me *everything*. So really, darling girl, if you still have any doubts or worries then for heaven's sake *ask Hermione*.'

'I already have, Mama,' Amelia replied, somewhat bleakly.

'Well there you are then,' Constance concluded, sitting back once more with another deep sigh and picking up her magazine. 'People the same age talk the same way, so it's much the best way. Now why don't you ring for some tea? And come and sit here beside me and tell me what you think of the latest fashions from Paris. I think they're quite appalling.'

After tea Amelia took Sam, their jolly little fox terrier, for a walk, having arranged to meet George on the Downs. With the little dog barking happily at her heels Amelia set off out into the cool of the early summer evening. When they got to the Downs the dog ran on ahead, nose to the ground as he endeavoured to pick up the most recent rabbit scent, the success of his searches flagged by the activity of his stumpy little white tail. As

Amelia strolled onto the springy downland turf she selected a fresh grass to chew, called to Sam not to run too far ahead and scanned the landscape for a sight of George.

As she walked she began to recite a verse from one of her father's war poems.

'They shall not sleep now
Nor shall their eyes
Lose sight of the bitter darkness
In which they fought
Beneath the glare of a foreign sun.

'I wonder if that's true of George, Sam?' she continued out loud, addressing the dog who was not in the least bit interested. 'Maybe once you've experienced something quite dreadful you just can't ever forget it, however hard you try. Except George is different from most men, Sam. He's the stuff of heroes. George once dived into the Solent to rescue a drowning man with absolutely no thought for his own safety.'

A moment later she saw him on the horizon, followed by his dogs. At once Amelia changed direction and hurried up the hill towards him, calling his name while keeping her sunhat on her head with one hand. As soon as she reached him he kissed her on the cheek, smiled and took her hand, leading her off on a long walk that encompassed all the old familiar and favourite places. For a while they were happy just rambling, caught up more in their past than in their future, remembering childhood days spent up in the green hills long before the roof of the world had fallen in. The dogs dropped back to follow quietly at heel as if they sensed the importance of these shared memories, and for a long while as they walked it was as if life had always been like this and they had simply picked up where they had left off five long years ago.

As George pointed out all the old familiar landmarks, Amelia kept glancing at the handsome man beside her, unable quite to believe that now he really was hers. What made her even happier was to see him so much more relaxed and so much more himself, restored it would seem nearly to his old self. His open face seemed to have lost its look of perpetual worry, his blue eyes were bright and clear again, and even the set of his jaw appeared to have regained its determination. He was almost absurdly good-looking, Amelia realized, recalling how everyone had thought just the same about him when he was a boy. *Like a little Greek god*, her mother would laugh when the two of them would return tousle-haired and flush-faced from some daunting tree climbing expedition, or some journey of exploration up on the Downs.

A little Greek god and a little tangle-haired wood sprite found on the Downs, Clarence had written under the photograph he had taken of them one day in fancy dress.

Yet she was never the tomboy, always just what she was: a pretty dark-eyed and dark-haired girl with what George called *a permanently startled look*, as if she had been suddenly surprised. Her mother used to tease her, saying that she must have got a fright being born, so that for a long time as she was growing up Amelia would try to change the nature of her expression by affecting a deeply puzzled frown.

She only abandoned the attempt to alter her natural appearance when George told her he actually thought hers was the most beguiling look he had ever seen on a girl, the evening of her sixteenth birthday when he had danced with her for most of the party. Amelia had at once pulled a funny face and told him in reply that she was plain and her look simply a *silly* one, but George had insisted she was wrong. So persuasive had he been that Amelia had believed him and begun to look at herself differently, now seeing quite a pretty face gazing back at her from her looking-glass rather than one she considered plain and frankly boring. The more she looked the more she realized George was right. Her wide eyes were her best feature, so instead of frowning all the time and trying to hide them under a fringe of dark hair she wore her hair differently, pulled back from her face and tied into a long plait down her back, a style which made her appear faintly Egyptian, for in spite of her large round eyes she had what her father called a Mesopotamian profile, with her straight nose, high cheekbones and a pretty mouth albeit with its slightly protuberant upper lip. *You're not going to be a beauty in the classical sense of the word, Amelia*, Clarence would say as he sat her on his knee, *but you will be a beauty certainly in a most distinctive way*.

In fact the only thing about herself she really still regretted was that she never grew to be tall. She felt that with more height she might the better match up to George. George on the other hand would not hear of such a thing, even when they had finished growing, assuring Amelia that he had no wish for competition.

By now they had climbed to Peter's Point, a beacon on top of their favourite hill, and George had fallen silent, slipping free of Amelia's arm and walking on ahead of her to stand on the highest point gazing southwards to the sea, as if looking beyond the horizon to France and the days of his warfare. Amelia rested on the pile of old stones which marked the site of the beacon, waiting for George to break his reverie so that they might continue their walk in the same relaxed frame of mind. But when he did decide to go on he did so without calling her to him, suddenly walking briskly away from the Point with only a whistle to his dogs.

As soon as she heard his signal and saw his dogs jump up to follow their master Amelia jumped up too, catching him up before he had gone more than a hundred yards. She grabbed his arm again, this time in an attempt to halt his progress, but George seemed hardly to notice her or the fact that she had hold of him, walking on steadily with his eyes still fixed on some unknown mark.

'George?' Amelia tried to catch her breath. 'George – what is it? Is something the matter?'

Her question must have momentarily caught his attention because he came to a sudden halt, looking at her for a long moment before walking on. Still attached to his arm, Amelia was pulled along with him, at a pace too fast for her.

'George?' she protested. 'George – please slow down! Please – and tell me what is the matter with you.'

'Nothing,' George said, screwing his eyes up at the horizon. 'It's just – sometimes it's just these things get into my head, that's all. Things that have happened. I'm sorry.'

'Would it help if you talked them out?' Amelia wanted to know. 'I know I can't really have any idea of what you've been through, but perhaps if you talked about it, it might help us both?'

'I wouldn't know where to start.'

'Just say whatever's in your head. Whatever's bothering you.'

George thought for a long while, then took a deep breath and shook his head. 'No,' he said quietly. 'I don't think so. I really don't think so, thank you all the same.'

He walked on again, with Amelia following in silence, knowing better than to prompt him any more.

'What this is like, if you understand me—' he said finally after they had walked another couple of hundred yards. 'I'll try to explain. What this is like is— It's like a dream. Try and imagine if you can being used to waking up with the air full of the noise of gunfire. With the whole sky alight with the blaze of the big guns. Think of practically every waking minute being like that – because that's how it seems – the noise seems eternal, although sometimes you would go days without a shot being fired. Yet all you remember is this incessant noise. Fantastic noise. Noise such as you have never heard before, noise like a thousand thunderstorms happening all at once. Then think what it's like to wake up at night and see a sky that is dark. And silent. With no shells screaming through the air and bursting or bullets flying past your head but just the sound of perhaps an owl hooting and nothing else. Not a thing. Then in the morning someone brings you breakfast in bed and you find you're lying in clean crisp linen instead of filthy, freezing mud. And the summer sun is streaming in through the window and there's the sound of birdsong outside. Over there – if you even *saw* a bird it was like a miracle, particularly a songbird. I remember once – it was at Ypres – after one particularly bad bombardment when the guns had fallen silent – a song thrush began to sing. Right out of the blue. Listening to it, it was as if you were home again, sitting in your garden some early spring morning and just listening to the birds sing.

Instead of lying up to your waist in mud with the dead and the dying all around us. Think of that, imagine that if you can, then tell me I'm not going mad.'

Amelia stayed silent, aware that anything she might say would only sound absurd. She took one of his hands and held it. What George had endured was so far beyond her understanding there was nothing she could say or do.

'I'm sorry.' George looked down at her suddenly, as if sensing her helplessness. 'But you did say, didn't you—'

'I did and I meant it,' Amelia interrupted, hoping to ease his discomfort. 'Just talk whenever you feel like it. And if I'm not around then come and find me. One thing I am quite good at – or so you've always told me – is listening.'

'I'm just indulging myself.' George gave an angry shake of his head. 'Good God, there are thousands of men who have been through far worse than I have. I'm sure they're not all sitting around crying on someone's shoulder and feeling sorry for themselves.'

'I bet they are. I would be if I was them. But what you mustn't feel is guilty.'

'Guilty? How so?'

'Because you survived. It isn't your fault others died. Men in your battalion. Friends. Even your enemies. You were only doing the duty which you were called upon to do, and while I'm sure it was perfectly dreadful – and that nothing anyone can say or do will remove those memories or heal those scars – you can't feel guilty because you're alive and the others aren't.'

George was staring at her in surprise, although Amelia doubted he was actually half as surprised as she was at what she had just said.

'I know I'm only a woman and so don't know anything about war,' she continued. 'But I do know that the one thing war is not about is fairness. It's not like a cricket match with the best side winning and then going off to drink beer together. It's about life and death, and sometimes – not always – about right and wrong. You fought on the side of right, there's no doubt about that, George. And if you had not done so, if people like you hadn't taken up arms against the enemy, wrong would have triumphed and *then* you would have had cause to feel guilty.'

George suddenly smiled. He smiled at her just the way he had used to smile at her before he had gone to war, a smile from the innocence of his boyhood and one which now marked not only their enduring friendship but their undoubted love.

'I survived because of you, Amelia,' he said. 'Or maybe I survived *for* you. It doesn't matter which. We've always loved each other, haven't we? Ever since we first met under that oak tree in the park. At the cricket match. Your father scored a century, and you applauded every single run, even though you were only – how old were you exactly?'

'Eight.'

'Even though you were only eight – and I said to my mother as we were walking home, "Mother? I've just met the girl I'm going to marry."'

For one moment more he looked at her the same way, the way they were, the way they had been – and then he leaned forward and kissed her again.

But this time she was not smiling. She simply sat on the table with the other men around her and looked at him, her mouth open, as were her eyes. He did not want to kiss her – that was the very last thing he wanted – but somehow she was making him, and then he knew why. If he kissed her now he would save her life, because the man holding the gun to her head would not shoot her after all. And then he realized another thing, just at the moment all the others started to laugh and jeer and call to each other that he wasn't going to kiss her, that he wasn't brave enough, that the medals on his chest were toy medals made of tin: he realized that if he did kiss her he could snatch the gun, turn it on the man and shoot him in the face, just as he had seen Simon his school friend shot.

This time when George screamed she went to him, ignoring the general's direction that she was to stay in bed. She went straight away to him and found him still shouting and screaming, sitting up in his bed in the dark, soaked in the sweat of his nightmare.

'What is it, George?' she asked. 'George? George, it's me. Your mother.'

'The girl. The girl.'

'What girl, George? There is no girl. You've been dreaming.'

'We have to save the girl.'

'George . . .' his mother repeated, switching on his bedside light. 'George, there *is* no girl. You've been having a bad dream.'

He looked at her. He was awake now, at least his body was.

'You were dreaming, George. It's all right now, you can go back to sleep. It's all right.'

'It isn't all right. Not at all. It isn't at all all right.'

'It is, George. You're home, you're in your own bed, it's me – your mother – and you're all right now.'

'Yes?' He looked round at her, now back to full consciousness. 'What happened? Was I dreaming?'

'Apparently.' His mother got up to fetch him some fresh pyjamas. 'Something about a girl. I do hope it wasn't poor Amelia.'

'No. No, it wasn't Amelia.'

'Who was it then?' his mother asked, handing him the fresh nightclothes. 'Who was it if it wasn't Amelia?'

George shut his eyes and shook his head.

'No-one. No-one.'

Four

The wedding was held in April, at St James's Church, Piccadilly. The war was over and the two families were determined to throw their only children a jewel of a wedding. As befitted the only son of a distinguished general it was also a very grand one, attended by royalty as represented by the King's brother the Duke of Connaught and his duchess, the armed services by Earl Haig and politics by a sprinkling of Asquiths, while the guests of Clarence and Constance Dennison included many Society painters and musicians, not to mention a scattering of famous West End actors who did not have a matinee that day. The radiant Amelia won the hearts of all the men present while the dashing, dark-haired war hero in the dress uniform of the Royal Artillery elicited private but none the less heartfelt sighs from every woman.

'You look heavenly,' Hermione told her as she prepared to help carry Amelia's train down the aisle at the start of the ceremony. 'The prettiest bride I have ever seen.'

'Be sure to catch my bouquet later.'

'Too late!' Hermione sighed. 'You've got the chap I want.'

George never looked once at Amelia as she took her place beside him, staring straight ahead of him just the way he had done when they had walked the Downs that lovely summer evening. Amelia on the other hand had eyes only for George, trusting that he would not falter, thinking that he was as strong as he looked. It was only when at last his eyes met hers that she realized with shock that there were tears in them.

Defying convention the young Dashwoods came down the aisle to the thrilling sound of Widor, past a sea of faces all of which seemed to be smiling on the slim, dark bride wearing her mother's dress and carrying a bouquet of flowers from the families' Sussex gardens.

However, no sooner had the car taking them on to the reception carried them out of sight of the church than they both burst into fits of laughter, Amelia finally managing to say, 'George darling, it is the *bride* that's meant to cry at weddings!'

The reception was held in the ballroom of Lord Harrington's town house off Curzon Street. Amelia happily circulated amongst all her friends and relatives, showing off her wedding ring and telling everyone of their plans to honeymoon in Scotland.

'Rather you than me,' Hermione said dolefully,

when she was helping Amelia change into her navy blue and white going-away outfit.

'A few minutes ago you were saying quite the opposite,' Amelia reminded her.

'I wasn't thinking of your gorgeous husband, Amelia darling,' Hermione replied. 'I was thinking of the flies. Scotland is always full of flies.'

'I don't care if it is full of snakes.' Amelia adjusted her fetching hat to a more rakish angle. 'We're going on honeymoon – not a walking tour!'

Amidst a throng of well-wishers whose already large numbers had been swelled by members of the general public waiting outside the house, the newly married couple left to catch the overnight train to Edinburgh en route to the Dashwood family's hunting lodge in Perthshire. For the first few minutes as they sat in their reserved compartment neither of them said a word. Amelia looked at George with a perfectly straight face while George looked at her with deliberately over-widened eyes. Amelia was the first to crack, dissolving into helpless laughter as the train with a great heave and a clank began to draw out of the station. George used the sudden movement to pretend that he had been thrown forward out of his seat, ending up with Amelia in his arms. He was just about to kiss her passionately when the corridor door opened and a very large and smartly dressed woman entered.

'Is this a Ladies Only compartment?' she enquired in a Scottish accent. 'I have mislaid my spectacles and am looking for a Ladies Only compartment.'

'This is a reserved compartment, madam,' George said, resuming his seat while Amelia straightened her dress.

'Splendid,' the woman replied. 'Don't worry, if you are a married couple I have no objection to you both sharing it with me.'

'No, I'm afraid you do not understand, madam—' George began again, only to be quickly interrupted.

'Are you travelling all the way to Scotland?' the woman asked, settling her large frame in a corner by the door. 'I myself am, so I do hope you are. It's a long journey without company.'

'We are indeed journeying to Scotland, madam, but—'

'Allow me to introduce myself. I am the Lady Donaldson, and when in Scotland I reside at Castle Cullen. Are you familiar with it? It is one of the most notable forts on the eastern seaboard.'

'I have heard of it, Lady Donaldson,' George said, beginning again. 'But, with the greatest respect, I would like to point one thing out to you—'

'Your name, sir, if you would be so good,' Lady Donaldson replied. 'You have omitted giving me your name.'

'Of course.' George took a deep breath, glanced at Amelia as if to reassure her, then returned to the lady opposite him. 'Allow me to present myself.

Captain George Dashwood, Royal Artillery, and . . .' he hesitated before saying proudly, 'and this is my wife Amelia.'

'Dashwood indeed, General Sir Michael's boy?'

'The same.'

'I am acquainted with your father, young man,' Lady Donaldson returned with a satisfied nod. 'Indeed we have stalked some fine deer together. Are you to Scotland for the sport?'

'Not exactly, Lady Donaldson—'

George was not allowed to go any further for from the expression on his face Amelia knew that he was about to announce exactly why they *were* going to Scotland.

'We're going to visit some relatives,' she put in quickly, throwing George a quelling look.

'Ah. Good,' Lady Donaldson sighed, folding her hands in her lap. 'You look so young and fresh, for one dreadful moment I imagined you might be off on your honeymoon. In which case I would naturally have found myself another compartment.'

'It didn't matter at all,' Amelia laughed as later they made their way down the corridor towards their berth.

'But to be so sure of her ground that she even joined us for dinner!' George protested, rolling his eyes. 'In fact I should not be in the least surprised if there's a knock on the sleeper door at midnight and the mighty Lady Donaldson heaves

74

into view asking *if this wee berrrrrrth's reserrrrrved.'*

As George finished speaking in his awful Scots accent he opened the door to let her into the cramped quarters where they were to spend their wedding night.

'It's all right,' George said, reading the look on her face. 'This is not going to be – it's not to be our wedding night. This doesn't count. We have to think of this—' He indicated the tiny cabin. 'This is *en* transit.'

Amelia smiled, suddenly grateful that they had known each other so long, before George leaned down to lift her chin and kiss her once on the lips.

'You get yourself into bed,' he advised, 'while I go and have a wee drammie. I'll be back in about twenty minutes or so.'

As it transpired George did not return for the best part of an hour, but since they were as he said only *en* transit, Amelia really saw no point in staying awake for him. Besides, for some reason train journeys always sent her quickly to sleep, particularly once she was abed in a berth. By the time George did return she was only vaguely aware of him. She remembered waking up and seeing him sitting on the edge of the berth below her, his shoes off and his braces round his waist, and she remembered a strong smell of whisky and the way he was just staring at the floor. After which she fell happily asleep again, only waking as the train pulled into Edinburgh station.

The Dashwood hunting lodge was a fine stone house built at the turn of the century by General Dashwood to accommodate him, his family and his friends when the urge to kill a salmon, bag some grouse or stalk some deer came upon him. It stood on high ground overlooking the Tay in over five hundred acres of mixed moor and woodland which made it an excellent small sporting estate.

It seemed that the immaculately maintained house had always been serviced by the Muir family, an entourage of four taciturn Highlanders who lived in a small cottage by the main gates, while the estate was managed by an immensely tall Sutherlander called Eoin MacIndroe who, as far as Amelia could make out, seemed to speak only Gaelic. When she wondered to George how he understood his estate manager when he himself spoke no Gaelic George assured her that when Eoin spoke to him he did so in English. It simply sounded like Gaelic because his accent was so impenetrable to newcomers. Yet despite the fact that the Muirs were taciturn and Eoin awe-inspiring, Amelia fell in love with Killie Lodge the moment their carriage turned in the drive. Given its dramatic and wonderful setting in a woodland and by water it was without doubt the most beautiful place she had ever seen.

There were welcoming fires burning in the hearths of every room, and while the outside of the large stone house seemed daunting Amelia was delighted to find the interior comfortable and informal, furnished as it was with well-worn but inviting leather armchairs and sofas. The bedrooms were similarly welcoming, with their old-fashioned beds covered with goose-feather eiderdowns, heavy tartan curtains hanging at the windows and matching rugs thrown over the chairs. Amelia expressed her delight to George at the comfort of what from the outside had appeared to be a somewhat austere Highland lodge, and learned that since the house was such a distance from Sussex his grandmother had left the furnishing of it to old Mrs Muir, who being a good Scotswoman had been both thrifty and sensible, buying all the furniture second-hand at auction. The result was a house which looked as if it had been regularly lived in for at least a hundred years, rather than a recently furnished hunting lodge which was only visited by the family twice a year at the most. Best of all, as far as Amelia was concerned, there were resident dogs, one huge hound of indeterminate breed called Rollo and a sanguine bearded collie bitch called Ellie. Amelia befriended them both immediately, as they did her, almost dragging her off for a walk before she had time to get her bearings.

'They're incorrigible,' Mrs Muir told her as she took Amelia's coat, shooing the dogs away to no great effect with a brown leather booted foot. 'They think folk belong to them, they do, rather than the vicki verka. Down, Rollo, boy, get down now. Och, he's a way with him that would whiten the skin of a tannery worker.'

It was by now early evening, and by the time Amelia came back downstairs having washed and changed her dress after their long journey, George was nowhere to be found.

'Well he'll be away in the hills, that's where,' Mrs Muir told her as she threw some more logs on the fire. 'Since he came here as a bairn, first thing he must do is walk the hills. Now let me get you some refreshment. Sit there be the fire and I'll fetch ye some tea and scones just made.'

Amelia felt more than a little peeved that she had not at least been invited to join George on his walk but her sense of aggravation passed as she ate her delicious tea in front of the fire, burying herself in her copy of Wilkie Collins's *The Moonstone* which she had packed to read on the train journey. But even though she was enthralled by the book she found she could not settle to it, since half her mind was occupied in wondering when exactly her husband might return. Mrs Muir had told her that due to the hour of their arrival they would be eating later than usual at seven o'clock, but with no sign of the errant George by half past seven Mrs Muir came into the drawing room to announce that dinner would be served at a quarter to eight *regardless*.

Ten minutes later, as Amelia prepared to go into the dining room whither she was now being summoned by a gong, she bumped into the returning George plus dogs in the hallway.

'Sorry I'm a little late, everyone,' George apologized as Mrs Muir hurried out to take her master's coat and hat. 'I lost Rollo the far side of the loch.'

'He'd have made his own way back as usual,' Mrs Muir replied. 'We were just about to start without ye.'

'Of course. Do go right ahead, won't you, and settle Mrs Dashwood here at table, while I pop and wash my hands and fetch myself a small whisky and soda. Since only my wife and I are dining,' George smiled, 'I doubt if we have to stand on ceremony.'

He pulled a face at Amelia behind Mrs Muir's back before disappearing to the cloakroom, leaving the housekeeper with an armful of coat and hat.

'Ach well,' she sighed, folding George's loden coat outside in. 'Since ye are here on your honeymoon I dare say we'll forgive your being two minutes late, but nae more, or there'll be ruin on the plates, not dinner.'

Everything was far from ruined, the delicious game pie in particular, and the rest of the excellent dinner which both George and Amelia ate with relish, hungry after their long journey and George after his over-extended walk.

'You might have asked me to go with you. Or had you forgotten you are a married man?' Amelia teased him. 'We always go walking together, so you could at least have asked me.'

'I thought you'd be too tired,' George replied in genuine surprise. 'Knowing you, I knew you'd say you'd come if I asked you, even though you were half asleep on your feet. So I thought I'd just take myself off for a while and leave you to the fire and one of Mrs Muir's excellent teas while I exercised the dogs.'

'I missed you.'

'I missed you too. But there'll be plenty of other occasions now. Anyway, it's a habit I've got into. Going for a hike as soon as we get here.'

'A habit that in future had better include me.'

'If you say so.' George smiled, and then raised his glass. 'To you.'

'To us,' Amelia replied, raising her own back at him.

They drank their toast in silence, looking across the table at each other shyly, before returning to their dinner.

'So what do you make of this place, Mrs Dashwood?' George wondered. 'It astounds me every time I visit it.'

'I think it is absolutely breathtaking, even from the little I've seen of it so far,' Amelia replied. 'I wouldn't mind living here for ever.'

'Oh yes you would. It rains an absurd amount of the time, and it's very cold in winter.'

'I wouldn't mind, really. As long as I had you.'

'We'll find somewhere special to live, Amelia, I promise you,' George said, looking up at her.

'Soon as we return south we shall start thinking very seriously where we're going to make our home.'

'Yes, I'd like that, George. I'd like to find us somewhere secret. Somewhere where no-one will be able to find us. Where we can hide away together from the rest of the world. Somewhere magical.'

'*Magical*?' George opened his eyes. 'Like an enchanted castle perhaps?'

'Nothing so grand,' Amelia laughed. 'Something much smaller. An old place. Somewhere perhaps that's been uninhabited for ages. That we can rebuild and make magic.'

In the place surrounded by four tall dark hedges two men sat listening intently to the young Dashwoods' conversation. The younger man, the Noble One, was clothed in a deep violet robe, his older companion, Longbeard, held a purse containing every known sort of jewel. Around them all was utter silence yet every word they wished to hear they heard.

'Now.' Longbeard nodded sagely. 'Now they will come.'

'You are sure,' the Noble One replied. 'Why? What tells you these are they?'

Longbeard shook his head once then nodded as he took from the leather purse a jewel of no known colour. He held it up and even though it was night-time the great jewel suddenly shone with a light as bright as the sun, a light which shone not on its outside but from within.

'This is why I know,' Longbeard said. 'The Stone of Quiz. When the light shines, the call has been answered.'

'What's the matter, Amelia?' George said suddenly. 'You look as though you've seen a ghost.'

'I think I'm just tired,' Amelia replied, with a puzzled frown. 'It has been quite a journey.'

'Why? What is it – don't you feel well?'

'No. I mean no I don't feel unwell. I feel fine, in fact. Never better.' Amelia smiled at George to try to reassure him, but in her mind all she could see was the image. 'For a moment I thought I had fallen asleep.'

'Thank you,' George laughed. 'Says a lot for my company.'

'Of course I didn't,' Amelia returned. 'As if I could. But it was really strange. It must have been a daydream. And because of what we were talking about.'

'We were talking about finding a house. Finding somewhere to live.'

'I know.' Amelia frowned again. 'And then – then I saw a house.'

It was George's turn to look bewildered. He put down his wineglass and stared across the table at Amelia.

'You saw a house,' he echoed. 'What sort of house? What did it look like?'

'I don't know,' Amelia replied. 'It was a house I'd never seen before – but it's gone now.'

'The house has gone? Or the image of it?'

'The picture I had of it, George. I had this really crystal clear picture of it, so clear I could have described every inch of the place. But now – now it's completely gone from my head.'

For a while they both sat in silence with the remains of their unfinished pudding still before them. Finally they resumed their talk, carefully at first in case – as Amelia teased – she had another vision, and then as animatedly as before, once George had convinced Amelia that what she thought she had seen was simply either the result of the wine, or just a daydream. The matter of where they might live had never been actually broached before since George had always been of the opinion that as long as he was in the army they could live at his parents' house until they decided exactly what his future was to be.

But now, since George had already hinted that he might not care to spend the rest of his life in the army, they had both, quite separately, started to dream the way most young married people do of where ideally they might live, given the choice. It emerged from their conversation that both were more than happy to stay in Sussex, with George stating a strong preference for living by the sea while Amelia was not so sure.

'You know I love the sea as much as you do, George. But the trouble with living right by it is there's no green – particularly in the winter. I think I'd miss the trees and the fields and the hills.

Looking out at a grey and stormy sea all winter might get me down.'

'I don't think so, Amelia. I don't think you would be got down by anything.'

'You don't know me, George.'

'If anyone knows you I do,' George replied with perfect seriousness. 'And what I don't know I intend to find out.'

Both the remark and the look in George's eyes silenced Amelia. She felt the blood rush to her cheeks and an odd feeling of excitement took her over, more so even than the first time she had jumped for a dare into the sea off some high rocks with Hermione, or the first time she had sailed the Dashwood dinghy by herself. It was odd that she felt such a sense of thrilling anticipation, since she thought she must have known the sort of adventure she was facing even if only in outline, yet now, as she found herself looking shyly back at her new husband with no absolute idea of what exactly her immediate future held in store, the colour in her cheeks lingered, and this despite knowing George all her life.

Sensing her sudden shyness, George put down his glass of wine and took the edge of the table in both hands.

'I'm sorry, Amelia. That wasn't the right thing to say. Will you forgive me?'

'There's nothing to forgive, George,' Amelia replied with a shy smile. 'It's you who should forgive me. Forgive my blushes, as they used to say.'

'I don't want to make you blush. At least not out of any sense of embarrassment.'

'It wasn't from embarrassment, George, I do assure you.'

George looked at her for a moment, then rose from the table.

'Let's go and sit by the fire for a while,' he suggested, smiling back at her. 'And make plans for the rest of the week.'

They sat by the great fire which had been left ready for them for a further hour, playing cards and talking about how they planned to spend their time together in the next ten days. George wondered if she would like to be taught how to fly-fish properly, since this was something the two of them had never done.

'You're more than handy with a coarse rod,' he said, pouring himself a whisky. 'And I know how much you enjoy angling, so perhaps if I taught you how to cast a fly—'

'Is it much more difficult?'

'It's a knack to be a fly fisherman, and a skill to be a good one. At least that's what Eoin has always maintained, and if ever there was a skilled fly fisher, it's he.'

'Can we have the first lesson tomorrow, please?' Amelia wondered, suddenly seeing herself on the river bank with George standing beside her, holding her by the waist while she carefully cast for a salmon. 'I really can't wait to get started.'

'Of course,' George agreed with a laugh. 'But in that case we shall need an early start – and seeing that it's nearly a quarter to eleven now, why don't you go on up to bed?'

Amelia was about to ask him whether or not he was coming up to bed as well before concluding that George was perhaps being tactful and giving her time to get undressed and into bed before him. Even though she had not considered in any depth what might exactly happen on her wedding night and in what precise order, Amelia still felt a peculiar sort of disappointment that her newly married husband was not going to accompany her to the bedroom, as if he was only going to join her halfway through a dance.

Since the installation of electricity had been confined to the ground floor only, upstairs was still traditionally lit by candlelight at night. Amelia found this wonderfully romantic, and since she was all alone it seemed even more regrettable that George had taken the decision to stay downstairs, for in her mind's eye she could see him lifting her up in his strong arms to carry her over the bedroom threshold before – and here Amelia gave a shiver of anticipation as the thought struck her – before perhaps helping her to undress?

Much taken by the thought, Amelia closed the door behind her, but instead of getting herself undressed and ready for bed she first extinguished the candles in the wall brackets and the two on the silver sticks placed on the chest of drawers, leaving only the ones by the bedside and on her dressing table alight, before sitting herself down in front of the looking-glass and beginning slowly to brush out her dark hair with long regular strokes.

This was a much-loved ritual and one she would happily prolong for upwards of a hundred strokes, since it provided what Amelia had always considered the best time for daydreaming, so even though George left another quarter of an hour before following her upstairs, when he did finally come into the bedroom he found Amelia still quite happily seated at the dressing table.

'I thought you might be in bed by now,' he said quietly, shutting the door behind him. 'If you'd rather I came back—'

'No, George, I wouldn't. I'd rather you stayed.'

From the short silence that ensued Amelia concluded with a certain amount of delight that it appeared to be George's turn to be at a loss for words.

'Is something the matter, George?' she enquired.

'Not really,' he replied. 'I really can come back if you'd rather.'

'George,' Amelia said with a small sigh, turning to him but still brushing her hair. 'It's all right – we are married now.'

'I dare say.' George breathed in slowly, widened his eyes and, puffing out his cheeks, slowly exhaled. 'It's just – it's just that neither of us have been married *before*.'

Amelia smiled and George smiled back at her, still firmly rooted to his spot. Amelia thought for a moment, then offered him her hairbrush.

'Would you like to finish brushing out my hair?' she suggested. 'It's very soothing.'

'For you?'

'For us both.'

He took the brush from her and frowned at it as if he had never seen such a thing before in his life. To prompt him, Amelia turned round on her dressing stool again to face the looking-glass, leaning her head back slightly so that her hair hung out and down from her head.

'Long, slow strokes,' she whispered. 'And don't say a word.'

He brushed her hair as if he had been brushing girls' hair all his life, yet Amelia thought that he could not possibly have done so before. Certainly his mother with her short hair and her oddly detached manner was not the sort of woman who would invite her little boy to come and help her with her *toilette*. Yet George was brushing out Amelia's hair carefully and tenderly, now putting the back of his hand under her tresses as he passed the brush downwards in long, slow strokes. Amelia sighed and opened her mouth to say something just as George leaned over her and kissed her upside down.

The next thing she knew she was in his arms and

he was kissing her right way round and oh so passionately. For a moment Amelia was caught breathless and had to ease herself away from him. Mistaking her intention George stopped kissing her, but Amelia just smiled, told him not to be sorry and began to return his kisses. He had one arm round her waist now, the other on her back, and he was bending her backwards to the bed, but carefully, so that he could ease her down onto it. She looked up at him in the flickering candlelight and he looked back down at her, slipping off his jacket and loosening his tie, taking it off and undoing his shirt. Amelia lay quite still, thinking that to start undressing herself would not only be forward but would spoil the intense excitement she was now feeling. Instead she just lay as still as she could while George stripped half naked before lying down on the bed next to her. He put a hand out, round her waist, to ease her nearer him, telling her how much he loved her before smothering her soft mouth with more kisses, kisses Amelia returned with ever-increasing passion as she put her hand up to the back of his head to bury it in his hair. For a moment George stopped kissing her, lifting his head to look at her, and in that second he saw only sockets without eyes, and blood streaming, a woman's face shot to pieces.

'Dear God!' he suddenly exclaimed, sitting bolt upright and holding his head. '*Oh my God oh my God.*'

'What?' Amelia said, immediately alarmed as she saw his look of anguish and heard the pain in his cry. 'George what is it? Are you ill? *George, what is it?'*

She had her hands on his shoulders now, holding him, but his head was bowed and he was sobbing, long racking sobs such as Amelia had never heard before. She had never ever heard a man cry, only girls, or little boys. These were terrible cries that shook his whole being, that made him gasp as if he was drowning.

'George . . .' she said urgently. 'George darling – please – please. *Whatever is the matter?'*

Still he said nothing, but now he allowed his head to fall on her breasts where he lay still sobbing. She put both her arms round him, rocking him as she would cradle, she imagined, a crying child, gently soothing him, one hand stroking his hair, the same hand pressing his head closer to her.

'You poor darling boy.'

She held him like that long after he had stopped crying, long after he had tried faintly to move when she would not let him, holding him until she was certain the pain had eased. Then she put both her hands to his face, either side of his tearstained cheeks, and tried to kiss away his sorrow. As she did so he just looked at her as if he did not know where he was, his eyes full of anguish, letting her ease him so carefully under the sheets and covering him with the goose-feathered quilt. He lay quite still on the pillows, white as a ghost even by the warm light of the candles, while she wiped his forehead with a cool flannel, and then his face, before putting her hand to his cheek and shutting his eyes, telling him there was no need to say anything.

'Sleep is the best thing, and in the morning, everything will be different.'

She waited until she knew he was quite asleep before she moved a muscle. Once she was certain she eased herself up off the bed, slipped out of her clothes and into her nightdress and slid under the covers beside him. The last thing she did was to blow out the candle by the bed, a candle whose last light illuminated the childlike face of her sleeping husband.

When she awoke the next morning, George was already up and gone. It was raining heavily so when Amelia went downstairs for her breakfast she was surprised to learn from Mrs Muir that the 'young master' had long gone out to have a few casts in the loch.

'Hardly fishing weather surely, Mrs Muir,' Amelia remarked as she lifted the silver lids on the dishes lined up on the sideboard.

'The young master's that good wi' his rod he'd catch fish in a hurricane, ma'am,' Mrs Muir replied, pouring some piping hot coffee ready for Amelia.

As she ate a delicious breakfast of salted porridge and cream followed by fresh haddock and poached eggs, Amelia thought over the events of the night. Her guess was an obvious one. George was troubled by some terrible event from his war service, which was hardly surprising, since she assumed most soldiers who had been in the front line carried mental images that would possibly last them their lifetimes. What she could not work out, however, was why George should be so troubled at such an ecstatic moment. Had it been in the middle of the night when they were fast asleep it would have been more understandable, but since they were both not only wide awake but in each other's arms and starting to make love, Amelia could not begin to understand what could possibly have triggered such a terrible and agonizing attack. Did she remind him of someone? And if so – who? For the life of her Amelia could not bring herself to believe that, like some of the married officers about whom Hermione had gossiped to her, George had kept a mistress in France, or made love to some other woman before returning home.

But even if this should be the case, Amelia reasoned, he was not engaged to Amelia at the time, let alone married, so it could hardly be counted as an *infidelity*. She also knew, from hearing the matter so often discussed between her parents, that given the circumstances of a war soldiers could not be expected to behave in the same manner as would be expected of them in peacetime. The same rules did not apply, and nor could any reasonable person expect that they should.

Nevertheless, Amelia assumed that whatever had upset George so terribly could have nothing to do with his own actions, since she believed what he had told her: that he had kept himself for her, and thought of her, and her only, all the time he was away. It had therefore to be to do with something terrible that he had witnessed in the war.

But what?

Only he could tell her that, but she knew George to be one of those people who clam up the moment they are pressed. When they were much younger Amelia had often pleaded with him too hard for information, with the result that she learned less than she would have done had she kept quiet and allowed him to volunteer the facts. So even though this situation was obviously a far more crucial one, this time the same rules *did* apply. She simply had to keep her own counsel.

By the time she had finished her breakfast the rain, which had been falling heavily, was easing, so taking directions from Mrs Muir Amelia left the lodge to find her husband. She soon caught sight of him not five hundred yards away on the shore of the loch, fishing by himself while the rain swept away across the water and the skies began to clear. By the time she was at his side the sun had come out, restoring the wonderful landscape to its morning glory.

'Amelia!' George said with delight when he saw

her. 'You've brought the sun out – which is no surprise.'

He leaned down and kissed her, smiling at her as if he had not one care in the world other than for her. Minutes later, once he had established Amelia's intentions, he began his fly fishing tutorial, patiently running through the basic technique right from the beginning so that his pupil would miss nothing.

'You're a quick learner,' he said, watching approvingly as Amelia began to flick the fly neatly and accurately through the air to land within ten feet of where he had instructed. 'You're also naturally sporting, so we'll have you landing your first trout tomorrow at the latest, no two ways about it.'

Indeed once Amelia had mastered the basic trick of the cast, the slow motion half delayed forward flick of the wrist designed to propel the feather-weight fly to land all but unnoticed on the water, she was ready to start that afternoon, but no sooner had they prepared to fish than the rains returned in earnest, driving the less robust Amelia back indoors. Despite being hardier, George accompanied her, insisting that he had done more than enough fishing for one day. Mrs Muir had a fire ready to dry them out before she served them a lunch of nourishing stew and home-made apple and blackberry pie.

The afternoon was spent in reading and playing more card games, the hours between tea and dinner by a long walk beside the loch since the rain had stopped once again, and the evening back in front of a blazing log fire after the second of Mrs Muir's ample dinners.

'This is heaven, George. Let's stay here for ever.'

'Seriously?'

'I'd be happy wherever we were, as long as I was with you.'

For some time before midnight Amelia sat at George's feet while he gently stroked her hair and they reminisced about their childhood. Then, as the clock chimed the witching hour, Amelia yawned and said she was ready for her bed.

'Are you coming up now, George?' she asked, standing up in front of the fire and slowly stretching. 'I need someone to do my hair,' she added, her head on one side, lightly teasing.

George looked at her, smiled, then bit his lower lip before answering, as if considering his reply. 'You go up first. I'm going to let the dogs out for a wander and I'll follow you up shortly.'

Half an hour later as Amelia sat brushing her hair at her dressing table, this time dressed ready for bed in yet another beautiful nightgown, George had still not appeared. Understanding that his absence might be deliberate, Amelia snuffed her candles out and slipped between the sheets. She intended to lie awake for as long as it took her husband to come to bed, but due to the wonderful food and the fresh Scottish air instead she was asleep within another five minutes.

*   *   *

The following day dawned clear but there was a strong north-easter blowing so Amelia dressed well and warmly against the Highland weather before setting off with her husband and Eoin to fish for salmon on the banks of the Tay. As they made their way to the beat, even though she was sorely tempted to take George to task for his non-appearance the night before, Amelia held her tongue and instead listened to what George had to say about the wiles of the Scottish salmon.

Again, just as he had been the day before, once he was outside with his mind occupied by other things George was as apparently happy as the proverbial sandboy. Certainly with his fly rod in hand and Amelia by his side anyone enjoying his company would put him down as one of the most contented of young men and rightly so, given the beauty and sweet disposition of his new wife. And because he was so transparently happy once night had changed to day Amelia was happy too, particularly as the fresh wind had cleared the sky of all the rain clouds, leaving the mountains and waters to bask in clear bright sunlight.

'Not the ideal conditions,' George opined, as he stared up at what looked like being a permanently cloudless sky. 'We could do with a bit of cover.'

'We'll need to fish the banks,' Eoin said, looking upriver. 'The fish'll be lying there in the shadows.'

'We'll try our favourite pools, Eoin,' George suggested. 'Clump Pool and The Basher.'

'Clump Pool and The Basher?' Amelia laughed.

'Don't ask me why,' George replied. 'That's how they've always been known.'

Amelia followed the two men upriver until they were opposite a high bank overhung with branches.

'Hardly beginner's water, George Dashwood,' Amelia observed, seeing how far under the branches the two pools that George had pointed out to her lay. 'You'll have to fish those, George. I'd get my line hopelessly snagged in those trees.'

'Quite so. It wasn't my intention to get you casting there, because even I find those pools tricky. But if you take this beat here, from where we're standing to where the bank rises upstream there . . .'

He pointed to the mark, a place where the bank rose steeply by a bend in the fast-flowing river.

'At least you'll be able to practise casting without anything behind you to snag your line, and without any trees ahead of you to do likewise. Just choose a spot on the water and practise landing your fly on it – remembering to keep that index finger in the slack . . .'

He stood behind Amelia as she prepared her rod, his arms round her as he reminded her of the positions for her hands.

'Then reel in slowly and rhythmically. What you must avoid at all costs is to show the salmon you're fishing for him. That fly must be all he sees. Not your line. And no movement on the water he can't recognize.'

Amelia turned her head to smile at him, suddenly so comforted by the feel of the two strong arms round her that all she wanted was to be kissed. She could see from the look in George's eyes that the same thought had occurred to him, and with Eoin now safely out of sight patrolling the bank a hundred or so yards ahead, Amelia thought it perfectly safe. She therefore deliberately moved her face just that bit closer so he would find her impossible to resist, which judging from the look in his eyes was indeed the case. Amelia closed her own eyes, only to feel George suddenly move away.

'No. No, not now. Not here.'

'Eoin's miles away, George. If that's what's worrying you.'

'That isn't what's worrying me.'

'What is it then? What is it that's worrying you – because obviously something is.'

As soon as her words were out, Amelia realized that she had made a mistake, even before she saw the change in George's look.

'Why don't you follow Eoin on?' he suggested, almost over-politely, just as he did when Amelia knew he was annoyed. 'I'll fish here for a while, then I'll come and join you in about half an hour or so. To see how you're getting on.'

'I'll only go if you kiss me, George,' Amelia half teased, hoping to make up some lost ground.

'Fine.' George shrugged, and leaning over kissed her on the cheek. 'Good luck.'

As she made her way up the bank to her designated station, Amelia hoped against hope that all George was upset about was the fact that she had wrong-footed him by making it so obvious she wanted to be kissed. Even though the river banks were deserted she thought George might still perhaps consider them to be a public place, so that his dismay had been caused by her wanting so much to be kissed rather than anything else – rather than, say, his not wishing to kiss *her* in case it led to the same sort of reaction as the night before last. Oh, she did so hope. Surely to heaven he had not been upset on that occasion by the fact of their kissing so passionately, because if that were so they might as well declare their honeymoon null and void here and now and return home at once. For a moment Amelia almost downed her fishing tackle to hurry back to George and have the matter out with him properly, but remembering his almost curt reaction when she had teased him a moment ago she thought better of it, making her way instead to her appointed rock where Eoin was waiting for her. And all the while the awful thought would keep coming back: *perhaps because they had been childhood friends they would never be able to become lovers?*

Eoin proved to be an expert teacher, instructing Amelia verbally rather than by example, a technique Amelia only truly appreciated once she had honed her new skill sufficiently well to land her fly within about six feet of the gillie's appointed target. Not that Eoin then felt it necessary to show off his own great skill in front of his pupil. On the contrary Amelia only witnessed it accidentally when, seeking help after tangling her line, she made her quiet way back to her husband's station and saw Eoin landing a fly repeatedly on the same spot of mirrored water under an overhanging branch.

'Heavens,' she whispered, standing just behind George's shoulder. 'How long does it take to get as good as that?'

'About four or five centuries,' George replied with a smile, his good mood apparently restored. 'Round these parts they say Eoin's family invented fly fishing.'

'We're on, sir,' Eoin muttered, having cocked his wrist. 'He's taken the fly.'

'You'll see some action now, Amelia. There are a couple of good-size fish in that pool – ten pounders possibly. Now just hold on and you'll see how to play a salmon.'

Linking her arm firmly through George's, Amelia watched enthralled as Eoin played the salmon, letting it run away from him downstream on an ever-shortening line, allowing the fish plenty of time to exhaust himself in the fight while patiently reeling him in a matter of inches each time he lifted the tip of his rod to shorten his line. Finally, after the best part of half an hour, he offered the rod to George who at once declined with a shake of his head.

'Never, Eoin,' he said. 'This is your fish, man.'

In response Eoin simply nodded once and began the process of finally landing his catch. As he lifted the end of his rod to turn the salmon towards the landing net that George now had in the water Amelia could see the silvery creature for the first time, twisting and turning in its torment as it tried desperately and possibly for the last time to save its life. But the fisherman's skills were too great and a moment later, after one final contortion, the salmon lay in the landing net, too exhausted now to offer more than token resistance as Eoin lifted it out to lay it on the bank preparatory to administering the *coup de grâce*.

'No – wait,' Amelia said as she saw the gillie taking his priest from his jacket pocket. 'Don't you think a fish as brave and as strong as that deserves to live?'

George stared at her, as indeed did Eoin.

'It's a fish, Amelia. You don't catch fish to throw them back. Certainly not salmon.'

'Just this once. He put up such a brave fight. And he's such a beautiful fish.'

George looked from her to the fish, whose only sign of life now was the occasional flick of his tail, then back at Amelia.

'George?' she asked him again. 'Just for me?'

'But you fish, Amelia,' he said in bewilderment. 'We've been fishing so often together. You understand fishing.'

'I always throw them back.'

'Not when we sea fished. Not when we caught mackerel over the side of the boat!'

'That was different, George. Don't ask me why now – it just was. Please put this salmon back. Please. Before it's too late.'

She was aware of the disbelief in Eoin's stare, just as she was of the confusion in her husband's eyes, but however feeble and sentimental she knew she might appear Amelia could not bear the thought of this brave fish being killed, even though she knew how good it would taste once Mrs Muir had finished with it.

It was different now, seeing first-hand how a salmon fought for its life, apparently not just by instinct but from a very real need for survival. After all, it had made the journey upstream to propagate and now, after surviving that long and difficult journey and after putting up probably the most heroic fight of its life, its reward was to be death to satisfy a sporting whim. That was all it was: a lust to kill a beautiful creature not because they needed its meat to survive themselves but just so they could say they had beaten a great brave salmon.

In spite of her pleas neither of the men moved, each seemingly waiting for the other to make the decision. So, sensing an impasse, and the distinct possibility that while they waited the fish might well die anyway, Amelia bent down, picked up the salmon, from whose mouth Eoin had already removed the hook, and prepared to put it back in the water.

'No,' George said, stopping her with a hand on her arm. 'If you must, then for heaven's sake put it back properly. Don't drop it in.'

'George! It was you who taught me ages ago how to return a fish to water when we were fishing for carp, remember?'

Freeing herself from his hand she knelt on the bank and carefully slid the great fish nose first into the shallow, where it lay for a moment as if already dead. Amelia watched and prayed, but the salmon showed no sign of life. Just as she was about to give up hope, suddenly it flicked its great tail, stirring up a cloud of mud, and a moment later slipped into the fast-running waters of the Tay.

'Thank you,' Amelia said, standing up and trying to keep sight of the fish who the next moment disappeared finally from view. 'I'm sure you don't agree with me, but since honours were about even, I think that was only fair.'

'Are we to throw every fish back now that we catch?' Eoin growled at his employer. 'For if so, I really see no point in continuing.'

'For today at least, Eoin,' George said with a wink clearly visible to Amelia. 'Although as far as that particular salmon went I must agree with my wife. I think the fish deserved his freedom.'

'Aye,' the gillie replied, with unveiled sarcasm. 'And I've no doubt there'll be plenty of grateful otters who think exactly the same.'

With a glower at Amelia the big Highlander set about changing the fly on his employer's rod while Amelia waited for her next set of instructions.

'Sorry, George. It wasn't my fish. I really had no right.'

'No you didn't. But – on the other hand, you did. You're part of a couple now, and that gives you a say in what we both do.'

'It never has, George. Not before. In marriage the woman has always been expected to go along with what her husband wishes.'

'Times are changing, Amelia,' George said, glancing up from the knot he was tying in his line. 'After all, there is even a woman Member of Parliament now.' He smiled back at her and, despite everything that had or had not happened, Amelia saw that his smile was full of love and understanding.

In spite of Eoin's dark mood, the rest of the day proved equally agreeable, with Amelia even managing to hook a good-sized salmon only for it to escape again almost at once. The gillie offered some grudging advice on how to play a fish once it was hooked, but the help was offered only in response to a prompt from George. It was clear that Eoin was not in a forgiving frame of mind. George, however, remained in a sunny mood all day, despite the fact that neither he nor Eoin managed to hook, let alone catch, another salmon before dusk.

Dinner was conducted in the same benevolent

mood, although Mrs Muir, having learned of the great salmon's freedom, had not taken the news well, to judge from her constant mutterings about the waste of a good fish as she went about serving the meal. George ignored her grumbling, asking Amelia instead what she wanted to do the following day.

'Have you not forgotten, sir?' Mrs Muir interrupted before Amelia could reply. 'Tomorrow was the day Eoin had set aside for a stalk.'

George glanced at Amelia to read her reaction, and seeing a frown cloud her pretty face dismissed the housekeeper and turned his attention to the sirloin.

'I know what you're thinking, Amelia,' he said, after Mrs Muir had left.

'Have we just come up here to kill things?'

'What would you rather do?'

'I'd actually rather not kill things, George. Fishing's one thing – but I'm not sure I want to go out shooting deer. Or birds.'

'Deer have to be killed. They do untold damage.'

'Not to their habitat. Only to ours. If we weren't here, if this was just the deer's natural habitat, which in a way it is – the moors, the woods, the glens – they'd only be prey to their natural predators. All they're doing really is eating what is rightfully theirs.'

'If we don't control their numbers, Amelia, there'll be deer everywhere.'

'Nature has her way of controlling her own

numbers really rather well, without our help.'

Seeming at a loss for words, George picked up his knife and fork, gave a deep sigh, then put them down again.

'What will you do if you don't come out with us? Eoin's laid it on specially.'

'Then of course you must go,' Amelia finished for him. 'You can't go upsetting your game-keeper.'

'There's no need to be facetious.'

'You don't have to worry about me, George,' Amelia said, taking a drink of water. 'I'll find some way of amusing myself. We women are quite good at that. Anyway, if I came out and you caught a stag you'd only have to blood me and I don't think I want that. I understand from my father that sometimes they cut open the stag's belly and push your head inside it.'

'Not always.'

'Is that what happened to you?'

'Yes.' George poured himself more wine.

'How old were you?'

'Ten.'

'Good heavens, George! It must have terrified the life out of you.'

'Of course it did. In fact I was frightened sick. Literally.'

'How ridiculous. What an awful thing to do.'

'It was my father's idea. He thought I was a bit of a cissy.'

'*You?*'

George smiled. 'He said I played with girls too much.'

'By that could he possibly have meant me?' Amelia wondered.

'Yes.' George looked at her and seeing the funny side of it at last they both laughed.

'And now you've ended up marrying me!'

'Yes.'

'So in a way you were blooded on my account?'

'I suppose so. Yes – in a way.'

'Then the very least I should do is come out stalking with you.'

'Why?'

'Because I'm your wife. And I think a husband and wife should share as many things as possible. If they want to get to know each other the way they should.'

'Well,' George said, giving the matter a lot of thought. 'Only if you're sure.'

'I'm quite sure,' Amelia replied. 'Anyway, if I am to have views on such things, then I should see them first hand. As I did with salmon fishing.'

Afterwards, as they sat by the fire with Amelia reading her book and George writing up his fishing diary, Amelia realized why she had stuck her neck out quite as far as she had. The last thing she wanted to see on her honeymoon was a stag being shot, so obviously the reason she had insisted must have been the hope that a show of such staunchness might in turn help George to overcome whatever inhibition it was which was

107

holding him back from loving her the way a husband should love a wife, whatever that way might be.

The more she thought about it the more she felt she was right, that she had shown willing in order to prove her courage so that he might overcome the fear that was so obviously haunting him.

Her challenge in fact took them back to their childhood, back to the time they had always matched each other's deeds to prove their undying friendship no matter how great the challenge: climbing the hardest and tallest trees, jumping the widest and most fast-running brooks, attempting to scale the sheerest hillsides, George stripped down to his undershirt and Amelia with her skirts thrown over one arm, both of them intent on not being outdone by the other. It had been harder for Amelia, encumbered not only by her clothing but by the protocol of her gender. Even so, as they had grown up and Amelia had developed into an athletic teenager, much to his surprise George had found he had a match on his hands, particularly after she had persuaded him to lend her some of his boys' clothes.

'What are you laughing about?' George said, looking up from his writing. 'Is it your book? I never found *The Moonstone* very funny . . .'

'No, not my book. I was just remembering when we had a bet about jumping the brook where we used to catch crayfish. I made you lend me some of your clothes—'

'And I fell in because I was laughing so much. Except I don't know *why* I was laughing because I remember thinking what a handsome boy you made.'

'I thought I must have looked stupid. Because of the way you were laughing. Anyway, I won. And not because you fell in – because I jumped further than you.'

'Like a rematch?' George's eyes lit up at the idea.

'Any time.'

'We'll have to find a good spot on the river.'

'And you'll have to lend me some of your clothes.'

'You wouldn't fit into them now. We were much more of a size then.'

'Perhaps Mrs Muir has got some bloomers,' Amelia suggested with a straight face.

'Or perhaps Eoin will lend you a kilt,' George replied with a smile. 'Anyway, we'll find a good leap before we go back south and have some money on it.'

'Done,' Amelia said, offering her hand. 'Shake on it.'

They shook, and Amelia *hoped* George would keep holding her hand, which he did for a moment, looking into her eyes and smiling.

'Bedtime, I think,' he said, after a second or two. 'We have a very early start tomorrow.'

Amelia followed the same routine as the night before, preceding George upstairs where she hopefully waited for him to arrive and join her.

Once again she was disappointed, for having kept herself awake by reading for over half an hour in her bed, there was still neither sight nor sound of him. This time, however, Amelia determined not to lie there tamely waiting, for that was to run the very real risk of falling asleep, so pulling on her dressing gown she went downstairs in search of her husband.

She found all the lights out and the fires doused. She also found the front and back doors were locked and bolted from the inside, indicating that George most certainly could not have gone for a midnight walk, unless he intended climbing back in through a window. Puzzled, Amelia returned upstairs, her way lit by the nightlight in her hand. When she reached the landing she nearly jumped out of her skin as a door swung open behind her and George appeared in his nightclothes.

'I was afraid you might be asleep,' he told her, before she could ask. 'I didn't want to disturb you.'

'Well as you can see I'm not asleep,' Amelia replied. 'In fact I'm very wide awake.'

'You really should be asleep. As I said, we have a very early start.'

'Why not come to bed, George?' Amelia suggested. 'Then we can both get to sleep.'

'I was going to sleep in my dressing room tonight. Because of the early start.'

'Don't be silly,' Amelia sighed, taking his hand. 'Come on.'

She dragged the obviously reluctant George

behind her along the landing and into their bedroom, where with a good deep yawn she took off her dressing gown and collapsed into bed.

'We do have to get up most frightfully early,' George reminded her, standing at the foot of the bed.

'I know, George, so you keep saying,' Amelia replied with another huge yawn. 'Good night.'

She turned over and pretended to go to sleep. Moments later she felt the covers lift and George slip into bed beside her. For a moment he did not move, as if afraid he might have woken her, then, when he felt sure she was still sleeping, he turned on his side away from her to fall asleep minutes later.

Amelia lay on her side of the bed facing her husband's back and wondering what precisely was the matter with him. Supposing he might be just terribly shy, she wondered what she might do to woo him, before realizing with intense embarrassment that there was nothing she *could* do since she herself knew nothing at all about the art of making love. So she carefully and slowly turned away from him to face the window opposite, staring out at the night sky until, after what seemed like an eternity, she finally fell asleep just half an hour before cockcrow.

Five

They were up high in the glen, several miles from the lodge. Again the day was fine but cold, due to the north-easterly still blowing in from the distant sea, but Amelia was well dressed against the chill just as she was stoutly shod in deference to the terrain. They had been out since dawn and it was now nearly midday, yet Amelia had kept pace with the stalking party, finally earning grudging praise from Eoin who like his employer had made no allowances for the supposed frailty of her sex, the two men having stalked their prey exactly as they would were she not with them.

They had spotted a magnificent stag about two hours after setting out and so far, due to Eoin's undoubted skills and cunning, the beast would seem to have no idea whatsoever of their presence, making its way across the hillside, stopping briefly to graze or help itself to some leaves from the branches of trees on the outskirts of small coppices around the glen. Several times it disappeared into the woodlands yet Eoin seemed to know instinctively where it would exit, swinging the party in a quick detour downwind of the copse so that they would be in position when and if the stag made its reappearance, which invariably it did. Only once did they lose it completely, when it began to run as if suddenly frightened, cresting a steep hill well ahead of where the stalkers hid and disappearing entirely from sight.

'A wild cat probably,' Eoin muttered as he searched the horizon through his field glasses. 'I could see something moving in the heather on his flank and it probably startled him. But he's no panicked. He's just putting distance betwixt him and whatever.'

'What's over that hill, Eoin?' George asked. 'If it's moor then he'll probably have bolted over it for cover.'

'There's quite a tricky burn, sir. Running through a gorge. He'll no make it across there, so he'll have to run north where there's a copse.'

'So if we were to cut through to the left of those trees,' George suggested, pointing to the woodland ahead, 'and along that track which must run parallel to your burn, we'd still be downwind and above the copse where he might have taken refuge, would we not?'

'Aye,' Eoin agreed. 'But we can only go as far as where the track bends, for if we go further we'll be on the wind and he'll pick us up. Are you set, missy?'

Eoin turned to Amelia, who secretly had been only too glad to stop so that she could catch her breath. In fact when she saw how the land unfolded ahead of them she would have been even happier to call it a day and turn for home. But her pride would not allow her even to contemplate such an attractive notion any further so with a nod to the gamekeeper she picked herself up, armed herself once more with her tall walking stick, and followed on the heels of her husband.

Half an hour later they found themselves at the point of the designated track where it turned almost in a U around a huge boulder. With one hand behind his back Eoin signalled to them to stop, dropping down below the ridge at the foot of the rock. George and Amelia at once followed suit, George ending up flat on his stomach like Eoin while Amelia sat with her back firmly positioned against the stone. They remained motionless like this, playing dead for maybe ten minutes or more as they listened to the sound of an animal very near by, its feet in the heather and its jaws slowly ruminating its food. Amelia looked at George, hoping to take courage from him, but to her astonishment she saw he was lying with his head in his hands and his eyes tightly closed. She began to edge herself towards him so that she could put a hand on his, but before she had moved an inch Eoin glared at her reprovingly and put a finger to his lips. So all Amelia could do was lie watching George, noticing with alarm that he now seemed to be shaking all over.

Afraid that he might be suffering from some form of fit, Amelia was just about to disobey all the orders she had been given to remain absolutely still so that she could see to her husband when almost right above her on the ridge the stag appeared, a magnificent ten pointer silhouetted against the sky, his great head tilted slightly upward as he nosed the air for scent. She had never seen such a mighty deer, certainly never one of this size and majesty. The deer in Sussex were beautiful little creatures, but tiny in comparison with this massive monarch of the glens, whose splendour was further increased by the fact that it was standing directly above them on a promontory. As she took in its beauty she knew at once that she could not bear it to be killed, yet she had absolutely no idea at all as to how she might prevent the slaughter, ignorant as she was how this huge fierce creature might react. She remembered stories about infuriated stags pinning people to the ground with their antlers and goring them to death, and certainly having seen this particular creature's horns at close quarters Amelia had no trouble in believing such a thing. So if she alerted the stag to the present danger there was every possibility it might turn on them before Eoin could get hold of his gun and kill it.

Worst of all, George was lying nearest to it, still with his eyes tightly closed, quite probably unaware that he was in danger. She realized there was only one thing she could do and that was to get close enough to Eoin to implore him *sotto voce* not to shoot, to draw his attention to George who was lying hidden from the gillie by a large rock which stood between them. But even as she turned to the gamekeeper she saw his gun was already at his shoulder and aimed straight at the stag's heart.

'No!'

Aghast, Amelia swung back round and saw George up on his feet, stumbling across the rocks in an attempt to reach Eoin. Above him, alerted by the sudden noise and movement, the stag had lowered his great head and turned to face its enemies.

'No!' George shouted again, almost now on top of Eoin who was still taking careful aim. 'No, you fool! Don't shoot, man! If you shoot they'll court martial you!'

He lunged for Eoin's rifle but he was too late to stop the gillie from shooting, although not too late to deflect the aim, so that the bullet fired almost directly up in the air above them well clear of the quarry. George struggled with the bewildered Eoin for possession of the rifle while above them the mighty stag lowered its head, turned tail and fled in a cloud of dust and dirt kicked up from the track.

'What are ye doing, sir!' Eoin was yelling. 'Have ye taken leave of your senses, man?'

George stared at him, both hands still on the gillie's rifle.

'You're the one who's taken leave of his senses, you fool,' he replied quietly. 'They'll shoot you.'

'Who will, George?' Amelia asked him, coming to his side and putting her hand carefully on his arm to remind him of her presence. 'Who will shoot Eoin, George? And why?'

He looked round at her with lost eyes, and she could see he did not know her.

'For God's sake,' he whispered. 'Don't you see? There's only one thing that can happen now. Don't you understand?'

He looked at her with anguish, before his legs started to buckle and it was only by using all her strength that Amelia was able to stop him from falling, while she called to Eoin to fetch up the bearers.

Six

The two workers off the estate who had been employed to follow them on the stalk helped bring home their employer on the old sure-footed pony whose job it should have been to bring home the dead stag. George had fallen into utter silence since his outburst on the ridge, allowing himself to be lifted onto the pony and held in position by one of the men, who kept a firm hold of him all the long way back to the lodge. Once home, while Mr Muir set off in pony and trap to fetch the doctor from the village, with the help of Mrs Muir Amelia took George upstairs to the bedroom where they laid him gently on the bed.

'He's such a braw man, I canna imagine what might be his trouble,' Mrs Muir said, looking down at the now comatose George. 'Maybe a brainstorm. Maybe a seizure, perhaps.'

'A seizure?' Amelia took the hand of her young, handsome husband who lay apparently blind and deaf to all. 'You don't think it can have been a seizure, surely, Mrs Muir? I think he's shocked. Something happened up there on the hillside, something which brought back some awful memory or other, and I think he's probably just very badly shocked.'

'The man could have had a heart attack for all we know, madam,' Mrs Muir sighed. 'We had best undress the poor soul, had we not? And it'll take the two of us, seeing the weight of him.'

'Perhaps we should just take off his top clothes, Mrs Muir, until the doctor has seen him,' Amelia suggested, unwilling to share such an intimate experience with her housekeeper, particularly since she had not yet herself seen her husband unclothed. 'We could take him down to his under-things and cover him with the eiderdown.'

'Very well, madam.'

Together they set about the task of undressing George, Mrs Muir proving herself so dextrous that Amelia got the impression she was well used to dealing with a man's dead weight, which given Mr Muir's high colour and apparently short temper would not prove surprising. But as to what could have caused her own husband's sudden collapse, Amelia had little idea. All sorts of alarms were ringing in her head although not for one moment did she believe it was anything as serious as a heart attack or a seizure. Having witnessed the whole thing at first hand she was inclined to stand by her own interpretations of events: that George had revisited some terrible scene from his not so distant past which had in turn precipitated his strange outburst and subsequent collapse.

'I'll need a more of a hand with his breeches, madam,' Mrs Muir said, bringing her back to earth. Looking up she saw Mrs Muir staring back at her as the housekeeper struggled to slip the unmoving George out of the last of his top clothes.

'Thank you, Mrs Muir, but I really don't think we need to bother any further,' Amelia replied. 'After all, I imagine what is wrong with my husband – if there is anything wrong with him – may prove to be mental rather than physical.'

'If he no recovers his lost consciousness you'll still need a hand to get him abed properly, madam,' the ever practical Scotswoman assured her. 'You'll not manage him on your own.'

Assuring her that if she was needed further she would be called, Amelia thanked the housekeeper for her help and dismissed her, and was left alone with her sick and silent husband.

'George?' she said, coming to his bedside in the faint hope that he might now be able to hear her. 'George – can't you hear me? It's me. George. Amelia.'

But all George could hear in his head was the thunder of the guns and all the sounds of his war. He was hundreds of miles away somewhere in the muddy fields of Flanders and could neither see Amelia nor hear her. What he could see was a man with a rifle and another man falling to the ground, his skull shattered by the close-range shot.

'I won't let them do it,' he told her. 'I shall tell

120

them everything. I shall tell them the truth. I shall tell them it wasn't your fault.'

'Tell who?' Amelia asked in a whisper, kneeling down carefully beside the bed so as not to frighten George in this moment of sudden consciousness. 'Who are you talking to, George? And what isn't their fault?'

George turned his head and gazed at her with a look of pure tragedy.

'He's killed Walker. And now they'll kill him.'

Before Amelia could discover anything further, he turned his head away again, closed his eyes, and fell back into a stupor.

Having finished his examination, Dr Macleod, a tall, thin elderly man with a profusion of black hair which sprouted from every visible part of his body, shut up his bag and shook his head sadly.

'Stupefaction,' he said with another sad shake of his head. 'I can recognize the malady now the moment I walk into a room. Even in these parts, remote as they may seem, I've seen more cases of stupefaction in the last two years than the whole of Scotland has seen in a century.'

'Stupefaction,' Amelia repeated as she walked him downstairs. 'I always thought the word meant astonishment. Or amazement.'

'Aye, lass, it does,' the doctor replied, allowing himself into the drawing room ahead of Amelia and heading straight for the whisky decanter. 'But our amazement is not always to our pleasure, is it?

Amazement can lead to shock and stupor, which I fear is what your husband is suffering from. He has been stupefied by his experiences.'

'Obviously by that you mean the war.'

'Precisely.'

Dr Macleod, having helped himself unasked to a large measure of whisky, sank into a chair by the fireplace and proceeded to fill his pipe. Amelia watched curiously, not at all taken aback by the man's lack of manners but rather admiring his individuality. As he got his tobacco lit, she sat down opposite him to hear what else he might have to say.

'We're all of us only just beginning to count the cost, Mrs Dashwood,' he said between puffs, spinning his exhausted match into the fireplace. 'In our wee village alone we had a population of eighty-three, and now we are but seventy souls. Eight of those thirteen fell at Loos. Men of the Seventh Cameron Highlanders who had knocked Fritz for six in the fight for Loos but were then shot down like rabbits on the pursuit into a nearby town. Ran into a barricade of wire hidden in the long grasses. The Germans were waiting for them in the town and when the Camerons were but a couple of hundred yards away they mowed 'em down. There was nowhere to hide, no cover, no trees, nothing. Just a bare hillside. It was wholesale slaughter.'

'Thirteen men. That has to be about a third of the village's male population, I suppose.'

'One third precisely, Mrs Dashwood. Thirteen boys I'd helped bring into this world who I knew like sons. One lad survived the battle and was later sent home, suffering just like your husband from stupefaction.'

'Can anything be done, Dr Macleod? Or must we just hope that time will do the healing?'

'I wish I knew the answer to that, so I do. They lose their senses, do you see? It's like a form of madness.'

'Madness?' Amelia leaned forward anxiously. 'You're not saying, are you, that my husband is insane?'

'He's no mad in the accepted sense of the word, no. But imagine if you can what this war must have been like. And what it did to men. Your husband, I understand from Hamish Muir, served through the whole shooting match. That's a terrible burden on a man, Mrs Dashwood, on any man. That is a terrible burden indeed.'

Dr Macleod fell silent, so deep in thought he allowed his pipe to go out. Amelia said nothing during the long silence, because all she could do at that moment was try to imagine.

'No, no,' the doctor said, coming back to life and tapping his pocket for his box of matches. 'No, your husband isn't mad as a lunatic is mad, Mrs Dashwood, but he has maybe been driven to a form of insanity by his ordeal. There are all sorts of treatments the medical folk are recommending nowadays, fancy remedies which are meant to deal with this sort of condition – Faradism and the like.'

'What is Faradism?'

'Electric shock treatment. Although how the administration of electric shocks to a man's brain is meant to bring him back to his senses the good Lord alone knows. I do not go along with that, do you see. Nor anything like it. Personally I simply live in hope that time, above all else, will prove to be the great healer.'

'So what will happen?' Amelia asked. 'What should I do now? Should we return home? Is my husband well enough to travel?'

'I do not think so, not at this moment. If he is as deeply shocked as I believe him to be, he must rest here in the hope that he recovers his senses. If and when he does – then you may return home with him, where no doubt you will seek advice from your own doctor.'

'Is our own doctor going to say anything different from you, Dr Macleod? Or is he going to offer some fancy, fashionable advice which might prove either useless or at worst dangerous?'

Dr Macleod looked up from relighting his pipe.

'Alas – you must be the judge of that, Mrs Dashwood,' he said. 'All I can do is to give you my opinion.'

'Which is to stay away from any so-called fashionable treatments.'

'In cases such as these we should really look

for the cause,' the doctor replied. 'And if we find it then and only then may we treat the illness.'

After a long sleep helped by some of Dr Macleod's powders, George awoke as if nothing at all had happened. From the time of the incident itself he had been insensible for over twenty-one hours, eighteen of which had been spent in actual slumber, so Amelia was more than a little surprised to be awoken herself by the sound of her husband calling.

She had spent the night in George's dressing room, allowing him to sleep undisturbed in the large four poster which should by now have been their marriage bed. Hurrying into the bedroom, she found George sitting up and wondering what he was doing there.

'Tell me what you remember of yesterday, first of all,' she said after she had sat herself down on the chair beside the bed.

'Yesterday,' George wondered, frowning hard. 'Yesterday we fished. Eoin caught a splendid salmon. And you made him throw it back.'

'That's all?'

'Of course not. I remember everything quite vividly. Why shouldn't I? We had beef for dinner, over which we discussed the matter of whether or not you should come out with us stalking today – and good heavens!' He checked the time on his wristwatch. 'If that's really the time Eoin will be up and waiting!'

'No, George.' Amelia put her hand on his arm as he made to get out of the bed. 'George, we went stalking yesterday. Don't you remember?'

George sat back in the bed, sensing the seriousness of Amelia's tone.

'What is this, Amelia? This can't be one of your teases.'

'Something happened yesterday, George. We were out stalking in the hills and you had – you sort of blacked out. There really is no other way of putting it. We had to bring you back here on the pony. Dr Macleod has been to see you – yesterday . . .'

'I don't remember a thing of this. Dr Macleod?'

'One of the things he wanted to know was whether or not this sort of thing had ever happened to you before. I couldn't really answer that.'

'Hardly,' George said quietly, lying back on his pillows to stare up at the ceiling.

'Has it, George?'

'Yes and no. Tell me what happened – yesterday. Don't leave anything out.'

Amelia told him, leaving out no essential detail. George listened, lying on his back staring above him and saying nothing, even after she had finished. Even though she spared no detail Amelia kept her account as undramatic as she could, so as to try not to alarm her husband with her own fears. After a long silence George wanted to know Dr Macleod's opinion, so Amelia told him everything that the doctor and she had discussed. She was completely frank.

'Did you suspect anything?' George asked, turning to her with a deep frown. 'Did you ever think there might be something wrong?'

'I don't understand the question. Wrong in what way?'

'It's pretty obvious, isn't it?' He shook his head and turned away again, this time right away so that he was looking out of the window. 'I have to be honest with you, Amelia. And I should have told you before.'

But he didn't tell her now. He just fell again into silence.

'Tell me what, George?' Amelia prompted him. 'George?'

She heard him sigh quietly to himself before answering the question, still staring out of the window.

'What happened yesterday – although it hasn't happened since I got home, I have to say – I think what happened yesterday happened several times when I was in hospital.'

'Just before you came back, you mean? But that's perfectly understandable, surely? When someone's badly wounded—'

'I wasn't wounded. Not in that sense. Not physically.'

'They said you'd been wounded.'

'Mentally. I collapsed.'

'You *collapsed*?'

'My nerves went. Had I not been an officer, and decorated, I know they would have shot me. Oh, what do they call it now? Yes, I had a breakdown.'

Amelia thought about this before replying, having frequently heard the term 'nervous breakdown' being bandied about without ever understanding quite what it meant. Now it was being applied to George it seemed too terrible to contemplate.

'I don't think so, George, really I don't. You were just tired. I mean, for heaven's sake – you had fought right through the war. It's a wonder you didn't collapse earlier. I mean, you probably had become neurasthenic.'

'It might have been better if I had.'

'You wanted to get out of the war?'

'You'd have to have been truly mad not to want to get out of the war, Amelia.'

Realizing the effect such a remark might have on his impressionable bride George glanced at her, and seeing the look in her eyes took and held her hand in one of his.

'It's all right,' he assured her. 'That doesn't mean I funked it – or wanted to run away. I simply mean that – well, that if perhaps I had been treated earlier it would never have come to this. You see, what happened was—'

He was on the verge of telling her everything. And in truth, right up until the very last moment he had fully intended to do so. He had formed the words in his mind. Amelia sensed this, and waited patiently, when he suddenly stopped.

'*You are quite certain of this?*' *the Noble One asked.* '*It does not seem necessary.*'

'*It is cruel,*' *Longbeard replied.* '*I grant that fact. But sir – we must think of the future. Not ours. Not theirs. But of the future. And, more than anything, of what is believed of you.*'

The Noble One nodded once as he slowly stroked his bearded chin. '*Propel them, therefore,*' *he ordained.* '*Advance them. Bring them closer to the time when they will know joy, when they may realize their bliss. Bring them here. Let them be in this place.*'

Longbeard nodded now, selecting a different jewel from his purse, holding the crystal clear stone up to the stars and releasing it so that it flew above them to vanish into the Milky Way. '*It shines over the place they are now,*' *Longbeard assured him.* '*The next die has been cast.*'

'Is anything the matter, George?' Amelia put her hand protectively over his, still not wanting to hurry him.

He shook his head, suddenly dismal. 'No, nothing's the matter. It's just that I can't remember what it was exactly that I was about to tell you, not exactly.'

'Perhaps it will come back? In a minute?'

'No.' To her horror Amelia saw her young husband's eyes once more fill with tears. 'No. I don't think it will ever come back. I think I have lost my mind.'

Seven

The fourth night of their stay in Scotland, Dr Macleod having pronounced his patient well enough to be up and about again, George and Amelia went for a long moonlit walk round the loch. It was a cold but windless evening, with a sky which was a blanket of stars.

'That's not the North Star, is it?' Amelia wondered as they stopped on the far shore.

'If you know what it isn't, why ask me?' George laughed. 'Anyway, I'm a useless astrologer.'

'That's the North Star there.' Amelia pointed. 'So what's that, then? That very bright star there – the one which seems to be nearer than most.'

'Probably just larger,' George replied, putting a hand over his eyes to squint above him. 'It isn't any part of the bits I know. Orion, the Great Bear, et cetera.'

'I agree. It's much too close, for a start – and a lot brighter.'

'Could be a shooter.'

'Except it doesn't appear to be moving.'

'It's very bright, you're right. Twinkle, twinkle, little star.'

'Not so little,' Amelia observed. 'It's probably

a thousand times the size of Earth.'

'Or maybe a millionth the size but just very, very bright.'

Amelia stood silently looking at the star which had so caught her eye.

'Is anything the matter, Amelia?' George wondered after a while, taking her hand. 'You've gone really awfully quiet for you.'

'I'm fine, George. But – but I think that we ought to go home now.'

'Back to the lodge?'

'No. Back home. In fact I think we should go tomorrow, and at once.'

Hundreds of miles away in Somerset two shadows moved among the ancient yews of an old priory and a sigh was heard above the sound of an owl's hunting cry.

'Time to go to work,' the Noble One urged Longbeard, but he only shook his head at his master's impatience.

Eight

On the train journey south, George and Amelia agreed not to say a word of what had happened to George to either set of parents. Amelia was only too happy not to do so, not only because the thought of their parents all discussing their personal problems was too much to contemplate but also because Amelia hoped that whatever difficulties George might be experiencing at the moment – difficulties which were obviously affecting their marriage – could perhaps be solved more easily with devotion and love than by any of the new-fangled medical remedies so feared by the redoubtable Dr Macleod.

Once home, however, their good intentions were more difficult to put into practice than they had imagined. Having as yet no place of their own, they were living, as they had known they might have to live, in a wing of the Dashwood family house. Although it was almost entirely self-contained, comprising as it did a living room, a sitting room and two bedrooms, because the newlyweds were living *en famille* they were forced, out of duty, to take all their meals with General and Lady Dashwood.

Amelia had been utterly against such proximity, and so too, in fairness to George, had he, suggesting from the outset that it might be more salutary to rent somewhere entirely independent of his parents while they decided where they were finally going to live, and even more importantly what exactly George was going to do. But Lady Dashwood would not hear of it.

'Whatever is the point, George? Whatever is the point of finding somewhere else to live which will not possibly be as comfortable as this? After all, this is your home. And until you find a home of your own, one expects you to continue to live here. Besides, you will soon be returning to your regiment, and then to whom will Amelia turn for company, pray?'

'But you said you were no longer thinking of returning to your regiment, didn't you?' Amelia asked George when they were discussing the matter privately in their wing after their return from honeymoon. 'When you were unwell in Scotland, you said—'

'I know what I said,' George interrupted. 'I was fully compos mentis at the time. But it's all a bit different now I'm back home.'

'But you're not at home, George. Not any more. We're staying with your parents, but we're not *at home*.'

'You're quite right. I apologize. But even so, as far as rejoining my regiment goes, I want a little time to think.'

'When you do, George, think about your health more than anything. Your health and your happiness, because that's just as important a part of your health as anything else. You can hardly go back into the army if you're – if you're still suffering blackouts.'

'It wasn't a blackout. Not like that.'

'According to Dr Macleod it was.'

'All right, just give it time, that is all I need – time.'

But as the months passed it seemed the more George considered his present position and the more the two of them discussed it the more it became apparent that George's basic attitude to the army had altered radically. Even his commitment to his regiment was no longer as before. It came as yet another shock to Amelia to realize the total and profound change that had come about in the man she loved. As always when shaken to the core, she sought out her father for advice, without of course revealing the true nature of her worry. She knew that he too had been brooding deeply on the war and its aftermath, judging from the amount of anti-war poetry he had been producing.

'But surely it can't all have been in vain?' she asked him one afternoon when George was out playing golf with his father and she had called on her parents to have lunch. 'I keep getting the impression from your latest poems that you think it's all been the most terrible waste.'

'Why mankind has never been able to resolve his problems without a call to arms I cannot imagine. Perhaps it's because we men actually enjoy killing each other.'

'*You* don't.'

'I tried to enlist.'

'But in retrospect—'

'Would I have done so? Probably not, knowing what I do now. In fact most certainly not.'

'Why? Because it hasn't made any difference?'

'Because it's made the greatest difference, more than any of us can ever imagine. We have killed most of our youth. The flower of it, certainly. If only we had thought a little more in advance.'

Slowly Amelia was beginning to put together some sort of theory as to what precisely might be troubling her husband the most, and after this particular conversation with her father she thought one of the most salient facts was that so *many* of George's contemporaries had been killed: friends from school, from the local village, or men he had befriended in his regiment.

'I think that's a major part of it,' he agreed, some few days later as he and Amelia walked the Downs, while holding back what he well knew was the major contributing issue. He stopped and pointed to a rolling field before them. 'Look,' he said. 'Let's say that in the middle of that pasture, we planted a copse of say one thousand trees, young oaks, England's national tree. Say we planted them in 1895, so that by 1914 they were just maturing. In fact let's say we planted six such copses along the hillside there, each of one thousand young oaks, trees which when they matured would make this landscape one of the finest plantations in the land. We go away then, to return six years later to see how our young trees are doing, only to be appalled. One in every six trees is dead. Instead of the great woodland we hoped to see, there are these decimated copses, four trees here then a gap of two or three, a single oak surrounded by more gaps, half a dozen trees still growing but next to them another four spaces. And so on and so forth. Even the trees which are left are suffering because they are trying to grow alone, without the protection and benefit of their dead friends – and why did they die? They died for a few yards of land. Someone uprooted them and moved them a hundred yards this way, or a hundred yards that way, then they moved them again another fifty yards, then another two hundred back again, another hundred and fifty forward again – and every time they were moved one in every six or seven trees died, so that finally when the powers that be ordained they had moved them far enough, they called an end to it. Only by then a sixth of the forest was dead.'

'But we stopped the Germans from annexing Europe, surely?'

'Maybe. But for how long, I wonder?'

'They said this was the war to end all wars. That no-one will want to fight again after such carnage.

We weren't the only country to lose so many men. Germany lost its millions too.'

'Its millions! There you are, you're saying it now. Yet only a short time ago you couldn't comprehend the fact that we had lost *thousands* of men, let alone hundreds of thousands – let alone *millions*.'

'You're right,' Amelia reflected. 'And soon those figures will just be another set of numbers, just so many noughts added together with so many other noughts. Yet all those noughts are somebody's sons.'

'All those men, young and some of them not so young, all those sons and lovers, husbands and bachelors who lie dead, they'll just be an entry for the record books,' George added. 'For people to study and frown over. *Would you believe it?* they'll say. *Just look how many fell in the war.* As if they were reading the cricket scores.'

'George,' Amelia said, having summoned up the courage finally to ask him. 'George – can I ask you something?'

'That depends, doesn't it? As you well know.'

'What is it exactly that happened to you?'

'At what point? An awful lot of things *happened*.'

'Whatever it is that haunts you.'

George stopped where she had stopped, looking not at her but at where his invisible forests grew.

'You wouldn't want to know, Amelia, even if I wanted to remember. All I can tell you is that I never ever want anyone too use the word "war" or "battle" in front of me unless they have been through the same thing. I never want anyone to glorify war, or tell me that it is a wonderful thing to do for your country, to throw away your life in a sea of mud, to kill someone else's son. Not ever. Do you hear? Not ever.'

Calling his dogs, he turned the collar of his coat up against the rain that had started to fall and turned for home.

Amelia had to run to catch up with him. 'But George, what does it all mean? What do you mean by everything you have just said? How does it affect us, darling?'

She felt selfish even asking the question, but it had to be asked. They could not just go on and on as they were, living with his parents, not being really married, not knowing, either of them, exactly what it was that was so wrong with him.

'What it means,' George said, suddenly sounding more himself than he had since he came home, 'what it means is that I cannot any longer stay in the army. Not feeling as I do, not for a minute. It would be completely hypocritical, dishonourable, what you will. I must resign my commission, even if it means I end up with a begging bowl in Oxford Street. I have to leave the army.'

In spite of everything he had told her and everything they had discussed, Amelia was still surprised. 'You have thought this through,

George?' she wondered. 'You have considered your family? I mean, what on earth will your father say?'

'I can't stay in the army just for my father.'

'I know. But he's so proud of you. I just worry what this might do to him.'

'Less than it would have done to him had I been killed, I imagine,' George replied ruefully. 'But there again, I'm not so sure.'

Amelia did not of course witness the actual announcement of her husband's intention to resign his commission. What she experienced was the aftermath in the form of George getting quickly and ferociously drunk before dinner. While he demolished three large whiskies in quick succession he said very little to her, other than the fact that he had broken the news to the General, and that it had not been at all well received.

Very little was said later over dinner either, in spite of Amelia's brave attempts to make conversation. In fact other than a token discussion of the weather very little was said at all, the meal notable otherwise only for the amount of wine and port consumed by the general and his son who never addressed one word to each other.

By the time Amelia and George returned to their wing to go to bed, George was the drunkest Amelia had ever seen him, unsteady on his feet and barely coherent in his speech. Realizing the best place for him now was bed, once she had led him safely upstairs Amelia began to steer him towards their bedroom with the intention of helping him get undressed.

'I can manage,' he said, beginning to take his shoes and tie off. 'I can manage perfectly well.'

'Very well then, manage. I was only trying to help.'

'You can help by coming to bed with me, Amelia,' George said, stopping halfway across the bedroom, his shoes in one hand and his shirt half undone. 'Come to bed with me now. Will you?'

Amelia hesitated. Even though she had no idea of how too much drink affected a man, she knew enough to think that this was not the ideal way to christen a marriage.

'Later, George,' she said, suddenly smiling to herself as she realized this was what a lot of much older couples must sound like. 'When you've sobered up a little.'

'I am not drunk, Amelia,' George insisted, holding on to a bed post. 'I am not even the slightest bit drunk.'

He eyed her, then let go of the post so that he might take off the rest of his clothes. As he did so, he began to sway rather ominously.

'He's going to cut off my inheritance, Amelia. My father is going to disinherit me,' he said, falling sideways onto the bed. 'We won't have any money.'

'That's too bad,' Amelia said, putting George's discarded clothes on a chair. 'You'll soon find another way to earn your living.'

'Ha,' George said, without humour. 'I don't think so, darling. Like what? As what? I mean like what, Amelia?'

'We'll think of something,' Amelia assured him, sitting him upright so that she could take off his shirt. 'There are all sorts of things someone as bright as you can do. You could teach.'

'Teach?' George echoed. '*Teach?* Teach what?'

'Teach boys.'

'Teach them *what*, Amelia? What exactly am I meant to teach these boys?'

'Whatever it is you're good at, George. Or you could go into business.'

'Business? That's like going into trade.'

'Don't be such a snob.'

'You want to be married to a tradesman?'

'Who I'm married to is you, George. I don't care if you go down the mines.'

'That's exactly what I probably will have to do, probably. Exactly.'

By now George was sitting on the bed in just his trousers with his braces looped down to his waist. Even though he was thoroughly drunk he still looked absurdly handsome, but because he was so thoroughly drunk he also looked at his most vulnerable, so that Amelia was unable to resist the temptation to kiss him, which she did. To her delight George wrapped his strong arms round her waist, pulling her towards him so that she fell on top of him, and then to her astonishment she

141

felt his tongue entering her mouth and exploring it. At first she tried to resist such an intimacy, but George was too drunk and too strong for her, holding her firmly to him. After only the briefest of struggles Amelia felt all resistance disappear and found herself kissing him back with a passion she did not know she possessed. George too must have been surprised, drunk though he was, for he murmured loudly enough at one point to make Amelia stop kissing him.

'Is something the matter, George?' she asked anxiously, pushing a loose bit of hair from her eyes. 'Have I done something wrong?'

'Lord no!' He was grinning like a boy. 'I should say not!'

He kissed her again, this time letting go of her waist with one of his hands, which she next felt, with a delighted start, on her breasts. With a sigh as the hand began to explore her, Amelia rolled sideways onto the bed, still kissing him passionately while George fumbled blindly at the fastening of her dress in an effort to remove it. Amelia eased herself away and smiled at him.

'It's all right, sweetheart,' she whispered. 'I'll go and take it off. Don't you move now. Promise?'

'I promise,' George stage-whispered back. 'I'm not going *anywhere*. Don't you worry.'

He waved a hand at her as she disappeared behind her screen to perform the rite she had so often practised: discreetly removing her clothes and slipping into her nightgown ready to get into bed with her husband. A matter of moments later she slipped back out from behind the screen only to find George completely unconscious on the bed.

'Oh, George,' she whispered. 'Oh, *George.*'

With a small sigh and a sad smile Amelia lay down beside him and covered them both with the quilt.

Nine

In spite of his drunken state the previous night, the next morning George was up and gone before Amelia was fully awake. When she came downstairs and went into the main part of the house for breakfast she discovered that he had in fact already eaten. According to Henry, the Dashwood family's butler, he had taken his favourite horse Beau for a long ride on the Downs.

Quelling a sense of being suddenly deserted and yet about to face a firing squad none the less, Amelia helped herself to some kedgeree from one of the large silver dishes on the sideboard and joined Lady Dashwood, who was just finishing her breakfast. As soon as Amelia was seated her mother-in-law set about cross-examining her about George, without so much as the briefest exchange of niceties.

'I sincerely hope this had nothing to do with you, Amelia,' she said as the maid set some fresh coffee on the table. 'George wanting to resign his commission. I hope this is not your influence coming to bear?'

'No, Lady Dashwood, I have never, as yet, had

anything to do with George's military career, or his decisions.'

'I am perfectly aware that George has been, let us say, a little tired since his return. But he is a soldier born and bred, as are all Dashwoods. However, now he seems to be coming back to himself I want to hear no more of this nonsense. I want you to see to it that this is the case, Amelia. I hope I make myself clear?'

'I'm sorry, Lady Dashwood. But I really cannot influence George in this matter, one way or the other.'

'Cannot? Or will not?'

Lady Dashwood, like most small women, was formidably aggressive and greatly preferred to have things her way. Having known her since childhood, Amelia was well aware of her mother-in-law's character, and although, as a small child, she had initially been terrified of her, she had soon learned that if she was to earn her place in the sun she would have to learn to stand up to her, which she finally did.

'It really doesn't matter whether it's *cannot* or *will not*, Lady Dashwood,' Amelia said quietly, leaning back in her chair so that the maid could take her empty plate away. 'George takes his own advice on matters as important as this. What I think about his resigning his commission is immaterial.'

'So what was your reaction when he told you, might I ask?'

'I admit I was a little surprised, Lady Dashwood. I had always imagined that like his father George would be in the army for life. But the war has obviously changed him profoundly.'

'War changes everyone, Amelia,' her mother-in-law insisted. 'Makes boys into men.'

'Perhaps that's what it's done to George,' Amelia replied, eyeing her adversary steadily across the table. 'Made him understand his own mind as men are meant to do.'

'*Men* do not resign their commissions, Amelia,' Lady Dashwood replied frostily. 'That is totally absurd.'

'Decisions such as the one George has reached sometimes require far more courage than we like to think, Lady Dashwood. A different kind of courage and perhaps an even greater one, in my opinion.'

Lady Dashwood narrowed her eyes and tapped her elegant fingers on the polished dining table.

'I have always had my worries about you, Amelia – as a daughter-in-law, that is. I have always been concerned about your background. It's so hopelessly artistic, so very *bohemic* as compared to our own.'

'Artistic I agree, Lady Dashwood. Hopelessly so – I'm not sure. Your husband and my father seem to find *Bohemia* no barrier to their friendship.'

'No, my dear. That is not what I mean. What I mean is that our family's points of view are very different. When I realized George's intentions towards you were becoming serious, I said to the general that, fond of you though I am, I feared *incompatibility*. I imagine I was right, now we hear the sort of nonsense that has started to influence George! You are aware, are you not, that if George insists on sticking to his guns, in all likelihood the general will disinherit him?'

'George told me that might be the case, yes.'

'You would have to move out from here.'

'Of course we would.'

'That does not worry you, obviously, Amelia?'

'I married George, Lady Dashwood. He's my husband and I am his wife. What George wishes to do he must do, and I will follow. When I married him I swore to love, honour and *obey* him, so that is what I shall do.'

'That is all very fine and large, the notion of marriage and one's proper duties, et cetera,' Lady Dashwood sighed, giving her a patronizing look. 'But reality is very different. Without money this is not an easy world to inhabit, my dear.'

'I'm sure you're right,' Amelia agreed, sounding almost affable about the difficulty of the world. 'But then it would be an altogether impossible world to inhabit, if we tried to do so in contradiction to what we truly believe, surely?'

'I see.'

Lady Dashwood looked across at her, wiped her mouth on her napkin, nodded once to conclude the interview, and rose and left the dining room. Amelia watched her go, knowing perfectly well that this was not a battle won, but merely a temporary ceasefire.

Since George made no reference either to his drunkenness of the night before or to their subsequent intimacy, Amelia imagined he must have no clear memory of the events of that night and so said nothing either, preferring to stand by her resolution to allow George any initiative. She did, however, mention the conversation she had had with his mother at breakfast time. George paid full attention while she recounted the exchange, then shook his head as if in defeat.

'That's why I went for a ride, Amelia. I needed time to sort things out. To clear my head.'

'And now that you have?'

'I'm not altogether sure I can go through with it—'

'Then don't, George.'

Her husband looked at her in amazement. 'Isn't that what you want? I seem to remember – at least I think I do – that you were shocked at the notion of my resigning my commission, but not displeased.'

'I wasn't shocked,' Amelia replied. 'I was surprised – and understandably so, I think. Whatever one imagines, it's always a surprise when the other person comes to the same conclusion. But once I had got used to the idea, in light of everything you've said and that we've been talking about together, it made absolute sense.'

'Yet now, when I say I don't think I can go through with it—'

'Look, George,' Amelia interrupted. 'Whatever you decide it's your decision, not mine. When it comes down to it, it really isn't for me to suggest anything or even to have an opinion. As I said to your mother, when I married you I promised to obey—'

'Yes, yes, yes.' George stopped her with a wave of his hand. 'But you don't believe that and neither do I. We've been friends most of our lives, Amelia. Because we've got married doesn't mean you now have to become totally subservient to my wishes. You've always fought for your corner and I expect you to carry on doing so, whatever we may have said in church. When I said I'm not sure I can go through with this, I was going to add I can't go through with it without your support – and I wasn't really sure that I had that. Not completely. I had a little bit too much on board last night.'

He grinned at her sheepishly, and Amelia laughed.

'A little? I'd hate to see you when you had a lot!'

'So? Do I have your support?'

'Of course you do, George,' Amelia assured him. 'What do you think?'

'That you just might be an angel sent from heaven.'

'So?' Hermione said, now tea was out of the way and she had invited Amelia to take a walk around her parents' garden.

'So what?' Amelia replied, knowing perfectly well the information her friend was after. 'Wild oats, as my mother always says to that particular question.'

'So-what-is-it-like-being-married?' Hermione sighed, as if speaking to a child.

'Wonderful,' Amelia said, carefully matter of fact. 'I thoroughly recommend it.'

'All of it?'

'Of course,' Amelia feigned surprise, hoping to throw Hermione off the track.

'Very well,' Hermione groaned. 'I can see I'm going to have to spell it out for you. What is *It* like?'

'What do you think?'

'I can't! That's why I'm asking you, you dope!'

'Ravishing, Hermione. Just as you thought.'

'I'm sure. *But what exactly happens?* I mean – *exactly.*'

'What exactly happens,' Amelia began hesitantly, trying to think of the best way to obfuscate the subject. 'He takes you to bed—'

'He kisses you first, obviously.'

'Obviously.'

'And undresses you? Did he – the first time, I mean, that is – did he undress you? I have always imagined that to be the most thrilling bit. Just to lie there and have all your clothes slowly taken off. All your buttons and hooks undone by a man's hand, then all your things very slowly slipped off, slipped off down your shoulders and your waist . . .'

'That's exactly what happens!'

'Your clothes dropping to the floor, your naked shoulders—'

'Hermione!'

'What, for heaven's sake? You're a married woman, Amelia!'

'And you're not, Hermione. Besides. Someone might hear.'

'Hardly. And you've spoiled it now,' Hermione sighed. 'Where was I?'

'Nearly naked with all your clothes dropping to the floor.'

Hermione put her arm through Amelia's and steered her round well out of sight behind some rose bushes.

'Did you nearly swoon?' she giggled. 'When he did It?'

'I don't really remember much,' Amelia lied, the fingers of her free hand tightly crossed out of sight. 'It was so – so ravishing.'

'Oh – *wow* . . .' Hermione sighed. 'I can't wait.'

'You're going to have to.'

'Sometimes, when I think about it,' Hermione replied, 'I don't think I will.'

'Hermione! Now you really *have* shocked me.'

'No – seriously, Amelia. Things aren't quite the same as they were. Things are changing, and some quite nice girls are doing it.'

'You've still shocked me none the less,' Amelia said, mock starchily. 'So in order that you don't go getting any more loose ideas, you're not to ask me anything more.'

Even though her tongue was firmly in her cheek, Amelia kept up the tease – but not for the moral good of her friend. She changed the subject for her own sake, since she really did have no idea how to break the impasse that had arisen between George and herself. As her mother would say, *Up a gum tree, darling!*

Concluding that it could perhaps be through some fault of her own, Amelia sought counsel. And when it came down to it she found her mother was, finally, the only person to whom she could turn, because both pride and honour and a great deal more ruled out everyone else.

'I don't see what exactly you're trying to say, Amelia darling,' Constance said after Amelia had euphemized herself into a corner. 'Are you trying to say that George is proving to be an unsatisfactory husband? Because all I can say to that is early days, darling child. It is very early days.'

'I'm not trying to say that, Mama, not exactly, no.'

'What, then? Because all I can tell you is that it took an awful long time for your father and I to become – how shall I put it? *Properly acquainted.*'

'Properly acquainted?'

'To get to know each other as a man and woman should. You and George have only been married – what? A matter of two or three months or something—'

'That isn't the point, Mama.'

'Then what is the point, darling? I can hardly tell

you what I think if you won't tell me the point of all this.'

'Oh, for heaven's sake!' Amelia blurted out. 'If you must know, George has hardly done more than kiss me!'

'I see.' Her mother sat thinking for a while. 'These things take time, Amelia,' she concluded. 'I know that sounds like hogwash, as if I'm trying to fob you off with bromides, but things like this aren't always as easy as the teacher makes them seem.'

'If only I'd had a teacher,' Amelia sighed.

'I was speaking figuratively, ducky. What I mean is the theory might be all very well, but the practice is so often entirely different. Some men are very shy, you know. Women often find this hard to believe, particularly women with no previous – with little previous *emotional* experience – but believe me it is often the case. Your father was a complete and utter innocent. We both were. It was quite funny really, when you think about it now, but at the time I was utterly distraught. Like you, I even consulted my mother. And do you know what she said? She said, *Wear a French scent and a black nightgown*, and do you know what, darling, I did, and it worked a treat!'

Confused and anxious as she was, Amelia could not help laughing at this, and of course it was comforting to know that her parents, however uninhibited and bohemian, had not just fallen into each other's arms.

Nevertheless, once she had parted from her mother, she realized that though it had been a great relief to laugh about it all it had not got her any nearer finding a solution to her marital problem. For what she had not been able to tell Constance was that she now suspected that the reason for George's reticence had to do with some dreadful association that he could not help making whenever he was about to make love to her. And that if this was the case, their problem could well be incurable.

'So what I must do is just be patient?' she asked her mother, on yet another day, knowing that she had already decided that this was the only possible conclusion.

'I know it's hard, darling, but men, in my experience, do not like women to take the initiative, at least not in the bedroom.'

'I see. Oh dear.'

'Oh dear?'

'Yes, oh dear. I mean, oh *dear* – why are men so complicated?'

'You mean women *aren't*?'

They both laughed.

'Just give it time,' Constance advised, turning back to some pattern books for drawing room curtains. 'For the moment, just pretend you are on holiday with a friend, and all will be well, you'll see.'

Amelia turned away. She would give it just a bit more time, but after that – she thought, in desperation, she might have to resort to wearing a black nightie and a heavier perfume.

The period of grace finally granted to George by his father was also a matter of time. Realizing that George did in fact truly wish to resign his commission, but seeing how desperately torn he was between loyalty to his family and the promptings of his conscience, Amelia solicited the help of her own father, asking him privately to take the general on one of their famously long walks where he might persuade the old soldier at least to try to understand his son's point of view. At first Clarence resisted, saying that he had no right to come between a man and his son, but Amelia persisted, agreeing in principle with her father while arguing that George was his own worst advocate and desperately needed someone to put his argument as objectively as possible.

'But I don't know his argument, Amelia,' Clarence had protested. 'I shall only go and say the wrong thing.'

'Of course you know his argument, Papa,' Amelia wheedled. 'It's the same as your own. The general listens to you. He thinks of George still as a boy who doesn't know his own mind, despite the fact that he spent four years fighting in the front line.'

'And won a VC.'

'Exactly. If you could only negotiate a ceasefire as it were, just buy a little time for George to try and work things out completely, that would be something, at least.'

That was exactly what Clarence did in fact manage finally to do, obtaining not as Amelia secretly hoped the unconditional peace for which she had prayed, but a six-month respite during which George could have full leave of absence from his regiment and all his duties.

'With the proviso, naturally, that you and I parley at the end of the said period,' the general confirmed to George that evening. 'Then we should know the lie of the land precisely. No-one will begrudge you your leave, not with your record, and we should not attempt to plead medical necessity as an amelioration. You fought the entire war, you were decorated for your actions, but there are plenty of others in the same boat, do you see? So we're not looking for special treatment, just some extended leave. Battle fatigue – that's all this is, and you'll soon get over it. So take this young wife of yours off with you, rent a house somewhere, and in the due and proper course of time you'll come back to your senses.'

'You were just about to argue with him,' Amelia said as they walked the dogs round the Dashwood estate that night. 'I could see it. You were just about to say that the due process of time was neither here nor there and that your mind was made up, but thank God something stopped you.'

'You stopped me. I could feel you stopping me. Even though I couldn't see you where you were

156

sitting, I could feel you. It was as if you were tugging my sleeve. The way you always have!'

'Have I?'

'You've always been tugging on my sleeve, Amelia,' George replied. 'Even in battle.'

'Really?'

'Sometimes it was just as if you were there hurrying after me. Once I swear you pulled me back, physically. It was one early morning when we were moving the guns up. We were cutting through what was left of this wood and there were two tracks, one going right and one left. I started to head the battery to the right and something – somebody – pulled me back. Do you remember once when we were on the beach, when we were little, and I nearly fell into the quicksand? I was challenging that friend of mine Robin to see who could jump the furthest?'

'Robin Fairfield. Yes, I remember.'

'You suddenly shouted, *No! Not there, George!* And pulled me back by my shirtsleeve—'

'I remember you were rather cross, in fact,' Amelia continued for him. 'But then when one of you chucked a piece of driftwood ahead of you—'

'Because you'd said it was unsafe—'

'It was quicksand.'

'That's how it was in the woods. I heard your voice shouting *No!* So I called the men back and redirected them down the left hand fork instead. We hadn't gone more than a hundred yards when this damn great shell landed – a twenty pounder probably – and it exploded right where we would have been on the other track.'

'I'm going to have a sit down.'

'Why? What on earth's the matter?'

'I just feel a bit giddy. I'm so sorry.'

He sat her on a nearby stone seat by the lake. 'You're as white as a ghost.'

'You're going to tell me I'm mad, but still. I dreamed what you just told me.'

'That's just what they call – no, what do they call it? When you think you've seen something or done something before.'

'No, George. It isn't like that. It's not déjà vu. I remember very well that I dreamed it. I dreamed it was night – and that there was a full moon. There was this little church. No. It was a ruined chapel.'

'Go on.'

'One of the men had a bandage over half of his head, and his arm was round another soldier's shoulder—'

'Bombardier Wiggins.'

'And this shell was coming through the sky very slowly. As if it was floating. I threw myself at you – and you fell over – tumbled down a bank. All the time the shell was coming straight at me. I put my hands up and I caught it – and I held it in my hands while I shouted at you to turn back and take the other road – and you did. I saw you running off with your men down this long road – miles away, smiling and blowing me kisses. After which, once

158

I knew you were safe, I put the shell down on the ground and lay on top of it, and woke up as it exploded!'

'Good God, Amelia. You have stunned me.'

'I even remember which day I dreamed it. Because when I woke up and went downstairs, still in my nightgown, my mother was decorating the Christmas tree which my father had cut down the night before. It was the day before Christmas Eve.'

'Dear God in heaven . . .'

'Now it's your turn to look as though you've seen a ghost, George.'

'And why wouldn't I? That was the day it happened.'

Of course when they returned to the house they could not wait to look it up in George's journals, where to their mutual astonishment there was the incident of 23 December recorded in detail.

'And you couldn't possibly have dreamed it since?' George said, staring down at his carefully noted log.

'I'd have had to have dreamed my mother and the Christmas tree too. And if I'd dreamed it since we were married, I certainly would have told you.'

'Yes – but you could have forgotten it until I prompted you.'

'Or I really could have dreamed it on 23 December 1917. That's the most distinct possibility.'

'Of course. You're absolutely right. Even though I don't want to believe it.'

'Why not?'

'Because it doesn't bear believing. It makes everything real unreal, and everything unreal – real.'

George sat beside her on the window seat in their bedroom and put his arm round her shoulders while they both stared out at the distant landscape. From the shadows of the cedar tree an owl silently rose, silhouetting itself against the full moon, while far away in a distant place, a mighty weapon from a long forgotten terrible war lay deep under the dark waters of a hidden lake, a lake which lay directly beneath a single bright star which seemed to have no proper place in the constellation.

Ten

Amelia saw the star again in Somerset. The four of them, Clarence, Constance, George and herself, had taken a trip to the West Country to stay with Archie and Mae Hanley, theatrical friends of the Dennisons who lived just outside Glastonbury, where Clarence was due to give a reading from his recently published volume of war poems in the famous ruined abbey. Constance had suggested the trip partly because she knew how much Amelia enjoyed hearing her father read his works, but more because she was well aware how much the young Dashwoods needed to get away from the atmosphere at Dashwood House. So first thing on a bright, early September morning the four of them set off to travel down to Somerset in Clarence's old Hillman, arriving at the Hanley household late in the afternoon having stopped for a leisurely lunch at an hotel in Hungerford.

The Hanleys divided their time between London and Somerset, which was Archie's home county, one of his most illustrious forebears having been a colonel in the army of King Charles I as well as one of the monarch's closest friends, close enough in fact to be consigned to the Tower by Cromwell for defending the Crown. The family seat was a splendid Elizabethan house set in a hundred acres of parkland below the village of North Wootton, just above the Whitelake which rises outside Evercreech to flow into the sea at Highbridge. It was a most enchanting place and one which Amelia and her parents always loved to visit, redolent of the past, steeped in legend, and set in a beautiful rolling landscape dominated in the distance by Glastonbury Tor.

'This place can hardly have changed since the time it was built,' George remarked as he stood in the Great Hall, surrounded by the Hanleys' pack of four dogs, all equally inquisitive. 'I feel we should all be dressed as cavaliers.'

'People frequently are, I assure you,' Clarence assured him. 'Archie and Mae delight in fancy dress parties.'

'Oh, rightly so too, Clarrie,' Constance called back to him, wandering about, lost in admiration. 'This dear place cries out for costume.'

Since there was no-one around to greet them, the party deposited their luggage in the Hall and went in search of their hosts, whom they found fast asleep in the rose garden, Mae lying in a hammock slung between two leafy trees and her husband stretched flat on the ground with arms and legs akimbo as if staked out. In fact so fast asleep was he that it took a combination of Clarence's shoe and the smallest dog's tongue to rouse him.

'My friends!' he exclaimed, rising with extra-ordinary grace from the grass. 'My dear, dear friends! Mae, my angel? Our lovely people have finally arrived!'

Soon they were all at tea, which the Hanleys' portly housemaid set as instructed on the grass while the party arranged themselves on rugs shaded by a vast lopsided parasol. The talk was non-stop, particularly once Archie began making his speciality, a cocktail of cold champagne, brandy and peach juice. Bottles of wine hung to cool in a net suspended in the waters of the river by which they were sitting, and Archie and Mae regaled their guests with hilarious stories of their latest theatrical enterprise, a tour of the Scottish play – as they like all their fellow actors insisted on calling *Macbeth*, despite being outside a theatre – stories so scandalous and amusing that even the normally reticent George was soon laughing more than Amelia had seen him do for weeks.

'Really what we are laughing at is Archie's face more than anything,' George remarked to Amelia later when they were getting ready for dinner. 'It's so enormous, and so sad, and so funny.'

'I'd sometimes love to be an actor,' Amelia sighed as George helped button her cream silk dress. 'To travel round the country with just a suit-case – playing a different theatre every week – sometimes every night. Play-acting your life away, not having to worry about reality.'

'If that's what acting is, getting out of touch with

reality,' George said with a wistful smile at his young wife, 'then I think I shall join up tomorrow.'

But what was to happen to them on the morrow was already written in the stars, as so many things are, and will be.

Amelia was sitting in the window seat of their bedroom when she saw the star again. Just as in Scotland by the shores of the loch, at first she once again imagined it to be the North Star, but then when she examined the skies more closely she realized that, just as in Scotland, it could not be, for the North Star was all too clear, or so it seemed to her.

'I think you're wrong.'

'Of course you do, George, while I, naturally, think I am right.'

'Archie must have a book on astronomy in that amazing library of his,' George told her, frowning. 'I will go and find one, and we can clear this up in no time.'

While he was away Amelia spent her time trying to work out the exact position of the strange celestial body. Once she had her bearings she fixed it as being five degrees to the south and east of the house, but since she had only the vaguest knowledge of the locality they were now in she went to join George in the library where she soon found a detailed book of maps, and together they returned to their bedroom and the window seat.

'This is quite an up to date book of the sky,'

George said, turning over the pages of a large tome. 'Drawn in 1910, so unless that is a bright new sun that has suddenly arrived in the firmament we should be able to identify it.'

'It seems to be in a line above this little town here,' Amelia muttered, the map book open in her hand. 'A small Saxon town called – Bruton.'

George put the book of the stars on the floor by the open bedroom window and began to identify the major constellations.

'Right,' he said, after he and Amelia had consulted both the sky and the book several times. 'It's directly under the third star in the handle of the Plough – so that should give us a definite fix. How are you doing?'

'Not very well. You see, all there is where there should be my wayward star is just space on the astrological chart. Look!'

George looked. Every star was noted and identified except for Amelia's so-called 'wayward' one.

'Has to be new then,' George concluded. 'And since we're no astrologers, either of us, it's not for us to say whether that is the case or not. Perhaps Archie might know some expert or other in the neighbourhood—'

'George?' Amelia stopped him. 'George, it seems to be moving. Look.'

George watched with her for a moment then shook his head. 'I can't see it moving, Amelia. But then stars are very deceptive.'

'It definitely moved, George. Downwards.'

'It could still be a shooter, as we thought up in Scotland,' George said doubtfully.

'That's no shooting star, George!' Amelia insisted. 'And it definitely moved.'

'Well it's not moving now,' George insisted. 'Yes it is!'

Again they stared at the brightly shining star as it definitely seemed to drop lower in the sky, almost as if it was hovering over something.

'Or somewhere,' Amelia said when they had discussed their mutual feelings. 'See here on the map? It seems to be somewhere directly over here – somewhere in the vicinity of this town. Because do you see this tower marked here?'

'Yes. It's some ancient monument or other. I would say. Definitely.'

Amelia got up and pointed out of the window. 'That's the tower – over there. You can see it silhouetted quite clearly on the top of that hill – so that would make the place the star is shining over about here . . .'

Now she was back at the map, tapping an area of green on the sheet spread before her on the floor.

'So?'

'So let's take a drive tomorrow morning and go and see,' Amelia suggested. She pulled George's sleeve in excitement. 'Oh, do let's, George. Papa's poetry reading isn't until evening, so we've got all day to explore.'

'And what do you think we're going to find?'

'Who knows?' Amelia laughed. 'A crock of gold perhaps?'

What they found was an area of countryside where it seemed time had stood still. Having borrowed his father-in-law's Hillman, George drove Amelia round all the lanes in the area that she had chosen for their search only to get hopelessly lost.

'Don't get cross,' Amelia begged, as she unfolded the driving map. 'This is fun.'

'I'm not cross. Not even remotely. I am utterly happy. And serene, if you really want to know, as if something marvellous is going to happen, but I don't know quite what.'

'My father always gets terribly cross if he ends up lost thanks to my mother. And I don't have a clue where we are.'

'Somewhere in the Dark Ages, to judge by some of the farms we've passed. Compared to Sussex, these places are positively Neanderthal. I mean, look at that one.' George pointed to the tall, handsome medieval house outside which he had stopped the car. Its windows were hung with sacking. 'Even their livestock looks antediluvian.'

'I'm never quite sure what that word means exactly, George.'

'Before the flood, I think. I'm sure those pigs never made it on board.'

Three men appeared at the gate of the unkempt yard where George had pulled up. They stared at the car and its occupants, three entirely different-looking men, one ginger-haired, one dark and one fair. The fair-headed one had the brightest blue eyes Amelia thought she had ever seen on a man, as well as the sweetest countenance. He was looking shyly at her, half smiling and twisting the cap which was still on his head round and round without stopping.

'You folk lorss?' the darkest-headed farmer enquired. ''Corse if 'ee are, then 'ee goner get e'en more lorss. If 'ee keeps drivin' up 'ere.'

'We're just touring,' George said, hoping to explain, although to judge from the frowns with which this pronouncement was met he had failed to clear the air.

'We're just driving around,' Amelia added, sensing confusion. 'Having a look at the country-side.'

'Ooh yar,' the fair-headed one said, sticking his tongue in one cheek. 'We got a lot of that roun' 'ere.'

'You wan' sum eggs or summing?' the ginger one suddenly wondered. 'Kill a pig if 'ee wan' 'im.'

'No thanks. We really are just looking.'

'Oh yar,' the fair-headed one said, shaking his head. 'Carn' see much poin' in 'at. Not if 'ee's not buyin'.'

'Thank you anyway,' Amelia said, with a smile which made the fair-headed one twist his cap round his head even more frantically. 'Goodbye then.'

The farmers watched them intently as they drove away. Noting this, Amelia turned and waved to them as if they had been their guests, but not one of the three waved back.

'I wonder if they fought . . .'

Amelia turned and stared at George and began to laugh. 'Oh, George! I shouldn't think they even know there's been a war!'

'Maybe not,' George agreed, grinning suddenly. 'Lucky devils! They certainly don't look the type to read newspapers.'

'Absolutely. And look – there isn't another building anywhere in sight.'

They had stopped at the top of the hill which led away from the farm. Down below they could see the old house and its land which stood surrounded by thick woodland and then a ring of hills.

'Look, George,' Amelia urged him. 'Look at this wonderful countryside. On an Indian summer's day like this, where else in the world would you rather be than here? In England.'

'The two most beautiful words in the English language.' George slowed the car to a halt once again. 'England and countryside.'

'Yes.' Amelia sighed and moved nearer to him so she could rest her head on his shoulder. 'I think you're absolutely right.'

'And you, Amelia, are absolutely – wonderful.'

George put his arm round her shoulders, and as he did so Amelia found that she had never experienced emotion such as she felt now. It was like a surge within her, a sensation so profound she could find no words with which to express it. For a moment she thought she might cry, so acute was her sense of joy. Instead, what she did to express the inexpressible depth of her emotion was to take the hand which rested on her shoulder and kiss it.

George said nothing, and when Amelia turned to look at him she saw that once again he was frowning that troubled, worried frown she had seen all too often; and always, it seemed, when they were intimate. Obviously, for him, there was no surge of joy, nothing but disquiet.

'Something's troubling you, George.'

'How do you know?'

'Because I can feel the moment when you suddenly become unhappy without you having to say anything. What is wrong? Can't you tell me?'

'I will, soon,' George said, turning away to look across the bold sweep of countryside. 'Be patient.'

'I am being patient.'

'I know. I know you are. Just be patient a little longer.'

Fortunately the day was too beautiful to be spoilt by the sudden dip in mood, as was the surrounding countryside. Neither of them was encouraged to be introspective for too long, and once George had managed to get the Hillman motoring again Amelia was able to forget that they had any problems and gaze out over the beautiful landscape that unfolded before them.

'This is a wonderful part of the world,' she said, as George drove slowly through the narrow streets of the pretty little Saxon town of Bruton. 'This is how England always was and always should be, glorious, peaceful and somehow – deep.'

'Deep?' George turned to look at her in surprise as he swung the Hillman up the narrow road which led across lush green valleys towards Evercreech. 'I don't see how a countryside can be deep?'

'Well it can, George Dashwood. It's deep because it feels as if it's always been here. As if this is England as it always was. As if it existed first, before any other part of England was here.'

'That isn't possible,' George laughed, not derisively but because he was still unsure of Amelia's exact meaning. 'How can something such as a mass of land—'

'I'm being poetic, George,' Amelia interrupted, putting a hand on his knee and smiling at him to show she wasn't taking herself too seriously. 'It's just that whenever I've come down to this part of the country with my parents, I've always had this sense of belonging. As if being English meant being here, in this part of England. And why that should be I have no idea, because the Dennisons certainly don't come from here.'

'It is a very ancient part of the country apparently,' George admitted. 'A place steeped in legend. As far as I can gather a lot of people think that the western tribes were the earliest settlers. I think I remember being taught at school that the kings of Wessex considered themselves the proper rulers of the country, even though they had no real idea of the size or shape of their supposed kingdom.'

'It's something more than that,' Amelia went on. 'It's as if this was a magic place. A place where the heart of England is and has always been. I suppose that's what I mean by deep, George. Its soul is very ancient, and its sense of history is very profound.'

'I don't know this part of the country at all,' George said, looking at the land around him. 'Yet I know what you mean. It has a very special . . . *resonance*.'

'Yes. It has a very special resonance. It's almost as if this is where we are meant to be.'

George looked at her. 'Do you think that's what your famous star was telling you?'

'I don't know if the star was telling me, George. I just know that is what I feel.'

There was a very good audience for Clarence Dennison's poetry reading that night in the ruins of Glastonbury Abbey, thanks not only to the fame of the poet and the vogue for war poems, but no doubt also to the fact that they were to be read in the main by Archibald Hanley, whose current popularity seemed to be immeasurable.

Seen in action George found that he was astonished by the man's artistry, particularly since he only knew the actor vaguely by repute, and until the moment he appeared on the rostrum in the ruined abbey had only seen him in the context of scandalously funny anecdotes told over champagne cocktails and fresh salmon sandwiches. His public persona was altogether different. Gone was the impish gleam in the eye and the waspish turn to the tongue and in their place instead was the famous mesmerizing look and the equally renowned sonorous baritone. To the last man and woman the audience was enthralled by the wonderful performance, whose climax was made even more dramatic by a sudden dry electrical storm which broke out almost overhead as Archie was reading the last poem, 'The Stranger on the Landscape'. But by the time he reached the last verse, and Amelia turned to look at George, she discovered that her husband was gone, overcome perhaps by the combination of the poetry, the thunder and the sheet lightning which, Amelia suddenly realized, must have all proved too reminiscent of recent events for him.

Her first instinct was to go after him, but she chose instead to remain in her place, knowing by now that if and whenever George wanted her he told her so. Whatever was troubling him, she knew he needed to be alone at such moments so that he could either overcome these hauntings or at the very least give himself enough time to recover.

She saw him later, leaning on a broken fragment of wall lighting a cigarette, his handsome face illuminated by a match. She went to his side and slipped her hand into his.

'Don't you want to come and say well done to Archie?'

'I'm not quite sure I know what to say. To him or to your father.'

'They'll expect you to say something. Particularly Archie. Actors always expect you to say *something*.'

'Even though they're saying someone else's words? And even though those words are only a reflection of someone else's deeds?'

'Does that bother you, George? I would have thought it was a mark of respect – if not honour. To have someone write verses about your deeds. And to have a great actor recite and give them meaning.'

'Yes,' George agreed, after giving the matter thought. 'Yes, you're quite right. I'm being churlish. Simply because I was so affected by it.'

'I don't see anything wrong in that.'

'Just a bit indulgent, allowing myself to be so moved by your father's verse. And by Archie's performance. For a moment I thought I might have been escaping from the reality, in fact I thought there was a danger that we all might be. Here in this magical setting, seduced by art – I mean even the thunderstorm.'

He looked to a horizon still lit by distant lightning.

'I'm not sure what this sort of thing proves,' he continued. 'Or even what it means. Isn't there a very real danger that because of the fineness and subtlety of great art what we all went through – the war – will become something to be enjoyed? I don't think it should be, you see. I think we should only be appalled and sickened by what has just happened.'

'I think that's a very good point,' Amelia agreed, sitting down on part of the broken wall next to him. 'In fact I think you should argue that with Papa over dinner. And with Mr Hanley.'

'No.' George shook his head and drew on his cigarette. 'No, I don't think it's something we should *argue* about. This is just me. I'm just trying to get my bearings, really. Trying to sort out everything that's going on in my head. Don't worry. I'm not going mad.'

Finally of course he was pulled into a discussion over dinner, a dinner which had turned into a splendid impromptu party thanks to the generosity and warmth of Archie and Mae who insisted that at least a dozen of their acquaintances who had attended the reading should come back to The Manor.

It was a very informal occasion, and since the storm had now completely cleared, leaving a fine and warm autumn night behind, everyone ate at

175

long tables set out on the terrace underneath a pergola covered in honeysuckle and deeply scented roses. As always at the Hanleys' table the wine flowed freely, as subsequently did the conversation, so that before long George forgot his introspection and found himself in a passionate debate about the role of the artist in a post-war society.

'Soldiers are not the only ones who make sacrifices, my dear young hero,' Archie informed him, clapping a hand on his forearm. 'This may sound like heresy to you, but artists also sacrifice themselves. We are like bees. We sting and we die.'

'It's only a cosmetic death, surely.'

'Art is a living death, sweet boy! We suffer so that the rest of you may see!'

'Hanley here is right, but only up to a point,' Clarence said, peeling a ripe peach with great precision. 'We artists have been described as being full of imaginings – which after we have told of them, everyone then sees.'

'It was a German who said that, isn't that so, Clarrie?' Archie thundered. 'That damnable know-it-all Goethe.'

'So what if it was, Archie? He it was who also said there is no patriotic *art* – nor any patriotic *science*. The two things cross all frontiers. As the true artist does.'

'So your poems, Mr Dennison,' George wondered, turning to Clarence. 'Your poems are not just in homage to English soldiers? They're meant for German ears too?'

'Of course!' Archie insisted, banging a fist on the table. 'But of course!'

'I can answer that for myself, thank you, Archibald, you old ham,' Clarence reproved his host. 'And yes, George, of course I would hope my poems were not chauvinistic elegies, but rather that they reflected the universal pain and suffering of war. Have you read any of Wilfred Owen's work? "Strange Meeting" for instance?'

'No, sir, I haven't. Should I?'

'Most certainly. No-one has put it better – what we're talking about now. *I am the enemy you killed, my friend. I knew you in this dark.* I'll give it to you to read when we get home.'

'*My hands were loath and cold,*' Archie continued, his eyes widening with the wonder of the words, his voice beginning to boom. '*Let us sleep now.*'

'Yes. But the point of art, that is what I am after.'

To a person the whole table seemed to be staring at George.

'The point of art?' a painter called Henry Hick echoed. 'The *point* of art, young man?'

'If the point of an army is to win battles, sir, then what is the point of art?'

'To *do* battle, I'd say,' Hick replied, pouring wine. 'To do battle with conscience. Art doesn't *answer* any questions, you see. It *asks* them.'

'I think what worries George here,' Clarence

said, taking hold of the wine bottle himself, 'is whether or not art is sometimes in danger of trivializing or romanticizing life – and man's achievements. Personally I don't think this is the case, George. I think that what the artist does – or should do – is to make us look at something afresh. Differently. This chap Nash, the painter.'

'I know him. We were at The Slade together,' Hick said. 'Then in the Artists Rifles. We fought together in the trenches at Ypres.'

'I was at Ypres. Royal Artillery, 29th Division.'

Henry Hick looked at him and nodded. 'I didn't survive it,' he said, looking George directly in the eyes. 'Did you?'

There was a silence, as George considered his answer.

'Paul Nash was also at Ypres,' Clarence volunteered out of the void. 'He personifies what I'm trying to say – do you know his work at all, George?'

George shook his head although he seemed not to really hear the question.

'Some call it surreal, but I think of it as expressive,' Clarence continued. 'He paints these savage landscapes, of land ravaged by war. Trees like amputated limbs. Holes filled with foul water. Blocks of broken concrete, woods reduced to matchsticks. One painting in particular shocks you more than any, a canvas called *We Are Making a New World*. Yet there are no living figures in it with which we can identify. Not a living nor dead soul.

Just this nightmare landscape of black twisted trees, mud humps and holes, and in the background these red hills with a setting sun behind. Red as if caked in dried blood. When you look at it, because of the artist's vision, George, you see far more than any photograph could show you. And because of it you feel infinitely more anguished, helpless and angry. That is what art does, George. As Degas said, the artist gives the idea of the true by means of the false.'

'Does that answer your question, sweet soul?' Archie demanded. 'Or do your devils still run?'

'I wasn't asking it as a question so much,' George said quietly. 'My mission is one of comprehension really. But I do have a question to answer – the one Mr Hick here posed me.'

'Well?' Henry Hick wondered. 'And what is your answer?'

'The answer is no,' George replied. 'If I am to be strictly truthful, I did not survive Ypres either.'

'Good,' Hick replied. 'Then you may come and visit me tomorrow and I will show you my canvases.'

'Thank you,' George said. 'I shall look forward to that.'

A moment later, privately, Amelia reminded George that they were meant to be returning home to Sussex the following day, but much to her surprise George expressed a wish to stay down in Somerset longer, perhaps at a pub or an hotel if the Hanleys could not have them. Amelia promised to find out from her parents – although knowing the sort of house Archie and Mae kept, she felt sure they would be welcome to stay on as long as they wished.

'Is there any particular reason? Or just a general one?'

'Is falling in love with a place particular or general? You tell me.'

Amelia found an early opportunity to make an enquiry as to extending their length of stay when Mae invited her to join her for a midnight walk around the moonlit grounds.

'Just me?' Amelia wondered, as they left the party on the terrace.

'We have not yet had a chance to *talk*,' Mae told her, as ever a little more dramatic than most people. 'Or to *conspire*. Most of all, I have not had the chance to congratulate you on your handsome husband.'

'I'm so glad you like him.'

'It's very touching. Both Archie and I have noticed that he rarely takes those great dark eyes of his off you.'

'It's absurd really, you know. We've known each other since we were children, so it is truly, really – absurd!'

'There is a world of difference between child and adult, as you've probably noticed.' Amelia suddenly found herself unusually silent, so Mae went on, after only the most imperceptible of pauses, 'A propos of which, I expect George is a perfectly sensational lover. But no, don't tell me. I will just be happy to guess from your expression.'

Amelia glanced at her companion and smiled uncertainly, at a loss as to how she might answer.

'As I said, Mrs Hanley—'

'*Mae*, poppet. Now you are married we can first name away like anything – after all, I am not some ancient aunt.'

'As I said, George and I have known each other since we were children—'

'And as I said there is no comparison. I only ask from mischief. So many dashing and beautiful men are utterly hopeless under the covers, you know. But no, don't say a thing, I can guess. I know I can.'

If ever there was a chance, it was now. Amelia already knew from her mother that even in their bohemic set Mae had always been considered *outrageous*, but much more to the point was the fact that – according to the nuances of gossip Amelia had either overheard or lately actually been privy to – Mae had, prior to marriage, been quite famous for her long line of lovers. If anyone could actually explain to Amelia the facts of which she was still so very ignorant, it surely must be she.

Fortunately Mae spared Amelia any unnecessary embarrassment by taking her by the hand, sitting her down on a bench beneath a vast and ancient oak tree, and coming straight to the point.

'One may know a woman better by her silence

sometimes, Amelia my dear, more than by – well, by her words, you know? As an actress one becomes more skilled at this than most, since one is forever trying to read the intentions of one's fellow actors. I sense a problem in your silence, in your lack of – let us say a nod or a wink in your troubled eyes. Tell me all. And I mean *all*.'

'Mae?' Amelia asked carefully. 'If I do, do you promise it shall go no further?'

Mae, who had now sat down beside her, opened her large green eyes as wide as she could and stared at her.

'Such a thing,' she gasped, putting a hand to her neck in mock theatrical style. '*Why, child – you would remove the very reason for my existence!*' She laughed, taking her hand from her neck and putting it on one of Amelia's cool ones. 'Just quoting the dear old Bard. It's like a nervous tic for me – quoting, quoting, always quoting. Of course it shall go no further if that is what you wish. I promise. Now tell me.'

So Amelia told her – everything. When she was finished Mae still had a hold of her hand, which she now squeezed firmly before attempting to reply.

'Well. Now then. To begin. The first part, the physical details rather than the metaphysical ones, is the easiest, believe me. And while it will sound perhaps slightly absurd in the telling I do assure you, poppet, it is no such thing in actuality. But as to the second part of your problem, as to why

George has not yet made love to you, that I can only guess at – and most likely *wrongly*. We must imagine – must we not – that it was either something that happened during the war, or even simply the fact of the wretched war *itself*. This friend of ours, you see, another actor called Herbert Greatorex – *particularly* good in Ibsen, whom personally I cannot abide. All that ghastly Nordic gloom – anyway, poor dear Herbie came home after two years in the mud and has been cold and complaining of the damp ever since. Sits all day and night apparently in front of a fire, and when Henrietta – his most darling wife – asks him what the whole ghastly business was like he simply says, over and over, *Not too good, Henny. Not too good.* Imagine. Can you? For the life of me I can't – and I am an actress, my dear. We cannot possibly know the half of it, precious child, and certainly, please God, I hope and pray that we never will. But if your beautiful George broods the way he does, and dreams the way he does, and goes off the way he does, we must suspect something *dread*. You can't ask him, my dear. Ask most normal men what the matter is and they either shout at you or shut up like a clam – so of course you cannot ask him. He will have to volunteer it to you, which if he loves you he most certainly will. But I suspect something *awful*, don't you? He has either seen something terrible or something terrible has happened to him – but no-one can face the beast down, alas, except himself.'

Amelia sighed. No matter who she consulted the answer was always the same. 'So I must be patient.'

'Yes, my dear, you must be patient – exactly. God knows it will not be easy—' Mae closed her dark painted eyes dramatically, to hint at the struggle ahead, before resuming. 'One day he will come to you and tell you, and when he does you two will be able to love each other as you assuredly are meant to do. But having said that, we must deal with the loving part, because when that particular day does indeed dawn you most certainly will want to be *well* prepared. When it comes to making love ignorance is certainly *not* bliss.'

And so Mae set about explaining to Amelia not just the facts of life but the art of lovemaking. Being such a consummately good actress she managed to invest the lesson with the right mixture of drama, poetry and good humour, so that far from finding it either embarrassing or awkward Amelia was enthralled and intrigued, the two of them finally laughing inordinately when Amelia finally confessed her version of what she thought might happen.

'*Moi aussi*, darling,' Mae admitted. 'You will never believe this, but in times of yore I was as green as the grass when it came to men, believe me.'

'I thought *I* was the only total ignoramus!'

'Ignoramuses don't come much more ignorant than I was, my dear one. We are only two of millions of women who have been or are in the same boat, I do assure you. Yet, still, I have a feeling that somehow, if we know too much too soon, some of the wonder must go out of life, and with a lack of innocence will go a lack of magic.'

Together they strolled back to rejoin the party, which was by now so busy arguing the merits of Henri Matisse's latest and most controversial work *L'Odalisque* that the two women rejoined the table without, it seemed, their absence being noticed.

Except by George, who looked round at Amelia and gave her such a sudden welcoming smile she felt she had been away for weeks.

The following morning found Amelia sitting in the drawing room of Henry Hick's house drinking coffee with Penelope, the artist's wife. When she was left alone for a moment she found herself watching George and Henry, deep in conversation either side of a table in Henry's studio.

They had been left there to talk further after Amelia had been shown the artist's latest works, a series of grim and graphic drawings of weary mud-drenched soldiers either waiting to go into battle or returning injured, concussed and exhausted from the trenches, works which, while quite telling, Amelia privately considered to be almost too intellectual. Penelope had invited Amelia back into the house for coffee, leaving the two men alone to talk about their mutual war experiences.

Henry's studio was a purpose-built shed situated at the bottom of the lawn, and clearly visible from the house. Amelia could see there was now an opened bottle of wine on the table and both men were smoking cigarettes.

But it was George who was doing the talking, sitting bolt upright his side of the table and looking just above Henry's head, rather than at him, as he addressed him, while as he listened Henry sank his head ever deeper into his hands until finally he covered his face with them both and remained so for a long moment – well after George had finished what he had to say. Finally, as George lit a fresh cigarette and continued to stare into the distance, Henry Hick took his hands from his face, shook his head before resting it on his forearms on the table in front of him.

'What were you talking about, George?' Amelia asked as they drove to meet Constance and Clarence, whom they had left walking the countryside above the neighbouring village. 'You seemed really very engrossed.'

'We were talking about the war. What do you think?' George returned, smiling at her affectionately but making it perfectly clear that he was stating the obvious. 'We'd both been at Ypres so we had a lot in common.'

There was a short pause while Amelia tried to quell a quite unreasonable anger. Finally she said, quietly, 'You can talk to *him* about it, but not to me?'

'Probably because you weren't over there fighting.'

'That isn't fair.'

'It's perfectly fair. Men can be war bores just as easily as they can be golfing bores.'

'That isn't what I mean, George.'

'No, but it's what I mean, Amelia.'

George slowed the car down as he saw Constance and Clarence waiting for them on a bench outside an inn.

'Feel like a drink?'

Amelia stared ahead, feeling suddenly almost bitter. 'I feel like several drinks if you really want to know. So look out, George Dashwood!'

George seemed not to realize anything of her internal struggles, but just wandered into the pub after Amelia, ordered them all some drinks, before sitting down with her parents to discuss the arrangements for going home to Sussex.

'I know you have to get back but Amelia and I rather wanted to stay down a few more days – and Mae very generously has said it's fine for us to stay on.'

'Borrow the car then,' Clarence offered. 'We can take the train back and you really will need a car down here, that I do know.'

'Are you sure, Mr Dennison?'

Clarence Dennison smiled. 'Perfectly. And I only hope that you find somewhere nice, George.'

'What on earth do you mean, Papa?' Amelia asked with a laugh. 'Find what exactly?' Her spirits as always restored by her father's outward-going nature, his natural optimism, his ease with himself.

'A house,' her father smiled in return. 'That's why you're staying on down, isn't it? For a house!'

That night after dinner when Amelia was exercising the Hanleys' dogs in the parkland, there was a full harvest moon shining, a moon so bright that at first when she looked for stars Amelia had to shield her eyes. Most of the cloud that had hung in the skies all day had now cleared, so that the full moon shone unimpeded, bathing the lovely grounds in a mysterious blue light. But once her eyes were used to the brightness Amelia soon spotted the body for which she searched. It hung in its usual direction, although it appeared to be even lower in the sky, and despite the moon's unusual aura it seemed to be even brighter than ever before.

George had just finished a long game of chess with Archie and was preparing to go up to bed when Amelia caught him.

'No,' she whispered, taking him to one side. 'Let's go out for a drive instead. It's a simply wonderful night.'

'A drive? At this time?' George smiled, even though he was well used to Amelia's often quirky improvisations. 'All right, if that's what you want.'

'I want to drive to where the star is,' Amelia told him as they made their way out of the house.

'Fine. Then we'd better take the spaceship and not the Hillman.'

'I want to go to the place below the star, nutty,' Amelia laughed, taking his hand. 'As it happens I think I know where it is. You know, like the Wise Men in the Bible! So this time let's try *not* to get lost.'

The moonlight was so bright that George drove without headlights, quite able to negotiate the deserted country lanes without a problem. Finding Amelia's so-called fix, however, was another thing altogether. For well over an hour they motored slowly round the tiny roads, George keeping his eyes firmly on the road while Amelia stared out of the window trying to deduce as precisely as possible the exact area over which the star hung.

'It's hopeless, George,' she finally confessed, sitting back in her seat with a groan. 'I mean, it could be anywhere.'

'What could be? What are we looking for? What do we expect to find?'

'How should I know?' Amelia replied impatiently. 'Your guess is as good as mine.'

'A wild-goose chase, that's my guess, Amelia Dashwood.'

'No! Stop!' Amelia suddenly cried, sitting bolt upright in her seat. 'My God, George! You were right! It is a shooter!'

'So?' George queried, pulling the car up to one side of the road and peering out through the windscreen. 'I can't see it.'

'Because it's gone,' Amelia said quietly. 'It just suddenly shot down out of the sky and disappeared.'

'It shot *down*, Amelia? Are you sure?'

Amelia nodded. 'It literally plummeted down like a brilliant stone dropping through water – and disappeared behind that wood over there.'

George looked to where Amelia was pointing and saw the dark outline of a small copse which lay about quarter of a mile ahead of them.

'Go on, George!' Amelia urged him. 'Get going! Let's go and take a look, for crying out loud!'

Still protesting, George drove on up the hill in front of them until he came to a dead end where the road as such ran out and turned into a narrow, overhung and overgrown lane. As soon as the car stopped Amelia hopped out and began to try to fight her way through the undergrowth which was congesting the path.

'Amelia? Where on earth do you think you're going?' George called after her.

'Where do you think, George? If it was a meteor or something—'

'If it was a meteor, we'd have heard a damn great bang if it had landed! Now wait!'

Armed with the sturdy walking stick Clarence had left on the back seat of the car, George went ahead of Amelia, beating a way through the mass of brambles and nettles which choked the pathway.

'I really don't know what you expect to find,

Amelia,' he grumbled, sucking a large thorn out of the back of one hand. 'A spaceship full of Martians, knowing you.'

'George . . .' Amelia sighed behind him over-patiently. 'George, don't you find it even the slightest bit odd that a star which we have both been watching should quite suddenly just disappear? Just drop out of the sky and fall somewhere in this very neighbourhood?'

'Apparently.'

'George – I saw it.'

'You saw what you *thought* was a falling star, Amelia.'

'All right, clever clogs. So if I was seeing things, where's the star now? Go on – look up at the sky where it was – which was there . . .'

Amelia stopped and pointed out the now vacant space in the sky. George ignored her, continuing to beat a way through along the path.

'George?' Amelia called. 'George, it has *gone*. Look!'

'Maybe it was never there in the first place. Or maybe it was one of those odd little suns you read about which suddenly burn themselves out.'

'Oh yes,' Amelia replied sarcastically. 'I'm forever reading about odd little suns burning themselves out and falling to earth in Somerset.'

'Well I never,' George suddenly said, coming to a halt. 'Well, I'll be blowed.'

'What? What, George?' Amelia bumped into George's back as he stood stock-still, staring ahead of him. 'What is it, George?' she repeated more quietly. 'What is it you're going to be blowed about?'

'It isn't a spaceship,' he replied. 'Or a star fallen to earth. Look – it's a house of some sort. Or rather a ruin.'

Coming to his side, Amelia could see the outline of just the top of some buildings which lay ahead of them behind a grassy knoll.

'How amazing,' she whispered, easing herself in front of her husband. 'I wonder if it's occupied.'

'Hardly,' George replied, following her up the knoll. 'With a drive in this condition?'

'Goodness,' Amelia exclaimed. 'Wait till you see, George – it's beautiful. Look . . .'

In the still bright moonlight the group of old ruined buildings which lay before them looked like something out of a fairy tale. Judging from the shape of the windows, at first Amelia thought the main building must have once been a church or chapel, but when she mentioned this to George he said he thought the disposition of all the buildings meant it was more likely perhaps to have been a small priory or convent, particularly given its position.

'Hardly the place for a church, however ancient, I'd have thought,' he said, walking slowly round the main building. 'Too far off the beaten track – and anyway, look – here at this side? There's what looks like the remains of a little chapel, see?'

Amelia leaned through one of the carved stone windows to examine the annexe.

'I think you're possibly right,' she said. 'In fact that stone table there under the main window – that could even have been an altar.'

'I am sure it was a priory. I mean, from the size of the main building it would seem to have been designed for residency.'

George took Amelia by the hand and walked round to what he thought must be the main entrance, an old oak door which was still on its hinges and, when he pushed it, opened on to a stone flagged hall.

'I'm sure I'm right, Amelia.' George stood aside to allow her to enter. 'This is definitely a hall, wouldn't you say? Rather than the chancel of a church – and this room to the right here . . .'

Amelia followed him as he pushed another door open to reveal a large rectangular room.

'. . . This was probably the refectory – and here—' George disappeared into another room off the one they were in, followed by Amelia. 'This was probably another living room – and there's another room running off at the end, I think. Yes, yes there is.'

'And there's a staircase,' Amelia called, having wandered through a stone archway into another hallway. 'So it has to be a house because you don't find a lot of churches with staircases, do you? You coming up, George?'

'Careful, Amelia!' George reappeared at the

bottom of the stone staircase, half of which Amelia had already climbed. 'You don't know what the floors will be like up there!'

'They seem to be fine!' Amelia called back, having carefully made her way along the landing. 'Most of the roof seems to be still in place, so the floors are really all right! Come up and see for yourself – it's like a rabbit warren up here!'

All along the corridor they were both now exploring they found a series of rooms which from their size and disposition could well have been bedrooms, while right at the end of the passageway there was an altogether larger room which judging from the serrated partition mid-way had at some time been divided into two. Spectacularly, the end wall of the large room was almost entirely taken up with an enormous Gothic window, sadly with only three or four panels of the stained glass still remaining, the rest probably having been stolen or vandalized.

'This must have some view,' George remarked, standing in front of the huge window. 'Down there below us – those must have been the gardens, I should imagine, and then beyond that wall there, it's just open countryside and then woodland, right up to the tower.'

Looking out at that landscape Amelia could see a broad sweep of fields and woodland, right up to the tall landmark tower which stood atop the highest hill in the neighbourhood.

'Do you know what that tower is, George?'

'No idea.'

'It was built where King Alfred is supposed to have erected his battle banner against the Danes. It's meant to be the site of a famous battle. One that saved England from evil marauders.'

'Alfred as in burning the cakes?'

'The very same. I told you this place was steeped in legend.'

'And *this* place,' George continued, taking Amelia's hand and leading her back through the building, 'I'd say this place has been lived in as a proper house, wouldn't you? And not so very long ago to judge from the way it's been fitted out. These doors here' – George pointed out some of the doors hanging in the entrances to what they supposed had been bedrooms – 'they're certainly not medieval. And downstairs, off the last room I was in when you came up here, there's a kitchen, of sorts.'

'Imagine living here,' Amelia whispered. 'It has to be the most enchanting place I've ever seen.'

'We must come back and see it in the daylight. I should imagine it's even more enchanting.'

'Do you think it's very old, George? It feels very old.'

'I think so. But we'll have a much better idea in daylight, wouldn't you say?'

'There's something else about it,' Amelia said, hesitating behind George as he began to make his way back downstairs. 'Besides feeling as if it's been here for ever.'

'What? What else is there about it?'

'It's – I don't know. I don't know how to say it, without sounding silly. It just sort of – it's as if it was a place of love. More than that. It feels as though it was once a place of *great* love.'

'You feel that too?'

'Really strongly. Isn't that odd?'

George stopped on the stairs, turned to her and shook his head. 'No. No more odd than you insisting we find the place.'

'What?' Amelia frowned back at him. 'I don't understand what you mean, George.'

'Have you forgotten your famous falling star?'

'Good heavens.' Amelia put a hand up to her throat. 'The star. You think the star actually brought us here, George?'

'Don't you?'

'Now it's my turn to be blowed.'

They returned the next morning, almost as soon as it was light. On their way George stopped the car outside a little whitewashed house which served as a post office to the little hamlet that lay no more than quarter of a mile away from the ruins they had discovered. Amelia waited in the car while George disappeared inside the post office, her thoughts completely taken up with their extraordinary discovery.

Try as she would she could find no logical explanation for the phenomenon of the star, and although not generally given to flights of fantasy she could not help believing that the two of them had somehow been guided to the place, although as to the reason why – as yet she only had the smallest inkling of an idea.

George on the other hand was happy to put everything down to pure coincidence, apparently seeing nothing remarkable about the fact that Amelia seemed to have spotted a falling star which would appear to have plummeted to earth right on top of a set of medieval ruins.

'Perhaps this is why they now lie in ruins,' George had joked as they had finally got to bed at half past two in the morning. 'Earlier this evening a family of four was seen to be enjoying a hearty supper of pigs' trotters when all of a sudden from a clear moonlit sky . . .'

Amelia now asked, 'So what kept you?' as George finally returned to the car from his sojourn in the post office.

'Sending a few postcards. You know. Wish you were here.'

'You were *truffling*, you truffle hound! Digging the dirt.'

'Don't tell me you don't want to hear?' George started the car and headed it straight for their destination. 'We were right. Originally it was a holy place, so my informant in the post office told me, some sort of priory founded early in the Middle Ages. Like most other such establishments it was dissolved and abandoned in Tudor times since when it has remained mostly unoccupied.'

'But we know someone must have been living in it recently, don't we?' Amelia argued. 'From some of the fittings – and the kitchen.'

'Precisely, my dear Watson. At the turn of the century this family got hold of it. The *de* something or others. Mad as March hares apparently, most of them. First the family lived here, then just the widow, who I gather was extremely dotty and stayed on with her dogs and her sheep after she had lost her husband until the war came, when for some reason she sold up and went back to Yorkshire. A farmer owns it now and wants to knock it down and sell off the stone.'

'Knock it down?' Amelia cried. 'He can't knock a place like that down! It's against the law, surely?'

'I don't think so.' George sighed dramatically. 'If you own a set of old ruins like that, you can do what you like with them apparently.' He gave Amelia a sideways glance which in her indignation she missed altogether.

'He can't knock that place down, George, I mean to say! That is a very special place.'

'Very special place or not, Mrs Dashwood – that is exactly what the said gentleman proposes to do.'

Amelia was still quietly seething when George stopped the car at the dead end of the road.

'Are you sure this is the right place?' she asked as she got out of the car. 'I seem to remember it from last night as being much more overgrown.'

George came round her side of the car, armed as before with his stout knobkerrie.

'This is the place all right. It probably just looks less overgrown in daylight. Besides, I gave most of these brambles a pretty good hiding last night.'

Amelia shook her head. 'It was much more over-grown than this.'

In fact the whole place looked not only considerably less sylvan but also less ruinous than they remembered it from their nocturnal visit, although George insisted this had to be an optical illusion since instead of moonlight they were now inspecting the place in bright and warm September sunshine.

Having once more climbed all through the house, examining every room and discovering that the main building was now more or less laid out as a family house, they inspected the grounds, making their careful way through small wood-lands, round overgrown paths, across a small field and back round a path which ended in a wall of trees. George pushed on ahead, holding back some sturdy branches so that Amelia could safely pass, but the way soon became impenetrable.

'Just as well,' Amelia said, testing the ground with the heel of her shoe. 'We wouldn't want to venture much further because the ground's quite boggy here. Very boggy, in fact.'

'That would make sense, would it not?' George wondered. 'Seeing how much of Somerset is half under water.'

'That's more to the west, George. Towards what's called the Flats. I should think all this water in the ground here suggests marshland pure and simple. There's a path we can take here,' she directed, pointing to a cutting through the trees. 'It looks as if we can get out that way.'

The two of them made their careful way out of the woods, Amelia protecting her clothes from the thorns while George did his best to spare her by holding back what branches he could. When they emerged they found themselves on the far side of the building, which they could just see beyond a huge hedge of brambles and wild dog rose.

'We shall have to walk all the way round again,' George said, looking unsuccessfully for a way through. 'This is like a wall.'

'Along here!' Amelia called from the end of the hedge. 'There's another hedge here at right angles, but there's a path to the side! Which runs back to the house!'

Following her directions they soon found themselves back in the land immediately surrounding the buildings, emerging on the side which contained the little chapel, which they had already found had been stripped of all its portable fittings.

'George,' Amelia said, as they stood beside the stone altar and examined the superbly carved and fashioned wooden roof. 'George, this place is unique. That stupid farmer simply cannot be allowed to knock it down.'

'Oh well, in that case,' George said with an

exaggerated sigh, 'we had better go and find him – and stop him.'

'Are you thinking what I am thinking, George?' Amelia wanted to know as, having ascertained from the post office where the farmer in question lived, George now drove out to find him. 'You have to be, don't you?'

'Of course. Of course I'm thinking the same as you are. We both thought it the moment we set foot inside.'

'If we do buy it—'

'*After* we have bought it—'

'If the farmer allows us to buy it, George, we shall need somewhere to live while it's rebuilt.'

'I'm going to ask Archie and Mae.'

'We can't impose like that. Rebuilding somewhere like that could take – I don't know. Ages.'

'The other night Archie said they were away so much that the house is empty for over half the year, except for Mad Betty and old Dan. I'm sure they wouldn't mind us either camping out in that little guest cottage of theirs or even keeping the house itself warm. Keeping the ghosts company, as Archie would put it.'

'You're right, George. The Hanleys *would* be only too happy to have us stay. Now I come to think of it they've often suggested the same sort of arrangement to my parents.'

'So there you are. All we have to do now is beat this farmer fellow down.'

*   *   *

The farmer lived high on a bare hill overlooking a valley grazed by black and white cattle. He was a big, ugly man dressed in a heavy brown overcoat and a vast floppy hat, even though it was a fine early autumn day. His coat was held closed by a length of twine, as were the bottoms of his heavy black trousers, tied tight above what appeared to be a pair of army boots. When George and Amelia approached him, he scowled and stood his ground, making no effort to greet them.

'Mr Crouch? My name is Dashwood. And this is my wife, Mrs Dashwood.'

'Whad 'ee wan'?' the farmer growled, poking his emaciated dog to heel with a long walking stick. 'Folk sed 'ey was sniffin' round 'e castle. Was 'im you?'

'The castle?' George said in surprise. 'If you mean the old ruined priory in the woods below Marlington—'

'I means 'e castle, thad's wad I means, squire.'

'I'm told you own it.'

'Wad if I does?'

'I'm also told you want to sell it.'

'Summun's bin doin' sum tellin' then, ain't 'ey?'

'I'd be interested in putting in a bid for it,' George continued. 'That is if you are wishing to sell. I need the stone.'

'Wad else 'ud un wan' 'im fer, ay?'

'Exactly. I'm also told the going rate – to

include the scrubland round it—'

'Scrub, 'ee say?' The farmer interrupted, before spitting hard on the ground. 'Er's thirdy acre gud meadow there, squire. An' another twenty scratch. Lan' alone cost 'ee twenny poun'.'

'Ten,' George said. 'You couldn't stand a donkey on it.'

'Twulve.'

'Ten,' George insisted. 'A hundred and thirty pounds for the entire holding, to include all loose stone.'

''Undred and fafty.'

'One hundred and forty. That's my last offer.'

''Undred and farty-five.'

'A hundred and forty-two.'

'Dun.'

'Done.'

The farmer spat on his hand and offered it to George, who without blinking an eye spat on his own and shook.

'I'll have my lawyer draw up the papers,' he said. 'Good day.'

'Be it cash, mine!' the farmer called after him. 'An' not to include 'em chairs in the parlour!'

'What chairs?' Amelia wondered *sotto voce*, as they walked away. 'He can't mean those dreadful old ladderbacks downstairs?'

'He's welcome to them,' George laughed. 'Even if they're Hepplewhite.'

'Which knowing Somerset farmers, they most likely will be.' Amelia suddenly stopped to stare at George. 'Is it really ours, George?' she asked. 'Really?'

'Looks like it. Bar a fall.'

'Then let's go and take another look, shall we? A proper look?'

'You took the notion right out of my head,' George replied.

By now it was late afternoon and the air was heavy with the drone of insects and the scent of wild columbine as they threaded their way back along the overgrown path to find themselves once more in the enchanted place. A family of young swallows were busy flying high above the chapel, building up their strength for the long flight south which was now imminent, while on the grass mound beyond the main window a hare sat watching the proceedings.

'What will it be like to live here, I wonder?' Amelia said, holding George tight by one arm. 'Can you imagine waking up in a place like this? And looking out on nothing but this wonderful view?'

'Living anywhere with you would be wonderful,' George replied dreamily. 'But here – here it's going to be heaven.'

'We can make a garden,' Amelia said suddenly. 'That's something I've always wanted to do – actually create a garden.'

'You've always been mad on gardens. Remember our famous garden? When we were small? You asked Old John if we could have a patch of our own?'

'All children do that, George. There wasn't anything extraordinary about that.'

'Not all children grew what you grew. Even Old John was amazed. He said you had the greenest fingers he'd ever seen on anybody.'

'Plants do seem to like me, I suppose. Let's go and look over there – where that high hedge is. I can't make out the lie of the land there at all.'

Amelia pointed to the hedge which they had been forced to skirt in order to return to the house earlier in the day, and led George over to it.

'I thought so,' she murmured, peering round the far end where they had not been before. 'It's a square – look, George? Do you see? It goes all the way round a square of ground, as if it had been planted that way deliberately.'

'Perhaps it was?' George strained his head to see over the top, which he failed to do, even given his height. 'From the look of how straight it is, it certainly suggests that it was planted quite purposefully.'

'Even though it's wild,' Amelia mused. 'It's not a formal hedge, at least not any more. It seems to consist mainly of bramble and hawthorn. But bramble and hawthorn doesn't grow in such an orthodox way. It would only grow this way if once there had been a proper hedge here. And yet even then—' Amelia stopped and frowned, looking back at the hedge behind her. 'Even then you would think that by now it would just have become nothing more than a tangle of scrub.'

'How strange!' George ran a hand through his hair. 'Why should it have kept its shape? When everything else around it has simply shot and run riot, how strange that it should be – kempt.'

'Look, George,' Amelia said suddenly. 'Look this end here – it isn't flush with the other side. It grows out two foot or so further, yet all the other corners, even though they're overgrown – you can see they're symmetrical.'

'Perhaps there's something behind it. Let me try . . .' He took hold of her arm, easing Amelia away from the corner. 'It doesn't matter if I get scratched.'

Wrapping a handkerchief round and round one hand, George pulled some thick and vicious-looking brambles out of the hedge and turned them back into the main growth to see what lay behind and beyond. Next he bent back some hawthorn branches, catching his fingers on the prickles as he did so, and complaining under his breath while making another attempt to clear a way. This time he was more successful and managed to raise a hefty-looking branch of hawthorn up above his head, fixing it in the growth there so as to make an entrance in the hedge itself.

'You're right, Amelia. There's a gap here, which again isn't completely overgrown. Look.'

Amelia ducked under the arm that was holding up another large bramble and saw the entrance.

'It's like one of those entrances to a maze – and yes – it is an entrance, George. It overlaps that hedge, see? And then beyond—'

She eased herself through and gasped.

'Come and see, George! It's a hidden garden!'

Inside proved to be a perfect rectangle of long grass threaded with wild flowers. There were no dandelions or docks, no nettles or bindweed, just delicate, pastel-coloured wild flowers which swayed in the gentle evening breeze. The grass was knee height meadow grass, lush, thick and green without a trace of cooch or briar, and was surrounded on all four sides by the hedge which seemed to level itself off at about seven feet. Amelia and George stood at the entrance in silence, both of them trying to work out how such a thing could possibly be.

'It must be the height of the hedge,' George said finally. 'It must act as some sort of buffer. It must protect this little patch. Preserve it.'

'I don't see how, George,' Amelia replied, without any answer herself. 'Seeds are carried on the wind. Why should the weeds bypass this place? And why haven't the brambles and briars overtaken the inside? By rights, as I said, this should be nothing but scrub.'

'Well of course!' George laughed. 'Somebody has made it their own! Someone has been tending it, for some reason or other – that has to be the answer!'

'I suppose so. But why just this place? Why not the rest of the gardens?'

'There's quite a lot of garden here. Maybe someone thought this was a special place, someone who loves wild flowers. And they tended it – I mean obviously that's what's happened, because otherwise as you say it would be completely overgrown.'

'I suppose you must be right. But it is peculiar.'

'We'll ask around. Somebody will know. There's obviously a logical explanation.'

'Why?' Amelia took his hand and pulled him back so that he faced her. 'Why does there have to be a logical explanation, George?'

'Because there has to be. Everything's explicable.'

'Everything?'

'Yes.'

'Including love?'

'To the scientists I suppose so,' George agreed, reluctantly.

'You don't really believe that. Not for a moment.'

'I'm not altogether sure I even know what love really is.'

'Nor me. So, perhaps it's time we found out.'

At this she kissed him. George did not kiss *her*. Amelia kissed him. Taking her emotional life in her hands, she put her arms round him, drew him to her and kissed him. She kissed him sweet and slow, slow and sweet, then long, long and ardently. As she kissed him she became him, entering into him and becoming one with him.

Now, he kissed her, he kissed her with long,

strong kisses, his arms round her, his mouth on her mouth. Their kisses turned to one kiss, one long breathless kiss until, at last, they loved each other fully, passionately, and completely on the warm grass while in the hedges, which gently moved with the warm breeze, bees sucked the pollen from wild honeysuckle as high above them swallows swooped and circled in the kind English sun.

Beyond the thick green leaves and twisted branches of the ancient hedgerow two men moved in shadow. Neither spoke as they moved noiselessly over the grass, but before they disappeared the Noble One turned to smile at the unseen lovers and raise one open hand in farewell, while the Bearded One stooped down to pick up a brilliant clear stone from the spot where it had fallen from the sky and replace it in his purse of jewels.

After which they vanished into darkness, high in a tree overlooking the secret place where the lovers lay, as a small brown bird sang a song it had never sung before, filling the air with thrilling music, while at the bottom of the thick wild hedgerow an ancient white rose began at last to grow.

Eleven

Now at last life was exactly as Amelia had always hoped. Not only had George and she found a beautiful place to live, but most important of all they were finally and properly man and wife. Reality was in fact even better than Amelia had privately imagined it, George proving himself to be a gentle and imaginative lover while The Priory was turning out to be a more enchanted and magical place than either of them had dared to dream.

With Archie and Mae departing their house the day after George and Amelia had moved into the enchanting little thatched guest cottage, they were left with the place to themselves. So while the purchase of The Priory was being legalized, inevitably they had time on their hands, time to take what turned out to be a proper honeymoon.

Of course neither of them made any reference to their previous problems, nor to the fact that George now seemed to find no difficulty at all in making love to Amelia. Privately, though, both of them believed that their ecstatic experience in the little hidden garden in the grounds of their future home had somehow exorcised the memory that had been haunting George.

Now there was no sign at all of his previous inhibition. Since that magic moment in the hidden garden it was exactly as if he was someone who had previously lost his nerve, only to suddenly recover it and to such an extent that often the mere exchange of a look would find them hurrying back hand in hand to the sensual privacy of their little cottage in the woods, where once, famously, they remained for a night and a day without re-emerging.

Amelia had never known such happiness, and she delighted in discovering the joys which resulted from their mutual passion. No longer was she just George's friend; now she was also his lover, and with the transformation Amelia too changed, from a girl into a woman – a woman who she was privately thrilled to discover was soon able to beguile her man as much as her man was able to enamour her.

Together they voyaged on a sea of discovery, finding themselves constantly amazed at the endless wealth of treasures the ocean of passion seemed to contain. What astonished them perhaps more was that, long-standing friends though they had undoubtedly been, they now seemed to be discovering each other properly for the first time, so that they spent as much time talking as they did making love.

'When one of us goes,' George said suddenly one day, 'we will know that a lifetime's talking is over, will we not?'

Amelia pretended that she hadn't heard him. Quite simply, the thought was unbearable. She refused to embrace it, and instead she started to sing and fool about to make George laugh, to make them both forget what he had just said.

Contracts had been exchanged on The Priory, and with the help of one Ambrose Philpotts, an architect friend bequeathed to them by Archie and Mae prior to their departure, George and Amelia set about looking for a capable builder. They finally settled on one of several craftsmen well known to Ambrose, a local stonemason and now master builder called Robert Stanley, someone to whom neither Amelia nor George initially warmed since he seemed both slow and truculent, but who Ambrose assured them, for all the apparent shortcomings of his personality, was in fact the most reliable and helpful of men. His problem was, Ambrose told them, that Bob Stanley himself did not take easily to people, particularly outsiders.

'And as far as Bob goes, that is anyone whose family wasn't living here prior to about twelve hundred.'

'AD or BC?' Amelia asked ruefully, having just been exposed to some of Bob Stanley's apparent inflexibility.

'His other trouble is he doesn't understand why

a young couple such as you should possibly want to restore a place like The Priory. To him it's nothing more than ruins. He told me he should be building you a nice warm, modern place, with all the conveniences.'

The idea was to restore the outside of the place while removing all the more modern additions that had been made inside. In place they intended to create a comfortable interior which would still be in keeping with the ancient house, using whatever old materials they could salvage from the site while at the same time scouring the countryside for wood and stone to match what they had found around the place.

In the event there was plenty in the immediate vicinity, the young Dashwoods getting the impression that whenever feasible and economically possible the local people seemed to prefer to start again and build from scratch for themselves. Luckily they also seemed to take little care as to where or to whom they disposed of what they considered to be the old rubbish, so that with patience and a lot of diligent searching Amelia was able to unearth practically everything they needed from old joists to unwanted floorboards, all thrown into barns, cowsheds, stables or outhouses, once or twice even on bonfire sites, just waiting for petrol and a match. On one expedition they even returned with a perfect Gothic stone window frame which Amelia had discovered being used as a doorway in a piggery and had purchased from the farmer for the sum of exactly thirty shillings.

Happily most of the original stone windows and old doors in The Priory were intact and un-damaged, other than missing panes of glass and the odd locks and latches from some of the external doors. The only blank they drew was on the question of matching roof tiles, since the roof had been repaired with a very catholic assortment of shingles.

After much prompting Mr Stanley finally admitted he knew of a place where he might be able to find old tiles while making it perfectly clear that he found it incomprehensible as to why anyone would prefer old to new. And so it was that by the time the day arrived for the building works to begin, all the necessary materials had been tracked down. By a combination of foresight and meticulous planning, George had mapped out an exact campaign for the restoration, much to the delight of Ambrose Philpotts who admitted that few if any of his clients had ever worked with such precision.

'And Mr Stanley isn't anywhere near as bad as we'd imagined,' Amelia told George one evening after he and his team had departed. 'He really loves this part of the world and little wonder. He told me Stanleys have been here since Domesday, first as farmers on Exmoor and then at Glastonbury where they moved in the seventeenth century, and where they learned their stone-masonry.'

'In that case you'd think he'd jump at the opportunity to restore a place like this. Instead of forever grumbling and wondering why.'

'It's only his way. People who live as deep in the country as he does are naturally suspicious of people like us. They see us as fly-by-nights. People with a whim in which they might or might not indulge. And they're afraid of being taken as fools, which is why they're so taciturn. Townspeople make fun of yokels. After all, you did – we both did, when we first came here.'

'I shall look at Mr Stanley differently from now on,' George promised.

While George concentrated on the actual building works, Amelia began a study of the part of The Priory which was going to be her province, namely the gardens.

It was obvious that no-one had actually been near the estate since the last year of the war, at least not to cultivate it. Ever since the last owner had sold it off to the farmer, the buildings had remained uninhabited and the grounds untended, with the consequence that the whole place had inevitably become a jungle. A long and careful search of the books in Archie's library finally yielded the one for which Amelia had long searched, namely a history of the locality which contained a whole chapter on The Priory, with detailed drawings of its elevations, interiors and – more important for Amelia – the grounds.

It seemed that originally the place had been laid out in the fashion of other self-sufficient religious communities, with a large walled vegetable and herb garden on the south side, meadows for grazing cattle and sheep to the west and two large carp ponds on the northern side, each on one side of a stone dovecote which supplied yet another form of sustenance for the monks. The ponds and the dovecote had disappeared within what was now the woodlands which lay to the north, but Amelia sensed that further exploratory work might eventually reveal their location, in which case she would return them to their original state.

To the south of the meadows there had also been a large lake surrounded by a thick belt of trees, in the exact spot where, when she and George had first walked the place, she had sensed the land turning to marsh, which seemed to indicate that the lake must lie within what now appeared to be just dense woodland. It was also quite clear from the drawings that in ancient times the lake was fed by a small river on its northern boundary.

When she showed George what she had discovered his initial reaction was that the lake could well have turned to bog by now, and if so clearing it would be – as he put it – the very devil of a job. Furthermore as far as he was concerned George reckoned he had spent more than enough time in mud to last him a lifetime. Amelia agreed to bide her time as far as the lake was concerned, before turning the pages to show him her other discovery.

'Our little hidden garden, do you see, George?' she said, tapping the page with her finger, this time to show a portion of the grounds to the south-west of the house. 'It was there all that time ago, as long ago as that.'

'That being?'

'When there first was a building on the land here. Which they think could have been as early as perhaps the sixth century.'

'Round about the time when the Stanleys settled these parts,' George grinned. 'But yes – you're right, Amelia. There it is – our little magical garden.'

Sure enough there on the page before him was a depiction of the rectangle made by the four hedges, the first drawing done as if from overhead and the second an elevation from the ground. The hedges seemed to have been as high then as they were now, the difference being that they appeared then to have been cultivated from privet or box rather than briar, hawthorn and bramble. It was a perfect geometric shape with what both Amelia and he assumed to be just grass in the middle, with the hidden entrance clearly shown from the over-head detail.

'Odd, though,' George added thoughtfully. 'Monks were famous for using every scrap of land to produce their food, yet our little garden would seem to have been purely ornamental. I tell you what – let's see if there's any mention of it in the text.'

Together they searched the chapter but could find no reference, other than the note in the plan of the grounds which simply described it as a *hedged enclosure*. 'Let's take a closer look at it tomorrow when we're on site, shall we?' George suggested. 'Maybe we will learn a little more about this mysterious *hedged enclosure*. Now, come on – well past bedtime.'

'It's only ten past nine, George,' Amelia protested, without thinking.

'Exactly,' George replied, lifting her up bodily in his arms and carrying her off to the cottage.

The first thing that struck them on revisiting the hidden garden was the height of the hedges.

'I don't remember them being this high,' Amelia said, staring above her.

'Nor me. In fact I recall being only just unable to see over the top. Now they seem to be a good foot or two higher.'

George stood by the nearest hedge. As soon as he drew himself up to his full height Amelia could see that the hedge was indeed over a foot taller than he. He could no longer see over.

'It has grown beyond belief. It's not just my imagination, is it?'

'No, George,' Amelia agreed, trying to find the entrance. 'It's not just your imagination. It's as if the garden wants us to keep its presence hidden from everyone. As if only *we* are to know of it.'

George frowned.

'This type of hedging normally takes centuries to grow.'

Not quite believing what he was seeing, George followed Amelia into the garden, where once again the place where they had first made love was to astonish them. For in contrast to the hedging the inside of the garden was as neat as anyone could wish.

'We haven't dreamed this too, have we?' Amelia turned to George. 'Or did we dream it all?'

'No, Amelia,' George shook his head and put his arm round her shoulders, 'we did not dream it and we are not dreaming now.'

'What can possibly explain all this?'

'I don't know. I have absolutely no idea at all, but I do know one thing. I don't think we should mention this to anyone. They won't think we're just fey, they'll think we're mad!'

There was one bit of news which they *did* make public some three months later. The day after Mr Stanley and his team had finished rebuilding the entire outside wall of the main part of The Priory, as well as nailing down the last of the restored roof tiles, to her own and to George's subsequent delight Amelia learned that she was expecting a baby.

Twelve

Feeling immensely protective of her in her new condition, George allowed Amelia to do only the lightest of work in the grounds while he helped on site with the continuing building work, which, due to a fine dry spring and Mr Stanley's unceasing labour, continued without hitch. For herself Amelia was perfectly content, spending her days exploring their land and her evenings sketching out suggestions for how the finished estate might look.

'Now, names? We must discuss names,' George said one evening as they were sitting by the fire.

'Yes, Captain Dashwood,' Amelia said, accompanied by the small salute she always gave him when he used what she called his military voice. 'Colonel if it's a boy, Miss Colonel if it's a girl.'

'You are a tease,' George groaned. 'And that wasn't my military voice. If I used my military voice you would have to stand down the fields to get away from it.'

'Oh yes it was, Captain Dashwood. Even the baby jumped to attention,' Amelia replied, patting her stomach. 'But before we get on to the business of names, don't you think perhaps we should first discuss the matter of your own particular future? After all, the six months you agreed with your father were up some time ago. I know it's not something you want to talk about, but—'

'It's all right. Ever since you told me you were expecting, I've been thinking about it almost incessantly. I just didn't want to talk about it until I was absolutely sure.'

'And?'

'And now I'm sure. In fact I was quite sure before, or at least I thought I was, but now we're going to have a child nothing would induce me to leave you.'

'Are you sure, George? Are you absolutely sure this is what you want? At this particular moment in time it may seem to be exactly what you want, but what about in three or four years' time?'

'No, I know now that I could never go back to the army. It isn't just you, or the fact that we're going to be parents, or that we're building a wonderful home – although these are all good reasons.'

'I wouldn't blame anyone for not wanting to leave The Priory, not once it's finished.'

'That would be reason enough for my change of heart. If nothing else, the thought of leaving you to go back into uniform fills me with dread, but it wouldn't be sufficient reason to make me change my mind. If that's what every soldier did, every soldier with a happy home, every soldier who loved his wife and family – well, we'd have been invaded again and again.'

'Then is it because you don't believe in war any more? I mean, have you become – a pacifist?'

The very idea of a Dashwood being a pacifist seemed too extraordinary for words, even to the former Amelia Dennison.

'No. No, I'm going to resign my commission not because of the war but because of the outcome. I think – I think it was wrong.'

'You think fighting the war was *wrong*?'

'No, I think the way we were *made* to fight the war was wrong. I think – I don't know – but I think it might well have been in vain, I think we were betrayed. I think the generals and the politicians betrayed us soldiers, not once but a thousand times. It is the generals and the politicians who should have been shot at dawn, not the poor men who went mad with the strain of the mud and the mustard gas.'

Amelia frowned at him, then stared into the fire for a long time.

'But that means – that includes your father,' she said finally. 'If you're saying the generals—'

'That includes my father, yes, theoretically. I can see how it happens. I quite understand that when a war becomes as big as this war did, when all perspective is lost, the generals and the politicians lose sight of two things. They lose sight of what they were originally fighting *for*, and they lose sight of the fact that the people who are fighting for this long and now lost cause are not numbers, but *men*. Their fellow men. Men with mothers and fathers, sweethearts, wives and children. Every war turns men into cannon fodder, but this war – no.' George stopped and shook his head. 'This war turned the flower of this country to dust. And I think that was too high a price to pay for the final outcome: a botched treaty and a few miles of mud.'

'Is that what you truly believe, George?'

'I think so,' George replied slowly. 'But the point is, whether or not I am utterly convinced doesn't really pertain. What matters is that if I have this sort of doubt then it simply is not fair to return to a profession where I am responsible for the lives of men. If there was another war – or, to put it another way, *when* there is another war, as there is bound to be just by the nature of things – it simply would not be right for someone who has doubts about its morality to be asking men to fight for their lives.'

'I understand, George,' Amelia said, stirring the embers of the dying fire with the poker. 'I think that's argued very fairly. But I don't like one thing you said – *when* there is another war, you said. Not *if*. Is that what you really think? That after this war to end all wars there'll still be another one?'

'I'm afraid so, Amelia,' George replied, sitting back and drawing on the cigarette he had just lit. 'In fact I'd say the next war will come about as a direct result of the one we've just fought.'

'In that case I think we should leave names till another time,' Amelia said, getting up and putting the guard on the fire, 'and go to bed.'

*   *   *

'If you're not going back into the army—' Amelia began again as she lay in the dark of their bedroom.

'*Since* I am not going back into the army.'

'How will we live?'

'I have enough put by for us to survive for the moment. Don't worry.'

'But if your father disinherits you – which he will.'

'I'll get a job. Don't worry, I've given the matter a lot of thought. But I'm not going to teach, thank you. Those who can't, et cetera. I'm not one of the can'ts. I'm a doer.'

'So what will you do-er, George? Become an actor like Archie?'

'I'm going to try writing,' George smiled, turning on his side and putting an arm round Amelia and pulled her towards him. 'That do you?'

'For now,' Amelia smiled at him in the dark. 'Tell me the rest tomorrow.'

'What I thought I'd try and write about is my life so far – but only in light of the war,' George told her at breakfast the next morning. 'How life was before the balloon went up, and how life is now.'

'What makes you think you'd make a writer, George?'

'You.'

'I've never said anything to you about being a writer.'

224

'You could inspire me to be anything.'

'What about your father? You know how this will hurt him.'

'I'm more concerned about my mother, as it happens.'

Amelia looked across the table at him in astonishment. 'Your mother, George? Why?'

'My mother comes from an even longer line of soldiers than my father. That was one of the main reasons they married. My father was deeply impressed by my mother's distinguished military lineage and in fact it was my mother who first put the idea of being a soldier into my head. She's the one who is not going to be able to forgive me for leaving the army. In which case it's going to be completely impossible for my father to keep me in his favour, even if he wanted to.'

Amelia put down her teacup.

'You do surprise me. But then you don't. The more I think about it, about your mother's attitudes, the more sense it makes.'

George picked up a piece of toast from the still warm pile in the white linen napkin beside his elbow.

'I think we should all live our lives according to the way we feel we should. Not in the way we're expected to. If my father wanted to kick over the traces and – I don't know.' George sighed in exasperation. 'I don't know . . .'

'Join Archie's travelling players? That do for you?'

'That will do just fine,' George replied, returning the smile.

'He'd probably be a star in no time. With those ultra-distinguished looks of his.'

'No doubt. But the point is – if that was what he wanted to do, so he should and good luck to him. Just as I should be allowed to do what I feel I want to do. I've done my duty. I've served king and country, and now if I decide that is that, that should be that.'

'Talk to him, George. Explain yourself to him the way you have to me and I bet he will understand your reasons.'

'I think you're right. Perhaps – better. I shall write the truth to him. That way we'll soon see whether or not I have a literary power of persuasion.'

For a whole week George did his best to write the letter. Each day on their return from the works at The Priory, while Amelia bathed and then cooked them dinner, George would sit at the desk under the window in the living room which overlooked the parkland and write page after page, all of which each evening were finally screwed up into little paper balls and consigned to the fire. Observing him, Amelia said nothing, sensing that George could well find the greatest difficulty expressing his thoughts, his feelings and above all his reasons for resigning his commission. But finally, unable to stand the slough of despair through which George was so obviously slogging, one evening when they sat together on the sofa after they had dined Amelia asked him whether or not she could be of any help at all.

'Yes. You can sit and listen to me while I tell you just what happened. That way – once it's out of my system – that way I might be able to put down something of it to my father. That way – he might understand!'

'Very well.' Amelia arranged herself on the sofa. 'Whenever you're ready, so am I.'

Having poured himself a large whisky for courage, George sat down opposite her, his tumbler held in one hand on the arm of his chair.

'You mustn't be shocked,' he began, after a minute's thought. 'You probably will be, and I don't blame you. But what I do ask is that you hear me out without asking me anything.'

'I promise,' Amelia said, outwardly calm. 'Whatever you say, I will not interrupt.'

'It was the year before the end of the war, 1917, and we'd just made a successful push, successful that is if success is to be measured in terms of winning thirty feet of mud. Anyway, it was spring, middle of May actually, a perfect spring day as it happened with the air full of swallows and the ground covered with the dead. Having made the push it was now my job to find a new site for the guns, since our next intention was to attack this ridge about four hundred yards away, just beyond a village called Crozy which until this success had been in enemy hands.

'I had a party of half a dozen men under me including a young lieutenant named Grace who had joined up the previous year, at the end of '16. We chose a mounting for the guns in a copse about a hundred yards south of the village, and then as ordered we made our way to the village to rendezvous with a second unit sent ahead to mop up under the command of a Major Walker. I failed to locate Major Walker until I saw one of his men coming out of a barn ahead of us. The man was then sick on the side of the road, and subsequently I discovered him to be very drunk. That's quite unusual, seeing we were still in action, so I went forward to investigate. As soon as I did, I became aware of someone screaming. Not that there was anything unusual about that since that's what you hear all day most days when you're under fire in the front line. But this was different because it came from the barn right ahead of me – and it was obviously a woman who was doing the screaming.'

George paused for a drink of whisky, looking over the edge of his glass at Amelia as he drank.

'Anyway. Anyway, I thought I had better see who exactly was doing the screaming and why, so with Lieutenant Grace and a couple of men I went up to the barn. I sometimes wish I hadn't. First of all, just by the door were the bodies of four dead German soldiers lying face down to one side by a wall. They'd all of them apparently been killed by a shot to the back of the head. I questioned the drunk soldier as to how these men had been killed and he said he understood there had been a machine gun nest in the farmyard and that the enemy soldiers had been shot on the retreat. I deputized a soldier to go and search for such a nest while noting that none of the fallen Germans had any weapons. It emerged later on that there was no sign of any machine gun post in the vicinity.

'Lieutenant Grace had gone in ahead of me and was shouting for me to come and see what was happening. I went inside immediately and saw a young woman surrounded by men . . .'

George stopped and looked at Amelia, uncertain whether or not to continue, but as agreed Amelia remained silent.

'She was surrounded by men in – well, let us say, no fit state. Lieutenant Grace, seeing what was about to happen, went to attack the major. Ridiculous as it sounds I then asked Major Walker what he thought he was doing – even though it was perfectly obvious. Pathetic the things you find yourself saying at times like that. Naturally he told me to forget it and get out and take my men with me, or he'd shoot the lot of us. I doubt if I'll ever forget anything I saw during that damned war, but the look on that woman's face has haunted me at every turn; and the fact that there was nothing Grace and I could do to save her!'

George shook his head, and sighed a sigh so profound that by contrast the silence that followed, which Amelia at last broke, seemed quite light.

'You mean there really wasn't anything you or Grace could do? I mean, surely you have military police for that sort of thing?'

'The reality of war is very different from the practices laid down in the drill books. All you can do is to follow the ground rules at times like this, or you run a very real danger of ending up at the wrong end of a court martial yourself. And the rule book says that when a senior officer issues an order to a subordinate, the subordinate must obey that order *without question*.'

'But aren't there any rules which generally govern how soldiers and armies are meant to behave in wartime?'

'Not as yet, no. All that's been established so far is the neutrality of medical facilities on the battlefield. No-one's given it any proper thought at all as far as offences against civilians are concerned. Anyway, it's pretty damn hard to take someone to court when you're waist deep in mud and corpses. And then again, a lot of people see war as being very different from peacetime, and what in peacetime might be considered as serious misdemeanours more than often are seen as understandable reactions in war. Rather like boys letting off steam at the end of term.'

'War is not quite what we are led to believe, then – no heroics, nothing like that, just – *horror* really. Oh dear, I don't really want to hear this. I mean, the waste.'

'Yes, really, just horror. As it happened Lieutenant Grace was a fluent French speaker and he found out the girl had been just a simple peasant whom the Germans had found hiding in the woods. They brought her down to the village where they kept her captive in the barn for their personal pleasure, and when we recaptured the place Walker found four of the Germans still hiding out in the barn with the girl held prisoner. He shot the Germans and kept the girl, until we chanced upon him and caught him in flagrante. According to the locals Walker then murdered her and made it look like suicide to cover his tracks.'

'And that was that?'

'Yes and no. It became a bit academic because Walker was killed soon after. I had prepared a report because I was determined that he shouldn't get away with it, but he was dead within a week of the incident – as indeed were most of the rest of his little band of villains. I doubt that my senior officers would have taken much note, however. Walker was considered a first-class officer himself, although most of us who served under him knew him as a thug and a bully, but good officers were always in short supply and never more so than at that point of the war. I'd probably have been told to do exactly what Walker told me to do.'

'Forget all about it?'

'I would imagine so.'

'Why didn't you tell me all this before? I knew you were hiding something terrible from me.'

'I didn't know quite how to. I suppose guilt does that to you. And then somehow recently it didn't seem to matter quite so much. Since we came here.'

'Poor George.'

'Not poor me at all,' George replied, putting his arm round her shoulders. 'More than anything I couldn't stop thinking about that poor peasant girl. That was why – I don't know whether you can understand this—'

'Of course I can. Because of what you had witnessed first hand, you made some sort of association between that and us. You and I. When it came to making love—'

'All I could ever see was her face. Not just in my dreams, which is where it started, but in actuality. Whenever – you know – even when I went to kiss you.' George stopped and shook his head slowly. 'I should have told you, I know. It was ridiculous not to, but I just couldn't think how to – the words.'

'But you're all right now, aren't you? You've been so well, so very much your old self.'

'Was I that different before?'

'You weren't so much *different*, George. Just rather introspective, which wasn't at all like you. Sometimes it was as if only a part of you was present. I knew that you just had to come to terms with whatever was worrying you, or wait until you decided it was time that I should know. But I don't think there's any point telling any of this to your father.'

'You don't?'

'No. Because this isn't the real reason you want to leave the army. The real reason you want to leave the army is because the war is over. That is all you have to say. The war is *over*.'

Thirteen

When George finally decided to go and see his father in person in order to explain his decision, loath though she was to be separated from him Amelia declined to accompany him because she thought she would be in the way. For his part George was just as loath to leave Amelia behind all alone in the cottage, but with the Hanleys' two servants caring for the main house Amelia insisted she would be perfectly safe.

'And I have a million and one things to do in The Priory garden,' she told him, to settle the argument. 'Besides having to find an actual gardener.'

So George went off to Sussex in the little Crossley 25/30 they had bought themselves as necessary transport when Clarence Dennison reclaimed the Hillman, leaving Amelia to get about in the pony and trap which Archie and Mae often used to take themselves around the neighbourhood.

From the woman in the village post office near The Priory, George's fount of all knowledge, Amelia collected a short list of names of skilled locals who might be able to help her with the task of creating a garden for her new home, and after extensive interviewing she offered the job to a quiet giant of a man named Jethro Blake. He had been the second gardener on one of the largest local estates, which had just been sold to a forage merchant for whom Jethro had very soon decided he just could not work.

Amelia's new gardener came to the job with a wealth of practical knowledge as well as a very real and deep affection for plants. He was a man of few words, but the ones he chose to use were always well considered and his advice – which Amelia was to find invaluable – was always based on first hand experience. As soon as she had spent half an hour in his company and once he himself had laid eyes on the grounds surrounding The Priory they both knew they were well suited.

'I have no hard and fast ideas, Jethro,' Amelia explained as they made their way round the estate for a second time. 'I would like to restore wherever possible various areas of the gardens to the way they once were, functionally at least. For instance the carp ponds which are completely overgrown would make a lovely water feature, wouldn't you say?'

'Keeping all the formal gardens, as 't were, to the front of the house?' Jethro wondered. 'It being south facing.'

'Quite so. While restoring the walled vegetable garden on the other side – and the avenue here – which you can still make out between this line of fruit trees—' Amelia pushed her way through an almost overgrown gap in a hedge to show Jethro where she meant. 'This could be two long herbaceous beds with a mown walkway between – leading back through gates onto formal lawns and rose beds perhaps.'

'Mmm,' Jethro grunted, rubbing his grizzled chin with one big hand as he surveyed the wilderness and tried to imagine what could be done. 'I'll need a lad, Mrs Dashwood. There's a boy in the village – young Robbie Spry. He might do.'

By the time George returned three days later, Amelia's gardening staff had already begun the long and arduous but exciting task of creating a beautiful garden to surround the old priory.

'Wine?' Amelia exclaimed when George produced a bottle from his case. 'What are we celebrating?'

'My father's clemency,' George smiled. 'And your foresight. What was it you once said your father had always taught you? Never complain and never explain? He was right. Instead of trying to justify my decision by a whole convoluted set of reasons, reasons which would have only made life impossible for the old boy, I simply told him I had arrived at a decision, a decision which I thought completely right for the way my mind was now set, and that was that. We went for a long walk on the Downs where we discussed the matter, and even though my mother knew perfectly well what I was there for, I kept it between my father and myself.'

'And?'

'And after he slept on it, and we went for another ten-mile constitutional, that was that. If that's what I wanted, then so be it, he said. A man with my war record could not be said to have arrived at such a decision lightly, and he said – very graciously I thought – that he respected me for having the courage to be true to myself.'

'And your mother?'

'She hardly addressed a word to me for the rest of my visit,' George said with a sigh. 'But then we rather saw that coming as well, did we not?'

'She'll come round, George. After all, you are her son.'

'That – alas – is half the trouble.'

After George had bathed and changed they drank their champagne in the early summer twilight on the terrace outside the cottage. As they sat talking about their plans for The Priory, Amelia suddenly stopped mid-sentence and frowned, putting a hand carefully to her stomach.

'Are you all right, Amelia?' George asked with concern. 'Is something the matter?'

Amelia smiled.

'Nothing that will not be resolved in a few months' time, George.'

By the time the baby was due, George and Amelia had been living in The Priory for three months. All the main reconstruction work had been finished on the main house and the building had also been plumbed and wired, leaving just the fitting and decoration to be done.

Meanwhile outside Jethro and Robbie had painstakingly cleared the entire estate, thinning out the trees and digging out all the scrub and unwanted growth. As the autumn leaves began to fall and the days to shorten, they began work on shaping the grounds into Amelia's design, cutting and trimming the fine old hedges, repairing the old stone and brick walls, digging the flower beds and relaying flagstone paths, so that, excitingly, now when she looked out of her bedroom window down on to the gardens Amelia could see how everything might look the following year when the lawns were sowed and the beds planted out.

'How I see it is just like the garden at Hidcote,' she would tell George as together they gazed out across the grounds. 'Each room with a different identity. More formal near the house so you see order and perspective whichever way you approach. Then when you leave to explore the rest of the gardens you are drawn away from the house by a series of walkways and paths, all of which will lead through gates and archways, stone and iron near the house and then natural entrances and exits cut from hedgerow and trees the further afield you venture. Beyond the herbaceous garden that's going to a Wild Garden, full of buddleias and other plants which attract butterflies, and all sorts of different long grasses to give movement.

Then I'm thinking of building a formal water garden as the next room, on the west side over there – behind those hedges. With a big round lily pond and steps up the hill which leads to the river. From the top of the hill Jethro suggested we build a water course, which I think is a very exciting idea, with a series of gently tiered cascades and ponds with slabs you can walk on . . .'

'Now it's cleared I can see we have a wonderful stretch of water.'

'Hardly Scotland, I'm afraid.'

'There are some half-decent trout in there, my darling. I shall be more than happy if I can hook some of those.'

'And you can fish for carp in the ponds.'

'What about all this water? I mean with children—'

'Everywhere there is water there will be a gate. You won't be able to get anywhere near any of the ponds without going through a gate, and every gate is going to have a lock,' Amelia assured him. 'The formal water garden will be completely surrounded by a high hedge with two entrances, both through gateways, which will be the only way you can get to the water course and the river. Likewise the carp ponds can only be reached through the gate at the end of the herbaceous garden and the old doorway at the back of the Wild Garden. Funnily enough the grounds were originally laid out as if they had children in mind.'

'Or monks who couldn't swim, probably! I

think it's a marvellous concept. Your garden will become famous.'

'Hardly, George. But it will become beautiful.'

The weather turned very cold the week the baby was due, causing George to consider bringing his exigency plan into operation.

Amelia would have none of it.

'No, George. We agreed. I want to have my baby at home.'

'Our baby, Amelia,' George corrected her. 'And since it's our baby I should have a fair share in the say as to where it should be born. And if the weather worsens—'

'It won't.'

'It could. And because it could I think we should make provisions for you to have the baby in hospital.'

'You can make provisions, George, but I'm still having the baby here.'

'Suppose the midwife can't get through? And Dr Lydford?'

'Then you'll have to deliver it, George.'

'Don't be loopy, Amelia.'

'I'm being perfectly serious, George. I do not want to have our baby in a hospital. I want it born here, at The Priory.'

'Even if it risks your life? And the baby's?'

'It won't. And don't ask me why it won't, but it won't. I just know.'

'More magic, I suppose.'

'Meaning?'

'Meaning more magic.' George raised his eyebrows. 'Isn't everything here done by magic?'

'Oh, you may sneer, Captain Dashwood,' Amelia replied airily. 'You may laugh until you are fit to bust, but you yourself admitted not once but several times that there's something very special about this place. The weather, for instance. There was that really bad frost everywhere else last Sunday, remember? Yet we had no frost here at all.'

'The old monks knew where to build their priories, obviously. In fact you could say they got their *prior*ities right – what a laboured joke.'

'It only ever rains here at night.'

'Darling, it rains here the same as it rains everywhere.'

'When did it last rain here during the day? It only seems to rain when we are sleeping.'

'I don't keep a rain diary. How should I know?'

'Then what about the weeds – or rather the lack of them? Jethro says—'

'Jethro, like most of the people round here,' George interrupted, 'is more than a little fey.'

'The last thing Jethro is, George, is fey. Jethro thinks *we're* fey. And he has said to me not once but on innumerable occasions that he can't understand why there's so little weed actually in the ground. Particularly seeing how overgrown it all was.'

'Probably something in the soil. And you can

argue till you're blue round the gills, but I'm sticking by my exigency plan. If the weather looks like being bad – you go to hospital, my girl, and that is that.'

'Fine.' Amelia sat back in her chair and glared at him. 'If you make me have this baby in hospital, George, I won't have it. I shall hold on to it. Like horses.'

'How do you know what horses do?'

'They tell me when I stop and talk to them.'

But behind all her jokes and banter Amelia was in earnest. She was determined to have their first child in their new home, since she had always believed very strongly that babies should be born in the place where their family lived and where they themselves were to live. She herself had been born at home and had always attributed the happiness of her upbringing and the love she had for her home to this fact. George, who prided himself on being altogether more practical in such matters – hardly surprising in a man of his background – respected Amelia's wishes but finally was of the opinion that common sense should and must prevail. He therefore duly but quietly made arrangements for Amelia to be admitted to the local hospital should the weather not improve.

He even consulted Jethro, a known weather forecaster, as to what the prevailing conditions were expected to be for the next ten days.

'Snow, Captain Dashwood,' he replied. 'And

when it snows in these parts, it snows.'

'And that means we probably wouldn't even be able to get out of the drive, Amelia,' George told her later. 'So let's be sensible, shall we? And take ourselves to hospital?'

'You go if you like, George. I'm staying here.'

'Amelia—'

'Dr Lydford lives only five minutes away, George. As does Miss Taylor the midwife. Five minutes, George, this side of the village. So if it snows, and we can't get out of the drive, they can still come up to the door. On foot.'

Convinced that Amelia would see reason before it was too late, but knowing that the more he pressed her the less likely he was to get a result in his favour, George watched the skies for snow. Just as Jethro had predicted, the wind dropped and so did the thermometer.

'Frost, perhaps. When it's about to snow it usually gets warmer. Ah—'

'Yes?' George said quickly. 'Ah? Ah what? What was the *ah* for?'

'Nothing,' Amelia said quietly, a hand on her baby. 'Just ah.'

At four o'clock that afternoon the telephone rang. It was Constance, wanting to know what the weather was like in Somerset since Sussex was fast disappearing in a blizzard.

'We're fine here,' Amelia assured her. 'Not a flake.'

'Perhaps George is right, Amelia dear. Maybe

243

you should pop off to hospital. Was that a yes?'

'No, as a matter of fact it was another pain.'

'Another? How many have you had, Amelia?'

'They're coming a lot more regularly now. George? Sorry – Mama – I have to go. George!'

Amelia dropped the telephone and gasped as yet another contraction all but knocked the breath from her body.

'George!' she screamed. 'Call Dr Lydford! And Miss Taylor – quickly! Quickly!'

Both helpers arrived together in one car, looking more than a little bewildered.

'Don't say anything,' George groaned as he opened the door to them. 'I was fully intending to get her to the hospital . . .'

'It isn't that, my dear fellow,' Dr Lydford said, taking off his hat and coat. 'You wouldn't have been able to make the hospital anyhow. The road's completely blocked.'

'I don't understand,' George said, hurrying upstairs with the doctor after the midwife.

'Snow, my dear fellow! A positive avalanche!'

'Snow? But I mean if the roads are blocked—'

'Not your road, old boy. The one from the village neither. The other side of the road – the far side – six inches of the stuff. But it's missed you altogether. And me so far. Someone must be smiling on you, George old chap.'

Longbeard never smiled, although he was in fact evidently much amused. He had always enjoyed taking on the elements, always loved the challenge of finding a spell which would confuse nature and make her blow her wind from east to west instead of north to south — or cause a frost to form in June. Or, as he had once done, cause the rain to fall upwards over the Wash. This task was easier than those, however, a simple dazzle which required him only to cast along the ley line that ran so nicely beneath two of the salient points, which he had done really most effectively, so that while the rest of the countryside lay fast beneath snow the ley ran warm as the gulf stream, creating what would once again be known as a natural phenomenon.

Now the Noble One and Longbeard stood beneath the yew beyond the house watching the yellow-lit window above and listening for the sounds. 'Next I must suppose you want me also to magick the child into existence, sir?' Longbeard sighed, opening his purse and looking at the starlights within it.

'I would have instructed you had it been my desire,' the Noble One replied. 'But it is not. For these things must happen naturally. We must play no part in these events.'

'No we must not sir,' Longbeard said. 'As we must not meddle with the elements.'

'They will explain that away, you know that,' the younger man replied. 'As mortals have always done. But we must not give them cause to wonder, at least not about matters understood. The child must arrive as all children.'

Both then looked up at the sound, a strange new cry that sang across the dark gardens. 'Yet you must name the child, sir,' Longbeard needled. 'You say you have decided on his name.'

'Because I was not so blessed, as you are aware. He should be named with the title my son would have borne,' the Noble One told Longbeard.

'And that might be, sir?'

The man in the robe smiled as he pointed his index finger at the lit window.

'Peter,' Amelia said, as they laid her son in her arms. 'Forget all our other ideas, George, let us call him Peter.'

Part Two
1926

'Those who want the fewest things
Are nearest to the Gods.'

Socrates

Fourteen

'You really were not brought up to write this sort of thing,' Lady Dashwood said, eyeing George from under the brim of her French felt hat with its broad silk trimming. 'Of one thing I am absolutely certain and that is that the older I grow the less I understand you.'

'The older I grow, Mother, the less I understand everybody,' George replied with a smile, looking round at the two families invited to The Priory by his wife to celebrate the success of his first novel. 'But then I have to say I did not expect you to enjoy my book.'

'*I* enjoyed it. In fact, Louisa, I have to tell you that I think it is a wonderful piece of work,' said Constance, who was sitting opposite. 'It thoroughly deserves every word of praise which has been heaped upon it.'

'By a lot of extremely radical freethinkers, Constance. I am hardly surprised that *Bohemia* likes it, that is only to be expected, but those of us on this side of the fence feel rather differently.' Lady Dashwood gave a small shudder, as if the better to express her distaste.

'Only natural, Louisa, you know,' Clarence

remarked. 'Dismay at the younger generation is a concomitant of middle age, along with attending church and reading aloud from newspapers the opinions of those with whom we're in firm agreement.'

Lady Dashwood tapped her glass for more water before continuing.

'It is a betrayal of class, Clarence. Writing a book such as this is flying in the face of family and heritage.'

'Perhaps that's precisely why it has so much power?' Amelia suggested. 'Why it's having such a profound effect? Because it's telling the truth about the war.'

The controversy over George's book had raged throughout most of the lunch, overtaking the initial debate about the social state of the country in light of the General Strike the month before which had been called off after only nine days. Naturally Lady Dashwood had set about her son over that topic as well, upbraiding him for not offering his help in keeping the country going as so many of his fellow officers and men had done. George had gently reminded his mother that not only was he no longer in the army but that he had, alas, every sympathy with the strikers. It was at this point that Amelia had been sure that her mother-in-law was about to up and leave the party very prematurely.

'Heaven knows what this country is coming to,' Lady Dashwood now continued. 'Heaven knows what you all fought and your friends died for. The wretched trade unions are holding us to ransom with their strikes, which simply should not be allowed. We've had a Labour government, albeit a short-lived one, under that wretched man MacDonald who was, if you please, a pacifist during the war. Can one believe such a thing? That a country such as this could be governed by a man who was too cowardly to fight for it?'

'If I may, Mother,' George put in quietly from his end of the table. 'I thought the whole purpose of the war was so that this country could remain what it has always been: a bastion of democracy and the home of free speech.'

'Well said, George,' Clarence agreed. 'The war was fought for exactly that. So that windbags like me could sit around excellent tables such as yours expounding our usually absurd ideas about life. And so that people like yourself could be free to write and to publish whatever they please, regardless of who else they may please, or may not. All you are suffering from Louisa my dear,' he remarked, turning his attention to George's mother seated by his side, 'is the usual embarrassment of families such as yours when one of the clan publishes something expounding views with which they happen not to agree.'

'All I hope is that my son is not turning into one of those wretched communists,' the general sighed from the opposite end of the table. 'Just to cap it all.'

'My husband is right to be concerned,' Lady Dashwood assured the assembled company. 'The country is fast becoming morally corrupt. One only has to look at the latest fashion to become aware of the fact. Skirts above the knee? I have never heard of such a thing.'

'Or even seen such a thing,' Clarence mused, straight-faced.

'And as for women sitting drinking in pubs,' Lady Dashwood concluded. 'Whatever next?'

'Women such as myself having the vote, probably,' Amelia said, 'instead of having to wait until we are thirty. As if all women are emotionally immature. I mean to say.'

'Good heavens,' her mother-in-law sighed without sympathy. 'I suppose you'll be chaining yourself to the railings any moment now, Amelia.'

'If you do, darling, I shall chain myself with you,' Constance promised. 'I couldn't agree more with what Mrs Pankhurst said. That the war was God's vengeance on the people who held women in subjection.'

'You surely do not believe any such thing, Constance?' Lady Dashwood enquired, genuinely shocked. 'It is simply a fact of life that our place, women's place, is in the home.'

'You may think so, Louisa, and no doubt many of your friends also,' Constance returned. 'But I'm afraid it's all changed now. Particularly since the war. Come now, what woman who has served as a nurse at the front or at the bench in a munitions factory, or in offices or other situations formerly closed to them – which of those women is going to happily return to scrubbing their doorsteps on a Monday morning and pulling off their drunken husband's boots every evening? And all for continued inequality? I don't think so, Louisa. I'm afraid those days are well and truly over.'

'The old order changeth. It always doth.' Clarence helped himself to yet more wine. 'Everything changes, that's the nature of things. The only thing that doesn't is the human spirit which, thank God, seems to be unquenchable.'

'Like your thirst, Clarrie,' Constance muttered, giving her husband a look.

'George is a typical example,' Clarence continued obliviously. 'Brave in battle and equally courageous in peacetime too. Takes a lot of courage to try and earn your living by the pen. Tremendous courage. You may not like his book, Louisa, but you should admire your son's courage for writing it.'

'Thank you, Papa,' Amelia said, with a smile to her father, who raised his glass to her in return. 'I think we should drink a toast to George for exactly that. For his courage in starting a whole new life. And for the success of his book. I know – just as George does – that his novel has not met with all of your approval. But then what interesting or important work ever did?'

'Quite right, Amelia,' Clarence nodded. 'Very few great poets have ever met with the approval of their contemporaries, let alone their families.'

'That is hardly the point, Clarence,' Lady Dashwood began, only to be stopped short by her own husband.

'Leave the man be, Louisa!' the general boomed suddenly, having been seemingly deaf to all that was going on around him. 'Clarence has a point and a good one too, as it happens.'

Amelia glanced down the table at her father-in-law. She had been as amazed as George when the old soldier had actually turned up for the celebration luncheon, since Lady Dashwood had given every indication that she would be travelling to Somerset alone. Yet at the last minute, for some reason no-one had dared to ask, General Dashwood had, it seemed, changed his mind.

From the look on George's face as he had seen the older man, as upright and white-moustached as ever, climbing out of the back seat of his immaculately polished car, his chauffeur standing at attention, his wife waiting with ill-concealed impatience for him to follow her up the steps of the house, Amelia had immediately known that her husband was as astonished as she was to see him arriving at The Priory, particularly since she knew from that morning's post that George's allowance still remained as it had been for five years – cut off.

'Oh dear, how dull, I can't remember where I was . . .' Amelia laughed, her train of thought interrupted.

'Encouraging us to raise our glasses to a great

254

writer,' Clarence told her, staring round the table as if to challenge anyone. 'Which I am quite sure your husband is going to be.'

'All I actually wanted to say and do is propose a toast to George,' Amelia said, with a shy smile down the table to her husband. 'I am very proud of him, and I am sure every one of us seated at this table will always have cause to be just as proud of him as I am.'

The general cleared his throat and stared up at the ceiling, while Lady Dashwood's mouth took an even more downward turn.

'So – to George. To his continued success.'

'To George—' Amelia began.

But stopped as she saw that her mother-in-law was quite obviously not going to raise her glass of water in a toast and elected instead to stare right past George to the garden outside.

'If you will kindly excuse me, Amelia,' she said finally, about to rise from the table to leave the dining room.

'Sit down, Louisa,' the general ordered. 'Whatever your feelings about George's book, this is not your house.'

Louisa Dashwood coloured at once and did as she was told, sitting back at the table, folding her hands in her lap and staring silently ahead of her.

'To George,' Amelia repeated, and in return everyone raised their glass, even – in response to another look from her husband – Lady Dashwood.

*   *   *

'George does look as though he's had kittens,' Constance said to Amelia as they were walking around the grounds of The Priory after lunch.

'I think he has, Mama. Or as near as can be.'

'Poor dear. The book doesn't pull any punches, does it? If he had not already had his allowance cut off it would surely be for the chop now, good and proper!'

Constance smiled at her daughter, pretending not to notice her inner anxieties, for if there was one thing on which Mrs Clarence Dennison was determined, it was that it was utterly useless to worry about anything, except perhaps where she had last put her spectacles.

'George was more than a little afraid at first, I have to say. Even though he and his father were finally in agreement over his decision to leave the army. But then he said if he had had the courage of his convictions – I mean, enough to leave the army, for goodness' sake – then it simply did not make sense not to turn that same courage to writing a book, and somehow trying to make sense of it all – of the war, of all his friends dying.

'That was how he reasoned, and I think he was right, as it happens. I do. He had to write what he felt, for all those who could not. He had to put back! Even if it has made him unpopular with all the old generals and set his mother's nerves on edge, being young is the time to try things. As a matter of fact I think we should always go on trying things, for ever and ever, or what is the point of anything?'

'Even so, Amelia, poor General Whiskers hasn't exactly had a good time of it since the war ended. With all those wretched politicians blaming all the generals for everything that went wrong, it has not been easy for anyone's generation, you must see that.'

'I know,' Amelia sighed. 'But then the generals have had a good go back at the politicians, so I suppose it's even Stevens really. Now come along, I want to show you the rest of the garden.'

'I can't believe you have done what you have done in such a short space of time,' Constance called after her, shaking her head. 'Nor did I ever know you had such green fingers.'

'It's coming along.' Amelia smiled back at her mother. 'Give it another fifty years and a few thousand pounds, and it will be quite presentable.'

'Talking of which, and I hate to ask this, but – but are you going to be able to manage to live on just George's writings, darling?'

'We don't want any handouts, Mama, if that is what you are really asking. George and myself had this absolute understanding that if he was to go his own way, leave the army and so on, take up the *uneasy business* of writing, as George calls it – then we couldn't possibly expect his family to finance us.'

'Fair enough,' Constance agreed, her maternal heart nevertheless sinking.

'We'll be fine, Mama. George has now proved that he is a very talented writer and since that is what he wanted to do, that is how we shall earn our keep.'

'With two children growing up, keeping up this place, Clara and the gardening boys – things could be more than a little tight, darling.'

Constance could have kicked herself for suddenly letting her anxiety for George and Amelia show, but it was like knowing your petticoat was showing: nothing to be done until you reached your bedroom.

'Of course things will be tight, and we will have to cut it very fine to stay here, but that is how it is. We are both agreed that Peter and Gwendolyn are not going to be spoilt by anything except fresh air, home cooking, and plenty of love.'

'Your father and I found it hard enough with just you, when your father was starting out.'

'Poets and painters don't earn as much as novelists, Mama. George has written a book that is being read by everyone, and taken up all over Europe.'

'Yes, yes, of course – and when all is said and done, after all, we *did* manage, even if I had to learn to disguise rabbit to make it look like chicken, and make my own clothes for those first few years. Confidence is everything. If you think you will win, you will. By the way, I wonder what's going to bring poor darling Louisa round to George's point of view? I do so hate to see mothers falling out with their sons.'

'I thought perhaps when Peter was born she'd unbend a bit, Mama. But she hasn't. And as for Gwendolyn – well, she has no interest in girls at all, which coming from a military family is not so surprising, I suppose.'

'Now you come to mention it, where is my granddaughter? And even more important, how is she?'

Together they strolled back across the main lawns to find Clara, George and Amelia's young nursemaid, and her charges, talking as they went about the health of the latest addition to the young Dashwood family, their beloved daughter born thirteen months previously.

'Edward – Dr Lydford, you know,' Amelia told her mother as they walked. 'I told you he said her health was a little frail, because Gwen was premature, and that we must take special care of her – did I tell you that?'

'You did, darling,' her mother agreed. 'But I still don't quite understand why being early should affect the health of the child.'

'He doesn't think it will affect her permanently, just initially. He said in fact a premature birth can harm both the mother and the child. But I could not be more well, and Gwen really is getting better by the day. She is quite bonny, as you'll see. At least for her.'

'And what about this nursemaid of yours? This *untrained* nursemaid, Amelia?'

'Clara is a first class nanny, Mama. Being the

eldest of what – six? – she's a natural nanny. She helped rear all her brothers and sisters. Besides which, she's a very nice girl.'

'You hear such awful things. Only the other day I was reading all about some young nursemaid or other who used to gas her charge each evening in order to get the baby to sleep, and the parents never knew anything about it, until she was found dead.'

'Clara's not like that, Mama. Clara's only vice would be to read Peter too many bedtime stories. Believe me, our Clara has been sent from heaven. Just a minute . . .' Amelia caught her mother by the arm as they were rounding the side of the house to the shelter of the walled vegetable garden where she knew Clara was sitting out with her two children. 'Look.'

Both women did not only look, they stared.

Obviously imagining herself to be safely out of the sight of the rest of the family, Lady Dashwood was, it seemed, paying a secret visit to her grandchildren. Bent over the pram which contained Gwendolyn, she had her back to Amelia and Constance as they rounded the corner and could be seen tickling the baby's tummy before gently taking hold of one of her tiny hands and kissing it. Straightening herself up with a devoted smile on her face, she then turned to Clara and took young Peter from his nurse quickly, hugging him to her.

'I think, just at this minute, we're needed in another part of the garden, Mama,' Amelia whispered. 'Don't you?'

*   *   *

A week later, George received a letter from his father which, once he had read it, he showed to Amelia.

Having read the letter most carefully Amelia gave it back to George. 'Well,' she said.

'Well indeed, darling.'

Amelia could see that George was upset, but she was determined not to show him that she had noticed. There was no point. It would not help anything.

'What your father is saying, if I understand it, George, is that while he respects your point of view, to resume your allowance would be to lend approval to your opinions and that he cannot do, is that correct?'

'Something like. The point is – I never asked him to resume my allowance. It did not occur to me to ask him. It hurts me that he thinks I might, that I am that sort of person. I know how he feels about the book, and about my leaving the army, but all I wanted was his respect, not his money.'

'I hate to be too obvious, George, but I would say that your mother is behind this. She thinks you have let down not only the side, your class and your regiment, but the whole country!'

'You may be right, but in the event it really doesn't matter. I just wish he hadn't written to me. Letters are somehow so cold, aren't they? Never mind, eh?' He turned back to Amelia, and she could see him almost physically kicking the hurt behind him as he smiled down at her. 'We knew we were going to have to tighten the purse strings, cut our cloth and all that!'

'We were not *not* counting on it, either!'

'It's all up to the muse now. Either that or starvation.'

'In that case I'd better lock you back up in your study, Mr Genius.'

'In that case yes – you better had.'

In future years George would count that time as being among their most idyllic, for nothing made him happier than to be at home living and working. From his study he could watch Amelia at work in her gardens, and his growing children at play, while around him the builders put the finishing touches to the old house. But more than anything it was the unlooked for joy that the children brought him that added such lustre to each day. Peter was a handsome boy, now almost five years old, with his father's blond hair and his mother's dark brown eyes, a mix which for some reason gave him an unusually dreamy look, while Gwendolyn had Amelia's dark hair and her father's bright blue eyes.

George and Amelia had often wondered at the strange genetic quirk that gave the children each other's eyes, as Amelia put it, but this singularity would have distinguished them even had not their handsome good looks done so. Peter, belying his appearance, was not at all wont to dream except in very specific terms. Already obsessed with aeroplanes, he had informed his father in no uncertain terms that he was going to be a pilot when he was grown up.

The young boy had first fallen in love with aeroplanes at the age of two, when playing out on the lawn one summer afternoon. He and his father had watched spellbound as a bright red biplane had performed aerobatics high above them in the sky. That day George had started to tell his son about aeroplanes while his mother dozed beside them, lying out on a rug on the newly cut lawn, but to his astonishment Peter remembered everything that George had told him, right down to the famous German who flew a red aeroplane in the war.

'The Red Baron. He crashed and died.'

'You remembered!'

In fact Peter appeared to remember everything and anything he was told, so much so that George nicknamed him 'Little Master Memory'. After that his father started to delight in seeing how much he could teach his son, soon finding himself not only teaching his little boy chess, but playing against him, only a matter of days after his first lesson.

'It happens quite a lot with children,' he assured Amelia. 'Particularly with chess, I mean. Their minds are quite uncluttered by prejudices so they easily pick up things that as adults we make difficult for ourselves because we put up objections.'

'I would hate Peter to be some sort of music hall prodigy, George.'

To Amelia's relief, Peter subsequently proved to be no genius, although there was no doubt that he was exceptionally clever and in advance of his years. In every other respect he was just like all other small boys, mischievous and inquisitive, or so they thought until one day when George was helping Clara put him to bed, when he piped up suddenly to Clara, 'I saw the man again.'

'Oh, now, Master Peter, none of your nonsense, please. This man you keep saying you see! My word, your mouth must be red from eating all the raspberries and telling Clara that they was greengages!'

'No, I did, Clarey, I did! I saw the man again.'

'He's always on about this man.' Clara shrugged her shoulders and looked sheepishly at George. 'He only ever has warm milk at night with honey in it, Captain Dashwood, nothing more, I promise you.'

'I did see him, Clarey, I did.'

'Did you indeed?' George replied with a wink to Clara. 'And where did you see him?'

'He took me to see the lake,' Peter told his father, before diving down his bed to retrieve his buried bear.

'He was never out of my sight for a moment, Mrs Dashwood.' Clara turned indignantly to Amelia who had come in on the tail end of the

264

conversation. 'Him and his imagination. Don't you listen to him.'

'Oh, but I shall.' Amelia laughed. 'You try and stop me, Clara. I love his stories. They're so inventive.'

'So he took you to the lake did he, young man?' George enquired when Peter re-emerged from under his bedclothes. 'What lake was this?'

'The one in the trees.' Peter sighed with the obviousness of grown-ups, while propping his bear up beside him. 'You know. The great big lake. In the trees.'

George looked at Amelia but said nothing. The one area in the grounds with which they had done nothing was where the lake used to be. The reason they had done nothing was quite simply because they had run out of funds. There had never been any mention made of the lake to Peter or to anyone, not even Nanny Clara, who had simply been told where it was safe to go and where it was not.

'Fine.' George sat down on the end of his son's bed. 'So why don't you tell us about it? About your trip to the lake?'

'Well.' Peter frowned deeply, as if trying to assemble all the facts. 'We were having tea. In the garden. And the man came and said would I like to see the lake?'

'Did anyone else see him?' Amelia now sat herself down in the nursing chair beside

265

Gwendolyn's cot, so that she could face him.

'I don't know.' Peter frowned, uncertain, as if it really was none of his concern. 'The man asked me to see the lake. Then I went.'

'You went with him to the lake?'

'Yes.'

'And what did Nanny Clara say?'

'Nanny Clara wasn't there.'

'I see.'

Amelia smiled at Peter while gathering Gwendolyn up from her eiderdown where she was crawling and lifting her onto her knee, as if by doing so she could prevent her from trotting off on her own down to the lake.

'So what was the lake like, Peter?'

'Big. Big and very dark. And flat. Very flat. With no ripples. So there can't be any fishes.'

'You never know, old chap. There could be lots of fishes deep, deep down.'

'I don't think so. The man said there were no fishes.'

'Did he? I wonder how *he* knew.'

'He said the lake was his. And that it was dead.'

'A dead lake?'

At this George exchanged a look with Amelia who was gently rocking little Gwendolyn on her knee, trying to pretend that she was not in the least interested in anything Peter was telling them.

'A dead lake with no fishes. Tell you what, Peter. Tomorrow you and I will go for a walk and you can show me where the man took you. All right?'

'Yes, please.' Peter looked at both his parents in turn excitedly. 'I'd like that. I know just where to get in.'

After they had tucked the children up for the night and left Clara to settle them in, George took Amelia by the hand and led her outside to the circle of trees which surrounded the place where the lake was supposed to be hidden.

'You're not going to wait until tomorrow, are you? Peter will be very disappointed if you don't.'

'He won't know. Unless you tell him. Now – look – this is extraordinary because according to Ambrose's old maps there *was* meant to be a pathway through to the lake here. In line with the house.'

George searched the line of trees busily for any sign of an entrance, but without success. Since it had been raining heavily earlier in the day, Amelia looked on the ground for footprints. Just when George was about to give up, she found a set.

'There's only one lot,' George stated, when she had summoned him to look. 'At least that's all I can see. And they look like – they look like Peter's.'

George looked up at her. Amelia looked back at him.

'They are Peter's. Those are his sandals.'

'Are you sure?'

'Not without actually going to fetch his shoes, no, George. Pretty sure, though. I mean there are no other children about here, are there?'

'No. And even if there were, what would

someone as small as this – what would they be doing down here alone?'

Amelia just shook her head and then tried to trace where the set of little footprints went. Straightening up she followed them slowly, carefully pulling aside the young saplings on the edge of the woods as it became apparent that the trail led into the very depths of the woodland. When she realized this, Amelia stopped and turned round anxiously to George, waiting for him to catch her up.

'This isn't possible,' she said, shaking her head. 'If Peter had been down here, how could Clara say he had been with her all the time?'

'You imagine for one moment Clara would let Peter out of her sight? She adores him. Anyway, it's more than her life is worth, she knows that.'

'So how could he have got down here without her knowing? And gone all this way into the woods? Look—'

Amelia pushed the branches which were just ahead of her to one side and nodded to the path which had now become visible. Not up the middle, but to one side, the trail of footsteps continued, almost as if the child had been walking along beside someone else. Yet there were no other prints anywhere – not one.

In silence the two of them made their way along the path, having to stoop, because of the overhanging branches. There was utter quiet around them, no sound of birdsong nor rustle of animal life, just deep, dark silence. Finally they came upon the lake, still and dark, circled by huge and ancient trees, the tops of which they had made out previously from the house although, because they were so tall, even from the very top of The Priory it was not possible to see over them.

Now, at last they could see the secret the trees protected, a stretch of dark mirrored water edged by enormous bulrushes which stood as still as sentries. No wind ruffled the glassy surface of the water, which was black from the shadows of the trees all around, black, unmoving, deep and dead. There was no way from the path to reach the water's edge either, not without cutting a way through the thick belt of rushes which circled the lake without a visible break anywhere.

'What a simply amazing place,' George whispered. 'It's as if no-one has been here for centuries.'

'I've never seen water so still,' Amelia replied, taking George's hand. 'It's like varnish. It's as if it's been painted.'

George picked up a stone from the path, cocked his arm, then threw it in a high arc so that it landed in the middle of the lake.

'*Curplopp.*'

It sounded the same to both of them as it breached the water which swallowed it without leaving a ripple.

'Not possible,' George said, staring at where the stone had disappeared as if swallowed by a large, dark mouth. 'That simply isn't possible.'

He took another stone from the ground by his feet, cocked his arm and threw. Again the stone landed with the same deep sound, and again the water yielded no ripples.

'I have to see if it's water,' George said, as Amelia gripped his hand even more tightly.

'What do you suppose it is? It has to be water.'

'It's like – it sounds like – *black treacle*.'

He sat down, pulled his shoes and socks off, and rolled up his trousers.

'Be careful, George.' Amelia begged, holding on to him till the last moment as he made a path for himself through the thick rushes which now whipped angrily back at him. 'Do be careful!'

'My God, it's cold!' George gasped. 'It's like ice! This is the coldest water I have ever known.'

'But how can it be?' Amelia called. 'It's been so warm!'

'Lakes are another matter altogether, Amelia! They're always about ten degrees colder than you expect!'

'But not at the edges, surely? When you're swimming out deep, perhaps – but not at the very edge?'

'This one,' George called back over his shoulder as he neared the edge of the rushes, 'this one is freezing right from the word go!'

Then he himself was gone, straight down and out of Amelia's sight.

'George!' She started kicking off her own shoes. 'George! George!'

As she stumbled towards the water's edge she heard him splashing and calling back.

'It's all right! Don't worry! I can swim, remember? It's all right!'

Amelia stood right by the edge of the rush belt, skirt in one hand, her other to her mouth as she watched the sodden George emerging from the water.

'There are no shallows,' he said, with a shake of his head. 'It just suddenly goes deep. Without any warning. And I mean deep. And I mean cold.'

Back at The Priory George sat in a steaming hot bath with a large tumbler of whisky while Amelia set him out some warm, dry clothes.

'I don't think I've been as cold as that in the water since I swam in Scotland,' he announced after giving the matter much thought. 'In fact I think that water was colder than Scotland, much colder.'

'That is a very strange lake, George,' Amelia said, putting a clean vest and pair of shorts on the bathroom chair. 'That is a weird and an ancient lake.'

'We know it's ancient, darling, because we have seen it on the old maps. That lake was here when they built the priory. And weird – I agree. But Peter's prints are the weirdest thing of all.'

'I shall take his shoes down with me tomorrow.'

'There won't be any need. Peter will be in them.'

'What do you think about Peter's story?' Amelia

271

asked as she sat on the window sill of the bathroom, looking out over the gardens now lit by the evening sun. 'What do you make of it?'

'What do I make of it? You mean what do I make of the man? Well – remember those stories we heard about some old hermit who lived here? Maybe if Peter's been seeing anyone at all—'

'Rather than imagining it.'

'Rather than imagining it, precisely. Maybe he's seen the old hermit lurking around somewhere and made a story out of it. This is – what? The third time he's said he's seen him?'

'Something like that. Third or fourth. The first time he said he saw him in his bedroom. Standing by the window.'

'I discount that one, Amelia. No-one could have got all the way up to the nursery without someone hearing or seeing them. They'd have had to go through Nanny's room first. No, that time I think he was dreaming. This time I don't know. Maybe he saw him when they were out in the garden and then spun a story round it.'

'He's only four, George.'

'Four or not, you know what Peter's like, darling. Looks to me as if we've got another writer in the family.'

'The footsteps on the path, George?'

'That I can't explain.'

'And all the other things we can't explain. Such as the way the weather's always different here, the way things grow so well and so quickly, the snow on the night Peter was born – or rather the lack of it. In fact how we always seem to escape the worst of the frosts. Remember two years ago? That frost in May which killed the flowers on Archie and Mae's wisteria? And all their early rosebuds? We didn't lose one bloom, and our wisteria was better than ever.'

'The frost can be explained, surely. I mean there *are* places which are the opposite of frost pockets. Our garden in Sussex, for instance—'

'George. You're not really aware of this because you're usually hard at work in your study. At first I thought it was just Jethro and Robbie's hard work, the fact that I hardly ever have to do any weeding. In fact, to put it quite bluntly, since we cleared the place we've hardly seen any more weeds! I haven't mentioned it to Jethro, don't worry – I don't want him to think I'm dotty either. But I've been keeping a journal of garden jobs and duties, and making Jethro and Robbie fill one in, too. And neither of them ever seems to weed either. In fact only the other day Jethro complimented me on the way I keep the flower beds because it leaves them free for the fruit and veg and so on.'

'Hm,' George said thoughtfully. 'Hm.'

'You know as well as I do that there's something – something different about this place.'

'I know it's very special, certainly. But *different*—?'

'Different, George. I was going to call it something else . . .'

'What, for instance?' George looked at her suspiciously over the edge of the bath. 'Not magic, Amelia? Magical perhaps, but not magic.'

'Let's just say I think it's charmed, George. Maybe old places like this, particularly places which have once been sacred – or semi-sacred, or whatever – maybe they pass different things on, different things from other places, ordinary places. I'm not explaining myself very well, am I?'

'You're not saying it's haunted, are you?'

'Yes, but not in the way we normally take it to mean. I think it could be haunted by its past, or affected rather. Maybe what happened here before, all that time ago, maybe it affects the way things are today. Who knows? There is so much that we really don't know about the past, and maybe we spend all our time treading on and around it, or it drifts past us, or encircles us, but we are just too insensitive to notice.'

'Hm,' George mused again, not really listening. 'Hm. So this man Peter claims he saw—'

'That most probably was our famous hermit,' Amelia said crisply, getting up and handing George his towel. 'For goodness' sake though, don't go making any mention of ghosts or the boy will probably never sleep another wink here. Now I'm going down to get myself a drink and make us some supper. I don't know about you, but I'm starving.'

'Hm,' she heard from behind her as she left the bathroom. 'Hm hm *hm*!'

They ate their supper outside at a table in the courtyard where they loved to sit on summer evenings, listening to the birdsong and watching the colours of the skies as they darkened. That night they sat there until it was dark, until the air was full of hunting bats and the mournful sound of owls, they sat there with a bottle of wine talking until they could barely talk any more, yet they both knew that the subject was far from being exhausted; they were a long way off from coming to any conclusions. For most of these apparently phenomenal things there might, somewhere, be some sort of explanation.

The frost for instance, the odd rainfall, the peculiar waters of the lake, perhaps even the apparently inexplicable lack of weeds – when put before various experts, all those things might well have some perfectly natural explication, some exposition based on the lie of the land or a freak incidence of weather patterns. Just as the amount of mud and silt on the lake bed might be due to the same phenomena. Also, as George suggested, the strange lack of weeds could be because the place had been tilled so diligently by monks making their herbals and growing their vegetables; or it might be that their soil had a totally different chemical make-up. And too, the man seen by Peter could well be the hermit once rumoured to have lived in The Priory. The footprints on the path to the lake could have been made by some vagrant child. Equally Peter's supposed discovery of the lake could have been in his imaginings, since he could easily have overheard his parents at some point discussing what precisely lay within their boundaries.

Yet one thing could not be explained away, namely the secret of the hidden garden, and perhaps because it could not, it coloured George and Amelia's judgement about all the other incidents.

Had they been able to think of one reason for what had apparently happened in and to the hedged garden, or even the merest and vaguest theory, then they could have put aside the belief both of them felt that there might be some extra force at work in the place, other than the natural ones. Yet they could not think of one, or even the beginning of one, which was why, when they went to bed that night, before they fell asleep, they both lay silently in the dark wondering what precise magic it was that seemed to be intent on enchanting their home.

The next morning they took Peter to the woods which surrounded the lake and asked him to show them where he thought he had entered them the day before with the stranger. Peter stood chewing the inside of first one cheek then the other as he stood staring at the thick belt of trees.

'I don't know,' he said at last. 'I've never been to this place.'

'But you said you saw the lake, Peter,' his father

said, crouching down beside him. 'Remember? You told us a man took you for a walk to the lake.'

'This isn't it,' Peter insisted. 'I've never been here, Daddy.'

George glanced at Amelia. He stood up and, taking Peter's hand, pushed the branches aside at the place where they had found the entrance the evening before. He led the way up the overgrown path until they came to the lake.

'Here's the lake, old chap,' George said as they reached the end of the path. 'There you are.'

Peter stared at it silently, as if he had never seen it before. He shook his head and began to chew the insides of his cheeks once more.

'Don't do that, darling,' Amelia chided him. 'You know that's an awful habit.'

'I don't like this place, Mummy. I'm frightened.'

'This isn't the lake the man brought you to?'

In response to his father's question the little boy shook his head again, gripping his hand ever more tightly.

'Perhaps there wasn't a man after all, darling,' Amelia said, lifting the little boy up in her arms. 'Perhaps you just imagined it?'

Peter shook his head and turned away, embarrassed by so much attention to his chatter.

'Can we go back now?'

'He dreamed it maybe, rather than *imagining* it,' Amelia said, after she and George had deposited their son back with Clara in the nursery. 'You know what children's imaginations are like. But I really don't like the fact that he was frightened by it.'

'It is an awfully dark and gloomy place, Amelia. Anyone would feel frightened.'

'And it shouldn't be. It should be somewhere lovely. I love a lake – so I'm going to get someone to come and look at it. Give me an opinion. It shouldn't be a place where children get frightened. Just one other thing, George,' Amelia added. 'I don't know whether you noticed, but there weren't any footprints.'

A man called Sam Wakes, a small and wiry man with a face like a water rat, came to plumb the depths of the waters. He was a friend of Jethro's. A man guaranteed by the gardener to know all there was to know about water and the like, he arrived at The Priory with a cart carrying a small dinghy and pulled by a bonny cob which he rode rather than drove. With the help of the mighty Jethro he dragged the dinghy down the track and launched it on the lake, watched intently by George and Amelia.

Jethro waded into the water at the very spot George had disappeared from Amelia's view, but in spite of all warnings as to the depth he managed to push the boat out with Wakes in it at least four or five feet from the rushes without the water getting any higher than the top of his gumboots.

'It must have been a hole,' George observed,

sitting down rather suddenly on a fallen tree trunk as he watched the proceedings. 'I must have just been unlucky. That is the only explanation.'

'Seems to be shallow round the sides here, Captain Dashwood!' Jethro called out, making his way back through the parted bulrushes. 'Muddy, though. Which might explain this 'ere dark water like!'

It did not take Samuel Wakes long to paddle out into the middle of the lake, where he stopped, shipped his oars and dropped a long plumb line over the side. Amelia wondered out loud what the exact length might be, and George, speculating as he watched Wakes unwind it, reckoned it to be at least twenty feet.

'That would be deep?'

'Deep enough.'

'How will he know when it touches the bottom?'

'The line will fold, just as it does when you fish.'

They watched as Wakes pulled the line back up with a shake of his head, reeling it up before dropping another one over the side.

'Can't be,' Jethro observed, pushing his cap to the back of his head and scratching his scalp. 'Inland lakes like he be, from a spring like, they'd hardly be more'n twenty foot. Twenty foot's plenty deep enough.'

By now Wakes was bent over the side of the dinghy, as if trying to look down into the murky depths. A moment later he began to reel his longer line back up before slipping the oars back in the rowlocks to paddle vigorously, it seemed, away from the centre of the lake to the perimeter. As he did so he stopped several times to test various depths until, apparently having had enough, he rowed to the far end where he stopped in what looked like the shallows to take samples from the bottom with a small pan attached to a long pole. He did this in various other places on the perimeter before rowing back to where he had started, Jethro wading in once more to take the painter and secure the boat to a branch.

'I'm not quite finished yet,' Wakes announced, speaking slowly. 'But I thought you might like to know what I found so far. First things first. 'Tis very deep. Out in the middle there, I ain't done a lake as deep as he. Must be fifty foot or more. I dropped my first line as you saw, my twenty foot one, and he just swung there. So I put in my other line, and he's near fifty foot. Didn't touch nothing, he didn't. So lord knows how much deeper he goes. Your guess be good as mine. But I'll tell you, Captain Dashwood sir, he be plenty deep enough.'

'It's not man-made then, that's for certain,' George said. 'Not that I thought it was, but there's nothing to say it hasn't been altered since it was first sprung.'

'No-one's been near him for years, Mr Dashwood. I never seen such black water. 'Tis freezing too. Middle of summer though we are, he's as cold as can be. Course he might be too, being that deep. Even so, that be cold water right enough.'

'And not very clear either?' Amelia wondered, half to herself.

'No, ma'am. Should be. Should be clear as day, for 'tis not mud on the bottom, not round the sides. 'Tis stone, and pebble, though could well be muck and mud when he gets deeper. Even so, you'd not think he'd be that murky.'

'Can't be spring fed then?' George asked. 'If it was spring fed it would be running clear, wouldn't you say? Even if there was a lot of silt below.'

'With respect, Mr Dashwood sir, he'd have to be spring fed. Or fed be an underground stream or river maybe. If there weren't no source for 'im, he'd have dried up long ago.'

'So what accounts for the murkiness?'

Wakes shook his head and rubbed his stubbled chin.

'That I can't say, sir. I never seen a lake like him. There's another thing too, though. You see there be no current, be there? None at all. Lake's as calm as a mill pond. Yet when you rows away from the centre, 'tis like there's all manner of a stream running against you. Whichever way you rows, you feel like you're being held back, as if 'twere some sort of great magnet.'

On their way back to the house George reasoned that there might well be sub-currents running in a lake as deep as that. Amelia argued that if there were such things then surely some sort of movement would be clearly visible either on or under the surface of the water, but George stuck to his argument, saying that water was a very deceptive surface. Amelia agreed, adding furthermore that until their children had learned to swim properly then all access to the lake should be fenced off. After which George promised that he would put the matter in hand with Jethro at once.

But the truth was that neither of them were made any easier in their minds by their resolutions or their promises, and they were certainly not reassured after they heard what Samuel Wakes had to tell them when he returned from the lake to load up his boat.

Fifteen

'I'd gone back for a moment only, see?' he said, standing with his elbows leant on the side of his cart. 'For I'd dropped some'at, my pocket knife which I had since I were a boy. When I got back to the turn in the path, just before where you was both sat, there were this noise. I looked up to the sky thinking it must be a storm, for it were like all the trees were blowin' in the wind like. But the sky were as blue as he is now, with never a cloud in sight. Yet the trees all around the lake, mind, they was bent and whipped like by a gale. And the water. The water was rushing, do you see – rushing not across as if blown be the wind but round and round in these huge big circles. Just like it were being churned. I never seen the like of it in all my born, never nothing near the like, not on a lake. It was as if it were the sea. I tell you – my jaw it dropped down to my knees I was that astonished. Even more so a moment later, for no sooner had this great wind whipped up the waters than it stopped. Just as sudden as it started. And as I stood there it all was as if nothing had happened at all. Nothing. The water was as smooth as glass again, and the trees – not a leaf was moving. 'Twas that quick it were like a dream. 'Twas as if I'd closed my eyes and dreamed it. Except I didn't. But I tell you what it was like, shall I? It were like the whole place had suddenly lost its temper. That's what it were like. Just as if the whole place had suddenly lost its temper.'

'We've betrayed the place,' Amelia said after Wakes had left. 'We allowed a stranger in to examine something which obviously the lake did not want to be examined.'

'Amelia,' George groaned. 'You are surely not suggesting that something inanimate like a hole in the ground filled with water can have feelings? Feelings which can be upset?'

'A lake isn't inanimate, George. You know that. Lakes are full of life, of the past, of mystery. We often talk of hills being moody and the sea being angry, after all.'

'In a poetic sense. Not an actual one.'

'But we don't *know*, George. How can we? How can we know what lies within mountains, under the sea, or hidden by the dark waters of an ancient lake?'

'So what do we do, Amelia? Don't you find all this a little – worrying?'

'No, not really. Do you?'

'I must say, I do find it unsettling,'

'You don't want to move, do you?'

'From here? Certainly not. Do you?'

'Of course not, George. Don't be silly. I love this place. Don't you?'

And of course George did, but before admitting as much he had to hear it from Amelia herself, because if she had nursed the slightest doubt about living at The Priory, such was his love for her and for his family he would have upped and left it that day. As long as Amelia was still happy he had no reason to want to move, since personally he was happier and better than he had ever been, a state he ascribed to both the love of his wife and the perhaps magical properties of their ancient home.

Besides, like Amelia, and even before she had expressed her own thoughts on the matter, he had considered the so-called storm on the lake to be a direct reaction to Samuel Wakes's examination, even though he realized that such an opinion was totally without logic.

But then, as both Amelia and he were now agreed, logic was not something which could be applied to their own experience of the place. In their opinion The Priory and its enchanted grounds now stood well outside the pale of logical explanation.

So they stayed put, and, thanks to Amelia's vision and artistry allied to George's dedication and patience, they continued to transform what had been little more than ruins into a beautiful house, and one which was not only architecturally perfect but also a warm, light and welcoming home.

Certainly it seemed to be a happy place, a place

made for a young family to grow, where children felt safe and loved to play. It was as if the good people who had once lived there in prayer and contemplation had bequeathed a legacy of love, as if their spirits were watchdogs of the family's future, and that as long as the Dashwoods remained there in the house they would be safe-guarded by them. This was what Amelia felt and George did too. They both had a sense of belonging to The Priory, a feeling strengthened, not weakened, by its inexplicable manifestations.

Yet, for the time being anyway, and without regret, they set aside any further work on the lake, fencing off the entrance with barbed wire and a sign warning strictly against any trespassing. It was almost as if they had both acknowledged, in their own very different ways, that the lake was a mystery, and not one either of them wished to unravel.

With George spending most of the day locked in his study writing, Amelia continued her work in the gardens, which thanks to the hard and creative work put in by Jethro and Robbie were admired by all who visited. Amelia and her little team had been very careful to ensure that rather than creating a new landscape they should endeavour to make the surrounds of The Priory look as though they had, quite simply, been restored, rather than suffered radical alterations.

For example, the courtyard at the rear of the

house still had the feel of the cloister that had once formed one side of it, a covered and pillared walkway off which led what had once been cells for the monks but were now guest bedrooms; the end of the square was contained by the little chapel, now charmingly restored.

In the middle of the courtyard Amelia had fashioned a knot garden which she had interplanted with fragrant old-fashioned roses, so that on a summer's evening the air was full of their subtle scents.

Beyond the chapel to the west lay the herbaceous garden, walled on the north side in old stone reclaimed from around the site by Mr Stanley, and carefully rebuilt where an original wall had once stood. A large flower bed flourished on the warm sunny south side, stocked with pink and maroon day lilies, blue globe thistles, pink mallows, campanulas and white verbascums, while at the back of the bed, and trained along the wall, grew two productive peach trees whose summer fruit Amelia loved to make a point of picking in the early morning sunshine when the flesh of the peaches was warm and the skin of such a sensuous velvet that just to hold them made Amelia, as she said, 'believe in heaven here on earth'.

A smaller bed laid opposite was planted mainly with blue and lavender delphiniums and pale pink and occasionally lemon yellow roses, fringed with pansies and pink diascias, set against an old box hedge which had appeared to be dying when they first moved in but now flourished, shooting each May a mass of tender green shoots which Amelia carefully cut and pruned each year in order that the bushes should fill out below rather than climb skywards unchecked.

Hedging was just about the only planting that Amelia permitted to grow in any kind of solitary fashion. It was a sore point with Jethro and indeed Robbie that Mrs Dashwood would not leave anything *to hisself. Not nohow! 'Tis always got to have something jumbled up and round it, so 'tis.*

'Back along this would never be allowed,' Jethro would grumble as Amelia, determined on untidiness at all costs, encouraged every kind of flower to thread its way through every kind of tree.

'Roses through apple trees, clematis through pears, you'll be growin' them through the Captain soon. Back along this'd never be!'

Jethro would shake his head in dismay, and Amelia would laugh, but carry on just as determinedly as before. She knew how she wanted the garden, full of colour, and a kind of gaiety that more strictly formed gardens would eschew.

In fact now the grounds were fashioned more or less exactly as she had described them to Jethro when he had first come to work there, not only the river bank cleared but the river itself, which at this point of its course had long become clogged up and apathetic.

They had managed to divert it to refill and reconstitute the old carp ponds, which they had found to be almost entirely choked with weed and silt, linking the two pools to each other with an arched Chinese-style bridge overgrown with guelder roses and fringed with gunneras and slender blue and yellow irises.

The effect early on a summer morning when the mist still lay over the waters was one of dreaminess and tranquillity, a mood carried on into the long walk which they fashioned through the area she had designated as the Wild Garden: an acre turned over to swathes of long grasses, wild flowers, buddleia and trees carefully selected for the differing colour of their foliage, weeping pears for spring, tall slender willows for summer, and acers for when the days grew shorter.

The walk led to Amelia's formal water garden, which was contained by an ancient yew hedge she and Jethro had discovered growing underneath a blanket of bramble and briar roses. They had cleared the hedge then square-clipped the yew into a geometric border within which they had sowed a lawn and constructed a round pond twenty feet in diameter edged with cut flags and sparingly planted with white, crimson and pink water lilies and perimeter clutches of white and blue water irises. Amelia had been adamant they should not over-plant the pool, for its uncluttered position was perfect to mirror the sky in all its changing moods.

'We must take our visitors out another way, Jethro,' Amelia had instructed when they were laying out the design. 'The whole idea is for the gardens to flow, to grow out of one another if you like, so that wherever you walk you are drawn into the next landscape.' The only place to which the visitor was not guided was the hidden garden, privately dubbed by George and Amelia, ever since their initial discovery of it, the Kissing Garden. They kept this part of the grounds for themselves.

'I think we should respect the garden's privacy, George. And since I don't intend to plant anything here there's going to be nothing to see anyway. All I shall do in here is keep the grass cut, and trim the hedges myself.'

'I agree. I wouldn't be happy with other people walking through it. It asks to be kept private, and so it shall be.'

As it happened, unless they were told about it no stranger would ever be aware of the Kissing Garden's existence. Since it lay beyond the mound south of the formal lawns in an area behind a newly restored wall, all that could be seen from the house was what appeared to be nothing more than one straight line of hedge. Even from an upstairs window the actual rectangle could not be made out. And should a visitor happen upon it, there was little likelihood that they would linger long, for, in truth, there was nothing there to keep them, just a box of hedge with a lawn in the middle. Or so it seemed.

*   *   *

By the beginning of the following year George's novel *The Ridge* had achieved best-selling status in England amid unabated controversy. Its admirers thought it to be the first original piece of writing to come out of what was now being referred to as the Great War. Naturally the book's detractors thought it narrow and biased. But no-one questioned the writer's actual talent, even the book's most severe critics having to admit that George Dashwood had *an important original voice* and *undoubted literary skill*.

The most severe reaction to the book, however, came from outside the literary world, from people who considered themselves to be members of George Dashwood's own class. They considered George to have betrayed his background, the most militant among them even suggesting he should be stripped of his medals.

At first George weathered the storm, allowing himself to be interviewed for various journals and newspapers and even arguing his case in public debate in various forums, but finally, when the criticism became really too subjective, he retired to The Priory, letting it be known that from then on the book would have to speak for itself.

Yet it was not to be as easy as that, for unfortunately George's new notoriety pursued him everywhere, despite the fact that The Priory was well off the beaten track, hidden in the deepest countryside. Every week hundreds of letters arrived for him, forwarded to The Priory by his publisher, while the telephone hardly stopped ringing with invitations from pacifists wanting George to make an appearance in aid of their cause, or from women inviting him onto the suffrage bandwagon. He was once more a hero, but this time to a very different sort of person.

By June he was beginning to feel that he had endured enough. He telephoned his publisher Jack Cornwall and told him to forward no more letters, changed their telephone number and made up his mind to take time off from work, time for Amelia and himself to holiday. Since he was a member of Wimbledon, their first real holiday outing was to go to London to see Helen Wills contest the Ladies' singles final.

'I like your hat,' George said when Amelia had finally come downstairs into the lobby of the hotel. 'I don't think I've seen that one before.'

'Mr Finlay in the village had it made up in London to go with my coat, specially,' Amelia said, glancing in the looking-glass behind George's seat. 'He is so clever. Always thinking up new ideas and moving heaven and earth to put them into practice. I say, George. You don't think it's too far down over my eyes, do you?'

'Isn't that the fashion? Like your – how can I best put it? Your *bosom*-less dress.' George looked at her straight-faced.

'George,' Amelia sighed, the way women

always do when their men take an opposite view. 'Can you imagine women leading the sort of life they lead nowadays corseted the way we were before the war? I mean can you imagine it? Corsets mean you can't breathe. I don't know how Queen Mary can bear them.'

'Before the war you were hardly old enough to wear a corset.'

'Don't you like this look?'

'I'll get used to it, I suppose. My trouble is I like women to look like women.'

'Rather than?'

'Boys. And I think the king agrees with me!'

Amelia eyed him and would have not only pursued him further, but set about him physically, had they been at home, and not just about to leave their London hotel for Wimbledon.

'It's all right, Amelia Dashwood, I was only teasing you,' George whispered as he held open the door for her. 'You look quite wonderful.'

She also looked highly fashionable, she was glad to see, once they arrived at the Centre Court and took their seats among the other members and their guests. Despite Mr Finlay's minute attention to her coat and skirt, his exquisite tailoring and eye for detail, Amelia had been afraid that she might have got so out of touch with London Society that she would appear as a semi-rustic alongside her contemporaries, but thanks to both her tailor's lively interest in the latest styles and her own desire not to look provincial they had managed to come up with an outfit which was very much à la mode. It had to be said that it pleased Amelia even more to note that she still took the eye of the opposite sex, especially of several quite dashing acquaintances of George's who came up to exchange greetings with their old friend and cast roguish looks towards his beautiful young wife.

'You seem to be looking for someone in particular, George.'

'I was wondering if Grace might be here,' George replied, scanning the crowd. 'Ralph Grace. Remember? He's a great tennis fan. But I can't see him.'

'You should ask him to stay,' Amelia said, taking her seat in a wicker armchair. 'Ask him down to The Priory, now that you're on holiday.'

'Yes, I should, shouldn't I?' George agreed vaguely, treading out his cigarette.

The spectators broke into warm applause as the two women finalists stepped out onto the Centre Court.

'Helen Wills will walk it. No contest,' George murmured, as an official who had known George since he was a boy made his way over to them.

'Hallo, Captain Dashwood. I can't tell you how good it is to see you after all this time. Really, first class.' He looked admiringly into George's eyes. 'We were all so proud of you when we read of your decoration. Very proud indeed.'

'Thank you, Mr Collier. And it's very kind of you to come over.'

'Anything you need at any time just say the word, Captain Dashwood.'

He nodded and smiled, and watching him walk off Amelia felt that peculiar glow that George's achievements always gave her. She was more proud of him than she could ever say; most of all, she was proud of his modesty.

It was during the knock-up that another man, seated directly behind George, decided to make himself known to him, although in a rather less courteous fashion than Mr Collier's. He tapped George on one shoulder with a rolled-up newspaper.

'Excuse me. Heard the name and I thought as much. You're that fellow, aren't you? That Captain Dashwood?'

George turned to find himself being stared at by a florid-faced man with a black Kitchener moustache and small rheumy green eyes. He was wearing a heavy tweed suit in which he appeared to have already over-heated.

'You're that damn writer fellow, aren't you?'

'Not today he isn't,' Amelia interrupted. 'Today my husband is just another tennis enthusiast come to see the finals.'

'I wasn't addressing you, you jessy,' the man persisted. 'I was talking to the captain here.'

'What did you just call my wife?' George turned right round to look the man full in the face.

'I used the name her sort answer to, Captain Dashwood,' the man replied. 'Women who lie down with men like you, sir.'

'Leave him be, George,' Amelia begged. 'The man is quite obviously mad.'

'If I am mad, my dear, it's only at this husband of yours. A man who could write such things about his country. About all the boys who gave up their lives so that he could write the sort of filth he does. Well, I won't have it, *Captain* Dashwood, sir. Not for one damned moment I won't.'

Amelia looked hastily round for Mr Collier, but he had vanished.

'I think you had better apologize to my wife, and at once.'

'And I think you're the one who owes an apology to your king and your country, sir. You have desecrated the memory of the fallen.'

Some other spectators sitting nearby began to take more interest in George and his opponent than in the match. But in spite of Amelia's tugging on his sleeve, George was still determinedly facing the man behind him.

'If you don't apologize to my wife at once, I will not be responsible for my actions.'

'And if you don't apologize to those whose memory you have traduced, sir, I most certainly will not be responsible for mine!' The man was on his feet now and beginning to belabour George about the head and shoulders with his newspaper, keeping time with his words. 'I repeat! And I do so for all here to hear! You are a disgrace to your king and country, sir! And the Victoria Cross! You should be tried for treason!'

'Apologize to my wife, sir.'

'I'll be damned if I will!'

'It's all right, George!' Amelia persisted. 'He's just a madman!'

'I have better things to do than apologize to a whore!'

He had barely got the insult out when George, now on his feet, sent him flying backwards over his chair with one perfectly aimed uppercut.

'Bravo!' someone called from behind as the man crashed to the ground, legs in the air and one hand clapped to his jaw.

'You asked for that, you fool,' another spectator said, pulling George's antagonist to his feet. 'Now if I were you, I'd get going.'

'I shouldn't have done that,' George muttered to Amelia as she wrapped his bruised knuckles in her handkerchief.

'Of course you should,' George's immediate neighbour assured him, as several officials hurried towards them, followed closely by a police constable. 'Bounder asked for it. You don't come to the Centre Court to pick a fight. Let alone insult a winner of the Victoria Cross.'

'You haven't heard the last of this, Dashwood,' the man croaked from behind a hand held to his bloodied mouth. 'You'll regret this day, I'm warning you.'

'Everything all right, Captain Dashwood?' Mr Collier had rejoined them. 'Someone said there was a fracas.'

'This fellow here,' George's neighbour said, pointing out the assailant to the policeman, 'this lunatic insulted Captain Dashwood's wife in no uncertain terms and the good captain quite rightly put the fellow to rights.'

'That's perfectly correct, constable,' his wife agreed. 'Captain and Mrs Dashwood were minding their own business when this wretched little man set about insulting Mrs Dashwood most dreadfully.'

'Saw it all,' another man agreed from the row below George and Amelia. 'People like him shouldn't be allowed in places like this. This is the Centre Court, not Hyde Park Corner.'

'We'll soon have him out of here, don't you worry,' the constable assured everyone, taking hold of the offender, who pointed wildly at George.

'This man is a traitor, I tell you!' he cried. 'This blackguard is a traitor to his king and to his country!'

'That'll do, sir,' the constable insisted wearily. 'Unless you'd rather I called up some reinforcements and had you carried away bodily?'

'You wait, Dashwood,' the man shouted back as the policeman began to drag him away. 'You'll rue this day – just you wait!'

Inevitably the incident had badly disfigured the afternoon. George and Amelia were hardly able to enjoy the match, both agreeing to leave immediately it was over.

'That was jolly, wasn't it?' Amelia sighed, as they sat in the taxi taking them back to their hotel. 'Still, I suppose if you're going to be a controversial author, we must get used to – controversy.'

'Do you mind terribly, darling?'

'Mind? I'm even prouder of you than ever.'

It was hardly surprising that for a long time after this unpleasant incident George hardly ventured further than the boundaries of The Priory, seeming to wish the world would go away and stay away. Simultaneously he came to believe that there really was little point in going away himself from the beautiful place where they lived. They had started to create Arcadia, and that was where he would stay.

'I don't need town any more. I don't need that sort of life and I don't like it any more. This is all that counts. Being here at The Priory with you and the children.'

'Don't mind me,' Amelia said tartly.

'Of course I mind you. But I thought you loved it here as much as I do. More, even.'

'I love it here more than I can say, George darling. But I also quite like going to London occasionally. To see friends and go to the theatre. And look at all the clothes I can't possibly afford.'

'You can go to town whenever you want. All I meant was if I didn't have to go there ever again, I wouldn't mind. That's all. And who can blame me? Living in a place as wonderful as this – with a woman as beautiful as you?'

'Oh, George,' Amelia sighed. 'You always say so many of the right things it makes me feel quite sentimental.'

So George turned his attentions once more to his writing, this time a novel about the aftermath of the war, a story concerning the return of a soldier to a country he had defended with his life and for which hundreds of thousands of his colleagues had sacrificed theirs, only to find the country turned against itself. He jokingly remarked to Amelia that since he was thinking of ending the story with the returning soldiers overturning the government it was probably just as well for him to stay holed up in the country down miles of wooded lanes where only the very dedicated would ever find him.

'Not only that,' he confessed one evening, 'but for some reason, ever since that incident at Wimbledon, I have had this feeling of doom. As if something awful is going to happen, or someone is going to do something dreadful. Some people are truly crazy. It's strange, isn't it, that someone else's truth can drive them to such distraction.'

Amelia put her hand out to comfort him. 'I know. It was all most upsetting. Don't think about it.'

'I try not to, I really do. But I can't help it. I just

have this feeling that our whole world is going to change.'

Amelia turned away from the thought, shrugging her shoulders.

In fact their world did change, suddenly and for ever, in the summer of the following year. George was in his study reading the newspaper before dinner one evening when Amelia came down from the nursery floor looking pale and worried.

'It's Gwennie,' she said when he questioned her. 'I am quite sure it's nothing – but just to be on the safe side I'm going to call Edward.'

'I thought she'd been unusually quiet recently. For her, that is,' George agreed, nervously lighting a cigarette. 'She's usually such a bundle of energy, but she seems to have been sleeping rather a lot lately.'

'And yet she still complains of feeling tired. And she looks tired all the time.'

Amelia picked up the telephone and dialled the doctor's number.

'Probably just growing pains,' George said. 'Children get all sorts of things wrong with them. When I was her age I remember being sickly for a year. The doctors said it was my glands.'

However, after he had examined the little girl and put her back to bed in Clara's charge, Edward Lydford came to quite a different conclusion.

'You should take this child to a good specialist at once,' he said. 'I don't mean to alarm you good folk, but she is not well and it's much better if she's seen by someone who knows what they're talking about and not some old country buffer like me. How old is she now?'

'Nearly three and a half,' Amelia replied. 'What do you think it might be, Edward? Is it something serious?'

'I'm not even going to attempt a guess at that, old girl,' Edward replied, consulting his pocket book. 'I don't want to go sending you up some false trail or other. Now. There's an absolutely splendid fellow in Harley Street by the name of McAllister. First class man. Looks at children and children only. Top man in his field. I suggest I make a date with him pronto. Now, in fact.'

Edward picked up the telephone and began to dial a number while Amelia and George exchanged anxious looks.

'It's probably nothing to worry about,' George said, all the blood drained from his face. 'Probably just some kids' thing like the measles, or scarlet fever, or something.'

'She's also had diarrhoea recently, Edward,' Amelia remembered. 'I should have mentioned it. Clara said Gwennie hasn't be right for nearly a week now.'

'Fine, fine,' Edward grunted. 'Tell it all to the good Dr McAllister. Sounds as if he can see you tomorrow.'

*   *   *

Leaving Gwendolyn in a waiting room in the charge of one of his assistants, the specialist summoned both parents back into his consulting room.

'First and foremost Edward was quite right to send you to me, Mrs Dashwood, Captain Dashwood,' the tall, grey-haired consultant told them both. 'He thinks of himself as a bumpkin but he's actually a first-rate doctor. And he was quite right to send you here with Gwendolyn. Now, I have no wish to alarm you, but I must be frank. Naturally I need to await the results of the tests I ran this afternoon, and I shall no doubt have more tests to run in subsequent days, but my initial inclination is to suggest the child may be anaemic. You know of course what the term means?'

'It's a disorder of the blood, as far as I remember,' Amelia replied for both of them, as her insides turned to ice.

Dr McAllister nodded.

'Literally it means a lack of blood, but in fact it is a shortage of haemoglobin, the pigment which carries oxygen in our red blood cells. If we run short of haemoglobin we feel weary and inefficient, we are pale and weary, we have headaches, we may even run a fever.'

'Gwendolyn did have a slight temperature this week, and last. Nanny said it was just over 99.4 for a couple of days, which was why we kept Gwennie in bed.'

'Just so, Mrs Dashwood. But we know now that there are many reasons for anaemia, the most common being a deficient production of iron, or an inability to absorb iron from the diet. I doubt if this is the case with your daughter. Then we come to vitamin deficiency – vitamin B^{12}, to be precise.'

'Excuse me, Dr McAllister,' George interrupted. 'With respect, these are just theories, are they not, as to what *might* be wrong with our daughter? Surely until you have the result of the tests—'

'Yes, Captain Dashwood, of course. But you are here because children are my special subject. I am very familiar with the various syndromes which affect the young and the very young. And I will stake my reputation on being right in this case. Everything indicates a blood disorder and it is imperative we establish precisely which one little Gwendolyn is suffering from. With her background we can rule out poor diet as the cause. Therefore, if I am right in my assumptions, we are looking at something altogether more serious – which is why I must recommend that we have Gwendolyn admitted to hospital at once.'

Amelia looked helplessly at George who was staring glassy-eyed at Dr McAllister. 'Hospital, Dr McAllister,' he repeated. 'Do you have any idea for how long?'

'Not at this stage, no.'

'It was a ridiculous question. Forgive me.'

'It was not a bit ridiculous, believe me. But try not to be too alarmed. I hope it won't be for long, but I do like to take every possible precaution. I would recommend we send her to Lady Carnarvon's Clinic, just a few doors up the street, where they can run a full set of tests and all the top men in the field will be able to examine the patient. I can book her in today for you, if you so wish.'

Amelia thought her heart would break at hearing Gwendolyn called *the patient*. They had brought a little girl up to London and now she was to be a *patient*, designated to a nursing home to be examined by a host of doctors curious to see what disease the child might be suffering from and how it was affecting such a young body. Then, when they had run their tests and analysed what they had found, they would stuff her full of medicines in the hope that whatever it was that was making her so sickly would miraculously vanish, when all that would probably happen was that the pills and potions would make Gwennie ever more sickly until – until she—

'George?' Amelia said, rising suddenly. 'Is it all right if I have a word with my husband, Dr McAllister? This has all come as a bit of a shock.'

'Of course. Why don't you slip into the room next door here? I shall make sure Gwendolyn is looked after since I am sure you have no wish to upset the child.'

He opened a door behind him and George took her arm and led her into the sitting room where he sat her down in an armchair while he stood by the fireplace studying a painting with absolutely no interest whatsoever.

'Let's just take Gwennie home, George – can we?'

'I know just how you feel. Because I feel the same.' George stared blindly at the painting. 'But I don't think so. I don't think we can.'

Amelia got up and stood behind George, finding his hand and taking it. 'Please. George? Please let's all three of us just go home.'

'We can't, Amelia. Dr McAllister is a very experienced diagnostician. Edward says he cares for every child who comes to him as if they're his own. So I think we must do as he says. If it's something serious—'

'Not things wrong with the blood, George. Not things wrong with children's blood. When children Gwennie's age are diagnosed as anaemic, George—'

'No, Amelia. Don't.' George stopped her before she had time to lose her self-control, taking both her hands and looking into her eyes. 'It won't be anything like that. But even if it was, then we would have to put Gwendolyn somewhere where she would get the right care and attention. If it was anything serious the last thing you or I would want would be to have her suffer.'

'Of course. I'm sorry. It's just that – I love her so very much.'

'I know. So do I. I love her more than I can say.'

Amelia swallowed hard, bit her lip, dug her

fingernails deep into the palm of her hand as she always did when she wanted to stop herself crying. Because she knew that the one thing she must not do was give in.

They stayed in London while awaiting the result of the tests, once more booking into Browns Hotel, where they spent the rest of the day in their suite, having settled the bewildered Gwendolyn into the nursing home. First thing the next morning they returned to Harley Street where they found a frightened little girl.

'I should have thought of this last night, darling,' Amelia said, sitting one side of her daughter's bed while George pulled a chair up the other. 'Still, I shan't leave your side until they've finished doing whatever it is they're doing and we all trundle off back home.'

'I want to go home.'

'It won't be long, Tiger.' George squeezed her hand. 'We've brought you a brand new jigsaw puzzle which I suggest we all do together – and look, Matron's bringing you in a wireless set so that you can listen to the children's programmes. Now that *is* exciting.'

It took another two days for the doctors to run all their tests and study the results, during which time Gwendolyn was not left alone for one moment by her parents, the three of them spending their time doing puzzles and playing games. In fact they were just in the middle of a particularly hysterical game of Heads, Middles and Feet, always a family favourite, when Matron looked in to whisper that Dr McAllister would like a word.

'We won't be long, Tiger.'

'It's all right, George,' Amelia said quickly, with a don't-leave-her-alone look. 'If it's just a word, I'll go.'

'Are you sure?'

'Yes, George,' Amelia replied firmly, going to the door. 'You stay right where you are.'

'Mrs Dashwood.' Dr McAllister rose as Amelia came in, offering her a chair opposite him. 'Your husband is not with you?'

'We didn't want to leave Gwennie alone. So he's sitting with her.'

'I see. Very well, I'll come straight to the point then, Mrs Dashwood. And it's not good news. I'm afraid Gwendolyn is not at all well.'

Once again Amelia felt the ice cold hand grab at her stomach and twist her insides. She took a deep breath to calm herself before she replied.

'You mean she has to stay in hospital, is that it?' she heard herself saying.

'I'm afraid so. Yes.'

'How long for, Dr McAllister? What exactly do you think might be wrong with her?'

'Mrs Dashwood, this is going to be very hard for you,' Dr McAllister said quietly, getting up from his desk and coming round to sit down in a chair he drew up close to her.

'I think perhaps I had better go and get my husband, don't you?' Amelia said, staring at the man who she knew was about to break the sort of news every loving mother must dread from the moment their baby is put into their arms. 'If it's going to be very hard.'

'You must do what you think best, Mrs Dashwood. If you would rather your husband were here – but I'm afraid it won't make any difference to the diagnosis.'

Amelia looked at him.

'She's not going to die, is she?' she whispered. 'Please tell me Gwennie's not going to die?'

Dr McAllister put a hand gently on one of Amelia's.

'Your daughter has pernicious anaemia, Mrs Dashwood. I'm afraid there's no doubt about it. Every test we made points to the same conclusion.'

'Pernicious anaemia?'

They were the words Amelia had dreaded. In a way she had more than half expected them, yet even now the verdict had been pronounced it seemed totally impossible to accept such a finding. Gwendolyn was only a child, barely three years old. Children her age should not fall prey to terrible disease. They had not known enough of the world to earn such a sentence. Children were blessed, children were the innocents, God loved little children.

'How could God do this? How can He let her die?'

'Mrs Dashwood, I did not say anything about dying—'

'But Gwennie is going to, isn't she, Dr McAllister? I can see it on your face. I can see it in your eyes. I saw it the moment I came into this room. She's going to die and there's absolutely nothing you or I can do about it.'

'I wish there was, Mrs Dashwood. More than anything in the world. When I find a child has a disease such as this, I really would give my own life to find a cure.'

Amelia fell silent for a moment, before looking at the specialist with quite a different expression.

'Are you sure this is what Gwendolyn has? And that there's nothing you can do? Nothing anyone can do?'

Dr McAllister nodded, closing his eyes so he would not have to meet Amelia's.

'What will happen? How long will – how long will she live? How many years, or months, or days has she got?'

'Mrs Dashwood.' Taking courage Dr McAllister looked her in the eye, and she saw his infinite sadness as he saw her dawning grief. At that moment she knew it was not going to be years, that perhaps it might not even be months, that it might just be a question of weeks. 'Mrs Dashwood – I think it will be very quick, and of course we shall do everything we can to make absolutely sure she does not suffer.'

'No.'

'I know how you must feel, Mrs Dashwood—'

'No. No, that's not what I meant. That isn't what I meant at all,' Amelia said, getting up. 'What I meant was no she's not going to die.'

'All I can say is that while she is here, while we do what we can for her, something might happen which prevents what looks like the inevitable—'

'That isn't what I meant!' Amelia stood up, staring intensely ahead. 'You don't understand *me*! I understand you all right – but you don't understand me at all!' She dropped her voice to a whisper, still staring but this time at him. 'Gwendolyn is not going to die.'

'We will do our very best, that I promise you. We will do everything in our power to try and prevent it, but I'm afraid—'

'We're taking her home, Dr McAllister,' Amelia announced, turning for the door. 'Please tell Matron to see that her things are packed. We are taking Gwendolyn home at once.'

'Mrs Dashwood . . .' Dr McAllister got himself between Amelia and the door, preventing her from leaving. 'Mrs Dashwood, Gwendolyn cannot leave here. You couldn't cope with what is going to happen to her. Not at home. Not without a nursing staff, believe me.'

'She is coming home, Dr McAllister,' Amelia replied. 'Now if you don't mind?'

She tried to get past him, but the specialist stood his ground.

'Just think about what you are doing, Mrs

Dashwood,' he pleaded. 'Think of the good of your little girl. You don't want her to suffer – you said so yourself.'

'She is not going to suffer, Dr McAllister. And she is not going to die. She will only suffer if you make her stay in this place. If my husband and I do not take her home.'

Amelia's tears had dried up and she stood facing Dr McAllister with a look of such utter conviction that he stepped to one side to allow her access to the door.

'Perhaps you should speak to your husband first,' he said, as his last suggestion. 'Perhaps once Captain Dashwood is apprised of the facts you will see it differently.'

'I don't think so, Dr McAllister. Not for one minute. I am absolutely sure Captain Dashwood will be of exactly the same mind as I am.'

Amelia was right. As soon as George learned all the facts, he agreed with her at once, and quite unconditionally. They must take Gwendolyn home.

'Pain, you said, sir, must be suffered. We were not to allay it nor make interference in their distress.'

'This is a child, wizard,' the Noble One chided. 'We will not brook such agony.'

'Very well.' Longbeard consulted his purse, picking out a handful of stardust. 'This may cure ills, sir, although 'tis no certainty.'

'I want nothing that is not certain, wizard. We

brought them to this place, I will not watch the child taken before her time.'

'Then what, sir? I have no spells for such as this. If I had, should we have found ourselves here? I think not.'

His companion looked at him once then put a hand on his arm. 'There is magick here enough. We have no need of spells. Just lead her where she must go. Go behind her eyes, enter into her mind, and once you are there she will know what to do.'

'Very well.' Longbeard nodded, then took from his purse a tiny jet black jewel in the shape of a beetle which he placed in his mouth. When the moon appeared once more his companion found himself alone beneath the yew while somewhere on the wind of night a tiny insect was carried on a light breeze to its place of destiny.

They had brought her home sedated, in case she was sick on the long car journey, so now she slept deeply in her own bed, while Amelia and George sat by the fire in George's study, drinking cups of cocoa and wondering in silence what they could possibly do to prevent what they had been told was inevitable.

'Perhaps—' George began.

'No,' Amelia stopped him. 'There can't be any *perhaps*, George. If we had left her in hospital, she would have died there. And if she's going to die, then she must die here. Where she was born. This is her home.'

'It won't be easy, Amelia. What a ridiculous thing to say – of course it's not going to be easy.'

George got up from his chair and fetched the whisky decanter to pour them both a drink. 'What I meant was that we're going to have to – no we're not. As a matter of fact, I don't know what we're going to have to do.' He sat down again, staring into the drink he held in both his hands.

'Maybe she'll get better now she's back here? Maybe, just maybe, the doctors are wrong and she's suffering from something else altogether. Doctors are often wrong. So maybe they're wrong in this case. They could easily be wrong, George.'

And they could just as easily be right, George thought. What they had decided in London had seemed so obvious at the time, but now they were back home with a possibly mortally sick daughter lying upstairs in bed reality was beginning to come home to them both, and to George in particular. In his heart he agreed absolutely with Amelia, that rather than leave their beloved daughter to her fate in a hospital, even with themselves in constant attendance, they should have the child at home where they could nurse her with total love and devotion. Yet now they were actually home, the thought of what they might have to undergo made George fearful, not so much for himself as for Amelia, whom he could not imagine surviving such a terrible ordeal.

'Amelia darling,' he began again. 'Perhaps in the morning after we've both slept—'

'I shan't be able to sleep, George. I don't actually

think I shall ever be able to sleep again.'

'Of course you will. If we're going to help Gwennie we have to sleep. We have to sleep, and eat and, and – keep up our *strength*. We have to be strong if we're going to get through this, one way or another, and to do that we mustn't give in. We really mustn't.'

'No.' Amelia looked at him, her eyes large in her pale face. 'No, you're right, George. We mustn't give in. You're right.'

'Drink your drink, sweetheart,' George said. 'And I'll take you to bed.'

Before they settled down for the night, George opened the window. As he did he was surprised by a warm breeze which of a sudden seemed to be blowing in through the window. He stared out of the window, puzzled. The night was as still as the waters of the lake, dark and silent.

Amelia was lying on her back, propped up by two pillows. Her eyes were fast shut but he knew even before he went to kiss her that she was not asleep.

'Good night, my darling,' he whispered. 'Try to sleep.'

'Yes, George,' Amelia whispered back. 'I shall. Because we must be strong.'

George leaned down to kiss her, and stopped. 'You have a ladybird in your hair. At least I think it's a ladybird.'

He touched her head with one finger, lifting the

tiny insect out of Amelia's hair in order to take a better look.

'A ladybird? At night? They don't fly at night.'

'Probably because it isn't a ladybird. Look – I don't know what it is. I've never seen an insect like it. Look.'

Amelia looked, now putting out her own index finger and transferring the tiny creature to her hand. It was shaped like a ladybird but was even smaller, with a dark black shell covered in what looked like minute crescent moons the colour of primroses. Strangest of all were its eyes, unlike any other insects' eyes, and of such blue luminosity that Amelia found herself squinting away from them as if dazzled. Meanwhile, the insect walked slowly round the palm of her hand.

'It's like – it's like a tiny jewel.'

'A tiny flying jewel,' Amelia replied, smiling suddenly. 'Because now it's gone.'

'Where to?'

'I don't know. I didn't even see it take off.'

'But you were watching it.'

'I know I was, George,' Amelia agreed patiently. 'And now it's gone.'

But despite her over-patient tone, she smiled again at him, and after that they both slept.

Amelia was drawn to it all the time, without knowing why. As each day passed and their little girl seemed to be slipping quietly away from them, Amelia would find herself outside the house and walking across the lawns without knowing quite where she was headed. One moment she would be at Gwendolyn's bedside and the next she would be opening the heavy iron gate at the end of the formal lawns which led to the path along which, each and every day now, and sometimes even at night, Amelia would find herself creeping back to what she knew to be a place of peace.

Increasingly, particularly in the night when she seemed to wake up and find herself alone in a sleeping house beside the weakening Gwendolyn, she would steal off into the dark garden and open the gate before sitting enraptured by something magical and healing. Nothing had changed in the Kissing Garden by day, but at night it seemed to her that there were voices calling to her to fetch Gwendolyn, to bring her out with her, to carry Gwendolyn to the Kissing Garden.

After one such visit she found herself hurrying back to the house, breaking into a run. She knew that Edward, their kind doctor, had done everything he could, but now the situation was beyond his capabilities. Now she had to turn to something altogether different. Now she knew she had to rely on other, unseen, powers. It was mad to try something so illogical, but she hoped more than she could say that those same powers that had brought her and George together in the Kissing Garden would somehow bring Gwendolyn back to health.

With the child wrapped in a rug and half unconscious in her arms, Amelia stole out of the house
and back across lawns that were already stiff with
frost. A hunting barn owl flew silently out of a
tree by the gate as the two hurried by, back
through the gateway, up the stone steps cut in the
side of the mount and finally at last to the hidden
garden, its dark yew hedges seemingly as impenetrable as the walls of a small fortress. Flakes
of snow fell on Amelia's dark hair and brushed
her cheeks as she found the entrance and made her
way within, where all was quiet and the ground
unfrozen.

For a moment Amelia stood, uncertain as to
what to do, until she realized that no snow
was falling within the little hidden garden.
Everywhere around the rectangle a blizzard fell
silently and swiftly from unseen clouds, yet on
the dark green turf where they stood not a single
flake fell.

She knelt on the ground, laying her child on the
still warm grass, one arm round the sleeping body,
while in the four dark walls of the hedge, unseen
by her, full blooms of the white rose closed back
up into buds as from the darkest part of the
hedgerow a black snake with bright emerald green
eyes silently emerged to slide secretly towards the
mother and her child.

When it was at her feet the creature reared up,
darting an arrowed tongue into the air and hissing
the sound of a dry wind sweeping across a desert.

All at once it stood up on its tail, straight as a stick, a stick which became a tree whose branches were of golden willow. Night turned to dawn and then midday with a sun high in the heavens, its warmth bathing the hidden garden with a power so profound that the grass grew up round the sleeping girl as the white rose reopened its blooms to drink in the light.

Now, as suddenly as the sunshine, night fell on a million days, the million nights of the million days that rushed by in the blink of an eye, together making but a brief moment in the span of existence that is the universe. Centuries flew by in a cosmic blur, scattering things known and unknown from the past and the future, and time was all one moment.

Then the tree became the snake once more, and as the creature slid away the clouds in the night sky closed overhead and the snow began to fall within the hidden garden.

For one moment, as she awoke, Amelia had no idea where she was or why. She found herself at dead of night standing in the hidden garden, which was fast being blanketed by snow, alone except for Gwendolyn who was lying wrapped in a thick red wool rug asleep on the grass, so fast asleep that Amelia had to put her ear to the child's face to see whether or not she was still breathing. To her relief she discovered the little girl was warm to her touch and sleeping peacefully. Covering her daughter's face with the corner of the rug against the snow, Amelia hurried out of the hidden garden and back to the house.

As soon as she realized that all she had on were her nightclothes, she became freezing cold, where she had been warm. Unsurprised, and with her shoes caked with snow, she picked her way across the lawns. Looking back for a second she saw that there were no tracks running in the opposite direction. She must have been in the Kissing Garden for as long as it had taken for inches of snow to fall. Yet she had no memory of leaving the house.

I must have gone mad, she said to herself as she pushed the front door open. *I must have had a brainstorm and lost all my sense. What in God's name did I think I was doing?*

No-one heard them come back in, not even Clara, a self-proclaimed light sleeper. As Amelia gently returned the still sleeping Gwendolyn to her bed, she felt only relief that her moment of insanity would go unremarked. The little girl did not even open her eyes as Amelia tucked her back up, simply turning on her side and giving what sounded to Amelia like a contented sigh as she settled back in her bed. Amelia ran the back of her hand as lightly as could be over her daughter's forehead, but it was as cool as it should be, with no sign of fever.

Which meant that the colour in her cheeks just might be more than a simple result of the cold night air. Finding herself smiling for no apparent reason, Amelia bent down and kissed her daughter carefully on the temple, brushing back her hair before running her fingers down the little girl's cheek.

Having made one last adjustment to Gwendolyn's bedclothes, Amelia went to the window and drew the curtains tightly before leaving the room. And the tiny insect hiding in her hair crept out onto her shoulder, spread its black gauze wings and flew swiftly and silently out of the landing window and into the new day's dawn.

Amelia slept in late for her. Since nowadays George invariably rose before her to put in an hour's work before breakfast he did not find it even a little odd that Amelia had not come down to join him over coffee and toast. That was the way their life was now, with Amelia sometimes snatching some extra sleep when the house was quiet, particularly if they had both been working hard or, as in this case, enjoying a brief respite from worry.

When she finally awoke, the first thing Amelia did was hurry to her daughter's room to see whether or not Gwendolyn was suffering any ill effects from the night's adventure. She was stopped by Clara at the nursery bedroom door.

'She's sleeping that peacefully, Mrs Dashwood. I haven't seen her so quiet in an age, and no sign of a fever or any discomfort at all.'

Amelia eased the door open to look for herself, and sure enough Gwendolyn was lying fast asleep on her side with her teddy bear beside her on the pillow.

'I think we should leave her to sleep for as long as she feels like it, don't you, Clara?' she whispered, closing the bedroom door. 'She hasn't slept without waking or wanting something for days now.'

'They do say sleep's the great healer, don't they?' Clara agreed with a nod as she followed Amelia down the corridor. 'And did you notice what else, Mrs Dashwood?'

'Such as, Clara? What should I have noticed?'

'Her colour. She's got a lot of her old colour back, bless her.'

Amelia smiled and looked out on her gardens, which now lay beneath a good six inches of snow, snow that had gone on falling long after their return to the house, removing all traces of her steps from the lawns.

'Give me a call the minute she wakes, Clara,' she said, turning to go downstairs. 'I shan't be far away.'

For the rest of the morning Amelia kept Peter in her charge so that Clara could be at hand in the nursery when Gwendolyn did finally wake up. George, who knew nothing about the growing feeling of optimism on the nursery floor, worked in his study all morning, joining Amelia for a glass of sherry before lunch. When they had discussed the sudden and dramatic change in the weather, inevitably the talk turned to Gwendolyn.

'She's slept now without waking for the best part of seventeen hours, George. I mean proper sleep – there's no need to look anxious. She hasn't fallen into a coma or anything.'

'Seventeen hours? Are you sure?'

'Perfectly. She's sleeping the way only a child can. And wait till you see her – she even has some colour back in her cheeks.'

'Perhaps Edward's funny old diet is working after all. Although I don't think it is all that funny really. It makes a lot of sense when you think about it. There's an enormous amount of goodness in liver and green vegetables.'

'I don't know what it is,' Amelia replied carefully, even though she had more than a slight suspicion. 'And it's still early days, so although I am more hopeful it's only guarded. Very guarded, in fact.'

'Can I go up and see her, do you think?'

'Of course. But whatever you do don't wake her.'

They let her sleep right through until mid-afternoon. Indeed Amelia would have let her go on sleeping if George had not become quite so worried.

'I really don't think she should sleep this long, Amelia,' he said, shaking his head in concern as he paced the drawing room floor. 'It really isn't natural.'

'Perhaps if I telephoned Edward,' Amelia suggested. 'Just in case.'

'Yes. Edward will know well enough how long a child's meant to sleep. Go ahead.'

'You think she's dying, don't you, George?' Amelia asked him, telephone receiver in hand. 'And I know she isn't.'

'How do you know?' George groaned. 'You're her mother, dearest girl. Not a doctor.'

'And that's exactly why I know she isn't dying, George,' Amelia replied, beginning to dial the doctor's number. 'Because I'm her mother.'

'All I know is that Dr McAllister said—' George stopped and closed his eyes, putting a hand to his mouth. 'It doesn't matter what McAllister said. Just speak to Edward, will you?'

Having assured Amelia on the telephone that there was nothing to get anxious about as long as they were sure the child was just sleeping, none the less Edward called round shortly after tea, as he was finishing his rounds.

By now even Amelia was becoming anxious, since, according to Clara, Gwendolyn had barely stirred at all since morning. Yet whenever any of them went to check on her condition the child seemed to be sleeping deeply and without distress, breathing regularly, not tossing or turning. At one point during the vigil George consulted a medical encyclopedia in order to find out how much sleep a person could take, and was comforted to discover several case histories where the victims of deep shock slept uninterrupted for two or three days at a time, particularly young children.

'There was a case in Italy not so long ago after a volcanic explosion where a child the same age as Gwennie was pulled alive out of the debris where she'd been buried for three days,' Edward informed them after he had taken an initial look at the patient and announced that he was of the same opinion as Amelia. 'The doctors never thought the child would survive the shock she must have suffered, particularly when she fell into what they assumed was a coma for nearly four days. Whereupon blow me, suddenly up she sat, rubbed her eyes and asked for her parents – both of whom, as luck would have it, were still alive.'

'What would happen, do you think, if we tried to wake her?'

'Funnily enough this report covered that very aspect, old chap. The Italian MOs wondered the very same thing, but fortunately as it happened none of them tried. Just as well, it seems, because when some boffin arrived from Milan to see the child, chap whose main study was the effect of sleep and comas, he said that if anyone had tried to wake the child she could jolly well have died from the shock of it. So there you are. Let sleeping dogs – and in this case children – lie, obviously. Eh?'

'I agree.' Amelia nodded. 'Who knows what our bodies can do? Or our minds?'

'Who indeed,' Edward echoed.

'But you have to admit, it really is most peculiar. I mean – why? Why in heaven's name should Gwennie sleep like this? Since she's been ill, as you know, Edward, she's been sleeping more and more badly. Recently the longest she's slept has been about four or five hours. So why this change, do you think?'

'I have no idea, old boy.'

'Amelia? Have you any idea?'

Amelia looked up at him and shook her head. 'No, George, I have no idea at all. Not one that makes any sense, certainly.' And before George could ask her more, which to judge from the expression on his face he was just about to do, she excused herself and, wrapping herself up warmly, took herself out into the wintry landscape to try to make some sense of it herself.

'Won't she want something to eat?' Peter enquired as he sat with his parents before bedtime. 'I couldn't go that long without having something to eat.'

'You can't eat in your sleep, Peter,' George replied, smiling at his son.

'I could.'

'Yes, I imagine you could,' Amelia agreed. 'I expect you could eat under water.'

'Don't try that though, will you?'

'No, Daddy.' Peter frowned and thought for a moment. 'How long do you think Gwennie will sleep for, Mummy? I hope she doesn't sleep as long as Rip Van Winkle.'

'She won't, darling,' Amelia told him. 'Gwennie's not going to sleep for ever.'

'I hope you're right,' George said quietly.

'Yes. So do I.'

Amelia was convinced she woke up the moment Gwendolyn did. Even before she got out of bed to turn on the light in the room she was sharing with her daughter, she knew Gwendolyn had come to, and sure enough there she was, sitting up in her bed, yawning profoundly and rubbing her eyes, tousle-haired and pink in the cheeks and looking better than Amelia had seen her since she had become so obviously ill.

'Well, well,' she said softly, sitting on her daughter's bed and giving her a hug. 'What a long zizz. You all right?'

Gwendolyn stared at her mother, then behind her at what was after all her brother's bed.

'Why you sleeping here, Mummy?'

'Just to make sure you were all right, darling. You haven't been very well, if you remember.'

Gwendolyn thought for a moment.

'Haven't I?'

'Not really. Don't you remember?'

'Sort of.' Gwendolyn yawned again, deeply and luxuriously, as only those who have slept well for an age can. 'I'm thirsty, Mummy. Can I have a drink?'

'Of course. There's some all ready for you. For the moment you woke up.' Amelia got up and fetched the jug of fresh squash that she had asked Clara to prepare. 'How are you feeling, sweetheart?'

'I feel fine, Mummy,' Gwendolyn replied, taking the proffered glass and holding it two-handed. 'Much better for sleeping.'

'Do you remember how you felt before?'

'Sort of. I was a bit tired.'

'That's right. And now?'

The little girl frowned deeply, wrinkling her nose. 'I don't feel tired any more. Can I have a biscuit?'

Amelia got up again and fetched a plate covered with a napkin from the top of the chest of drawers. Just then Clara appeared at the nursery door, doing up her dressing gown.

'Oh,' she said with delight. 'We're awake, are we? My, that is a sight for sore eyes.'

'Nanny – I just want one moment, if you don't mind,' Amelia said, turning her back on Gwendolyn and dropping her voice. 'She seems absolutely fine, but I just want a moment.'

'Of course, Mrs Dashwood,' Clara agreed, going back out. 'I'll be right here on the other side.' She closed the door.

'Do you remember *anything* else about being unwell, Gwennie?' Amelia whispered, sitting on her daughter's bed. 'Anything funny? Or unusual? Anything say that happened just before you had that great long sleep?'

Again Gwendolyn pulled a little face and shrugged. 'No,' she said happily through a mouthful of biscuit.

'Nothing at all. Really?'

'Yes. Nothing at all. These biscuits are soft.'

'That's because they've been up here for—' Amelia stopped herself just in time. 'I'll bring you up some new ones. Those ones must have come from the bottom of Nanny's tin.'

'Can I come downstairs, Mummy?'

'What? At midnight?' Amelia laughed, and tousled her daughter's dark hair. 'No you most certainly cannot, young lady.'

'I'm not tired.'

'I'm very glad to hear it. How's your horrid headache? Has it gone?'

'Yes.'

'Tummy all right? And those beastly aches and pains?'

'All gone. Please please can I come downstairs?'

'No, darling. But tell you what   you can come and sit in Mummy and Daddy's bed.' Amelia lifted up her daughter and hugged her to her, careful not to make too much fuss. 'As soon as Nanny's put you into some fresh night things, I'll have her bring you along the corridor straight away.'

'Can I sleep there all night, Mummy?'

'If you're good.' Amelia smiled. 'And don't *snore*.'

*   *   *

329

With Edward Lydford in constant attendance the three of them carefully monitored Gwendolyn's state of health over the next weeks, all the time looking for the slightest sign of relapse, but by the time winter was at last in retreat and the March winds began to herald the advent of spring Gwendolyn was apparently so much better it was if she had never been ill. To all intents and purposes she was the same healthy and happy little girl she had been before she had first become sick, full of energy and fun.

She had in fact recovered so quickly that she had been able to enjoy the second heavy snowfall of winter which arrived in mid-January. In the glorious winter sunshine which followed hard on the blizzards she was busy building snowmen with her brother and tobogganing on a tin tray down the sides of the long garden banks.

'How will we know?' George had cautiously asked Edward that day as with Amelia they stood watching the children putting the finishing touches to their snowman. 'How will we ever know if she really has recovered? Isn't it true that those who suffer these sorts of illnesses often have periods when they seem to be perfectly all right, only for the sickness to strike again?'

'Yes and no, old boy.' Edward paused while ferreting for his pipe in a coat pocket. 'Things can come and go, certainly. But then, on the other hand, sometimes things can go altogether.'

'Alternatively she might have been misdiagnosed,' Amelia said, even though she did not actually believe it. 'It is possible, Edward, isn't it? For even the best doctors and specialists to get things wrong?'

'Absolutely, old girl. Happens every day of the week somewhere or other. Particularly, I have to say, with kids. They can't tell you as much as we old fogeys, you see. Particularly the nippers. So a lot of it, while not guesswork exactly, just ain't exact, do you see? One does wear a blindfold over one eye much of the time, if you like.'

'When I see how well Gwennie is now, Edward,' George said, wiping the condensation off the inside of the French door with the back of a hand, 'how much energy she has, and the way her appetite has returned, I have to believe she's well again. By that I mean completely well.'

'Couldn't agree more, old boy,' Edward replied. 'But of course this series of tests they're going to run in Bath should clear up any doubts once and for all.'

Naturally Amelia had been apprehensive about subjecting Gwendolyn to any more tests. She was nervous in case they showed Gwendolyn's apparent recovery to be a false dawn, and that George's expressed anxiety about periods of remission followed by renewed attacks had been justified.

Yet they knew the tests must be run, for without them they would all be living on hope rather than

331

hard fact, so on the appointed day they took the little girl into Bath. They had assured Gwendolyn that the only reason the doctors were going to take samples of her blood was so that they could compare it with Mummy and Daddy's, but luckily Gwendolyn was not in the least bit interested either in the reasons or in the tests themselves, which were nowhere near as stringent as the ones she had been made to suffer previously. Amelia had suggested that Gwendolyn should take her teddy bear to the hospital with her so that the doctors could take a sample of his blood as well, a diversion which proved enormously successful.

The afternoon's outing ended with the three of them having tea and cakes in the Pump Rooms much earlier than they had hoped, and a week later Edward arrived at The Priory with the result of the tests.

'I am delighted to tell you, everyone,' Edward beamed, holding the letter out before him, 'that Miss Gwendolyn Dashwood has been declared to be one hundred per cent free of any disorder of the blood. In fact, the doctor in charge of the examination is delighted to add that he has rarely seen not only such a pretty young patient but such a perfectly healthy one.' He turned away suddenly, shaking his head, and there was a small pause before he added, 'It's days like this that make it all worthwhile.'

*   *   *

'I feel like getting quite drunk,' George confessed to Amelia after Edward had left them to continue his rounds.

'Then do,' Amelia laughed. 'I shall most probably join you. I don't think I've ever been so happy or so relieved.'

George poured them both a drink, and for a moment they stood in silence.

'So either it was a misdiagnosis, or else Edward's diet did the magic.'

'That's right,' Amelia agreed. 'Although I'm more inclined to go for the latter, because to my mind there's no doubt at all that Gwennie was seriously ill.'

'You think it was Edward's treatment, then?'

'I think something did the magic.'

'You're not making sense. Either Edward's treatment did or it didn't.'

Amelia shrugged and shook her head. 'I don't know, George. I can't explain. I just don't think anything is as simple as that.' She finished her drink. 'Let's put on our coats and go to visit the Kissing Garden.'

'It's a bit cold for that, isn't it?'

'Have you forgotten, George? It's *never* cold in the Kissing Garden.'

George laughed. It was true.

What if she should remember, sir?' Longbeard asked. 'Once back, she might remember, might she not?'

'Mortals do not remember,' the Noble One replied

smiling, well pleased at the result of the beetle magick. 'Now since we find ourselves in their time we must have time to spare. Amuse me.'

'I could tell you something which might not amuse you, sir,' Longbeard replied. 'Naturally, it could be of no note, or it may simply have been a time reflection or a star flash, but it might interest you to hear it, and it might be important for you to know, sir.'

'Tell me then, if you must,' his companion sighed, watching the birth of a minor galaxy. 'There are an infinite number of deeds to do other than idle in chatter.'

'The one who was your friend,' Longbeard said, 'The one who loved your wife in your time . . .'

'Yes? What of him?' For the first time in many centuries the face of the Noble One in the violet robe grew dark as he held the forearm of the old man in an iron grip. 'What of him?' he repeated, 'What of him?'

'As I said, sir, it might have been a dazzle. But methought I saw him here, here in this very moment where we are, sir. I thought I saw his image behind us in the dark water. Again I saw it, this time beside us in a glass you held, sir. While you examined your own image on the near side of the glass, the far side contained none other than his own. Thus were two men one. The two men who loved her, each a reflection of the other.'

'Enough!' cried his companion, releasing his grip. 'We have a task to do! He must not come here! Never! If you should see him again, wizard, I command you to turn him to some small creature of the night, a toad, a bat, but never allow him to show his face here again! Not ever!'

Part Three
1931

'Anything more than the truth would be too much.'

Robert Frost

Sixteen

'How old are you now, Peter?' Lady Dashwood asked her grandson, smiling as he pulled on the bright red crêpe paper crown he found in his cracker.

'Ten, Grandmother. Why?'

'I am absolutely useless at remembering the age of my grandchildren, Peter, that is why.'

'You only have two, Mama,' George reminded her, unravelling a motto from his own cracker.

'I can barely remember my own age, George,' Lady Dashwood replied. 'Let alone the age of these two little people.'

Gwendolyn gave a small sigh and widened her big eyes patiently. 'Peter is ten next birthday, Grandmother, and I shall be seven next May.'

'You have grown, Gwendolyn,' her grandmother said almost suspiciously. 'In fact she has shot up, has she not, Amelia?'

'She's going to be much taller than I am.'

'All in favour of tall gels meself,' the general grunted, holding his motto at arm's length so as to read it better. 'Now then – someone tell me, right? Which king of Spain wore the biggest shoes?'

'The one with the biggest feet, Grandfather,' Gwendolyn told him, with another sigh.

'My word,' the General exclaimed. 'Not only are you going to be tall, young lady, you're going to be one of those – what do they call 'em? One of those blue-stockings. That's what you're going to be, young lady.'

'What's a blue-stocking?'

'Someone very clever.'

'I'm not – I just knew the answer! We had it last Christmas!'

'Still say you're clever meself,' the General insisted. 'Dashed if I can remember jokes.'

'If you are going to grow up to be clever, Gwendolyn,' Lady Dashwood added, 'be careful not to show that you are in front of the opposite sex. Men run a mile from a clever woman, most especially an English one.'

'With some notable exceptions,' George said with a look to Amelia.

'Now then, young man.' Lady Dashwood turned her attention to her grandson. 'And what do you intend to do when you are grown up?'

'I'm going to fly aeroplanes, Grandmother.'

'*I am*, not I'*m*, please, young man. So you intend to fly aeroplanes. I trust this does not mean you intend to join the Flying Corps?' Lady Dashwood raised her eyebrows to stare wide-eyed at her grandson. 'This is a military family, Peter. Gentlemen join the army. Gentlemen do not join the Royal Flying Corps.'

Constance Dennison, who had been unusually silent till now exchanged a look with her daughter and was about to say something when Amelia frowned and shook her head.

'Have you decided on schools yet, George?' Lady Dashwood continued, turning to her son. 'It surely is high time this young man was away at school, being taught the sorts of things boys of his age should be taught, instead of being at home all the time, listening to all sorts of bohemic nonsense.'

'Is that how you think of our family chatter?'

'Certainly not the stuff for a growing boy.'

'George and I enjoy having Peter at home. And as far as his education goes it certainly is *not* being neglected.'

'He certainly is *not* being taught the king's English.' Lady Dashwood sniffed. 'George? I trust you have the matter in hand?'

'Give me senseless Bohemia any day, Louisa,' Clarence sighed, 'rather than foolish Mars.'

Sensing another possible confrontation between George and his mother, Amelia invited Louisa, Constance and the children to withdraw, leaving the gentlemen alone to enjoy their port and cigars.

This was the first Christmas the three families had actually spent together at The Priory, and so far – perhaps to everyone's private surprise – it had proved to be a remarkably happy occasion, with even George's mother managing to *come off it*, as Amelia put it to George, joining in the fun and games her son and daughter-in-law had organized, although whenever the opportunity arose she still managed to either criticize her son for his present literary activities, or demean his past ones. Amelia had hoped George might not mind his mother's criticism, which always came masquerading as wit, but it seemed he did. He was very good about not getting into arguments, either ignoring his mother's remarks or seeming to take them only light-heartedly, but behind the closed doors of their bedroom it was a different matter.

Here George made it perfectly plain to Amelia that he much regretted his mother's all-pervasive disapproval, not to mention her inability to show anyone any real affection. The sad thing was that until the moment he had resigned his commission George had always enjoyed a good relationship with his mother. They looked upon and treated each other as friends, and although Louisa's outlook on life had been invariably critical, nevertheless she had, until that moment, seemed to have a deep and genuine affection for her only son – not because he was a hero but because he seemed to personify everything she and in fact most women would wish for in a son: courage, resolution, honesty and good looks.

Resigning his commission had, however, proved too much for her to take, and, although somewhat surprisingly his father had managed to come to terms with his son's decision, it seemed that his mother would never do so. Nor was she was able to find it in her heart to forgive him, still less when George's books became a dramatic talking point in Society, polarizing opinion between those who thought the author little more than a traitor to his country and those who considered him to be one of the bravest and brightest of the new literary talents to emerge since the war's end. Predictably enough Louisa Dashwood had pitched her tent in the former camp, believing her son had let down his entire side.

'As if it is not bad enough for one's son to resign his commission,' she would often remark to friends at luncheon, 'imagine what it must be like to have one who does so *and* writes books.'

So although it was in the hope of reconciliation that Amelia had suggested the three families should spend Christmas together at The Priory, realistically it was also with a feeling of trepidation. Until this year George and Amelia had spent Christmas staying with one set of parents or the other, and while this had provided some happy times, nevertheless the young Dashwoods had badly missed spending the holiday with their two children in their own home. Because their parents fortunately were good friends, there was at least no danger of any argument arising between the four of them, other than the usual banter at the card table or the ongoing but friendly dispute between Clarence and the General over the merits, or not, of the present Poet Laureate.

The only real danger of controversy lay between George and his mother, which meant that Amelia was constantly on her guard to defuse any possible confrontation, knowing as she did from experience that when her mother-in-law chose to argue with someone the outcome invariably cast a pall over the celebrations no matter what the result, such was the power of her formidable character.

So while the three men settled themselves down to enjoy their port and cigars, and Peter and Gwendolyn to play with their Christmas presents, Amelia diverted her mother-in-law's attention away from the quarrel that she had just been about to pick with her son, to talk about such safe subjects as Dodie Smith's runaway success in the West End with *Autumn Crocus*, which Clarence and Constance had taken the young Dashwoods to see when they had been staying with them at the beginning of the month.

Meanwhile in the dining room the talk had turned away from the current universal economic depression to the growth of the Nazi party in Germany.

'Violet Bonham-Carter was right,' Clarence said. 'She warned everyone of the consequences of the French action in the Ruhr back in 1923, but no-one listened to her. The Liberals were in chaos, and now the League of Nations, which was our best hope, so now that hope's gone as well.'

'I'm not altogether sure, Clarence,' the General said, 'how well informed this Bonham-Carter woman was, do you know. People had some pretty derelict ideas then.'

'If you're worried because as you soldiers would have it she's a *mere woman*, Michael, think again,' Clarence replied. 'The feminine point of view is often the most sanguine, the most practical and the most commonsensical. She said we must help Germany prosper or rue the day. Or words to that effect. And here we are, ruing the day.'

'Of course, we have to keep our eye on Germany,' the General said, tapping an inch of his cigar carefully into an ashtray. 'This Hitler fellow appears to have Hindenberg dancing to his tune, rather than t'other way round. Which is not what the wiseacres have been predicting.'

'I've just read *Mein Kampf*. The book he wrote in gaol. Have you read it, Clarence? Because if not, you should. I don't think we should underestimate Mr Hitler.'

'I don't know, George. I was dining with some members of the Cabinet recently, God forgive me.' Clarence paused to blow a perfect smoke ring and watched with satisfaction as it rose unbroken to the ceiling. 'Anyway, there was a lot of talk about Germany and her future, but the most interesting rabbit was that a lot of people, including the ones that matter in Germany, think Hitler is mostly hot air, a characterless little man, all sound and fury. And that for all his rantings he will easily be controlled by German big business.'

'Don't count on it, Clarrie.' The General looked up suddenly and stared across the table at his friend, and George noticed again how very large

343

his father's brown eyes were, and how kind. 'Personally I don't like what's going on over there one bit. Country's bankrupt – they had to close all their banks this year, that's how bad it's got – they have a growing population that needs to be fed and clothed, they have massive unemployment and totally weak leadership. Absolute blueprint for some sort of revolution, I'd say.'

'Like Russia, do you mean, Father?'

'Not entirely, my boy. Although there are plenty of Bolsheviks in Germany, I'll be bound. No. No, I think the danger is going to come from the right in this case. Which is why we have to keep our eye on this Hitler fellow.'

'I heard from some friends who've just returned from Germany that Hitler was being bankrolled by some of the German fat cats,' George said. 'Some millionaire called Hugenberg? And two or three others have followed suit.'

'That's what they were saying about big business controlling him.' Clarence nodded and stared at the tip of his now too-hot cigar. 'Three other millionaires have pledged their support to the Nazi party.'

'He who holds the purse strings doesn't always call the tune, Clarrie,' the General sighed. 'This fellow Hitler is working class. When they come from that side they have nothing to lose, know what I mean? They're takers. Particularly from business. Particularly from the rich boys.'

'Meanwhile we're raising some home-grown

Nazis all of our very own,' Clarence said, pouring some more port as the decanter passed to him. 'Oswald Mosley? Yes? Left the Labour Party now, I gather, to form his very own Fascist party. Make what you can of that, gentlemen?'

'I was at school with him,' George leaned forward, relighting his cigar by using the candle near to him. 'He was full of odd ideas then. In fact I think by now he's tried practically every political bed there is bar communism. He's been a Conservative, an Independent, a Socialist – and now he's gone back to the right.'

'Where did the word Fascist come from?' Clarence wondered, leaning back in his chair. 'Mussolini coined it, I know – but I'm never altogether sure what it means.'

'It comes from Ancient Rome, as a matter of fact. The *fasces* were a bundle of sticks tied to an ox, and they represented civil unity, as well as the power of the State to punish wrongdoers.'

'One thing I do know is that Mussolini began his political life as a Marxist. They don't half bed-hop, these politicians.'

'He's certainly no Marxist now.'

'So, Fascism is total subordination to the State?' asked the general.

'And unquestioning allegiance to the leader,' George added.

'A recipe for mayhem if ever I heard one,' the general opined. 'And one absolutely tailor-made for present day Germany.'

'And a Happy Christmas to all my readers,' Clarence concluded, suddenly looking and feeling far from festive.

Their mood soon lightened when they had joined the rest of the party in the drawing room. Once the family games were under way all talk of politics was soon forgotten, as it nearly always is when children have to be entertained.

On Boxing Day George took his father out for a morning's hunting up on the Downs with the South and West Wilts, while Amelia showed the two older women around the priory grounds, explaining what had been done and what she still intended to do as they walked through the gardens on an unseasonably fine and mild December day. Despite the season the estate still looked beautiful, reflecting all the hard work Amelia, Jethro and Robbie had put into its creation. Louisa was visibly impressed by what Amelia had achieved even during the past year.

'But what is that over there?' she wondered, when they had come to a pause. She pointed at the top of a hedge she could see beyond the high mound with the long set of stone steps. 'I do not remember seeing that particular part of the garden before, Amelia. In fact I imagine that is the only place we have not been.'

'That's because there's nothing really to see there, Louisa,' Amelia replied hastily. 'It's a corner we haven't really had the time to do anything with.'

'The hedge is well cultivated none the less.'

'Jethro likes to keep everything trim and neat.'

'All except for the areas round the lake,' Constance chimed in. 'He would appear to have lost the battle there.'

'We were hoping to do something with the lake – and in fact George even roped in some expert or other to come and give us his opinion. George thought it might need dredging because the water was so dark, but it appears the reason for that is because the lake is so deep. So until we can afford to attend to it properly, if we ever can, we've had it fenced off and declared as No Man's Land.'

'Very sensible too,' Lady Dashwood concurred, 'with two young children. However, I would still like to see over there, Amelia, if I may.'

'There really is nothing to see,' Amelia called after her mother-in-law, who was already opening the heavy iron gate and making her way towards the steps in the mound.

'That isn't the reason you don't want her to go there, Amelia,' her mother laughed behind her. 'I can see from the look on your face.'

'Can you?' Amelia said. 'Well you're wrong. The true reason I don't want her to get in is that it is so boring. There's nothing *to* see.'

'Get in?' Constance echoed. 'You mean it's some sort of enclosed garden?'

'It's nothing, Mama,' Amelia replied, hurrying on up the stone steps. 'It's just a piece of grass enclosed by hedges, just nothing.'

'Magnificent!' Louisa Dashwood called as she reached the hedge and began to inspect it. 'And frightfully ancient too, I should imagine!'

'That's what we too thought,' Amelia agreed, hurrying on to where her mother-in-law stood. 'But that's all it is at the moment. We really haven't time to do anything to it.'

'Perhaps if I can take a look inside I may have an idea. I may be able to come up with something.'

'You won't be able to get in,' Amelia warned as Louisa began to look for an entrance.

'It's all right, my dear. I have found the entrance here – neat and trim as can be!'

By the time Amelia and Constance had arrived at the corner of the garden Louisa had disappeared.

'I think I shall take a look inside, too,' Constance said, peering in through the gap in the hedge. 'It looks absolutely charming.'

'I'd rather you didn't,' Amelia said, without quite knowing why. After all, it was nothing more than a somewhat neglected patch of wild garden laid out between a rectangle of yew hedging. It contained absolutely nothing that Amelia would wish to hide – nothing visible, at least. Yet even so, and inexplicably, Amelia feared the intrusion of strangers within its boundaries.

'What is it, darling?' her mother wondered, hesitating in the entrance. 'Something's the matter?'

But before Amelia could begin to find an excuse for her reluctance both of them were stopped in their tracks by the sound of someone crying.

'Louisa?' Constance said in concern. 'What on earth . . .'

Amelia hurried after her mother, who was making her way as quickly as she could to Louisa Dashwood's side.

'Louisa?' Constance called once more. 'Whatever is the matter?'

Seeing the older woman within the enclosure Amelia knew that her feelings had been right. She should never have let her into the Kissing Garden. She would spoil everything, take away the magic that Amelia was quite sure was there.

'Are you all right, my dear?'

'I am absolutely fine, Connie dear,' Louisa assured her, turning her face so that over the handkerchief she was holding to her mouth both Constance and Amelia could see the transparent look of happiness in her eyes. 'Most assuredly I am.'

'Then whatever is the matter, Louisa?'

'Just look, Connie. Just *look* – have you ever seen such a beautiful place?'

Amelia watched as her mother looked around her in astonishment, seeing only what Amelia saw: the rectangle of grass and the four tall and somewhat austere yew hedges. There was nothing else to catch the eye, nothing to make the spirit dance.

'If you don't mind, Mama,' Amelia said, taking her mother to one side. 'If I could just have a moment or two with Louisa alone.'

'Very well, dear. But if you want me I shan't be very far away. I shall wait at the top of the steps.'

'Of course.'

After her mother had left the little garden, Amelia took hold of her mother-in-law's arm. For once Lady Dashwood seemed to take no notice.

'What is it?' Amelia wondered quietly. 'What is it you can see exactly?'

'Oh, Amelia dear,' Louisa whispered back, surprising Amelia by the sudden apparent affection. 'This surely is the most beautiful place I have ever been?'

'But there's nothing here—'

'Why did you not want me come to this place, Amelia? It is a place of such peace as well as beauty, dear child.'

'I – I was afraid you might be disappointed, Louisa,' Amelia said quietly, seeing the look on Louisa's face. 'So often when one talks about a place that is special to one, a special place, people are disappointed when they actually see it.'

'You could never exaggerate the beauty of this place, Amelia dear,' Louisa assured her, taking her daughter-in-law by the hand for the first time ever. 'Least of all you, the most modest of people. You know, dear child, I have seen some very beautiful sights, and been to some truly remarkable places. When for the first time I stood in front of the Taj Mahal as dawn broke, I actually thought I might die from joy. And the first time Michael and I climbed a mountain in Scotland one summer's day and seemed to be standing on the very roof of the world – well, words can't describe the feeling. Yet this place . . .' Louisa stopped and sighed a sigh of such pure bliss that Amelia herself felt she might weep. 'Darling girl, this is the most beautiful place of them all.'

'Would you rather I left you alone?'

'Yes, I think I would like that.'

That evening when Amelia went looking for George before dinner she failed to find him. She had gathered from Clara that the men had returned from hunting well before dark, and she could see from the state of George's dressing room that he had already bathed and changed out of his hunting clothes.

Wanting to talk to him about the events of her own afternoon she pursued her search, trying his study in case he had suddenly got lost in a book as was often his habit nowadays, and then the stables in case he had returned with a lame horse and was checking on the welfare of the animal. Thinking he might be with his mother, she asked after both of them, but it emerged that no-one had seen his mother either, not since she had returned by herself from the Kissing Garden to disappear upstairs to her room.

Giving up, Amelia went and soaked in a long hot bath before getting ready for the last dinner the families would take together that Christmas, both sets of parents being due to go their separate ways the next morning. Mrs Hiscock and Amelia had designed and prepared a special feast for the evening, and given the good mood which everyone seemed to be in for once Amelia found herself looking forward to the gathering without any reservation – until emerging from the bathroom she found George in their bedroom lying flat on his back on the bed staring silently up at the ceiling.

'George?' she said, coming over to him.

'Hm. Hm hm hm.'

'Don't start that business, George,' Amelia warned him, selecting a silver evening gown from her wardrobe. 'And you'd better get into your dinner jacket because you're going to be late down otherwise.'

'What's been going on, Amelia?' George wondered, still lying flat on his back. 'I don't know what you said to my mother, I don't know what you've done to her, but she is quite herself again. In fact more so.'

'How do you mean?' Amelia wondered, although suspecting she might already know the answer. 'I haven't said or done anything to your mother.'

'You must have done something. She thinks the sun shines out of your two lovely big eyes.'

'Meaning she hasn't always,' Amelia said with a smile, sitting on the bed beside him. 'You look a little bemused. What exactly happened?'

'I'm not sure,' George replied, turning on one side to look at her. 'I mean I think something must have happened because I've never known her like it. Not recently. Not for a very long time, in fact. Before I joined the army, really. Look – you know my mama. Never use two words when one will do the trick, that's her motto. I have never known her so talkative. This afternoon when Papa and I got back from hunting – and a rotten day was had by all, you'll be delighted to hear—'

'Good,' Amelia teased back. 'I hope Charlie gave you a good run for your money, you all got lost and he got home safely to his family.'

'More or less the whole day summed up pretty neatly. Anyway – once we were home and bathed and all, Mama summons me to her room. Thinking I'm in more trouble – that some high-up friend of hers or other has taken real umbrage at my latest book – in I go, only to find her in the most benevolent mood I can recall. We talked for hours – for what seemed like hours – and she did most of the talking. But it wasn't just the fact that we talked. It was what we talked about. What she said. You won't believe this, but do you know what she said, Amelia? She said she was truly sorry – her exact words – that she was truly sorry for her lack of understanding and compassion. I didn't quite know what she was referring to, so I sidestepped a bit. Said she had no need to be sorry for anything, et cetera – that she was the best mother anyone could have – but she wasn't having any of that. She gave a laugh, made me sit in the chair in the window and told me to keep quiet until she had finished. For a moment – for quite a few moments actually – I thought she had been drinking.'

'I can hardly imagine your mother getting even the slightest bit tipsy.'

'If you'd heard what she had to say, the thought would certainly have crossed *your* mind, too.'

'She was with me in the garden until teatime. And you were back from hunting at what? Only half an hour after I was back in the house, so I heard.'

'Of course she hadn't been drinking.' George sat up and shook his head. 'I was joking. It was just – well. She was in a sort of way intoxicated. That's the only way I can describe it. I can't actually remember seeing her in such a – in such a *euphoric* state. Even though the content of what she had to say was serious. She was smiling the entire time, as if she was happy to talk about it at last. To get it off her chest. That's why I asked you what you might have said or done with her?'

'As I said, George, *nothing*, really. Go on. I'm riveted, fascinated in fact.'

'She said she had been completely selfish in the attitude she had taken about me and the direction in which I wanted my life to go. That what she'd been thinking of was not me and you and whatever family we might have and our future together, nor what I'd experienced as a soldier, but

354

simply what people might think and say about her and Papa. As well as about that indefinable and completely ridiculous thing called family history – her words, not mine – a history which she then announced had no proper merit, not in real terms, not in the actual world of the living. You don't seem very surprised, Amelia.'

'A woman of your mother's intelligence and character couldn't seriously live out the rest of her life at loggerheads with her only son. With the son she so obviously loves.'

'She could have done, Amelia. My mother is a stubborn woman. When she sets her mind against something, or someone, I can't remember her ever changing it.'

'Go on. Because I know you have more to say.'

'I know how difficult love is – not between us, I don't mean that. I mean that sometimes we simply take it for granted, particularly in families. We don't feel it's necessary to express our emotions to each other, especially if we're British.' George smiled at her. 'She's never been one to express her emotions. Sometimes as you well know it's as much as you can do to get a smile out of her. But then that's the way she was brought up. To think that a show of emotion equalled a sign of weakness. That sentiment was sentimentality and that love was something unspoken. Above all the honour of one's family was paramount. My father really loves my mother and I know that she worships him. Yet I'm sure they have never said as much to each other – at least not until now. But now, my mother is full of – full of the fact that she loves us all. I was quite overcome, I am afraid.'

'Of course you were, my darling.' Amelia leaned over to kiss George's cheek. 'And you have every right to feel the way you did.'

'It wasn't just that – although that would have been quite enough. She also said she was proud of me. Not for my war record. Not for what I was as a soldier, not for my VC . . . you won't believe this.'

'Well?'

'What she is really proud of is the stand I've taken since the armistice. She said she had been terrified for the whole war. Expecting to get a letter or a telegram any moment saying that I'd been killed. How she prayed this might not be so, and how she thought her heart would burst with happiness when she saw me finally get off the train at Midhurst. But because of her upbringing she couldn't show it, much as she wanted to. It was the same when I resigned my commission and wrote my book. She said she wanted nothing more than to talk to me about it, but because of her friends' reaction she thought there was something improper about it. Funnily enough it wasn't that she thought my father would disapprove. It was more she thought I might have caused harm to myself. And to us. Truth is, she found herself in an awful muddle and couldn't make any sense of it. She had no-one to talk to about it, either.'

'She could have talked to my mother. My mother would have listened and understood.'

'She thought your mother thought her stuck up and starchy.'

'No, she's always felt most affectionate—'

But George interrupted her. It seemed that he could not stop talking.

'Oh, Amelia, we're all so afraid of being made to appear in the wrong that we say things we think we should say, instead of the things that we really feel. And then we all pass away, leaving the things we meant to say still unsaid, and the people we leave behind are never any the wiser.'

'Your mother is right to be proud of you, George, because you have had the courage to stand up and be counted for your beliefs. You've been rebuffed, insulted, and vilified, and by people who really should know better, yet you have always stood your ground.'

'I think I may have to stand my ground again. Don't ask me why – I just have this feeling.'

'Well, if you do, darling, I shall be here by your side. I won't waver, I promise you.'

'I know you won't, and I love you for it.' George leaned over to kiss her. When he had done so, he smiled at her the way she loved him best to smile, then stood up and smiled at her again. 'I still think it was something you said. Or something you did.'

'No, I promise,' Amelia replied, getting to her feet and putting her arms round him. 'It wasn't anything I said, or anything I did.'

'You're saying that as though it was someone else's doing.'

'Not someone's, George. Some*thing's*.'

'Something's?' George pulled a bewildered face and shook his head. 'How come?'

'This place. That is what *did* it!'

It was the best party of the whole Christmas celebration. Peter and Gwendolyn were allowed to stay up until it was time to go in to dinner, at which point Peter went round to say good night to each of his grandparents individually while George carried Gwendolyn round on his shoulders for the same purpose.

To everyone's astonishment, which they kept concealed, the longest good night came from George's mother who seemed reluctant to let either of her grandchildren out of her arms.

'Next Christmas Michael and I would like nothing more than for you all to come and spend the holiday with us,' Louisa announced as the meal drew to its conclusion. 'We have had such a very happy time here with you both.'

'Hear hear,' said the general.

In the drawing room, to round the party off, Amelia sat at the piano and everyone sang a selection of the latest songs, including 'Button Up Your Overcoat', 'You're the Cream in My Coffee', 'Tiptoe Through The Tulips' and 'Singing in the Rain', ending up with 'Blue Skies' which to everyone's delight and astonishment Louisa sang as a solo in really rather a beautiful soprano.

When George put Amelia's Jack Russell terrier Tipsy and Burt, his Irish water spaniel, out for their last walk of the day, he noticed that the unseasonably mild spell of weather had changed dramatically. There was a bitter east wind which, judging from its rawness, must have swept in straight from the Urals. In fact it was so cold that before he and Amelia undressed for bed George lit the fire in their grate and fed it logs until the unlit room glowed with the dark red warmth of the burning wood. Once the fire was burning brightly, they buried themselves under a mountain of bedclothes to make love while outside the countryside silently disappeared beneath a mantle of deep snow, a fall which covered every foot of the countryside around them and every single inch of exposed ground – all except the strangely perfect grass in the Kissing Garden, which once again remained like a patch of green carpet in an otherwise totally white landscape.

But when dawn broke and a weak sun rose on the blanketed countryside, the household learned the tragic news that Michael Dashwood had awoken to discover that during the night his beloved wife Louisa had passed peacefully away in her sleep.

Seventeen

Later Amelia would mark the death of George's mother as the turning point in their lives, but in fact the seeds which brought about the apparent change in George's mentality had been sowed well before. Even so, the sudden loss of Louisa Dashwood had a profound effect on her only son; so great in fact that for a long time afterwards Amelia was concerned that George might well regress to a state similar to the one in which he had been when he had first returned from the war.

At times he would sit and talk to Amelia for hours, able it seemed to express his inner fears and doubts, while at others he would remain completely incommunicative, disappearing off on long walks or rides whenever Amelia – sensing that he was about to be engulfed by another depression – asked him if he was feeling all right.

She soon discovered that the best approach was to carry on as if nothing had happened, helping to look after the children and run the household, knowing that if and when George needed to turn to her he could do so, for the simple reason that she was always there.

'Do you ever think of death, Amelia?' he asked

her one night. 'Of course you do – let me put it another way. Does it frighten you?'

'I wouldn't be human if I wasn't frightened by it, George,' Amelia replied. 'My father says that we're only afraid of it because it's the one experience which we don't actually go *through*. But to tell the truth I've never found that much help, actually. What we have to think is – if we lived for ever, would we appreciate life? I don't think so.'

'What about an afterlife? I know we've talked about this before, but do you really believe there is one?'

'I know I shouldn't, but I do. My father on the other hand is firmly of the opinion that this life is reward enough. He says if you have a good and happy life why should you need heaven? According to him Paradise should be reserved for those who have a really bad time of it here on earth.'

'I wouldn't know where that put Mama.'

'I'm sure your mother went straight to heaven.'

'Because she had such a terrible time of it here on earth?' George widened his eyes disbelievingly at Amelia before lighting a cigarette and staring into the fire.

'I didn't say that was what *I* believed, George,' Amelia corrected him, picking up her embroidery. 'What I meant was that if there is a heaven then I'm quite sure your mother went there straight away.'

'Suppose she hadn't talked to me the way she had that night,' George wondered. 'The night that she died.'

'She did, and that is all that matters.'

'Yes, that's true. But I wonder *why* she did. Don't you ever wonder why she did? I certainly do. It was as if she had a premonition.'

'No, George, I don't think so.' Amelia glanced up at him over the frame she was holding on her knee, but George was still staring into the blaze of the fire. 'I don't think she had a premonition at all. She was altogether too happy that afternoon, and that evening, remember? You said yourself you had never seen her in such high spirits. The way she behaved that night – laughing and singing – that wasn't the way of someone who had just had an intimation of their mortality. At least, I wouldn't say it was.'

'So what would you say it was?' George challenged her, now looking up from the fire and holding her gaze.

Amelia hesitated before telling him about the visit to the Kissing Garden. It was as if by telling George she might be somehow betraying Louisa. And, too, she hesitated because to discuss magic, or what she thought might be magic, might be to erode it in some way. They had never discussed what had first happened in the Kissing Garden. It had been a sort of secret compact, not to talk about it, in case it went away, or became debased in some way. But now, seeing how grief had taken so much of George's vitality from him, she finally gave in, and told him how his mother had insisted on going into the garden, and how she had told

Amelia that it was the most beautiful place she had ever been, and how as from that moment she had been like Pilgrim when he had been through the Slough of Despond and his burden had fallen from his shoulders.

George was silent for a long time after Amelia had finished, silent for as long as it took him to smoke a fresh cigarette. When it had gone he stood up and, after staring down into the fire a while longer, left the room without saying another word.

Since he had not even looked at her once she had ended her account, Amelia thought she had upset him and that possibly he was even angry with her, but much as she was tempted to go after him when she heard the front door bang she remained where she was, sitting doing her embroidery by the fire, until George returned some two hours later.

'Why didn't you tell me?' he demanded, as he poured himself a large whisky. 'Why didn't you say anything about this nearer the time? Why wait for so many weeks to pass?'

'For two reasons, George,' Amelia replied. 'And I'd quite like a whisky as well, if you don't mind.' After she had taken a restorative sip of her drink, she went on, 'I didn't say anything to you because I thought you might think I was being fey, and if you did, then that would minimize the importance of the conversation you had with your mother later that afternoon.'

'How so?'

'If you thought I believed that the Kissing Garden had anything to do with what happened between you and your mother, you could well have thought it contrived. Or you might even have believed that she had been – well, let's say for the sake of it that she'd been *bewitched*. Which would mean you might think that what she said to you was as a result of something other than her true emotions. As if – well, she had been intoxicated.'

George interrupted angrily. 'For God's sake, woman – talk sense, will you!'

'I am talking sense,' Amelia outwardly calm. 'And please don't address me as *woman*, if you don't mind. It makes me feel like your servant.'

'I didn't mean it like that. I'm sorry. As you were saying—'

'George – after all that's happened we have to accept there is something extraordinary about this place. And if it isn't a matter of spirits or you can't embrace such a notion, then let's just call it *enchantment*, shall we? There are plenty of places which are haunted by their past – affected, if you prefer – and this may well be one of them. But that isn't the point. The point is that whatever your mother saw or experienced in the Kissing Garden, it wasn't what she saw—'

'Or didn't see,' George interposed gruffly.

'It was what she *felt*, George. Standing there in that little garden she came to a different understanding of things. She saw what she thought she had done wrong, how she thought she might have failed – and she wanted to make amends. Why it happened we don't know, and we'll never know, nor does it matter. Maybe why she thought the little garden was the most beautiful place she had ever been was because she suddenly came to this understanding, and when she did she felt so different she thought she was in paradise – who knows? Nothing strange happened there, nothing odd. There wasn't any manifestation, or spooky sights, or ghostly sighs and whispers. It was just a realization. Your mother suddenly realized, just as anyone her age might suddenly realize – anyone her age and with her terrific character, that is – she suddenly realized that she must put things right with you, with the son she loved so much. Before it was too late. The fact that it happened in the Kissing Garden – well, who knows? Coincidence, possibly. Remember, George, this is a very ancient place, a place once occupied by monks who spent an enormous amount of their time in contemplation, so the Kissing Garden might well have been one of those areas especially set aside for their private devotions.'

'What you're saying – no, I don't understand what you're saying.'

'Yes you do, George. What I'm saying is that even if something did inspire your mother to think the way she did, they were her thoughts and hers alone. What your mother said to you wasn't because she had any sort of intimation, but because she suddenly saw the truth. She suddenly realized she had to say those things to you because she wanted to. Because she loved you.'

Amelia had little idea whether her outburst had helped George or not, because although he gave it long consideration he said nothing in return. Not that she had been expecting miracles. Whatever else may have happened to them since they met, and particularly since they found and moved to The Priory, she knew that one thing was constant in their existence and that was her husband's character. George thought about things for an age. He brooded on them, turned them over and over in his mind, argued with both himself and Amelia, then wrestled some more before coming to any conclusion, so whatever effect her words might have had on him Amelia knew that she would have to wait some time before learning the results. That was how George was. That was his character.

Or so she thought.

So while he grieved and tried to come to terms with the change in his life brought about by the sudden death of his mother, Amelia retreated into the shadows and left him alone with his anguish. She did not withdraw an ounce of the love she felt for him; that would have been impossible. She had loved George all her life, and now she was married to him and the mother of his children she loved him more than she dared to contemplate. He was her whole life, but nevertheless she took care not to smother him.

But then, as quickly as George's moodiness and heavy drinking had started, it stopped, and he began work on a new book, which immediately preoccupied his every hour, for once he started on a new book he made sure not just to write, but to walk or ride for several hours a day.

Amelia herself had become a passable horse-woman by now, thanks not only to George's tuition but also to his generosity. No sooner could she sit to a canter than he bought her a good-natured bay gelding who went by the name of Max, and, with George comfortably mounted on Beau, they could ride together across the Wiltshire Downs and through the forests surrounding the Longleat estate.

Other than her gardening there was no pursuit Amelia enjoyed more, although she soon discovered that riding out daily with George required not just skill but endurance. Happily Max was able to keep up with Beau, which was more than Amelia could with George when they went walking. Amelia liked to stroll and saunter, examining the flora and fauna as she went, while George preferred to stride through the country-side at a steady and very demanding pace, stopping every now and then only very briefly to admire a view before exhorting his less robust companion onwards. Consequently when George was *cooking a book*, as he called it, and invited Amelia to go for a walk with him, more often than not Amelia declined, preferring to garden and leaving George to stride round the countryside on his own.

So it was that at the start of what was to prove a long hot summer George at last pulled himself out of his despair and exercised himself back to fitness, while Amelia went on working diligently in her garden, which was becoming almost as famous as her husband's works of fiction.

And in the soft and temperate Somerset air their two children thrived as well as, if not better than, their mother's plants. Gwendolyn in particular was growing as tall as her mother had predicted she would, well on her way, it seemed, to becoming a slender, beautiful, but most importantly healthy young woman. Peter meanwhile was enjoying his spell at a preparatory school run from a fine old house outside Shaftesbury. He was driven there daily by Amelia, who, living deep in the Somerset countryside, had learned to drive from sheer necessity.

From his mother's small legacy to him George had bought Amelia an Austin 7 to which she was now devoted, a miraculous little car which had never let her down. In contrast to George's Bentley tourer – purchased from the proceeds of what they had both nicknamed his 'traitor's novel' – with which, it seemed to Amelia, he was forever tinkering. Amelia had become a familiar sight at Peter's school, arriving to watch cricket matches in her little burgundy-coloured open-topped car, straw hat tied under her chin with a coloured scarf to prevent the wind from stealing it, picnic basket safe on the back seat packed with teatime treats for her son and his friends.

Sometimes George would insist on accompanying Amelia, often using the excuse of having to see his son's progress on the rugby pitch as a reason for escaping the horrors of creation. In this case they would arrive in the Bentley, which by now had been upgraded to the superb four and a half litre open model. It was the car which attracted the boys' attention when they arrived in the tourer, not the driver, whereas when Amelia arrived in her little Austin 7 the opposite was the case.

While his school friends nurtured romantic fantasies about his mother, Peter's passion for aeroplanes continued to grow. His school books were covered in drawings of not only the latest aircraft models but also those he had designed himself, sleek futuristic monoplanes with guns mounted under their wings; or vast passenger airliners which would be capable of flying round the world non-stop. And most adventurous of all, a plane without any propeller at all, powered instead by a rocket. He had learned to fly, too – in his head.

As luck would have it his mathematics master, Percy Framlingham, had served with distinction in the Royal Flying Corps in the Great War. And so it was not too long before Peter discovered that Mr Framlingham had, in his spare time, gone as far as building a mock-up of his Sopwith Tiger's cockpit, with a working joystick controlling invisible ailerons, elevators and rudders.

It was in this rudimentary classroom that Peter learned the principles of flight.

'Take one morning, Dashwood, that's all, one morning and you'll have your wings. You're a natural, d'you see? A natural pilot, there are such things, d'you see? Like yachtsmen, or jockeys, what have you. Just that we're a bit unrecognized, as yet.'

The sports-coated teacher with his ruddy complexion, although much older than his pupil, was in fact a twin soul for Peter. It was just one of those things. They both knew it. The only trouble was Mr Framlingham was not Peter's father – George was.

Approached by the teacher to allow his son to take to the skies, George argued that Peter was only ten years old and far too young to be taken up in a plane. This argument was soon demolished since both Mr Framlingham and Peter reasoned that if a boy was allowed to ride a horse, which was a wild animal and less controllable than a plane, or taken daily to school by motor car, there was no logical reason for not allowing him to fly. It was no more dangerous.

Amelia was horrified, but her resistance only encouraged Peter. 'Flying is the newest mode of transport – you just have to get used to it. Granny Dennison told me that Grandpa used to have a fit before the war when you started going about in motor cars.'

'That was different!' But Amelia already knew that she was on a sticky wicket, and so she carefully avoided both George's and Peter's eyes. 'I don't want you flying, Peter, and that is that.'

But Peter persisted, as she knew he would, leaving it one day and returning to the argument the next. If she let him ride, or go in a motor car, what was the difference? Finally, as they all knew she would, one morning Amelia walked off into the garden, secateurs at the ready, and dread in her heart, having at last given in to cold logic.

It was a bright afternoon in the summer holidays, cloudless, perfect flying weather, when George drove the buoyant Peter and Mr Framlingham to an airfield south of Bristol to meet a famous flying ace who, because he was a friend of Framlingham's, was, it seemed, willing to take the boy up in his private biplane.

'Known Beaufort all my life. Splendid chap, you know,' Framlingham enthused. 'You can trust him with your boy, Captain Dashwood, believe me.'

As it turned out Beaufort was a raffish blond-haired chain-smoker who thrust out a yellow-fingered hand to greet his pupil, and after a short lecture on safety had him up in the air before George had time to collect his thoughts.

Beaufort flew a bright yellow biplane with his

name and logo painted on the fuselage in brilliant red and he flew it with rare skill, climbing, wheeling, diving and finally looping the loop, a stunt which George had seen many times but now – given the passenger in the biplane was his son – made him turn away and close his eyes.

'May I sit the lad up front with me, Captain Dashwood?' Beaufort enquired when father and son were joyfully reunited, Peter speechless with excitement and George silent from shock. 'He seems to know a heck of a lot about this game so I said I'd let him have a go at the old stick. If it's all the same with you?'

'I don't think his mother would allow—'

'Please, Daddy?' Peter begged, before George had time to finish. 'Mr Beaufort is the most terrific flyer.'

'So I see. Even so, I don't think your mother—'

'Oh, thanks, Daddy! Really! I'll do anything you say! Promise!'

Before George could insist that he stay on the ground with him, before he could form his firmest refusal, Peter had gone, running after Beaufort, zipping up his thick borrowed jacket.

'No fancy stuff this time please, Mr Beaufort,' George called after them, trying not to think of Amelia's face, of what she would say, if she was there. 'No loops and no nosedives,' he finished, feebly.

'Righto!'

The last was said in farewell, and the flyer was

gone before George could admonish him. He was about to go after him when Framlingham put a hand on his arm.

'He'll be fine, Captain Dashwood! Believe me. This chap shot down eight Germans, had a scrap with the Baron and lived to tell the tale.'

'Be that as it may,' George said, through tightened lips, 'but not with my son beside him!'

This time George watched with a hand over his eyes as the bright yellow aircraft climbed into a clear blue sky before circling steadily round the airfield. It did half a dozen laps all told before descending in a perfect approach to make an equally faultless landing.

'Not bad for a rabbit,' Beaufort said with a grin as he ruffled his co-pilot's blond hair, while the father of the said co-pilot felt the blood returning to his face for the first time in half an hour. 'We'll have him flying solo in a week. Less, even.'

'Dad?' Peter looked beseechingly at his father, his secret wish being to leave school that moment and devote his life to flying.

'That's enough for one day, I reckon,' George said, quickly shaking Beaufort's hand and hoping the wretched man would not think of yet another thing that would scare George witless. 'By the by, did you let Peter have a go at all?'

Beaufort smiled at his pupil in a secretive way, as much as to say should he let on, while Peter merely shrugged his shoulders and grinned.

'Apart from take-off I didn't do a thing,'

Beaufort confessed, looking momentarily embarrassed. 'Just shouted him through it, that's all.'

George stopped in his tracks and stared back at the ace in disbelieving silence. 'But you were in control just the same?' he heard himself begging.

'I didn't need to be, Captain Dashwood. Your boy can fly that plane as well as I could after two weeks' intensive training.'

After that nothing more was said about the venture, apart from a brief and much censored account given to Amelia on their return home. It was as if father and son had come to a silent agreement, since both Peter and his father knew that once that little yellow biplane had ascended like a bright and gorgeous butterfly into the clear blue English skies the die had been cast.

Peter was of course overjoyed that the ambition he had been nursing for as long as he could remember was not going to be an idle dream. As soon as he finally left school he now knew he would join the air force. On the other hand his father, although proud of his son's precocious skill, and admiring of the boy's courage, remembered what he had seen of the remains of those who had been shot down in flames by the enemy during the war and feared for him.

George tried to make as little of the matter as possible, doing his best to convince Amelia that Peter's flying was nothing more than a boyhood obsession, and that by the time he started his new school some craze would take the place of aeroplanes, and they would find themselves worrying about something entirely different.

'That's children, darling,' he said after dinner as they sat discussing the matter in the drawing room, watching what had been a clear summer sky slowly becoming overcast and ominous. 'That's children, and boys in particular.'

'I think that's my trouble. I've never been a boy.' Amelia shook her head and smiled, while the look in her eyes stayed worried.

'I wanted to be a train driver, just like every other little boy,' George remembered. 'That was all I wanted to be for practically all my childhood.'

'I don't remember that. I don't remember that at all.'

'It was my guilty secret. I kept it well hidden from you. I thought if you knew I wanted to be an engine driver you would never even contemplate marrying me.'

'Are you trying to tell me, George Dashwood, that you were thinking of matrimony while you were still in short trousers?'

'I'm afraid so,' George sighed, relieved to see that he had distracted her. 'I told you, after I met you at that cricket match I started drawing up a list of the friends I wanted at my wedding.'

'I didn't want to marry you at all,' Amelia returned, still watching a sky that was becoming more threatening by the minute. 'I wanted to run away with you and live with you in sin. I remember one day when we were sailing at Itchenor, I just wanted you to put the boat out into the Channel and sail us over to France where we'd take to the roads, living on our wits and talents.'

'What particular talents were these, Mrs Dashwood?'

'My musical ones – I would sing by the wayside and in cafés and taverns—'

'The French don't have taverns,' George laughed. 'And what was I going to be doing?'

'You were going to be fighting. Not as a soldier, but as a prize fighter. Taking on all comers in illegal boxing matches held in the back rooms of whatever the French have if they don't have taverns.'

'You should have said. It sounds a splendid idea. How old were we at the time?'

'Let me see.' Amelia frowned, pulling an over-studious face. 'I was ten, I think. So you'd have been a pompous fourteen.'

George roared with laughter and took her in his arms to hug her. As he did the first roll of thunder rumbled from not so distant clouds.

'What can you have you been reading?' he said. '*The Beloved Vagabond*, no doubt. You were forever reading that book.'

'Yes, I probably was,' Amelia agreed. 'Fancy you remembering that.'

'You hardly ever had it out of your hand at

about that time. Your head was always full of these wonderful romances.'

'You're my best. You know that, don't you?'

'And you are mine. Now come on – let's go to bed early and watch what promises to be a rather spectacular storm break.'

By the time they had hurried upstairs the evening sky, which had now turned ink-black, burst into a tumult of rain while a clap of thunder directly overhead seemed to shake the ancient priory from the roof to the cellars.

'This is going to be a spectacular display.' George walked quickly between the bedroom windows shutting out the rain that was just beginning to drive towards the house.

Amelia watched as the lights started to flicker. 'Storms really frighten me.'

'I know. Remember the famous storm on the Downs?'

'When you held my hand properly for the very first time.'

George turned back momentarily from the window, smiling at the memory, while a brilliant fork of lightning sizzled out of the storm clouds. 'Do you know, when I held your hand that day, I'd never known such a thrill of excitement.'

'Just from holding my hand?'

George nodded as another fork of lightning danced across the landscape. 'Just from holding your hand.'

As another bolt of thunder crashed just above

them, Amelia tried to pull George away from the window. But he stayed transfixed by the way the countryside outside was being lit up by the lightning.

'Doesn't it worry you?' she asked anxiously, clinging tightly to his arm. 'It must be just like the war, surely? I don't know how you can stand it.'

'It's not remotely like the war. This isn't man-made. There's no-one being deliberately killed or blown to pieces for the sake of a few feet of mud. This is nature at her most magnificent, and that's why I can watch it.'

'Well I can't, so I'm going to go to bed and hide under the covers.'

'You do that. But I want to watch this.'

Amelia undressed, climbed into bed, and hid her head under her pillows, while George stood at the window and watched the worst storm suffered by the West Country since the turn of the century.

It was in the absolute calm which followed it that Amelia found herself dreaming a nightmare which would haunt her for years.

378

Eighteen

'Peter!'

She woke up shouting his name, sitting up in bed drenched in the sweat of a nightmare. She was gone from the bed before George was sufficiently awake to find out what was the matter, gone down the corridor to their son's room, pulling the girdle of her gown around her, pushing the damp hair away from her eyes.

'Peter!' she called again. *'Peter!'*

George was only half a second behind her. 'What is it?' he asked as he found her by the boy's bed. 'Whatever is the matter?'

'I don't know,' she whispered, shivering with the chill of her perspiration. 'I must have been dreaming.'

'What? What were you dreaming?'

'It was Peter. It was Peter, George.' She whispered, half to herself. *'It was Peter – and he was dead.'*

George leaned down and gently shook their son awake. Peter stirred, but did not wake up fully, looking up at his parents with only one eye, not knowing who they were or where he was.

'He seems fine.'

'I must have been dreaming. But it was so – real.'

She crept back to their own room, followed by George. He took her in his arms. 'Want to talk about it?'

'It was Peter. He was a young man – I don't know. Eighteen, nineteen. But he was a young man, not a boy any more, and he was sitting in this deckchair somewhere, I think it was summer. Yes, it was summer, and he was sitting in a field, and in the middle of this field there was a long straight road. The sky was clear blue. There weren't any clouds at all, just blue. Miles and miles of blue that seemed to go on for ever. And there were all these other young men the same age, all lying on the grass sleeping, or sitting in deckchairs reading magazines and smoking cigarettes, and Peter had on a sort of short leather jacket, I've never seen one like it, but I saw this one very clearly because he showed it to me. He said, "Do you like my jacket, Mummy?" And he zipped it up the front and laughed. Then I noticed something hanging on the back of his deckchair which looked like a knapsack. I said something like "Is that your lunch?" and he shook his head and said, "No – silk. It's silk." I saw all the other young men had them and as I looked they all smiled and said together, "Don't worry, it's silk, Mrs Dashwood." And then everyone began to laugh and smile and I suddenly realized I was wearing the silk dress I had made to go on honeymoon with you. But the young men weren't laughing at me, even though I was dancing by myself. They were laughing at something in the sky above them, something they were all pointing to.'

'What? Did you see what they were pointing to?'

'No. But I heard this alarm ringing – a sort of klaxon – like a very loud donkey braying, and when I looked again all the young men were running towards this road. Peter was leading them, running backwards and waving to me. He called to me but I couldn't hear what he said, so I tried to run after him but the heels on my shoes broke. "Mummy! Mummy! Tell Daddy it's all right – I won't need Mr Framlingham!" Then everyone laughed, and they started to pull on these sort of helmets.'

'Helmets – what? Flying helmets?'

'Yes – perhaps that is what they were – because they had flaps over their ears – and then I could see the planes. The planes were all coming towards them down this road and the young men stopped them by holding the tips of their wings so they could swing themselves up into the cockpits.'

'What sort of planes were they? Were they biplanes, or what?'

'I don't know what sort of planes they were, George! I have no idea about planes! All I know is they were planes I've never seen before! Single-winged with these big markings on them and cockpits that pulled over the pilots' heads. The next minute they were in the sky while I was stumbling about this long road in my broken-heeled

381

shoes which I couldn't get off. Then another plane came past, a yellow biplane, and you were flying it and I was in the front seat and I could see Peter quite clearly. He is in another plane beside me, us, talking into something round his face, pointing to something up in the sky beyond. I can see what he's pointing at – enemy planes, and they are vast. Much, much bigger than these tiny little things all the young men are flying – and they make this terrible noise. I block my ears and Peter laughs. I can hear him saying, "You always block your ears! When you don't want to hear me!" Then suddenly his plane is on fire—'

Amelia stopped.

'It's all right. It was only a dream, darling. Just a dream.'

'I know it wasn't a dream, George,' she asserted sadly, as they breakfasted alone out on a terrace bathed in warm sunshine. 'It was a vision.'

'I don't see how you can *know* that.'

'It's hard to explain, except to say you know when things are a dream. There's a sort of feel to them, and also a sort of lack of sense, and cohesion. This just wasn't like that. But I can't explain why. It's just what I felt. No – no, it's what I *knew*. I knew as I was dreaming it that this was a vision of the future. This is what is going to happen.'

George drank some coffee and stared up at a perfect cloudless summer sky. Around them the lawns and flower beds steamed a soft mist as the sun began to dry them, while in the distance could be heard the waters of the swollen river in what had to be full spate.

'If, at some point,' George said, refilling his now empty cup, 'Peter *does* want to join the RAF, if when he grows up he finds he still wants to fly, you know I'm not going to be able to stop him.'

'You can stop him doing anything until he is twenty-one.'

'Let me put it another way. If that's what Peter still wants to do when he leaves school, I don't think I should stop him. Do you?'

'Yes, George. Yes I do.'

'But that's not really the point, is it?' George asked her gently. 'The point is what happens if there's a war.'

'Is there going to be a war, George? I thought what you all fought and died for – I thought that was the war to end *all* wars.'

'I don't know if there's going to be a war. No, that's a lie. Of course there'll be another war. Man can't stop fighting wars, but if you mean is there going to be another war *soon*, I don't know. All I can say is that there shouldn't be.'

'There shouldn't be, George? How do you mean?'

'I mean if there is another war it will be through bad government. Mismanagement. We won the last war and Germany lost it. If she ever becomes strong enough to fight another European war, it will be our own fault. That's why there shouldn't be another war, and believe you me, Amelia, I shall make it my business to make as sure as I can that there isn't one.'

'But suppose there is, George. Suppose there is and Peter joins the RAF, which he will—'

'If he's old enough, or still young enough – who knows?'

'George—'

'You are saying,' George said slowly, looking at her carefully across the table, 'if there was another war within – I don't know – let's just say if there was a war for which Peter would be eligible to fight, you would like me to stop him from fighting? While other people's sons fight for our country and our future and our safety – you want me to say to our son I forbid you to do what you want to do? Do you want me to make a coward of him? Is that what I'm to do?'

'Will *you* fight? If there's another war, George?'

'I'm not a professional soldier any more, so I don't *have* to fight.'

'I thought you were a pacifist now – so that you believed you *shouldn't* fight.'

'I've never declared myself a pacifist. All I've spoken out against is the last war. The way it was mismanaged. The waste. The futility of it, if you will. But I have never said that war is wrong per se. Aggression is wrong. Annexing other people's territory is wrong. Wholesale slaughter of innocent people is wrong—'

'To *us*, George. As you always say yourself,

people seem to be able to justify anything. Look what's happening in Germany. The Nazi party is getting stronger and stronger every day, they've started persecuting Jews, limiting freedom of speech – things we all hold to be wrong but which they are convinced are right.'

'The German politicians maybe. But not the German people – I doubt that.'

'But if say the Nazis really come to power, if Germany becomes the sort of danger so many people think it will, would you fight then? If it came to another war?'

'The first thing I would do is fight to prevent such a thing happening.'

'I don't want to lose my son, George.'

'I would do anything for you, Amelia. You know that.'

'Then stop Peter from flying.'

'It was a dream, darling. Something you dreamed because it was something you're worried about. It was only a dream.'

'No, George. It wasn't. What I saw was the future.' Amelia got up from the table, touched George on his cheek, and began to head back into the house.

'Where are you going?' George asked, turning round in his chair. 'I thought we might go for a walk.'

'I think I'm going back to bed, George. And I don't think I'm ever going to get up again.'

*   *   *

Afraid to dream, she did not go back to bed, but the nightmare stayed with her all that day, none the less. Everywhere she looked she could see the burning plane spinning in the sky. When she tried to read a book all she could see was her son's face melting in the flames and his stricken plane crashing into the sea.

Finally in despair she turned her wireless on at full volume, changed into her riding clothes and hurried out to the stables to get Max ready for the hack she hoped would at last clear the terrible pictures from her mind.

'Can I come with you?' she heard a voice behind her enquire as she brushed Max out as vigorously as she could. 'I can get Taffy ready in a minute.'

'Of course you can, Peter,' Amelia answered, smiling at her son who had come to stand beside her. 'I thought I'd ride up through the woods and onto White Sheet Down.'

'Daddy coming?'

'No, Daddy's working,' Amelia replied, taking a rope halter to help Peter catch his crafty old Welsh mountain pony. 'He's designing us a brave new world.'

'I don't know what that means, Mummy.'

'And I don't know why I said it. Come on, sausage. Let's go and try and catch old Taffy.'

They rode for three hours high on the Wiltshire Downs, across prehistoric burial grounds, past ancient forts hidden deep in the chalk turf and along bridle paths which had borne the footfall of Roman soldiers. The sun was hot and the air was so clear Amelia felt that if they looked long and hard enough they would be able to see all the way across the plain to Salisbury Cathedral. They talked very little until they turned their horses for home, heading west through the ancient woodland of Snail Creep Hanging, Great Ridge and Stonehill Copse, forests formed of old trees, twisted giants with gnarled faces, the way bisected with historic tracks that had once led pilgrims to Salisbury.

As they slowed to a walk Peter turned the conversation to the subject of Amelia Earhart's amazing feat in becoming the first woman to fly the Atlantic ocean solo.

'For a woman to fly the Atlantic is pretty incredible.'

'We girls aren't entirely feeble, you know, darling,' Amelia teased him. 'We're capable of doing more than just cooking and having babies.'

'But I mean flying an aeroplane across the Atlantic, that takes guts.'

'So does having a baby. I am sure I could learn to fly an aeroplane. Not that I'd want to.'

'No, Daddy says you get lost going from home into Bruton.'

'You mark my words, young man. Before you know it girls will be doing practically everything that boys can do. You just wait.'

'I don't mind,' Peter replied with a shrug. 'Just

as long as we don't have to do everything girls have to do – like having babies.'

'Do you really want to fly, Peter?' Amelia asked him cautiously.

'You bet. More than anything.'

'There's nothing else which really takes your fancy?'

'What I really want to do more than anything actually is to fly all the way round the world, in a plane of my own design.'

'Do you think that's what you'll end up doing. Being a pilot?'

'Yes.'

Amelia kicked Max ahead of him suddenly. It was everything that she had dreaded to hear, but there was nothing that she could do, and for the first time, she knew it.

Although Amelia's despair about her dream abated over the next few weeks, just as George had predicted that it would, the images were locked up fast in her mind, so securely that if she allowed her thoughts to turn for one moment to flying she at once saw her nightmare vision. To dispel them she determinedly concentrated on practical things, like gardening, as well as playing hostess to the various friends and colleagues George had begun to invite down for weekends.

Most of their guests were friends of them both, acquaintances from Sussex who would happily drive all the way across to Somerset to enjoy what were becoming known as *typical Dashwood week-ends*. Weekends where they knew they would be sure to have fun.

The Dashwoods had laid out a fine lawn tennis court in what had been just a patch of wilderness the far side of the Kissing Garden, so the summer weekends were normally taken up with energetic games of mixed doubles and histrionic games of what was soon dubbed *Dirty Croquet* on the formal lawns in front of the house.

These gatherings generally left Amelia in a state of pleasant exhaustion by the time their guests had left on Monday morning, and it was to one of them that George suddenly decided to invite his publisher, Jack Cornwall, a man Amelia hardly knew.

On first sight he seemed strangely unaesthetic for a man of letters, a strong but stocky individual with a heavy face and a seemingly permanent frown. He wore heavily framed spectacles with very thick tinted lenses which because they were to correct short sight made his eyes look small. In fact, on the rare occasions when he took his spectacles off, he was revealed as having large, dark and very kindly eyes, quite at odds with the pugnacious set of his face. Nor was he very communicative, at least not with Amelia.

'He's a very shy man, that's all,' George explained to Amelia when she reported on his publisher's odd behaviour. 'He doesn't have children of his own and he always says they frighten him.'

'Well, I'm not sure about children frightening him, but he certainly frightens the pants off them.'

His apparent virtues were his perfect manners, his undoubted mental brilliance, his immaculate sense of dress and his extraordinarily beautiful voice, a voice so seductive that Amelia had no difficulty in believing George when he told her Jack was married to one of the most desirable women in London.

Even so, on their initial encounters, she could not establish any sort of rapport. Usually she had no difficulty in dealing with any of George's male friends, since she liked the company of men as much as George enjoyed the company of women. Not Jack Cornwall. He was fastidiously polite, extremely interested in her horticultural skills, admiring of what she had managed to do with what had been nothing more than a set of ruins, and appreciative of what was put in front of him at the table, but other than that he appeared to have no interest in Amelia at all. By the end of the first day of his visit Amelia had stopped trying, keeping out of his and George's way as much as possible and preserving the formalities as best she might whenever their paths collided.

'You don't seem to like Jack much,' George observed after their guest had left. 'Did you argue or something? He's normally a very amicable chap. Taciturn, I agree. But usually amicable.'

'I like Jack. It's just that Jack doesn't appear to like me.'

'Ah.' George smiled. 'If that was the impression he gave you, Amelia, he likes you all right.'

Jack began to be asked down to The Priory regularly after that, eventually bringing his wife. On that first joint visit Miranda Cornwall proved herself to be not only the beauty she was rumoured to be but an expert tennis player. Amelia, who was no beginner, simply could not live with her on court.

'Something tells me you've played this game before,' Amelia laughed after the game as they sat drinking lemonade. 'And I have a rather wicked idea. Would you like to make a few bob? And help me get my own back on a chum?'

'You will never find Mrs Cornwall averse to a tilt at the ring,' Miranda sighed, stretching her extremely long legs out in front of her.

'This is hardly the *ring*, Miranda,' Amelia explained while she refilled their glasses. 'But we could make some nice pocket money. A dear friend of ours called Archie Hanley is forever taking bets on our tennis matches – and always cleaning up. So, as Mr Damon Runyon has it, the man *owes*.'

'Wonderful,' Miranda reached for the gin to add to her lemonade. 'Tell me the plan.'

The next day, invited over for a drink by Amelia, Archie was duly taken on a walk which included a stroll past the tennis court where he observed an apparently heavenly apparition called by the equally heavenly name of Miranda losing hands down to a lead-footed, stout and extremely short-winded man in steamed-up spectacles.

'Alas,' he muttered to Amelia. 'To look at her you would imagine she would be a goddess on the tennis court. The conformation is exquisite, the execution appalling. Ah well, beauty and brilliance rarely combine.'

As a consequence of the beautiful Mrs Cornwall's performance on the tennis court, the next day when Archie opened his usual book on the Dashwood Tennis Tournament the coupling of Miranda Cornwall with Amelia was freely available at 10/1, even though Amelia was known to be the most competent of the women playing.

'Very generous of you, old boy,' Edward Lydford said when he had laid a bet of £5 to win £50. 'But seeing the amount of business you've been doing at that price, don't you think you should trim the odds a bit? Yes? Yes?'

'It is money for the oldest of rope, dear friend,' Archie replied, beaming, all confidence. 'You have not observed Titania here on the court as I have.'

'Oh yes?' Edward beamed. 'You mean yesterday when she was playing her old man?'

'I could not have put it better, dear doctor, had I tried.'

'Ah, but what you didn't know, old boy, was the dear pretty thing was playing him left-handed, don't you know. And with a pebble in her plimsolls. Yes? Only way the old boy can get a game.'

Consequently Amelia and Miranda won the tournament at a canter, never dropping a game until the final when they put George and Hermione to rout 6-4, 6-4, even though Hermione could also play a useful game of tennis. No-one could have been braver about paying out than Archie, although privately he was calling imprecations of the vilest kind down on Amelia's pretty head when he realized just how he had been fooled.

'Miranda Cornwall has to be the maddest woman I have ever met,' Hermione, also staying for the first time, confided to Amelia as they sat drinking cold lemonade after the match. 'Have you ever met anyone who sings while they play tennis?'

'Not just sings, but sings opera. She got through most of the first act of *La Bohème* by the end of the first set!'

'I would kill for those legs.'

'That is the difference between us – I would kill for that first service. And that drop volley.'

'She really is married to that odd man? Well, maybe he's not so much odd as original.'

'Jack Cornwall is a very influential chap, George tells me. Knows all sorts of interesting people in all sorts of interesting places. He's also a first-class publisher.'

'Your hubby . . .' Hermione said, patting her face carefully with a towel. 'He has become quite a literary number, *n'est ce pas*? Not only writing all these controversial books, but now all these articles in the newspapers.'

'I know. I never imagined the sort of life we have now when we first got married. I thought I would be an army wife for ever in evening dress being kind to lower ranks – and here I am practically joining the dirndl and rope-sole shoes set, all home-made broths and fruit picking.'

'Do you like the sort of country life you have now? I mean do you really, really like it?'

'I love it. Don't you?'

'I hate it. But then, hardly surprising.'

'You never really did like the country though, did you, darling?'

'What we knew when we were growing up wasn't *country* – it was fun, all our parents did was to arrange fun things, and we met new people all the time, and we enjoyed ourselves, always making dresses and putting on the gramophone to learn new dances. We had fun. You are having fun. I have no fun. But then. You haven't met my husband, and really, when I think about it, I hope you never do. I must have been desperate. I was desperate. So few men after the war, had to be married, or become a spinster in an attic with a parrot for company. Although, come to think of it, a parrot would be better than His Always Crossness.'

'I thought you said your husband was ill, Hermione. Which was why you couldn't bring him to stay?'

'I haven't brought him with me, darling, because if I did, I really think I might have murdered him. He is not just ghastly, he is double double ghastly. And as for *It* – well, His Always Crossness makes me wish I *was* a spinster in an attic.'

'Oh dear,' Amelia said, studying her friend's appalled expression. 'What do you think we should do? I mean do you think you should call it a day, and have a divorce?'

'First let's find me a scrumptious gentleman with whom I may have a raging affair, and after that we will talk about what to do with His Always Crossness, and his horrid, horrid ways. I truly think I might go mad otherwise.'

'Ralph would do her just fine,' George mused, when Amelia told him that night about Hermione's disastrous marriage. 'Pity she's married.'

'Ralph,' Amelia said blankly. 'Which particular Ralph are we talking about, George? And I don't think Hermione's going to be married for long.'

'Ralph as in Lieutenant Grace, remember? And Hermione is surely not going to get divorced?'

'Oh, I know what everyone thinks of divorce, but really, George, it's a much better thing to face a divorce court than a murder charge, surely?'

'Meaning?'

'Hermione will *murder* her husband if she doesn't escape. He sounds *appalling*.'

'How *appalling*?'

George remained straight-faced with difficulty, as always at moments such as these.

'You'd faint if I told you, George. I wouldn't know where to start. So why don't you ask Ralph down here? Just to cheer poor Hermione up – she's going to be here till next weekend.'

'I have work to do – and anyway, I thought we weren't having any more guests until after Peter's gone back to school?'

'One more guest is not going to make much difference, George. Besides, you haven't seen Ralph Grace since the war, have you?'

'No,' George said a little too quickly for Amelia's liking. 'No, I haven't.'

'Come on, George,' Amelia teased. 'Come clean.'

'I saw him briefly some time ago. He'd got into a scrape and needed to borrow some money.'

'But you're still friends.'

'Of course!'

'Then ask him down. I'm sure you'd like to see him.'

'Oh, very well,' George sighed. 'I shall call him tomorrow.'

But seeing how little difficulty George had in locating his old friend, it occurred to Amelia that some time ago was not in fact so very long ago.

They were sitting under the trees having tea when he arrived on a motor bicycle, dressed in a long white duster coat of the sort she remembered her father wearing when he used to drive his open-topped Renault, a pair of huge shiny goggles and a battered old leather flying helmet. He parked his bike against the cedar tree, took off his goggles, exchanged his flying helmet for an old straw Panama and, pulling a shiny brown leather Gladstone bag off the pillion, waved at the tea party. As she watched Amelia noted that he was also tall, not quite as tall as George but six foot even so, slim, with long thick black hair and the most doleful countenance she had seen in an age.

'Excuse me?' he called. 'This is The Priory? There's no sign at the gate! Not that there's a gate, come to mention it!'

'You must be Lieutenant Grace!' Amelia called back, getting up from her seat and walking towards him. 'Sorry about the lack of sign, but George won't have one. When we did put one up, all sorts of strange religious people kept trekking up the drive. I'm Amelia Dashwood, George's wife.'

'Just as described,' Ralph Grace replied, doffing his old straw. 'No, even more beautiful. I am thoroughly enchanted to make your acquaintance.'

'Described,' Amelia wondered as they crossed the lawns to where Hermione, Clara, Peter and Gwendolyn were having tea. 'My husband has described me to you?'

'George got letters, Madam Dashwood. I got

curious. George got depictive. These are your lovely offspring?'

'Yes. And this is Mrs Baddeley, an old friend of mine, Clara our children's nurse turning housekeeper, Peter our son, and Gwendolyn our daughter.'

'And a future breaker of hearts,' Ralph said with a forlorn sigh. 'How do you do, how do you do, how do you do, how do you do. Is there some hot tea still in that fine silver pot, Clara the children's nursemaid turning to housekeeper, please?'

'We have just been discussing the kidnap of the Lindberg baby.' Hermione said to fill in the small pause that inevitably followed. 'Such a strange business. Why take a *baby*?'

'Let's change the subject,' Amelia suggested, and she nodded to Hermione, prompting her to find another. Hermione shook her head, and turning from Amelia smiled at Ralph.

'Very well, Hermione, if you are going to be a party pooper – Peter, can you find us a safe subject? Something which will not make us sad, please?'

Peter frowned. 'One day we shall fly so high we shall be able to reach the moon.'

'Now that is high, very high – as a subject, I mean.'

'Don't talk tosh, Peter,' Gwendolyn said through a mouthful of cake, earning a finger-wagging from Clara. 'You do talk such tosh.'

'Wait and see, Miss Clever Boots,' Peter replied.

'I'll bet you anything you like that in fifty years we'll have sent a rocket to the moon. Soon as we can work out how to cope with the pull of earth's gravity – although the problem isn't so much getting out of it, it's coming back into our atmosphere, if you ask me.'

'And you really think that if the scientists can find the way, we'll be able to put a man on the moon, boss?'

'Rather than in it,' Amelia said with a smile.

'Yes I do, sir,' Peter said, ignoring his mother's facetiousness. 'And why do you call me *boss*, if you don't mind me asking, sir?'

'Ask away or ye never shall find. It's a habit, I'm afraid. I have cultivated this habit of giving people names and labels when I meet them.'

'I see.' Peter began again, his favourite topic never far from his mind. 'I think it will probably be the Germans who put a man on the moon, myself.'

'The Germans?' Ralph frowned, putting down his teacup on the table and taking off his long white coat. 'So why do you suppose the Germans will be more able than us? Or even the Americans?'

'Because they have the best scientific brains, sir,' Peter replied. 'They have all these brilliant Jewish scientists.'

'Who are all leaving Germany for – America.'

'Your son is button bright, Madam Dashwood,' Ralph said after Clara had taken Gwendolyn off

399

for her bath and Peter had disappeared to fish a safe pool in the river. 'Your son is button bright and your daughter most fair.'

'And you are very quaint, if you don't mind me saying,' Hermione laughed. 'It's a long time since I heard a girl called *fair*.'

'It's a nice word though, don't you think, Mrs Bradley? *Fair*?'

'Yes I do, Lieutenant Grace – and the name is Baddeley, and you may call me Hermione.'

'Atrocious, is it not, Madam D?' Ralph said, turning to Amelia and widening his dark green eyes. 'How all the fairest of the fair are wedded.'

Amelia laughed and took a few seconds to examine their guest. He was not as classically handsome as she had first thought when she saw him standing in the shadow of the cedar of Lebanon against which he had parked his motor bike. In fact, the more she examined his face the less conventionally good-looking he appeared, yet this did not detract from his attraction.

Despite being married to an almost absurdly handsome man, Amelia had found that nowadays she had come to rather suspect sheer good looks, since too often those who were blessed with beauty seemed not to care much about their other graces. She had come to prefer people like Jack Cornwall, people who were more than they at first seemed. And now as she found herself regarding Ralph Grace she decided that he fell very much into this category. His face was not handsome but droll. His eyes turned down at the sides, giving him a Sad Sam look. His nose was long and aquiline and his hair a great mane of floppy shiny black hair. The final impression was of someone who might well be found sitting at a café table on the Left Bank of the Seine, drinking anise while watching the world pass by before annotating its foibles in an old pocket book.

'Have you seen something of interest, *chère Madame*?' he suddenly wondered, as if reading her thoughts.

'I'm sorry? I was staring at something over there, Lieutenant Grace.'

'Ralph. Let us go mad and first name each other indiscriminately.'

'Very well – Ralph, this is Hermione, and as you know I am Amelia.'

'And so where is – George?'

'Finishing an article commissioned in haste by some lunatic editor and keeping him up all night and all day, because he writes very, very slowly.'

'Do you know something, Amelia?'

'No, Lieutenant – no, Ralph.'

'I would just love a drink.'

Ralph smiled at the two women, challenging one or the other of them to wonder whether it was still not a little early, but neither of them did. Instead Hermione, possibly having taken her cue from Miranda Cornwall, started to sing an aria from *La Bohème*. Ralph Grace at once joined in and made it a duet. With some reluctance Amelia left them singing and went in to supervise the dinner. She had asked Ralph down specifically to meet Hermione, but now that he was here she found that she wished, for no reason that she could name, that she had not.

But while they seemed able to sing together in perfect harmony, dinner proved to be several bridges too far for any hopes Amelia might have nourished that George's old friend would become enamoured of her old friend. They were clearly not just chalk and cheese, but salt in each other's wounds, able to agree on nothing at all. Their hosts found themselves umpiring their arguments during dinner, arguments that led to George's removing the wine bottle from his old friend's reach, and Amelia's 'withdrawing' the ladies to the drawing room, where Hermione did nothing but complain about Lieutenant Grace's manners and compare him unfavourably even to His Always Crossness.

'Not a marriage made in heaven.' George sighed theatrically as he slowly started to undress, much later.

'That wasn't the point, George,' Amelia replied, already in bed and reading. 'Hermione already has a husband. The idea was just to let her perhaps indulge herself in a mild flirtation.'

'No such thing, Amelia, as a *mild* flirtation. Anyway, I don't think we need to worry too much on that score since they obviously can't stand the sight of each other. So what do you make of Ralph?'

'What do *you* make of him? After all, he's your old friend, not mine.'

'Meaning?'

'Has he changed, George? Is he the same old Ralph Grace you knew, or has he changed? I'm sure he's found *you* changed. At least I hope he has.' Dropping her book on the floor, Amelia turned to George.

'Won't you get cold without anything on?'

'Not if you have anything to do with it, Captain Dashwood.'

'I thought you wanted to know about Ralph?'

'Later.'

'He's still the same old Ralph. Funny, cantankerous, argumentative and b-minded. What do you make of him?'

Amelia thought for a moment, her hand resting on the flat of George's stomach.

'I think he's outrageous, but – rather fun.'

'As I said, sir, as I did warn,' Longbeard groaned, as he and the Noble One sat high in the yews watching the darkened house.

'He has no right!' the Noble One repeated under his breath. 'This is no business of his!'

'Good sir, with respect,' Longbeard said, polishing the tip of a jewelled stick on the silk of his robe. 'There is no known way to forfend such an exigency. He belongs to our time, he is in the same sphere. We shall

never be rid of him, sir, and no magick in the skies shall remove him.'

'You can make matters difficult for him. You can cast some dazzles which will distract and divert him.'

'I might, sir, and I could. But think on it. Perchance his presence may prove of value. If you consider my crystal and look to the end, there might be purpose here.' Longbeard opened his hand and there in the palm a crystal glowed with ice-blue light. The Noble One took the jewel in his own hand, holding it so close to his face that its light gave him the appearance of an ice warrior, a man with frozen eyebrows and lashes and a frosted beard.

'Yes,' the Noble One said after a while, once he had watched the events which were to come unfold. 'I take your meaning. I would have had it otherwise, but his presence may indeed prove opportune.'

'Not that we can discharge him, sir,' Longbeard reminded the Noble One. 'Now he has found us, we are as much in his hands as he is in ours.'

'You forget he has no magick, wizard – no spells, no dazzles. He cannot confound us as we can him.'

'Yet he may confound us in another way. He can win a game at which we cannot play.'

'Yes – yes!' the dark-haired white-robed man standing in the hidden garden agreed. 'Yes, I may play and win at a game in which you can take no part! And play it I shall – and win it I will!' So saying he put his clenched hand on his heart, closed the night from his eyes, and silently avowed her name.

Nineteen

The following day Hermione made some going-home noises to Amelia about the drunken and disagreeable behaviour of her fellow guest, wondering aloud why someone as perfect as George could possibly be friends with someone so obviously louche as Ralph Grace.

'I don't think he's louche, Hermione. I think he was rather drunk last night, but then you weren't exactly totally sober yourself.'

'Even more reason for him to be polite to me. A real gentleman never takes advantage of a lady. Not even His Always Crossness argues with me when he is drunk. He waits until the next day when he has a hangover, as is proper.'

But when Ralph finally emerged nursing a sizeable hangover, all was soon forgiven, since he made sure to appear kneeling on all fours out into the garden where Amelia, George and Hermione were sitting drinking large glasses of Pimms.

Having crawled across the lawn he rolled over like a dog in front of Hermione to beg her forgiveness, then presented Amelia with a huge bunch of her own roses, before rounding off his performance with an impersonation of Charlie Chaplin complete with George's shooting stick.

'Bravo!' a delighted George cried. 'I'd forgotten what a blisteringly good mimic you are, Ralphie.'

'Can you do Buster Keaton, sir?' Peter asked, having been drawn by the sounds of laughter to stop the game he was playing with his sister to come and watch.

'I can, I can, boss,' Ralph said, collapsing in a chair. 'But not now, guvnor. Later perhaps?'

'I'm going back to school this afternoon,' Peter said.

'After lunch, I promise. Prep school?' He squinted up at Peter, shading his eyes from the sun.

'Yes.'

'You dreading it?'

'No I'm not actually. I think it's good fun.'

'More fun than Eton?'

'Much more fun than Eton,' George put in.

'And a whole lot nearer,' Amelia added. 'He's only an hour away by car.'

'Excellent,' Ralph agreed, pouring himself some Pimms. 'I hated Eton.'

'Were you there at the same time as George?' Amelia asked with a frown.

'I was two years his junior, and didn't know him at all. And then I was expelled.'

'Good lord!' Amelia laughed.' May we ask for what?'

'Smoking,' Ralph replied with a grin.

'And drinking,' George added, straight-faced.

'But did you know each other?'

'Only by repute,' George said. 'We all heard about Grace Junior's expulsion, of course.'

'And we all knew about Adonis Dashwood,' Ralph replied. 'Captain of everything including captain of everyone's sisters' hearts.'

'Tut tut, George. I never realized I married a Romeo.'

'You didn't.'

'Nonsense!' Ralph carolled with his hands to his mouth as if loud hailing. 'Rubbish! George Dashwood was a roué!'

Seeing Clara appearing at the door with a tray of food, Amelia got up to help her set lunch on the terrace. By the time she returned to the company an argument was in full swing about the role of women in the post-war world.

'There is one school of thought,' George was saying, 'which thinks women should return fully to the subjection of man.'

'By that do you mean that since the war man has been subjected by *women*?' Ralph asked mischievously. 'What have I been missing living in France?'

'By that I mean – as well you know, Ralph Grace,' George continued, 'that a whole school of thought has it that by reason of his strength and his intellect man is woman's superior – that women should recognize their own spiritual and economic inferiority and concentrate purely on maternity.'

'You don't believe that, George, surely?' Amelia said, as she resumed her seat.

'I do! In fact I raise my glass to the man who propounds such a splendid philosophy,' said Ralph.

'Then you'll be raising your glass to Mussolini, Ralph,' George told him. 'As if you didn't know.'

'To Benito!' Ralph toasted, teasing the assembled company with gusto. 'To Benito Musseleeny!'

'I bet Milton's your favourite poet, too! *Man speaks to God, but woman may only speak to God in man* – I expect you can quote him all right!'

'Undoubtedly, Signora Dasherwood!' Ralph cried in perfect mock Italian. 'Away-a with all this-a pernicious doctrina of this-a feminis-ma! This-a is-a all the talk of Boleeshavisa-ma!'

Hermione laughed at Ralph's cabaret, but George just shook his head sadly.

'Ralph is making fun, but what he says is true, I'm afraid. This is how a lot of people are thinking nowadays, particularly Mussolini's Italian Fascists. They think that while the sexes should be reconciled—'

'Meaning we're not at the moment?' Amelia interposed. 'So what on earth have we been doing up till now? If not being reconciled?'

'I'm talking about the militants. The people who say men and women should be reconciled but on *male* terms. They actually believe women lack the spiritual qualities of men and as a result are—'

'—are morally decadent,' Ralph said, finishing the sentence before him. 'You lot have obviously not read George Dashwood's latest article in the *Telegraph*. Which I read while waiting for the hammers in my head to stop pounding. According to our pundit here, we live in dangerous times. Hey, that's something else we can drink to – to dangerous times! And moral decadence!'

'Does your friend here never take anything seriously, George?'

'He takes everything seriously, Amelia. That's why he's forever making jokes.'

As they moved to the lunch table the talk grew ever more heated as the debate continued, Ralph deliberately playing devil's advocate while George did his best to explain the complexities of the arguments about feminism, Bolshevism and Fascism to Hermione who had long declared herself to be hopelessly out of her depth. None the less she was appalled to learn that both Fascists and Nazis believed that women were by their very nature immoral and should be treated as second class citizens under the complete authority of men, and made to bear as many children as possible.

'I really don't see the point in our having won the war and defeated them,' Hermione said in dismay, 'if this is the way they're thinking.'

'Ah, but you see we didn't really win the war, Hermione,' George told her, quietly. 'In fact some of us are not at all sure we even defeated them.'

The whole table fell to silence at this pronouncement, everyone turning to George in expectation of an exposition.

'Some people think that Germany sued for peace for reasons other than because they thought they had been vanquished,' George said. 'My father told me only recently that no-one was more surprised when the Germans sued for peace than the Germans themselves. They had no Eastern front to worry about, and Ludendorff had damn near beat us on the Western Front before the Americans arrived. And remember, they went over our heads when they sued. They went straight to the Americans and deliberately so, according to the old man. Exploiting the rift between our government and President Wilson.'

'I never knew that,' Ralph said, suddenly serious. 'You mean the Germans weren't actually on their knees at all, George?'

'I don't know about on their knees, Ralph, but they were certainly demoralized after the defeats at the Marne and Amiens. And they knew the Americans were coming. But a close friend of my father's was at a meeting with Lloyd George not long after the Germans began making overtures and Lloyd George didn't like it one bit. Apparently he made some sort of comparison with what Carthage had said after the First Punic War: that conceding defeat gave them the chance to be the better prepared and organized the *next* time.'

'Oh ho.' Ralph widened his eyes in pantomime fashion. 'I *see*. So what to do, old bean? What to do, eh?'

'Looking to the past again, I think we have to do

everything in our power to make sure we don't find ourselves in the same position as the Romans when Hannibal nearly drove them into the sea. I think we have to try and avoid another war at all costs. Otherwise it really will all have been a terrible waste.'

'Shall we dance? This is becoming really quite dreary.' Getting up from the table, Ralph stood by Hermione's chair as if at a ball.

'I can't hear any music.' Hermione looked round.

'You will,' Ralph replied, offering her his hand and then leading her off to waltz around the lawns singing *The Blue Danube*.

Later, when George, Clara and Amelia had finished packing Peter's school trunk and the rest of his belongings into the Bentley, Ralph and Hermione were in the middle of a game of blindfold tennis which by now had Hermione in near hysterics of laughter.

'Do you think it's safe to leave them together?' Amelia wondered as Peter went to wish them goodbye. 'I'm beginning to think this wasn't such a bright idea.'

'Of yours.'

'Of mine,' Amelia agreed.

'They're grown up people, darling. We can hardly go and wag a finger under their noses and tell them to behave. Or lock Ralph in his room.'

'I would imagine there aren't that many rooms which can contain Lieutenant Ralph Grace.'

'Look what I got!' Peter exclaimed, running back across the lawn from the tennis court. 'Lieutenant Grace gave me ten shillings!'

'Which he just borrowed off me,' George whispered to Amelia before their son had reached them. 'Jolly good, Peter! That should keep you in tuck for the whole term!'

'And we hope that the tennis will leave our guests too exhausted to even think of anything else,' Amelia said *sotto* to George as Peter settled in the back of the car.

'And hope is all we *can* do,' George agreed, winking at Amelia. 'All aboard!'

When Amelia and George finally returned home some four hours later and found no sign of either of their two guests, they feared the worst.

'It's all right!' Amelia called to George across the lawn after they had decided to mount a search party. 'I've found Hermione! She's asleep in the summer house!'

'And Ralph's fast asleep in his bedroom,' George said as he came to join Amelia where she was waiting for him in the herbaceous garden. 'Obviously the tennis wore them out.'

'You hope. Hermione's sleeping like the dead.'

'If anything had *happened*, one of them would hardly be out here in the summer house and the other miles away upstairs in a bedroom.'

'Hm,' Amelia said, mimicking him. 'We shall see.'

After George had hurried off to answer his study

telephone, Amelia promptly returned to the summer house and had no hesitation in waking Hermione.

'You look as though you've been knocked out by something. Have you?'

'No.' Hermione answered, with a weary yawn. 'Not that, I assure you. Although – oh, it doesn't matter.'

'Come on, Mrs Baddeley, tell all. It won't go any further.'

Hermione looked at her, before beginning to rearrange her tousled head of hair with her fingers.

'Very well, if you must know – he *tried*.'

'Surprise, surprise.'

'And if you must know, I didn't exactly object.'

'No comment.'

'Just as well.'

'So?'

'So what, Mrs Dashwood?'

'Come on,' Amelia urged her. 'I thought you said nothing happened.'

'No, I didn't. Not quite. What happened was, if you must know—'

'Which I must, I must,' Amelia assured her happily. 'Did he kiss you?'

'He tried to.'

'And you stopped him?'

'Of course not! I was all ready for him to kiss me! And he was all ready to kiss me!'

'And someone came in,' Amelia guessed, with a sigh. 'Clara, no doubt. It would be.'

413

'We weren't even in the house! As if I'd be so indiscreet. No, we were outside, in the garden. In that little hidden garden, if you really must know.'

'The Kissing Garden?' Amelia said in surprise, before she could stop herself.

'Is that what you call it? How appropriate.'

'It doesn't matter. The little hedged garden at the top of the mound?'

'Yes. Anyway, for some reason or other we found ourselves in there—'

'How? I mean whose idea was it to go there?'

'Ralph's. He suddenly said, "I have a brainwave!" And started spouting Shakespeare or something. The bank where the wild thyme grows – you know the bit. And the next thing I knew he was leading me into this enchanted little garden.'

'Hm,' Amelia sniffed. 'And *hm* again, as George says.'

'It really is the most enchanting place, Amelia. Don't you find it so? There's something about that little garden that as soon as you find yourself in it . . .' Hermione stopped, smiled and gave a little shiver of delight.

'Go on,' Amelia said, as coolly as she could.

'I think Ralph was as taken with it as I was, from the look on his face. He went awfully quiet, which as you've probably gathered by now is quite unusual for Ralph Grace – then he took me by the hands, both hands, and looked me right in the eyes in – well, all I can say is in a very *powerful* way. Does that make sense?'

'Yes. Go on.'

'So there we were, both sort of hypnotized if you like, and I heard him saying something about finding me terribly attractive and that he knew we shouldn't but he just had to make love to me. Which was when I thought he was going to kiss me – which was when I hoped he was going to kiss me – so I shut my eyes – and the next thing I knew I heard this cry. And when I opened my eyes Ralph was clutching his head and groaning.'

'Good lord! Whatever was the matter?'

'Don't ask me! He said when he tried to kiss me it was as if someone had hit him around the head.'

'Really?' Amelia frowned, waiting for her friend to continue. 'So?'

'So – so it happened every time he tried to kiss me! So he said. Every time he touched me he said he got this terrible pain in his head. I mean really. I mean *really*, Amelia! He said it was like the kind of electric shock you can get from car handles and so on.'

'You think—'

'You bet I do. I felt such a fool! He was obviously just getting a rise out of me. Teasing me. I mean the man is totally deranged!'

'I see.' Amelia bit her bottom lip and frowned in an effort not to smile. 'So then . . .'

'So then I told him what I thought of him and where to go, and he went. Still holding his head.'

'Hm,' Amelia said. 'So. He banged his head and

went to bed and didn't get up until the morning. Literally.'

'And if so, Amelia darling,' Hermione concluded, 'I could not care less.'

'He's such a tease. I should put the whole matter out of your head.'

Hermione looked at Amelia. 'You can say that again, and again and again, Mrs Dashwood.'

Amelia laughed, trying not to look what she felt, which was for no reason she could think, oddly relieved.

Once Hermione had returned to Yorkshire and Ralph back to London and thence to do business on the Continent, The Priory settled back more or less into its old rhythm, with both George and Amelia getting up early to do an hour's work, George in his study and Amelia in the garden, planning the day's tasks with Jethro and Robbie, before meeting again over breakfast. After they had eaten George would return to his work and Amelia to hers, not seeing each other until half past one when they took lunch together and discussed their joint efforts. In the afternoon they would either walk or take the horses up for a hack on White Sheet Downs before returning to The Priory in time for tea, after which they would both put in another two hours' work, stopping in time for a long hot bath and a well-earned drink before dinner.

This then was the shape of their days, a pattern

which left them both tired but happy by nightfall when they would retire to bed to read, listen to the wireless or more often than not, make love.

Being completely happy with each other's company, when George was writing they hardly ever entertained or accepted invitations. Amelia was always glad to use George's writing as an excuse to stay at home because home was where she loved to be. They had both long come to the conclusion that a day away from their beloved priory was a day wasted.

So it was with some surprise that less than three weeks after the departure of their last guests Amelia heard that George had asked Jack and Miranda Cornwall down for the following weekend. Not that she minded, she was merely surprised, for when George was working at full steam he confessed he simply did not have the necessary spare energy to deal with visitors, least of all his publisher and his overactive, restless if delightful wife.

In deference to Miranda, therefore, Amelia suggested that she would have to throw at least one dinner party, if not a Sunday luncheon as well, since Jack's wife was hardly the sort of woman who would be quite happy sitting around with no-one to talk to other than her hostess. George merely said they could play tennis and go riding, which exasperated Amelia since, as she further explained, his publisher's wife was a social creature, who quite rightly considered herself important enough to be awarded the courtesy of at least one formal occasion. But having just finished a long summer of entertaining Amelia had, quite literally, run out of guests.

In the end, having rung around the neighbourhood, she contented herself with arranging a simple family dinner for the Saturday night, while encouraging Archie and Mae Hanley to bring their own house guests to lunch the following day, should they be back in time from their latest tour. George had seemed happy enough with this plan, only to surprise Amelia by suddenly announcing two days before the Cornwalls were due to arrive that he himself had invited half a dozen people for the Saturday night.

'Who, George?' Amelia asked in open astonishment. 'You don't know half a dozen people round here, so who on earth are you thinking of asking?'

'Look, if it's awkward—'

'It's not awkward, George. I'm simply curious. First of all I'm curious as to why you suddenly decided to ask Jack and Miranda down when you've just started a new book, and now I'm curious to know who these six people you've suddenly met and want to ask to dinner might be.'

'I haven't *met* them, Amelia,' George confessed finally. 'They're acquaintances of Jack's.'

'They're friends of Jack's? You mean we are turning into some sort of catering service for people your publisher wishes to entertain in the country? A novel arrangement, surely?'

'It isn't that,' George said, stopping her in mid-flow. 'These are people Jack thinks I should meet. People who could help me in – help me with this book I'm writing.'

'Do we have to ask them to dinner here?' Amelia continued in dismay. 'This just isn't us, George. We never have people here to dinner whom we don't know. Why can't Jack take you and these people out to dinner in London, if it's that important?'

George shook his head. 'It'll be all right, really.'

But it was far from being all right. In fact the evening was as difficult and as uncomfortable as Amelia had dreaded. Not only did neither she nor George know any of the people whom Jack had invited, but it seemed that they were strangers to Miranda as well, with the consequence that Miranda, who as Amelia soon discovered bored easily, proceeded to get aggressively drunk before they had even sat down to dinner and pick arguments with whoever happened to be nearest. Just before Amelia was about to call everyone to table, she saw Jack take his wife aside and speak to her slowly and very seriously. Miranda listened to him with obvious impatience, tapping her expensively shod foot and only half attending to her husband until he, leaning even closer to her, whispered something effective enough to gain his errant wife's full attention, and after that she behaved herself, if sitting in a sullen silence throughout a four-course dinner can be construed as good behaviour.

As for Jack Cornwall's friends, Amelia had never met a collection of more flint-hearted people. From the moment they arrived she knew just from their aura that they were all extremely rich. Yet far from being patronizing, which seemed to Amelia to be a habit of the very rich, they all but ignored Amelia, as if her home was a restaurant where they had been invited to gather, and she was the cook, albeit a cook who sat down at table with them.

Over dinner the menfolk made the sort of coded and exclusive small talk such men so often do, bewildering Amelia even more, since if this was all they had come to talk about she could not imagine what the point of the party could be at all. Their wives meanwhile talked lightly and fancifully to the men on either side of them, men they already seemed to know intimately, to judge from the conversational shorthand they employed and the private jokes they exchanged. Meanwhile Amelia was completely ignored by the man seated on her right, whose only conversation with her consisted of his briefly expressed surprise that she could live all the time in such a barbaric place as Somerset.

Fortunately she had placed Jack Cornwall on her left, but Jack was not the most fluent of conversationalists. Amelia, however, could talk *small* with the best, so she kept up a stream of chatter with Jack in an attempt to instil some life into the group at her end. But it was an uphill struggle, with Jack – as it appeared to Amelia –

considerably more anxious to stop any conversation from getting established than the opposite. George on the other hand was being ardently besieged by the two women placed either side of him, both very blonde, and dressed in expensive black dinner dresses, discreetly bedecked with old and quite beautiful jewellery. In such company Amelia suddenly felt dowdy and rustic, and even more so when, the ladies having withdrawn leaving the men to their port, she found herself without support among the still silent Miranda and her other unknown female dinner guests.

It was soon all too obvious that the women were as bored as Amelia was uncomfortable, none of them making the faintest effort to talk to their hostess, apart from an initial brief exchange about the number of children they all had or had not, and how many houses and yachts they all owned. However, once they were on to gossip, their conversation became more animated. It became positively excited as names that Amelia knew only from reading the social columns flew about her drawing room and she and Clara dispensed coffee and ashtrays, feeling very much the staff. Miranda, on the other hand, was made of sterner stuff. She was also, once more, quite drunk.

'What a bunch of Fascist bores,' she announced, smiling, to Amelia. 'You poor darling, having to ask them here, what a *martyrdom.*'

Amelia was at once plunged into a dilemma, not knowing whether to ask Miranda to leave the room, or to leave it herself. In the end she opted for neither course since, as she very soon realized, Miranda was unstoppable. By the time the gentlemen finally joined their ladies, after one of the longest after dinner separations Amelia had been forced to endure, Miranda had won a complete victory. The women sat smoking, in silence, and she sat smiling at Amelia.

'Somerset and Sussex three, the rest naught!' she announced, as the gentlemen rejoined them from the dining room, and Amelia went hastily to the piano to provide a diversion by singing one of Noël Coward's latest songs.

'So what was all that about, George Dashwood?' Amelia asked wearily as they prepared for bed. 'I have never been so bored in my own house, nor, I have to tell you, so insulted.'

'All I can say is that I am terribly sorry,' George said, sitting her on his knee on the edge of the bed. 'It won't happen again.'

'You look as though you've run into a wall.'

'I feel as though I have. I really am sorry.'

'What was it all in aid of? And what on earth did you find to talk about with those awful men after dinner? You were closeted away with them for hours.'

George looked at her, sighed, then hugged her tightly to him before getting up and starting to undress.

'I don't want to bore you with it,' he said

with his back turned to her. 'It's all to do with this book I'm writing. Jack knew I needed some first-hand material, and thought this was doing me a favour.'

'All I can say is that I hope it did,' Amelia said, yawning and stretching. 'I have never met such a group of appalling people.'

'They weren't a lot of laughs, were they?' George agreed. 'But I did learn an awful lot of things I hadn't known before.'

'Such as?' Amelia asked, sitting on the bed and carefully unrolling her silk stockings.

'You really do have the most fantastic legs,' George told her dreamily. 'In fact you really do have the most fantastic body.'

'Such as, George? I want to know what you learned. Such as?'

'Such as?' George said, sitting beside her and kissing the side of her neck. 'I learned that you have – the most beautiful body.'

'George?'

'Yes?'

'Don't ever do that to me again.'

'Kiss you on the neck?'

'Ask people like that to our home.'

'I promise.'

'And George?'

'Yes?'

'Kiss me again. Just where you did.'

'Yes, Amelia.'

'Oh, and George—'

'Yes, Amelia?'
'Nothing.'

The next day George shut away himself up in his study with Jack Cornwall while Miranda nursed her hangover in her bedroom. This had meant that Amelia could spend a sunny morning in the garden. She was also happy that Archie and Mae had returned home, but declining Amelia's original invitation had instead asked them all to luncheon, because one more social event at The Priory might, as she said to Clara, 'drive her dotty'.

As always the hospitality at the Hanley household was first class, as was the invited company, so that the rest of Sunday was spent most enjoyably. The Cornwalls drove directly back to London from Archie and Mae's so that on their return to The Priory Amelia and George could take an early bath and collapse happily and privately in front of the fire in their dressing gowns.

At one point during the evening, while George had gone to fetch a bottle of white wine from the cellars, Amelia padded into his study to look for a book on old and medieval plants which she had lent George for his research and, she now remembered, she needed to help identify what appeared to be some strange herbs and flowers she and Jethro had discovered growing at the back of one of the borders. The room was in the usual ordered state of chaos George created whenever he was working, so Amelia took great care not to disturb anything as she searched carefully for her precious volume.

At first she could see no sign of it anywhere among all the piles of books which stood on top of the large partner's desk at which George always spread himself out to work, but then, just as she was about to give up and go and ask George in person where the book might be, she spied it at the bottom of a pile of books right at the back of his desk.

Normally she would not have paid any attention to the books George was reading for his research, but, of a sudden, as she unpiled the books, this collection struck her as odd since it was still all bundled up in a loosely tied cradle of string. When she lifted the bundle up to reach her own book the string slipped off one corner and the pile came apart, spilling several volumes.

With a sigh of irritation Amelia began to collect them together, noticing their titles as she did so. Among them was a copy of *Mein Kampf* which someone had bookmarked in several places as well as underlining a great many passages in pencil. There were two books by Friedrich Nietzsche, a German philosopher whom as Amelia knew from her conversations with George many considered to be the father of Fascism, as well as works by several political philosophers who were unknown to Amelia. Yet as soon as she started leafing through their various works it became very apparent that they shared much the same extreme right wing views as Hitler, for most of the underlined passages she read as she stood at George's desk extolled the need for action and the control of power. More than a little frightened by the potency of the expressed philosophies, Amelia read on, bent over the desk with the books open in front of her and concentrating so hard on their content that she did not hear George come into the room.

'Ah ha,' he said, putting both his hands on her waist and startling her. 'I see we have a spy in our midst.'

'I thought you were writing a murder story, George,' she said, trying to wriggle free.

'What's to say I'm not, Mata Hari?'

'All these books on how to rule the world.'

'Jack lent them to me. I told you, he was helping me with my research.'

'What's the thriller about? I thought it was about a murder at a village fête?'

'Then if that's what you know, Little Miss Nosey,' George said, beginning to shepherd her out of the door, 'you don't need to know anything more.'

'Oo-er!' Amelia exclaimed theatrically as George continued to ease her out of his study. 'The vicar's a crypto-Fascist!'

'Every possibility, Mrs Dashwood,' George replied. 'Still waters and all that stuff. In this country you never know who is quite who.'

'Seriously, George,' Amelia continued, once they were settled back in front of the drawing room fire with a bottle of Chablis and a plate of delicious ham and cucumber sandwiches Amelia had prepared earlier. 'All those books Jack left you. Aren't they a bit on the heavy side for what you're writing?'

'It isn't really for the book,' George confessed, pouring the wine. 'It's sort of general background stuff. For a series of articles I've been asked to write.'

'What – on Fascism?'

'The point is,' George continued, not answering her question, 'the point is a lot of people think there's some sense in what all these people have to say. Particularly in the present economic climate.'

'Are you attracted by what they have to say, George?'

'Of course not. So saying, I don't know that much about it, hence all the homework.'

'Why should Jack be the one who supplied it? Jack doesn't publish this sort of stuff.'

'He knows what everyone else is publishing. Jack's not just what he seems, Amelia. Jack's . . .'

'Yes?' Amelia prompted as George fell silent. 'What is Jack then, if he's not what he seems?'

'Nothing.' George half smiled and shook his head. 'I was merely going to state the obvious: that Jack is much more than the dogged old plodder he appears to be. But then I realized someone like you would have worked that out ages ago. Are there any more of these incredible sandwiches?'

'There would be if I made some more,' Amelia

sighed, getting up. 'You're not telling me the truth, are you, George Dashwood?'

'Of course not, Mrs Dashwood,' George replied easily. 'When do I ever?'

For the next couple of weeks Amelia saw very little of George other than in the evenings, by which time he was too exhausted to do much more than drink his whisky and soda and eat his dinner before collapsing in front of the fire and shortly afterwards collapsing into bed. Despite being well used to living with George's moods when he was writing, it did occur to Amelia that his new book seemed to be taking more out of him than the previous ones. Night after night he would take himself back to his study after dinner leaving her alone with her tapestry, while hardly had the dawn chorus struck up first thing in the morning before he seemed to be back in his study, hard at work once more.

'There can't be that much further to go, surely?' Amelia asked him at the end of one marathon stint. 'A couple of weeks ago you told me you were on the home run.'

'It fell to pieces,' George replied simply. 'Now you see it, now you don't. Jack told me this often happens with thriller writing. You think you have it all beautifully worked out, then right at the last moment you find a flaw, usually one which unravels the entire piece of knitting. That's just what I did. And now on top of everything I have to dash up to London.'

'To London?' Amelia repeated as if he had said 'China'. Since this was the last thing she was expecting. 'But when? And why?'

'The end of this week. Look, I'm sorry, but Jack rang and—'

'Can I come?'

'There wouldn't be anything for you to do.'

'Nothing to do, George?' Amelia laughed. 'I can go shopping! Have my hair done properly! See all those lovely clothes in all those lovely shops which I know I can't possibly afford! Go to some art galleries! Go to the theatre! Nothing for me to do? You're getting as bad as Hermione's husband! His Awful Crossness.'

'I thought you were happy in the country,' George replied with a worried frown. 'I didn't think you liked going to town that much.'

'I'm a woman, George. And still quite a young one, in case you had not noticed. So however much I love this place – which I do – I like going to London. I don't want to spend the rest of my life with straws in my hair!'

'Of course not.' George fell silent, standing with his back to her staring out of the window across the lawns. 'Damn,' he said finally. 'Oh, damn it anyway.'

'George?'

'It's just that I have to go up for more than one day and night. I have meetings all day Wednesday, a dinner to attend that night, business most of the next day and another big dinner on Thursday.'

'Am I not invited? To the dinners?'

'They're not dinner parties, they're business dinners. Come by all means, but I won't be free to take you out in the evening as usual. Or even to see much of you during the day.'

Amelia considered the prospect and finally thought better of it. Had Hermione settled in London rather than Yorkshire she could have happily spent the time with her, but it was far too short notice to expect Hermione to drop everything and dash down south merely to keep Amelia company, and so, rather than face the prospect of spending nearly three days on her own in town, she soon saw there was far more sense in remaining behind at The Priory, where even at that time of year there was always plenty to do in the garden.

So on Tuesday afternoon she helped George to pack, at his request carefully puffing his favourite photograph of herself into one of his crocodile skin cases and kissing him goodbye upstairs in the bedroom, downstairs in the hall and outside in the driveway, before finally leaning down to kiss him inside the Bentley as he settled himself behind the wheel.

'I love you, Mrs Dashwood,' he smiled, pulling on his leather driving gauntlets. 'More than I can ever say.'

'And I love you, Captain Dashwood,' Amelia

returned. 'More than anyone will ever know.'

She stood in the drive waving to the car long after it had gone, because she was still so suffused with love for George, and then, realizing that he had truly gone, she dropped her hand, and turned to go back into the house. As she did so it occurred to her that The Priory perhaps more than anything else in their lives, had helped them through all their difficulties, and not just because of the Kissing Garden. There was so much besides. Even the fabric of the house made a statement about life and how it should be lived, the kindness of its old stone having about it a noble simplicity, with no silly values like those with which, she was suddenly sure, the city abounded.

Twenty

'I should imagine that was something you didn't bargain for,' Amelia said, throwing that day's copy of the *Daily Mail* onto George's lap as he sat with his evening drink before the fire.

'Whether I did or did not, Amelia,' George groaned. 'So what?'

'So what?' Amelia picked the newspaper up again and waved it in his face. *'There'd be nothing for you to do, Amelia! It's all boring meetings and business dinners!'*

'That *was* a business dinner,' George said patiently.

'A private party at Lady Astley's Mayfair residence? With half of London Society present? And you photographed with the hostess having cocktails? Some business dinner. A *monkey* business dinner if you ask me.'

'If you would listen – just for a minute—'

'There's a whole report on the Society pages, George! I've never seen such a glittering guest list! And yet, for some reason I cannot fathom, your wife was not invited.'

'If you would just listen for a minute?'

'Very well. But what I am about to listen to had

better be good.' Amelia lit herself a cigarette, picked up her drink, and sat down opposite George, glaring at him.

'I had no idea there was going to be any such dinner, I give you my word. It was sprung on me at the last moment.'

'I'm sure.' Amelia seethed. 'I mean this looks like one of those parties they throw together at the last moment. Doesn't it?'

'I was at a reception the night before—'

'Where? What sort of reception?'

'It really doesn't matter where.'

'You bet it matters where! Receptions are generally preceded by invitations. So was I excluded from that one as well?'

'It was at The Ritz. It was thrown by the news-paper I'm meant to be writing these pieces for—'

'And I wasn't invited?'

'Yes of course you were invited – but knowing how much you hate these things – and since that was the only invitation which actually included you on this particular trip – I didn't think you'd mind.'

'So you lied.'

'Of course I didn't lie.'

'Of course you lied, George. You said there was nothing for me to do and that none of your appointments included me.'

'I didn't lie. I just didn't mention that boring old reception because that's all I considered it to be. A boring old reception, which it certainly was.'

'At which it just so happened you were invited to Lady Astley's swanky soirée.'

'At the last minute.'

'Why?'

'Oh – thank you,' George said in mock surprise. 'Why do you think? They were short of men, obviously. Since the war everyone is always short of men, darling, *you* know that. You and Hermione are always talking about it. It was the apparent reason why poor Hermione got herself hitched to His Always Crossness, wasn't it?'

'There is no need to be sarcastic, George. Hermione is living the life of the damned and trying to make the best of it. She thought the beastly man was nice. It wasn't until the gates of that horrible house in which he has her incarcerated slammed behind her that she realized he was some sort of Bluebeard. He keeps her so short of money she has to beg the servants to give her some of their grub. I mean to say – but that has nothing to do with the matter in hand. Tell me why you were at the Astleys'. And no half-truths, George, or I promise you there will be hot tea everywhere except in your cup.'

'My story is quite simple. Jack knows the Astleys, he introduced us, and Lady Astley asked me if I would like to go to dinner. End of story.'

'I could have caught the train.'

'You could. But then you weren't invited.'

'You could have made sure I was invited.'

'Would you have come?'

'Of course I'd have come! I mean look who was there!'

'It was very short notice.'

'You didn't want me to come.'

'Of course I wanted you to come. It just wasn't – it wasn't—'

'Convenient.'

'Politic. It just wasn't politic.'

'It was certainly a political enough party, George,' Amelia said, snatching the paper back from him. 'Half the Cabinet was there. Lord Upton—'

'I know who was there. It just wasn't possible to invite you.'

'There just happened to be one chair free for you.'

'It just happened that they really rather wanted me to be there. For purely business reasons.'

'What sort of business do you do with these people, George?' Amelia asked in disbelief. 'Old Sir Marmaduke Astley made his money out of shipping—'

'Ships' rivets to be precise—'

'So don't tell me he's gone into potboilers now? Or maybe you were doing business with Lady Astley? She's renowned, isn't she? For doing business with handsome young men?'

George said nothing. He just took the paper away from Amelia and threw it on the fire before lighting himself another cigarette.

'You're being a little childish,' he said, after he

had allowed her a short but potent two-minute sulk.

'I am not being childish, George! I am being feminine! I'm a woman! A wife! Someone with a very attractive husband who says he's going to London for one reason and then gets caught out going to a party with one of Society's most notorious hostesses!'

'Purely for business, Amelia.'

'What sort of business, George?'

'That I can't tell you, I'm afraid.'

'Why? Why should it be such a secret?'

George looked at her and shrugged. 'Because that's how it is, I'm afraid.'

'Is it to do with your work?'

'Yes.'

'Do you promise?'

'I promise.'

'Do you *promise* promise, George? Do you swear?'

'I *promise* promise and I swear, Amelia.'

'Hm.' Amelia, who had got up again to pace round the room, gave George a long look and then sat down opposite him again. 'Is she as beautiful as everyone says? In person, I mean.'

'Deanna Astley?'

'No, George, her cook. Yes of course Deanna Astley! She certainly looks it. I saw all these pictures of her in the *Tatler* at one of their famous parties at their house on the Thames. She's quite tall, isn't she? And she looks as though she has a fabulous figure. As well as being about fifty years younger than her husband.'

'Not *quite*,' George laughed. 'She is a lot younger, twenty-five years perhaps? And she certainly is very elegant, and tall, yes – I would think she's about five feet ten – and she is formidably bright, although she's one of those women who manages not to put men off by appearing *too* intelligent. I mean, she is a very skilled woman, socially that is. And so she should be, given the exalted circles she moves in.'

'Is she attractive?'

'Very. But there's no need to look like that, Amelia – I didn't find her attractive. But she obviously is because she was continually surrounded by the best-looking as well as the most powerful men present.'

'They say her husband turns a blind eye to her affairs.'

'Perhaps he does,' George replied. 'I don't know. But from the way he looks at her I should imagine he is still madly in love with her.'

'You obviously talked to her, probably at length.'

'Obviously, and probably.'

'Just before dinner? Or after dinner as well?'

'During dinner.'

'You were sitting near her?'

'I was sitting next to her.'

Amelia stared at him. 'Even though you were a last-minute invite? Even though she had only met you the night before?'

'It seems she had read my books,' George said with a sigh. 'C'*est la vie*. People do.'

'It had better not be c'*est l'amour*.'

'Don't be silly, Amelia.'

'I am not being *silly*, George! I am being the very opposite!'

In a fury of jealousy and resentment Amelia put down her drink and, followed by their dogs, went out into the garden to cool off. It was a cold evening but Amelia was past caring about her comfort, too upset by this turn of events and too dismayed to think that George might have been lying to her. She could think of absolutely no reason why he should have gone to all these lengths to take himself off to London by himself other than the fact that he had already arranged to go to dinner with Deanna Astley. The only point on which her reasoning kept floundering was that as far as she knew there had been no other occasion in recent memory when George could possibly have met Deanna Astley, unless he had been lying about some of his previous visits to London when he had ostensibly been meeting Jack Cornwall.

She stood on the Chinese bridge over the carp ponds watching the reflection of the moon as it slowly rose in the clear night sky, staring at the stars in the dark waters which rippled in the night wind with the slow movements of the large fish lazing just below the surface, occasionally rising to catch a last meal of the day. The dogs had disappeared down the watermeadows, where she could hear them happily barking as they chased some poor bewildered bird or startled rabbit, and when they stopped their barking and began to pad their way back to the bridge in answer to their mistress's whistle she could hear the sucking of a carp as it searched for food in the rushes near by and the quiet call of a night bird high up and invisible in a tree somewhere.

But she could hear nothing of the man who stood watching her from the opposite bank, even though he stood in full moonlight, even though the stars reflected in his dark green eyes and the night light caught the gold on the girdle of his gown.

Days later Amelia was out working in the garden, her first task of the day to cut back the climbing rose which seemed to have lost its way around the wall outside George's study. As she carefully placed her wooden ladder against the stonework four feet from his window she saw him sitting at his desk with his back to her, taking a telephone call. Unwilling to overhear his conversation without his knowing, she was just about to call out and warn him of her presence when she made the mistake of stopping and listening.

'Because it just isn't fair on Amelia – puts such a strain on the family.'

George stopped to listen to what whoever it was on the other end of the line had to say, and Amelia found herself flattening herself against the wall, just as she had seen people do in films when they were overhearing things which were none of their affair.

'It's not the same for you. You've lived your whole life as a lie,' George went on when the other person had finished, and he ended with 'very well, I'll think about it' before replacing the receiver once more.

Amelia at once eased her way back along the wall and jumped down into the garden, and very relieved she was that she had when she saw George's study window swinging wide open. She immediately bent over some plants.

'Amelia! Where are you?'

'Here!' she waved one garden-gloved hand back at him as she began to pick her way back towards the study.

'What are you doing?'

'Just thinning out the sedums, actually.'

'We thinned the sedums out at the weekend.'

'Yes, so we did.'

She straightened up and looked over at him. She knew she should say something to him yet she did not. She knew absolutely that something said now would prevent the pain which would inevitably follow, but she still said nothing.

This is what it is like, Amelia thought, as she watched him. This is what deceit between a man and a woman is like, what it feels like, this is how it hurts, this is how despair tastes. Yet all I have to do is reach out – I just have to put my hand on his and say, *George who were you talking to?* And if he pretends he wasn't speaking to anyone, or if he tells me a whole conversation which I know he hasn't had, then I shall know he's being unfaithful. But if he doesn't – if he sighs that great sigh of his and says, *Why do you always get the wrong end of the stick? It was a surprise – a surprise I was organizing for you and it was all backfiring*, or some such typical George excuse or reason, then I shall know it was all a misunderstanding. That George is as he always is – that I have made a fool of myself – and then we'll laugh, and he'll kiss me, and we'll laugh some more, I'll tell him what fool I am, he'll assure me I'm no such thing and the whole thing will be forgotten.

Yet I can't. I can't say a thing in case I'm wrong. In case I'm wrong to hope what I hope and right in suspecting what I fear to be the truth. So because I'm so frightened, so terrified in case this is the case, I'm not going to say a thing – and George is coming out to have a cup of coffee with me, but he's not going to say a thing either.

For a moment George stood by the table. 'Amelia,' he began, closing his eyes and taking a deep breath. Thinking he was about to confess his infidelity Amelia suddenly pushed back her chair and stood up, panic-stricken. 'You will always love me, won't you, Amelia?'

'No, I won't, George. Certainly not.'

441

George stared at her in disbelief. 'You surely don't mean that?'

'George, be reasonable. If I say "yes" I could be giving you a pink ticket to do anything you want.'

'Is that what you think? Do you really imagine I would ask such a thing of you?'

'I don't think it, no, but I do fear it.'

He leaned over and kissed her once, sweetly, on her mouth, touching her hair, running his hand down one side of her face before cupping his palm under her chin so that she had to look up at him. He smiled at her, suddenly, and went.

He waited until Amelia had taken herself up for a pre-dinner bath before writing the words of the telegram he now knew he must send. In fact he hardly needed to pen them out, so thoroughly had he run them through his mind beforehand. Once he had heard the water running into the deep old-fashioned bath he shut his study door and lifted the telephone receiver for the operator, only to find there was no dialling tone. Several energetic jiggles on the cradle having produced no result, George whistled for the dogs, called up the stairs that he was just going to run them round the grounds, and slipped out before Amelia had time to reply.

Amelia's car was parked in the drive but, unusually for her, without the ignition key. Determined to try to find her keys, George let the dogs into the back and went to return to the house, only to run straight into the arrival of a torrent of hail, complete with lightning and thunder.

'To hell!' he muttered, turning back for the dogs. 'I'll send the damn thing tomorrow!'

'Yes,' the Noble One said. 'A timely storm and well summoned, wizard. But we shall have to do better now or the cause may be lost. I had not foreseen this new interference. You with your crystal may well have done – though if you had you should have acted – yet knowing your ways you most like enjoy such diversions.'

'Ah no, my liege, no,' Longbeard sighed. 'I too lose control – more frequently it seems now as the centuries roll. Perhaps this Lady is in truth a witch herself and, if so, then my powers will be vexed.'

'I think not,' the Noble One replied. 'I think this Lady is not a sorceress but a temptress, yet even so I fear we must do what we supposed.'

'There is a risk, sir, you know that – and you know how great it may be – for loosing such dread sights means that they stay here in the ether, and once here in the ether, sir—'

'I know, wizard, I know!' the Noble One told him sharply. 'But just consider what happens if we lose him to his heart and not his head. Consider my vow, consider our beloved land, consider the consequence, then tell me 'tis not worth the risk.'

'There is no reason other than that, sir,' Longbeard agreed with his most solemn nod. 'Oft-times I forget when I grow weary, I forget.'

443

'Not long, old man,' the Noble One said. 'Not long. And then we shall see you float among your beloved stars and see your ancient face made young again by the music of the spheres. But now one last dazzle – find the stone of darkness, and let it loose this very night.'

He did not keep the stone in the purse but locked it in a cave of ice on the dark side of a distant star. Now he held it in his hand the wizard could feel the heat within, a heat which had been fired millions of years before when Satan kicked a chip from the sun and, cursing it for ever, turned it into a cyclops. No sun shone in or near this stone. When it fell to rest in a desert it burned through to the core of the earth, landing in hellfire where Satan sealed it in a case of such evil that nothing could ever melt it other than God's love. How it came into the wizard's possession is a story for another time. Suffice that when the wizard found it, it was only due to the nobility of his liege that he was not taken to be one of Satan's foot soldiers. Instead, in gratitude to his lord he buried the black stone in a dark star, the very coldest and most distant within their firmament, dreading that he might be called upon to use its power. Now was such a time. Already he could feel the throb of heat and hate within its skin of darkness as it floated above his outstretched hand. Worse, as it floated he could see a future that was blackened with evil. He could see men, women and children in dull grey uniforms with numbers on their sleeves, walking, their faces skeletal, their eyes lost to everything that makes the world bright, their suffering so terrible as to be indescribable.

*   *   *

George awoke with a start, sitting up in bed in a moment of terror such as he had never known. He had no idea what had caused the terror or why he should have woken with such a fright. He was cool, his heart was steady and the night was calm – except for a slight breeze which lifted the curtain momentarily at the window before dropping away to stillness.

He crept out of bed, not wanting to wake Amelia but needing, for some reason, to breathe the night air, to get back in touch with reality. He had had a nightmare, that was all. It was a clear night, with a moon that seemed to light every part of the garden except for the deep shadows under the trees, and so brilliant was it after the earlier storm that he was drawn to go outside.

Pulling on his dressing gown and slippers, he let himself out of the bedroom. A minute later he found himself in the middle of their beloved garden, asking himself, 'Why am I here?'

Something had fallen to earth in the shadows under the yews. Walking over to the old trees he saw an object no larger than a sixpence, but when he bent down to examine it the forgotten images of his nightmare returned at once. With a gasp he straightened up, shaking his head as if he had been hit by something.

In the morning when he awoke and dressed he found a strange note in his jacket pocket. It read: COUNT ME OUT. CANNOT HELP YOU AS YOU

WISHED. PERSONAL PRICE WOULD BE TOO HIGH.

He stared at it, and then, thinking it was some note he had forgotten to send to Jack Cornwall, he threw it into the kitchen fire, and went to the dining room to have breakfast with Amelia.

Twenty-One

For the first time in her married life Amelia felt unhappy. She did not feel it all the time, for whenever she was with George everything seemed to be as it always had been between them. George was as attentive to her as ever, and just as kind, while she herself still loved to try to enchant him. And of course they still shared all their free moments at The Priory together, lunchtime and early afternoon and the evenings after they had both finished work. Yet something had changed. Amelia sensed it and this despite George's seeming to be outwardly his old, loving self.

But Amelia could not find peace, as before.

She realized that she could well have become bored by country life, it being so very uneventful. Or perhaps she wanted another child?

'Maybe we should get a small flat in London somewhere?' [she wrote to Hermione]. 'Maybe I've got to the age where if I don't keep mentally fresh I shall start to stagnate and if I do I shall lose George. I see it all around us in the countryside – women left to their own devices while their husbands follow their careers or lead their own lives, coming home to wives who have lost not only their appeal but their figures and their looks. Maybe this is what's making me feel so unsure of myself, that I see myself turning into one of them, and fear that when I do George will leave me. As I say, I don't think it's anything to do with *George* – except that he doesn't seem to take me into his confidence as fully as he always used to – about his work, that is. Then perhaps this is because I have been somewhat critical about some of the things he's been writing in newspapers and magazines – views I don't fully understand, and which George doesn't see fit to explain to me. All this stuff about appeasement and the need for understanding Germany's problems. As I said to him – not once but often! – I thought the whole point of fighting that awful war was so that we could give up worrying about Germany's problems. But all George will say is that it's a lot more complicated than that.

Then there are all these strange new friends of his – I can't say ours first because I didn't make them and second because I don't much like any of them. We now have a succession of extremely rich and deadly boring people at our dinner table – and sometimes for the weekend (help!), and in return have to attend reciprocal parties either in London or at some fancy address where I feel like Little Miss Country Bumpkin. We can't possibly afford to keep up with these sets of Joneses, but George insists on accepting all their invitations because he says it's all to do with his work. Since he hasn't written a book since his detective one, which was not a success, and is concentrating on writing articles for papers and magazines, I can only imagine this is the direction in which he sees himself going – yet when I ask him about it he clams up, and although he's much too sweet and kind to say that it's none of my business I get the distinct impression that's what he feels! And now, my dear – guess where we've been invited? Only to Riverdean – the Astleys' famous house on the Thames! Oh for an attack of measles or something really catching so that I can stay in bed here reading about how to make my gardens more beautiful instead of having to go to some ghastly house party where I shall spend the whole weekend being ignored. I do so hate grandeur, and snobbery only a little less!

Lots of love, old friend,
Amelia.'

Although she considered herself to be fairly sophisticated, Amelia could not help feeling nervous about being asked to such a very grand country seat, a house so well run and with so many servants that even the royal family was pushed to match the extravagance of the Astleys' hospitality, not to mention the undoubted celebrity of their guest lists. The newspapers always took a particular interest in who was invited to Riverdean, since it was known to be a seat of much political influence, a place where reputations could be made and broken.

Amelia would have really liked George's help and advice as to what might be required of her in the way of a wardrobe, as well as to find out whom he expected to be on the guest list, but as usual he was closeted away in his study working feverishly to meet some deadline or other. Since Amelia knew the problem of what should constitute her wardrobe was hardly on a par with the problems with which her husband was wrestling, she kept well out of his way and instead used her dearly loved Clara as a sounding board.

'I've always loved this dress,' Clara said, holding up a silver lamé copy of a Molyneux made by Amelia's dressmaker. 'You'll have to take this, Mrs Dashwood. It's so lovely.'

'I don't know whether it's *right*, Clara,' Amelia sighed. 'I doubt if it's formal enough. Whenever we go to these house parties the women seem always to be dressed entirely in black. It's either black, or according to the magazines back to the style of the eighteen century, which is apparently all the rage. It's so awfully difficult with places you haven't been to before – particularly places quite as grand as Riverdean.'

'How grand is grand, Mrs Dashwood? Are there really forty bedrooms?'

'Forty bedroom *suites* apparently, Clara. All

done up by famous interior designers like Syrie Maugham.'

'Well, I never, Mrs D. I'm glad I don't have to help out there, I am.'

'They have two butlers, two housekeepers, a major domo, and six footmen,' Amelia told her, while rifling through her minimal wardrobe of dresses. 'And near enough a hundred gardeners, or so I am told. They are rich enough to move entire barns – and even a church, so my husband informs me – putting them where they just thought they looked better around the estate. My husband said someone remarked that the Astleys have done what the Almighty would have done if He'd had the time and the money. There's nothing here for me to wear to a place like Riverdean. Honestly, Clara, I could weep my eyes out.'

'You'll be all right, Mrs Dashwood,' Clara assured her. 'You always look the thing.'

'It's just that you need so many changes of clothes,' Amelia complained. 'For shooting, lunching, walking, rowing, playing tennis, taking tea, drinks, dinner – they spend the whole day changing into something different. Look, Clara – we've filled three suitcases already and we've only dressed me till Saturday lunchtime. I think I'm going to have to trundle into Bath and buy myself a couple of extra outfits from somewhere. I don't know what my husband thought he was doing when he accepted this invitation.'

'I'm ever so glad he did,' Clara grinned. 'I'll

be able to hear all about it when you return.'

'*If* we return, Clara,' Amelia groaned. 'This is a foray deep into enemy country.'

It seemed to Amelia that attending these occasions caused George no undue worries while her stomach was always full of butterflies. She envied his sang-froid, but then, as he teased her as they drove to Riverdean, had she spent four years in the mud of Flanders parties such as the one they were on their way to attend would hold no fears.

'Even so, George, you were never much of a social animal,' Amelia replied. 'Yet now we seem to spend more time going out than anything else.'

'At the risk of being boring, Amelia—'

'I know. It's for your *work*. But it still doesn't make sense. All these super-rich and powerful people constantly begging for your company.'

'Our company, darling.'

'Oh, like heck, George. I can't remember when I last exchanged more than two consecutive sentences with anyone at one of these dreadful occasions. People are very odd, and none odder than the very rich.'

George laughed. 'The rich enjoy collecting people – and obviously for some reason or other they consider that at the moment I'm collectable.'

'You're always trying that one on and it simply doesn't hold up. We've been places where the host and hostess don't even seem to have heard of you and I always feel we must have been asked for quite another reason. And actually I'd quite like to know what that reason is now, please.'

'It's Society, Amelia,' George insisted. 'It's the way these people go on. They can't bear to admit they don't know the right people personally, so they ask their friends and guests to invite those they consider to be the right people to swell their guest lists. That's how one finds oneself at places where the host and hostess don't know one.'

'I could believe that to be true about some places, but not Riverdean. According to what I've heard you only ever get asked there if you are a personal friend, or someone *really* important.'

'I've met the Astleys on several occasions.'

'George – you're only a writer, and, let's face it, not that renowned. It's not as if you've won the Nobel Prize or anything.'

'So maybe they're just hard up for decent tennis players.'

'No, George. You are up to something – and I want to know what.'

George looked round at her from the driving seat, then shrugged. 'Very well,' he admitted. 'I want to get into politics.'

'You what?' Amelia looked at him in utter amazement. 'You? Who always said that politicians were the most untrustworthy, useless people on earth?'

'Which is why maybe we're going to need some better ones.'

'So.' Amelia said after a moment's thought.

'Suppose you do want to go into politics. Why not start off at grass roots? At home in Somerset?'

'I was going to. But then some of the people I've met recently suggested there were better ways of going about it.'

'Such as contesting a safe seat?'

George shook his head. 'On the contrary. Such as being backed by the right people.'

'I take it you're going to be a Conservative?'

'I haven't actually joined any party yet. But when I do, yes, I suppose it will be the Conservatives – but you're not to say anything.' He looked round again, this time very seriously. 'Not a word. Do you hear? Promise me, Amelia – I want this to be a secret at the moment. And it's very important that it stays so.'

'Why?' Amelia teased, relieved that there was an obvious reason for the change in George's social behaviour, and this was it. 'Why the big secret?'

'For I'm to be Queen of the May,' George joked. 'For I'm to be Queen of the May.'

Yet, judging from the look in his eyes, Amelia thought that perhaps the joke had a little more import than she was meant to realize.

The house party at Riverdean was at least as bad as Amelia had feared. The house was huge and daunting, the guest list enormous, distinguished and equally unnerving, and the entertainment itself formidably formal. Every meal was a set piece and every moment of recreation choreographed, the guests going through the motions as if the entire event had been thoroughly rehearsed with the particular intention of removing all show of sentiment. Once Amelia was discovered to be not only lowly but unknown she was discarded from the pack like a sick animal, left to fend for herself when George was not in attendance, which was often, due to his very apparent popularity – especially with the women and most particularly with Deanne Astley.

In the flesh the famous hostess was even more beautiful and alluring than Amelia had been led to believe, with a perfect figure, extraordinarily long legs, incredible elegance and the strangest and most compelling gaze Amelia had ever encountered, a look which changed character entirely depending on which sex the pair of pale turquoise eyes was fixed upon. When Deanna Astley looked on her rivals the look was chilling and disdainful, but when she gazed upon men the objects of her attention became like rabbits mesmerized by the headlights of a car.

From the moment Amelia set foot inside Riverdean, Deanna Astley singled her out for especial contempt, either ignoring her entirely or if forced to address her treating her as if she were only one step up from a maidservant. Except when George was present. When George and Amelia were in their hostess's company as a couple Deanna Astley treated them both as if they were royalty.

'You're exaggerating,' George said, predictably enough, when Amelia fell into the trap of complaining about Mrs Astley's rudeness to her, as they changed for dinner. 'And if I didn't know you so well, Amelia Dashwood, I would say it was because you were jealous.'

'If you think I'm capable of being jealous over that sort of woman, then you don't know me at all! Not one little bit!'

'I was only joking,' George said lamely, making a mess of his bow tie.

'No, you were not joking,' Amelia seethed, taking the strip of fabric and starting to tie it for him. 'You're like a cat with a bowl of double cream whenever she comes near you. What is it with you? Or more to the point, what is it with *her*?'

'I don't know what you mean,' George said, trapped by the firm hold Amelia had of his tie. 'One has to be polite to one's hostess.'

'Polite, certainly. But not lickspittle, George Dashwood. You're worth a million of most of these people. And I hope I'm worth a little, but more to you than her!'

'Amelia—'

'I mean it, George,' Amelia said, finishing with his tie and standing back to glare at him. 'If I see you fawning around her again like a little puppy dog I shall come over and kick you up the backside.'

'In front of all these eminent people?' George smiled. 'In front of most of his majesty's Cabinet ministers?'

'Most of *them* need a jolly good kick up the derrière, too,' Amelia concluded. 'I've rarely met such a bunch of boring stuffed shirts in my life. They don't have a thing to say for themselves.'

'Try asking them about their childhoods,' George suggested. 'Ask them about their mothers and especially their nannies. You won't be able to stop them talking after that. You'll see.'

Amelia did as advised throughout dinner and Sunday, carefully questioning two Cabinet ministers, one eminent banker and a boring earl about their childhoods. Her success was so entire that by the time they came to leave on Monday morning Amelia found she had acquired a whole list of rich admirers and subsequently a whole new set of social venues to which they were about to be invited.

'Thank you, George,' she groaned in the car as they headed back west. 'I think you made me do that deliberately. It seems I've even got us invitations to spend the New Year in Scotland.'

'I think we'll pass on that one,' George said, changing the Bentley up a gear. 'Even so, you were an enormous success.'

'In a field in which I have no ambitions to be successful, I may say. There were some really odd women there – did you notice? There was a whole bunch of them who seemed to hang around together all the time. You couldn't miss them because none of them seemed to wear any make-up. I know it's not the *done thing* in the country

457

anyway, to wear lipstick with tweeds and all that – but at that sort of extremely grand house party you'd have thought they would. It was so deliberate, the way they looked with no make-up and all in practically the same little black dress – it was as if – I don't know. It was as if they were some sort of sect.'

'That's interesting,' George said, glancing quickly at her. 'Do you know who they were, any of them?'

'No. I was introduced to some of them and their husbands, but as to who they all were . . . One of them's married to that rather handsome banker I sat next to.'

'David Montmorency-Hughes.' George smiled. 'He's a bit more than a banker, darling. He's the Governor of the Bank of England.'

'Had a rotten childhood, apparently. Nanny used to beat him with a stair-rod and shut him in cupboards. His wife was one of "the sect." And Lord Upton's wife. She seemed to be another.'

'Mmmm.' George nodded thoughtfully. 'Interesting.'

'Actually practically without exception they were all the sort of people you can't abide. Or couldn't abide.' Amelia looked round at him. 'They were all what you used to call *flinty hearts*. The sort of people who've always given you the ab-dabs. Yet there you were accepting their hospitality as if they were blood brothers.'

'That's what would-be politicians have to do.'

'You always said people like that are pagans. That they have no feeling for the humanities. No interest in any ideas which are kind and good.'

'Yes I know – and you looked sensational in your silver dress, by the way. I meant to say.'

'Sensational as in an embarrassment,' Amelia countered.

'Not at all. None of the men could take their eyes off you.'

'None of the women either.'

'They were jealous of your daring.'

'Actually, by then, George, I'd really stopped caring,' Amelia confessed. 'They were all being so frightfully snooty I'd have quite happily trotted down that very grand staircase totally in the buff. That might have actually got some of them talking. But then I remembered your ambition to become Prime Minister and thought better of it.'

George laughed – genuinely, Amelia was glad to note.

'I did hear some quite interesting gossip,' Amelia remembered. 'Or rather overheard it. About the Duke of Windsor – and his *cutie*, as apparently they all call the duchess.'

'I'm surprised,' George remarked. 'The Astleys are very friendly with the Windsors.'

'So you probably know that the duke and duchess plan to set up home in France.'

'I've heard the rumours. I know they were keen on making him the Governor of the Bahamas, but that the Queen won't have it.'

'Actually the only thing that really seemed to matter to most of those silly women was whether or not people should make a full curtsy to the Duchess of Windsor – which they think people should. And that she should be accorded the title of *Your Royal Highness*, and not *Your Grace*. As if it matters, George. There are far more important things that matter – such as making sure England doesn't give in to Hitler. And that's something else I noticed. That most of the people there were much more pro the Duke and Duchess of Windsor than they were the King and Queen.'

Again George glanced at her before turning his attention back to the road.

'Is that the impression you got? Probably just party talk. People talk awfully big at parties.'

'I have to say I didn't actually like anyone there, George,' Amelia sighed. 'And neither did you, surely?'

'The point is they're all influential people, Amelia,' George replied. 'The sort of people would-be politicians like me need to know.'

'I can't stand the thought of you going into politics. I far preferred it when you were just a novelist,' Amelia continued, as the car started to descend the hill which led down into Bath. 'When you were an *enfant terrible* and everyone was attacking you – I felt so proud of you. So proud that you were prepared to stand up for what you thought was right, and in print. You didn't care what anyone thought of you. Not a jot.'

'Meaning I do now.'

'Politicians have to suck up to people all the time. That's something I can't see you doing. At least not the George Dashwood I married I can't.'

'It's something I'm going to have to do whether I like it or not.'

'And what about whether I like it or not?'

'It's just something I have to do,' George reiterated. 'Now can we please talk about something else?'

'For the moment, if that's what you want,' Amelia agreed. 'But it's to be continued, don't you worry.'

Despite Amelia's obvious dismay at George's newly chosen career path, almost everyone else became extremely excited at the prospect of someone with George's war record and distinguished military family going into politics – a prospect which much to Amelia's surprise had very shortly after the weekend at Riverdean become public knowledge. One depressing result of this disclosure was that George and she were invited out with ever-increasing regularity to dine at the tables of those Amelia so heartily despised and whose company George had similarly once avoided, particularly the dining tables of those who believed in what was now commonly called the policy of appeasement. These were powerful people, as Amelia very soon discovered, with the ears of the politicians whose belief it was that the only sensible approach to what others saw as a growing threat from Germany was to keep Hitler sweet, arguing that German expansion to the east would be a good thing since it would surely divert any danger from the west, and although George never went as far as to endorse these sentiments in print, Amelia began to form the very distinct impression that this was a concept to which he too subscribed.

'You don't know what you're talking about!' he said impatiently when the subject came up at home. 'This is something which I am afraid is a little above your head.'

'I do so hope you're not flirting with Fascism,' Amelia replied, ignoring the put-down. 'You may not want to call it that, but from the sound of all these arguments I spy Fascism.'

'Is that what you really think?' George sighed in exasperation. 'You don't seriously imagine I'm attracted to that sort of thing, do you? Surely you know me better than that?'

'At the moment I don't think I know you at all, George.'

'If you want it in simplistic terms—'

'I had better have it in simplistic terms. In case it goes too far over this pretty little head of mine.'

'What some people are trying to do is to make the world a better place to live in now, or else our generation died in vain. And for those of us who fought and survived the war, it's important that we should help to try and build a world where such a terrible conflict won't happen again. If such a thing is possible.'

George stopped, and looked at her in a very different way, the way he had started to look at moments like this, as if he wanted to tell her something but could not. Amelia read these looks perfectly correctly, but she failed to understand the reason behind them, thinking that why George seemed reluctant to continue with these arguments was because he thought she was not up to him intellectually. Since that was what she thought and it put her on the back foot, Amelia became more aggressive, and then George would shake his head, apologize and shut himself away in his study. Usually Amelia just let him go, realizing she could not force him to discuss things which he thought were beyond her, but on this particular occasion, when they had just returned from yet another high-powered social gathering, there was one hook she would not let him off.

'I know you're all for putting the world to rights, George,' she said. 'But that's no excuse for anti-Semitism.'

'You're not accusing me of that?' George said, with genuine hurt. 'I don't believe it if you are. How could you even begin to think that of me?'

'Let me see,' Amelia replied, mock-thoughtfully. 'It must be because tonight you just sat there while certain people made anti-Jewish remarks and said nothing.'

'It wasn't my house.'

463

'Meaning it's bad form to pick an argument on away ground.'

'In a way, yes.'

'You never minded before. I've seen you taking other people to task before around other people's dining tables and not caring one hoot about it, let alone two.'

'This is different, Amelia. This is a political thing.'

'A political thing? To disparage Jews?' Amelia said sharply. 'Is this going to be part of the brave new world you're hoping to build? Because if it is—'

'Stop it! Do you hear? Stop it!' George cried, getting to his feet, his face contorted in anguish. 'You have to stop asking me all these questions, do you hear? Just stop it! No more. You are not to keep pressing me and needling me and asking me all these questions!'

'Why not?' Amelia returned, suddenly worried by the look in George's eyes, a look which seemed to carry her back all the way to a dreadful day up in the glens of Scotland. 'I'm your wife, George. I love you. I have a perfect right to ask you what I like!'

'No, Amelia,' George said suddenly, very quietly. 'No you don't. You don't have any such right. No-one has the right to know! I have a mission – do you understand? All this – what I'm doing! You mustn't ever ask me about it! Never! Not ever!'

'Why not? Why has this got to be some sort of secret?' Amelia protested, on her feet as well and confronting her husband, who was staring at her dementedly. 'There never have been any secrets between us, so why should there be any now?'

'Because that is how it is!' George said with a passion which genuinely surprised Amelia. 'And if you ask me to explain – I can't! If I could, I would, believe me – but it just isn't possible! So you're going to have to trust me. Please. Remember what you promised me and trust me. Please.'

'If that's what you want, George,' Amelia said uncertainly, 'then of course. Of course I trust you. I don't think you're capable of doing a bad thing. At least that's what I've always believed until now.'

'Then please just keep on believing it. Please believe in me. If you don't – I don't know what I will do.'

He looked so completely and utterly lost that Amelia could do nothing but take him in her arms, where he stood silently for an age, his arms round her, his head bowed over her shoulder. When she moved at last to kiss him, she saw there were tears in his eyes.

'George,' she began, but he just shook his head mutely at her and took himself off to his study.

From then on he would say nothing more on the subject, and once she realized the moratorium he had imposed was in earnest Amelia declined to

465

press him further. Instead she busied herself in her beloved garden and left George to his readings and his writings, noting only that he spent longer and longer shut away in his study and less and less time with her. Whatever free time he did have was immediately taken up by social engagements they attended together or George attended on his own. The time he had once spent with his wife and family was now passed in the company of financiers and politicians, and since the habitat of such species was urban rather than rural George spent more and more time away from The Priory: up in London, or Manchester, or York, or Paris, and even on one or two occasions in Munich.

And because they never discussed the matter of George's public life or his new political ardour Amelia could only guess at the reasons for his actions and his attitudes. Unfortunately the conclusions she reached were a very long distance from the truth, and because she guessed wrong the bewildered Amelia found that where there had been only the greatest and most loving intimacy between herself and George there was now an ever-widening gap, a gap that was soon to become an emotional abyss.

Particularly now that Deanna Astley had entered their lives.

Amelia's fears and suspicions came to a head when, two months after their weekend at

Riverdean, she and George were accorded what was considered to be one of the greatest social accolades of the day, an invitation to a soirée in the Astleys' famous London residence, two houses knocked into one in Mayfair. Unfortunately the day before the engagement Amelia fell ill with a stomach infection, severe enough to confine her to her bed.

'I shall telephone and cancel,' George said after the doctor had left.

'No,' Amelia said, although that was precisely what she wished him to do. But she knew how important the party must be to her politically ambitious husband, and she insisted he went without her. 'There's no reason for you not to go,' she assured him. 'This is the best chance you will have of meeting all these important people you have been dying to meet and who obviously are dying to meet you, so you really ought to go.'

'It's only that the Prime Minister is going to be there, otherwise . . .' George hesitated, standing at the end of her bed watching her anxiously.

'Go, George. I mean it.'

'But what about you?'

'I shall be perfectly all right. I have Clara if I need anything, and Edward said he would look in again in the morning. So go on – go. You keep saying how much this will mean to you.'

'No – you don't understand, Amelia.'

'Of course I don't. We established that months ago. But then that doesn't seem to matter so much now. Not as much as it once did.'

'Don't say that. It just isn't true.'

'Of course it is. You used to take me into your confidence completely, but now I'm not allowed to ask you anything. Or if I do you just hole yourself up in your study and lock the door. So go on – go off to your party.'

'It isn't my party,' George protested. 'And I don't really want to go without you.'

'Of course you do,' Amelia replied, lying down and turning her face away from him. 'Now go away and leave me in peace. I'm really not feeling at all well.'

Amelia remained miserably in her bed for the next forty-eight hours while George took himself off to London, just as miserable but unable to refuse the invitation since, as Amelia had said, this was the best and possibly the only chance he had of meeting on a social level the people he had to meet if he were to have any chance in succeeding with his mission. He was miserable because he could not tell Amelia why he must go, knowing that if he could only do so she would understand what he knew must seem to her like his completely irrational behaviour. But it was not possible. He was forbidden to mention to one living soul the nature of his intent. He understood one careless word to the wrong person could ruin everything and endanger the future.

Yet who had instructed him in this way he had absolutely no idea.

*　　*　　*

Amelia read all about the glittering party in her *Daily Mail* the next day. There was a picture of George standing with the Prime Minister, Deanna Astley, more glamorous than ever by his side. There was also a report of a skirmish on the doorstep of the Astley residence when George was leaving the reception in the company of a party of friends which included Jack Cornwall and Ralph Grace.

'I'm not surprised to see Jack's name,' Amelia said to George on the telephone when she had read the item below the photographs. 'But Ralph? I didn't realize he was part of the smart set.'

'Just read what happened, Amelia,' George replied at the other end of the line, sitting in a chair in the corner of his hotel bedroom, drinking a large cup of black coffee. 'It wasn't that amusing.'

'This is the same man who attacked you at Wimbledon, surely?'

'The man who insulted *you* and whom I attacked, you mean,' George replied. 'We were all just leaving, and Ralph had gone to hail a cab, when this madman – who must have been waiting all evening – this madman rushed up from the service area and had a go at me.'

'It says here he had a knife,' Amelia said in quiet dismay.

'It's all right, Amelia. Jack and I overpowered him easily.'

'But he had a knife, George. He could have killed you.'

'I think that was the general intention.'

'George—'

'It's all right. I didn't even get a scratch.'

'He called you a Fascist.' Amelia put the newspaper down.

George laughed. 'He called me a lot worse than that.'

'How can you laugh when someone tries to kill you?'

'Darling,' George sighed. 'Probably because I've had the whole German army trying to kill me.'

'Why did he call you a Fascist?' Amelia persisted. 'Why, George?'

'Because the man's bonkers, darling.' George laughed again. 'Stark and staringly so. Now how are you? Are you feeling any better?'

'I was,' she replied. 'Now I'm not so sure. When are you coming home?'

'Er – tomorrow,' George replied after a brief hesitation. 'Tomorrow or the day after. I have to go to a meeting tonight – some sort of political rally – and tomorrow I have to have lunch at the House of Commons. It all depends what happens at the lunch when exactly I'm coming home. But I'll be in touch all the time. As long as you're all right.'

'I'm fine. Please hurry home.'

Before she had even put the telephone back in its cradle Amelia realized how much she missed George – her old George – and even her new one. Life seemed suddenly so utterly pointless and empty without him, and she realized that even despite her anger over the way he had deliberately distanced himself from her, she still loved him with all her heart.

The next day she read another report in the newspaper which caused her further anxiety. It seemed the political rally which had taken place the previous night was yet another organized by England's very own self-styled Fascist leader, Oswald Mosley. Among those attending were Sir Marmaduke and Lady Astley, several other well known Society names, and the popular author and political commentator George Dashwood.

Breaking all the rules, as soon as George returned home Amelia demanded to know what he had been doing at such an affair. Far from being perturbed by the question George was unruffled, explaining that it was his job as a writer and commentator to find out exactly what was going on at these rallies and what was being said. Attendance, he argued, was not necessarily concomitant with agreement. These rallies and the growth of the Mosleyite party were an important political development which could not and should not be ignored.

'That satisfy you, Twinkle-toes?' George was standing at the end of Amelia's bed. 'Or do you think I've come back with a suitcase full of black shirts?'

Amelia was bested, as she knew George's argument was perfectly plausible. Since he was writing increasingly for one of the major newspapers, it was obviously vital that he kept abreast of all the latest political developments, so whatever her private fears Amelia knew perfectly well that George had answered that particular question satisfactorily. What she found almost impossible to accept, however, was how over the next few months George's name became more and more closely linked with Deanna Astley's, as George absented himself more and more from The Priory to attend more and more functions and social engagements. Naturally Amelia was included in the invitations, but she very soon gave up accepting most of them once she discovered not only how unimportant she was to most of the people she met there but how much of a hindrance they considered her, as if she was the apparent wrongdoer rather than the notorious Mrs Astley.

'It doesn't look good me turning up without you,' George would say, increasingly tired of the ongoing argument.

'You're the person they want to meet,' Amelia would retort. 'And I want to see my family, rather than a lot of right-wing stuffed shirts. So go on – off you go and have fun.'

'I'm not going to some jolly schoolboy tea party, Amelia.'

'I know you're not. But since you don't seem to think it worth your while to enlighten me as to what precisely you are up to, what am I *meant* to say?'

Time and time again George would hesitate, since what he wanted to do more than anything was stay at home with Amelia and his family and try to recapture their previous idyll. But fate and those who haunted their former paradise had unbeknown to him decreed otherwise. So time and time again he would find himself having to tear himself away from The Priory, knowing full well that by doing so he was estranging himself more and more from the person he loved. But he could not stop himself. It was as if unwittingly he had got on a merry-go-round and now found he could not get off. Even worse, deep inside he knew that he must not get off, not if he was to play his destined part in the darkening future.

Summer passed and autumn came, and with less to do in the garden and the children back at school Amelia found that for the first time in her marriage she was desperately lonely. Archie and Mae were away filming somewhere, Hermione was not only still up in Yorkshire but expecting her second child, and all her Somerset friends seemed to be either away in town most of the time, busy on their land or fully occupied bringing up their hunters. For a desperate moment Amelia even considered joining the hunt simply for the company it would afford her, only to remember Mae's warning that it was *so bad for the complexion, darling*. So she resigned herself to facing an increasingly lonely winter with George destined to be away more than ever, following his political and literary businesses.

George was spending so much time in London that he finally yielded and rented a small service flat, but it was not somewhere that took even two people comfortably, and Peter and Gwendolyn had no interest in going to London other than at Christmas. As the October winds began to howl around the old priory Amelia built herself huge fires in the drawing room and immersed herself either in her reading or in her needlework. And so the months passed, but slowly, so slowly, each day seeming like a fortnight with Amelia quite alone, until a neighbour chose to call, or she drove herself to the village. Sometimes she would try to delay Jethro or Robbie from returning to their families at teatime, or, if the weather was exceptionally bad she would sit listening to the wireless, aware that she was lonely but incapable of doing anything about it.

What better moment than now, thought the Tall One, leaning nonchalantly against the old wall, when you feel unloved, and sadly ignored? What better moment than this? Rubbing his thumb against his finger he flinted stardust and blew it through the crack in the old window. It flew across the room and into the flame in the fire into which the Lonely Lady was staring.

When the doorbell rang it startled her, yet as she heard Clara going to answer it she had the strangest feeling that she knew exactly who was ringing. Now he stood at the door, with Clara behind him, peering around him and saying his name. Amelia was on her feet, putting down her book, brushing the dog hair off her skirt, excusing her appearance while he just smiled.

'I was passing the gate, and better to ring the bell, I thought, than walk straight in and give you a fright. Better to have myself announced formally by my charming old friend M'moiselle Clara, who could tell me to run along should you be otherwise engaged.'

'Ralph,' Amelia heard her voice somewhere saying. 'I can't tell you how very good it is to see you.'

'Wasn't it George himself who told me to come and see yous,' Ralph said, affecting a bad stage Irish. 'Sure wasn't I in this neck of the woods doing a spot of business, and since he knew that I was, didn't he ask me to keep an eye on yous all?'

'You've seen George?'

'Haven't you?'

'Well of course!' Amelia laughed. 'What I meant was you've seen him recently?'

'Haven't you?'

'Stop it, Ralph,' Amelia said, laughing once more. 'You're incorrigible.'

'I am I am,' he said. 'I am I am I am. And I would kill for a whisky.'

They sat in front of the fire. There was never any small talk it seemed with Ralph Grace – it was straight in at the deep end.

'George seems to spend an awful lot of his time in London. For such a home dog.'

'Not so much a home dog nowadays, Ralph. More of a gun dog.'

'A gun dog? Our George? I thought George had become a spaniel.'

'Are you sneering, Ralph? Because if you are – don't.' Amelia glanced at him, then threw her half-smoked cigarette into the fire.

'Of course I am not sneering. What I meant was – when you said he was a gun dog – I meant to say I thought he had changed his spots. You know – George No-More-War Dashwood.'

'I don't really know what he thinks any more, Ralph. He doesn't include me the way he used to.'

Amelia stopped. It was out, and nothing to be done. She had betrayed George.

'I'll tell you what I admire about your mister,' Ralph continued, as if she had not spoken. 'What I admire most was the book he wrote straight after the war. He must have known the sort of furore it would create, but he stood his ground – in typical Dashwood style – and that took some doing.'

'You know much more about us than I know about you. What have you been doing since?'

'Not what I intended to do, Mrs Rafferty.'

'That isn't my name.'

'I warned you about this thing I have about giving people names.'

'Anyway, go on. About what you've been doing.'

'I meant to go back to finish my studies at

476

university, which were somewhat interrupted by *la guerre grande*. I was studying modern languages – French and German.'

'I knew you spoke French.'

Ralph looked at her, eyebrows raised. 'George told you? Of course he would have told you.'

'Not immediately. It took a bit of time.'

'How much did he tell you, Mrs Rafferty?'

'He told me about that poor girl . . .'

'Ah yes, and Walker no doubt.'

'It took for ever for him to be able to talk about it.'

Ralph nodded again, smoked some more of his cigarette and looked up at the ceiling. 'Anyway,' he continued, as if making a fresh start. 'I didn't go back to university because I thought I'd lost too much time because of the damned war. I went into the Diplomatic, and since then I've been all over the shop. The Orient, Russia, Germany – you name it. But I'm stationed in Paris at the moment. Or rather, more accurately, I was.'

'I've never been to Paris,' Amelia admitted. 'We're always meaning to go, but somehow after the war George wasn't very anxious to return to France, which is quite understandable.'

'Oh, you must go to Paris,' Ralph insisted, and threw his finished smoke into the fire. 'I shall take you and show you around.'

'What a lovely idea,' Amelia agreed, quickly. 'We can *all* go together, George and I and you and – is there a Mrs Grace?'

For some reason Ralph found the question hilarious.

'Why's that so funny?' Amelia wondered, finding herself laughing as well. 'I don't see why that's so funny.'

'Of course you do, Mrs Rafferty!' Ralph hooted. 'Is there a Mrs Grace? You sound like something out of a play! You *know* there is no Mrs Grace.'

'I don't see how. How do I know?'

'Because you do.' Ralph stopped laughing, pushing his dark hair back from his forehead with slender fingers while he stared at her suddenly.

'So,' Amelia said with a shrug, in an effort to lighten the atmosphere, 'we shall all go to Paris, George, you and I – and you will show us around.'

'If that's what you want. But that isn't what I want.'

'I don't think I'm going to ask you what you want, *Mr* Grace.'

'I would prefer to show you around Paris by yourself.'

'I don't think you should say things like that. Do you?'

'No. In fact I don't even know what made me say it.'

Another silence fell, as Amelia suddenly wondered what she was to do with her unexpected guest. He had arrived by motor bicycle, apparently on his way to Bath, and she fell to wondering if she could tactfully suggest that he should be on his way quite soon. Instead she heard herself saying, 'Have you had anything to eat, Monsieur Grace?'

'Non! And to be honest – I am starving.'

Excusing herself, Amelia went out to the kitchen, stopping on the way to lean against the closed drawing room door and catch her breath.

'What's that you said?' Clara asked as Amelia found herself standing in the kitchen looking at her housekeeper, who was sitting at the table reading a magazine. 'What are you going to make so sure of, Mrs Dashwood?'

'Was I talking out loud, Clara?'

'I heard you say, "I must be quite, quite sure".'

'Did I say that?'

'Yes, you said, "I must be quite quite sure to tell Mr Rafferty" – is he the new plumber?'

Amelia laughed. 'No, no, that's just Lieutenant Grace's nickname for myself and Captain Dashwood. But thank you – I must ring Captain Dashwood in London and tell him that Lieutenant Grace is here and wants to stay the night.'

As luck would have it George had returned to his hotel only five minutes earlier to change for dinner.

'Ralph's there?' George said, with little apparent surprise. 'Well, that's Ralph all over, of course. A great one for doing things on the spur of the moment. Why didn't he telephone?'

'I'm not sure. He was passing the gate and thought he'd look in.'

'Typical Ralph. Look, Amelia—'

'Is it all right if I give him supper?' Amelia asked, interrupting.

'Why are you asking me that? You don't have to ask me whether or not you can entertain my best friend.' George laughed. 'You can give him supper and put him up in the cottage.'

'I don't see why we should have to put him up. He's got his motor bike – and anyway he's on his way to stay in Bath, or somewhere.'

'No, no, I won't hear of it. Of course we must put him up. All being well I should be home tomorrow by midday or early afternoon. See you then. I can't wait.'

'I can't wait either. George—'

Before he could reply there was a ring on the outer door of the flat.

'George?' Amelia said on the other end of the telephone line. 'George – are you still there?'

'I think it's the porter come to leave some coal.'

'Take care driving home.'

George replaced the receiver and went to the front door. As he had expected his visitor was not the porter, but Deanna Astley.

Returning to the drawing room Amelia found Ralph standing by the sofa table going through the photograph albums.

'This is – as the Americans would say – one hell of a place, Mrs Rafferty, but obviously a complete ruin when you bought it.'

'All but,' Amelia agreed. 'Someone had been living here, but an awfully long time ago.'

'Round about the Dark Ages?'

Amelia laughed. 'Round about then.'

'I could have taken you out to dinner. I suddenly thought.'

'What's that got to do with what we were discussing?'

'Nothing. I just suddenly thought I—'

'—could have taken me out to dinner,' Amelia interrupted. 'You don't have to worry. Dinner's in hand.'

'I should have thought of it earlier.'

'It doesn't matter, really. We can have dinner here, and George insists you stay the night, in the cottage.'

Amelia looked at him again, trying to decide what sort of man he was. At that moment she felt that had Archie and Mae been searching for someone to play Feste in *Twelfth Night*, Ralph Grace might have perfectly fitted the bill. He had about him a strangely doleful air, which made her feel suddenly protective, particularly as he went on to say, 'There really is no need to put me up.'

'You don't want to stay?'

'That wasn't what I said. I said there was no *need*, Mrs Rafferty. I could quite easily hop on my bike and vanish out of your life as quickly as I gate-crashed into it.'

'Don't you think you've had a bit too much whisky for that kind of caper?'

'Good God no. I've driven Bessie before with the best part of a bottle on board. I'm not going to leave because I don't want to.'

'Tell me,' she said, wishing Clara would call them in to dinner. 'What are you doing in the area? This isn't exactly the sort of location where old friends just drop by. Or in. Were you already in the neighbourhood?'

'Yes and no. More no than yes, really.'

'I don't have the beginning of an idea what you mean by that, Ralph.'

'I mean I was in the neighbourhood but not already. I was passing through. Rather than staying.'

'Passing through. Where from?'

'From Paris.'

'From Paris?' Amelia echoed in amazement. 'Aren't you a little out of your way?'

'Certainly,' Ralph replied. 'That's the whole idea – when you're on the run.'

'Dinner,' Clara said, having given a quick knock on the door. 'Sorry it's taken so long.'

Over dinner Amelia successfully avoided falling into what she thought might have been one of Ralph's bear traps by asking him to explain his enigmatic statement about being *on the run*. Instead she drew him out about his travels and his experiences in the Diplomatic Corps. Inevitably the conversation came back to Paris.

'The famously benevolent Sidney Smith said he

thought that every wife had the right to insist on seeing Paris.'

'I really must go, mustn't I?'

'We shall make a party of it. You, George, and me as your guide. You shall come too, M'moiselle Clara,' he said to the housekeeper, who had just returned with the pudding. 'It will do you all good to get out of the countryside for a while and enjoy some cosmopolitan life.'

Privately Amelia wondered how a man who had apparently just fled the city because of some incident from his past could possibly hope to return there so soon.

'I remember George telling me you're a bit of a pianist,' Ralph said when they returned to the drawing room after dinner. 'Did he also tell you that I was an excellent listener?'

'I can't say I remember him saying *that*. On the other hand he might have told you that I hate it when somebody *asks* me to play. I immediately become all thumbs.'

'In which case I won't ask you again.'

Inevitably Amelia did play for him, lured to the keyboard by the simplest of tricks.

She was pouring them both a second cup of coffee when Ralph sat himself down at her piano and began leafing through her music before proceeding to murder all her favourite melodies. By the time Ralph was three-fingering his way slowly through 'Smoke Gets In Your Eyes' she could bear it no longer.

'Oh very well – what would you like to hear?'

'It never fails.' He looked up at her, mischief and mayhem in his eyes.

With George away so much Amelia's enjoyment in playing the piano had somehow foundered. There seemed little point in playing to yourself. This evening, however, she had an audience, which was perhaps why she found she could not stop, so that by the time she had worked her way through 'Stormy Weather' and all her other favourites, the fire had died down, and Clara had popped her head round the door to say good night.

'You play beautifully,' Ralph told her, still leaning on the piano watching her. 'I don't suppose you know "I Can't Get Started with You"?'

'I don't think I've even heard it.'

'It's new. And it's going to be a smash. Let me play it for you.'

He went round to where she was seated at the piano but before he was only halfway there Amelia was already protesting.

'Why don't you try and sing it? Or hum it, or something?'

'I don't think you'll pick this one up easily. It has a very difficult middle eight. Let me just map it out for you.'

Reluctantly Amelia made room for him at the piano stool.

'Don't get up. There's plenty of room for both of

us on a duet stool, I am happy to say, Mrs Rafferty.'

Now Amelia found that it was Ralph playing and singing to her, and as he did so it seemed to Amelia that the duet stool was becoming less and less roomy.

Each verse ended the same, and each time Ralph sang the words they seemed to have more and more import.

'Yes,' Amelia said hastily, for want of anything else to say, when he finished. 'I see what you mean about the middle eight.'

'Mmm, tricky, isn't it?'

The middle eight was not the only thing that was tricky: not looking at Ralph was tricky too. She knew that she must not look up, least of all look round, because if she did she knew he would kiss her.

'I'll show you to the cottage.' She tried to spring up from the stool, but that was as far as she got.

They couldn't hear his laugh; no-one could, except the two men sitting high in the yew trees. 'Damn him,' the Noble One said. 'May fire rain on his cursed head.'

'I warned you, sir,' Longbeard sighed, stroking the soft white hairs of his whiskers. 'I said he was here.'

'Then kindly be rid of him, wizard! Send him flying! Do you not see, the wretched knave shall ruin everything! Just as he did before! He already has her in his thrall.'

*   *   *

Try as she might, Amelia could not get rid of the sense of that kiss. It was only the lightest of kisses, but as she tossed and turned in her bed before sleep finally induced oblivion, she could not forget the sensation.

How could she have let him? she kept asking herself. How could she have liked him kissing her? She was a married woman – she was married to George. She rolled over yet again on her pillow, holding it in her arms while she struggled to make some sense out of the evening, and, failing, fell asleep.

The next day Amelia was up early, as always. By breakfast time there was still no sign of Ralph. Imagining that he must be a heavy sleeper, Amelia returned inside, and had a cup of coffee and a slice of toast in the kitchen with Clara before beginning her day's work in the garden. At half past ten she saw him emerging from the cottage to stretch and have a good yawn in the sunshine before he noticed her. Amelia at once busied herself, nevertheless watching him out of the corner of her eye as he ambled across the lawns.

'Morning, Mrs Rafferty,' he called, without a trace of the embarrassment that Amelia herself was feeling. 'What an extraordinarily perfect morning. All right if I go and help myself to some breakfast?'

'Yes, of course,' Amelia replied, determined to

be as formal as she could. 'Clara will show you where to find everything.'

As he thanked her and turned to go, Amelia straightened up, about to call him back, but then thought better of it. It hardly seemed quite the right time nor perhaps the place to ask a man she barely knew what exactly he had meant by kissing her the night before. They had after all parted in complete silence. Amelia fleeing upstairs while Ralph made his way, albeit possibly a little hazily, to the guest cottage.

So, not really knowing what she should say, she let him go inside to be ministered to by Clara while she went on working in the garden, all the while wondering how and when exactly to approach the subject.

Since she did not expect George home until early afternoon, she decided that perhaps it was best left until Ralph and she sat down together for lunch, when she could more easily bring the subject up – if indeed she had the courage to bring it up at all.

'You look as though you are sitting on an egg, Mrs Rafferty,' Ralph said as he helped them both to some sherry in the drawing room at midday. 'Do you have something you wish to hatch?'

'To be hatched, actually. It was something you said last night. Just before dinner.'

'About being on the run? I was wondering when you'd get round to it.'

'You could have volunteered the information.'

'And have you drop dead from shock? *Oh la la.*'

'That bad, is it?'

'*Terrible, madame.*'

'Who are you on the run from? The police?'

'Worse. Must worse – from someone's husband,' Ralph said, poker-faced.

He looked so droll that Amelia found herself laughing, but even as she smiled her heart sank as she realized that he was, quite clearly, some sort of professional adulterer.

'Do you want to elaborate, Lieutenant Grace?'

'Would it be wise to follow one indiscretion with another?' he wondered, refilling both their glasses with sherry. 'I shouldn't have even mentioned it. In fact I don't actually know why I did. I was probably just being provocative. In fact I'm sure I was, because since I arrived here I seem to have lost most of my common sense.'

He lapsed into silence, but Amelia refused to prompt him out of it, just sipping her sherry and staring out of the window, wishing hard that George would be back soon so that he could take charge of his friend and she could return to her gardening and forget all about what happened between them the previous evening.

'About Paris,' he said finally. 'And my voluntary exile. Well, not so voluntary an exile as it happens, since I was actually sent home.'

'Really?' Amelia's look contained as little interest as she could pretend.

'Yes.' Out of the corner of her eye she saw Ralph thoughtfully rub his chin, as if not quite sure how to play his next move. 'Yes,' he continued. 'It was the wife of someone rather important as it happens, although I hasten to add it was none of my doing.'

'These things never are, are they? At least not as far as my understanding of them goes.'

'What started out as a mild flirtation,' he continued, ignoring her, 'turned serious – but not on my part. That really wasn't my intention.'

'You were just amusing yourself.'

Amelia turned to look at him, and knew at once from his expression that she had him cornered.

'Touché,' Ralph shrugged, smiling ruefully. 'It wasn't actually quite like that, but fair enough – I concede.'

'So. They booted you out from Paris – what? For good? And you came back to England to lick your wounds.'

'Not for good – an enforced long leave, shall we say. Until the smoke dies down. I'm too valuable a member of the service for them to get rid of me.'

'He said with due modesty.' Amelia laughed. 'You are too much, Ralph Grace, you really are.'

'There's more to it than that, if you're interested, Mrs Rafferty.'

Amelia said nothing, leaving it to him to decide whether or not to continue.

'The woman in question was being wronged,'

he said, realizing he was not going to be prompted. 'I know you'll say it was no excuse, but her husband is a well-known Casanova, putting himself about not only in Paris but in every city to which he is delegated, while she is expected to stay at home darning his socks, or whatever women do – bottling and salting beans, making chutney.'

'In that order?' Amelia teased. 'Hardly the chic Parisienne.'

'Very well, ironing his shirts. Sitting sighing over his photograph – we both know what I mean. And that's precisely what Madame X did. She stayed at home and was a good wife. Until finally Monsieur X started bringing his women home and – well. And entertaining them, shall we say, under her nose, and when she protested – he beat her up.'

'And you came to her rescue?'

'I came to her help.'

'Sir Galahad.'

Ralph turned and stared at her with a look of bewilderment. 'Don't mock, Mrs Rafferty. Marriage can't be a prison for women. Although it seems that's what many men would like to make it, particularly in countries where the religion denies women the right of divorce. Think of yourself in such a situation. Your husband fornicates, interminably. Everyone knows he is being unfaithful – in fact your best women friends vie with each other to be the next one in his bed, leaving you alone and friendless, trapped in a

490

loveless marriage. Then as the icing on the cake he makes sure to beat you up. Wouldn't you long for someone to come to your help? Someone to take some care of you? To amuse you? To love you?'

Amelia shrugged her shoulders. 'I would run away.'

'You discover George is lying, that he's not the man you fell in love with and married. And that he is having let's say just one affair, rather than a whole string. Then you meet someone who treats you as you should be treated, do you think that's a mortal sin? Or some sort of heinous social crime? Surely not. I don't think that's what you think.'

'You hardly know me,' Amelia said quietly, taking his empty glass and getting up from the window seat. 'You really only met me yesterday. And now it's time to go into lunch.'

But Ralph was not to be diverted merely because he had food in front of him, and the truth of the matter was that Amelia was more than happy to listen to him, because he talked to her, not *at* her, as so many of the men she had recently met in George's company seemed to do.

'Has George spoken much to you about the war?'

'He told me all sorts of things about the war. Why?'

'If it hadn't been for George I would have shot myself on several occasions. No, that's ridiculous,' he said, stopping himself and smiling. 'I could only have shot myself once. What I mean is that on more than one occasion I was quite ready to shoot myself. It's strange. You're fighting for your very life and then suddenly – you want to end it. But there you are. There isn't a lot of logic where war is concerned. Particularly when you're as young as I was. One moment I was in the classroom, gazing out at a sunny landscape and dreaming of going to Oxford – and the next I was waist high in mud and gore, wondering just how long I might live.'

'I know,' Amelia said quietly. 'As I was forever saying to George, I don't think the rest of us have any way of even beginning to understand it.'

'Why should you? We didn't – God knows we had no idea. We might as well have been going off for a rugger match. What saved me was George. I don't know how we became friends – it was nothing to do with having been at the same school because we didn't know each other – and he was older than me – and my senior officer. A captain to my humble second lieutenant. We weren't even from the same sort of family. My family are all painters and sculptors—'

'Really? Mine too. My father is a poet although he is much better known as a painter.'

'Of course. I know of him, as it happens, quite well, because both our fathers were in the Artists Rifles. Anyway – where was I? George. Yes, well I really admired George. In fact I think I probably hero-worshipped him. He was a remarkable soldier, you know. Never gave a thought to his own safety, only to that of his men. And not un-naturally his men adored him. Would have gone to the end of the world for him. Except – that's exactly where most of them were already.' Ralph stopped.

'Don't go on if this is painful for you . . .'

'What George was, when I come to think of it, was – *inspirational*, that's the word I was looking for. Just when you thought you could go no further, there would be George, looking for all the world as though he just stepped off the parade ground – or out of some Boys' Book of Heroes – and you'd get an infusion of courage. We instantly became friends. Whenever we got some time to ourselves, we'd shack up in some billet and we'd talk, and talk, and talk. I'd sit and sketch while George would read. He had this little volume of Shakespeare's sonnets—'

'Bound in blue leather,' Amelia said, inter-rupting with a smile. 'I gave it to him. For his birthday.'

'I know. His eighteenth. He'd carried it in a breast pocket of his uniform ever since. By the end of the war he knew every sonnet off by heart.'

'No, that is something I didn't know.'

'He'd sit and recite them, even when we were in the front line and there was a lull in the action. He'd ask for requests, and one of us – usually one of the bombardiers, one of the men – someone would request a particular sonnet and George would recite it. Sitting in what was left of a wood somewhere – with the guns charged and ready – with the dead and the wounded lying all around us while we waited for the next bombardment, Captain George Dashwood would recite Shakespeare. Until Major Walker came along. He was a brute of a man who seemed to hate us – more than the enemy I sometimes thought. Of course he didn't dare confront George, for not only was George a hero, he was also a hundred times the man Walker was. Knowing that George and I were friends, he picked on yours truly. He would send me on suicidal sorties, make sure I was attached to a battery in the most vulnerable position, assign me the most menial jobs you can assign a lowly second lieutenant. I tell you, if it hadn't been for George, I think I might have turned my gun on myself.'

'But you didn't.'

Ralph smiled impishly. 'Or if I did, seeing where I am today, I must have missed!'

Amelia laughed.

'Anyway, just when I'd got myself sorted out and was turning into not a bad soldier – not a brilliant one like George, but not a bad one – I did something that could have had me court martialled and shot, albeit this time by a firing squad.'

'What?'

'I shot Major Walker,' Ralph said, raising his eyebrows. 'I still can't believe I did it. I shot and killed a member of my own army, and a senior officer to boot.'

'I see. At least I don't see. I don't see at all.'

'George didn't tell you everything?'

'Obviously not.'

'I thought I did it for what he did to that wretched little French girl, but I don't think I did. I think I did it for what he did to *me*, and all the rest of us who went to Malvern or Marlborough or wherever he so disapproved of people being schooled. Young men plucked from the sixth forms of England, who'd been thrown into the melting pot without an idea of how to fight or be a soldier. Young men whom he made absolutely no effort to help. I shot him point-blank.'

'How? I mean – I mean did you really do it in cold blood?'

'No, I didn't do it in cold blood. George knew that, and that made the difference, I think.'

'George knew? George knew you had shot someone? That you'd shot Major Walker?' Amelia looked at him in amazement as Ralph continued with his story.

'We'd been ordered to take up new gun positions but had run into a totally impenetrable barrage. The few of us who survived took cover in an abandoned foxhole and when there was a brief lull in the barrage George suggested making a run for it to a ruined farmhouse about a hundred yards ahead. Major Walker, who'd really taken no part in the fighting at all, suddenly yelled he'd had enough, and started to make a run for it back to the line. Cowardice in the face of the enemy. So I drew my pistol and shot him. Not in the back. I called to him first – and when he turned, I shot him.'

'You were mad.'

'If he'd seen an ordinary bloke deserting under fire, Walker wouldn't have hesitated. The only difference was he would have shot the chap in the back.'

'You don't have that right, Ralph. To judge a man and be his executioner.'

'Oh, I think you'll find war abnegates all so-called *rights*, Mrs Rafferty.'

'Did George report the incident?'

'He should have done, but when, as my senior officer, he wrote his report, he merely put that Walker had been killed "in action". So, you see, I owe George my life.'

Amelia picked her pudding fork up as if to try to finish her dessert, only to replace it almost at once with a sad shake of her head.

'Why did you tell me? You didn't have to tell me. George didn't tell me.'

'George promised he would never tell anyone. Not for himself, but for my sake. Even after all this time, I could still be charged.'

'Hardly.'

'Most certainly.'

'So you're a wanted man.'

'I very much hope so,' Ralph said, and his impish smile returned.

'That's not what I meant,' Amelia retorted, getting up from the table. 'And you know it.'

'If you really want to know, I don't know why I did tell you,' Ralph said, as he followed her back into the drawing room. 'It's most peculiar, but since I found myself back here, I told you because – how can I best put it? Because I felt compelled to do so. As if someone was willing me.'

'I thought I was the only fey one round here.' Amelia turned round, teasing him, as she put another log on the fire.

'Fey,' Ralph mused. 'Isn't that akin to being a pagan?'

'No, anyone can be fey. It's a sort of second sight, or seeing things before they happen, or being aware of the spirit world – that's what it is, really.'

Ralph took his packet of Turkish cigarettes out of his pocket and lit one, pulling on it with great satisfaction.

'I still don't know what to think,' Amelia said, putting distance between them by going round behind a sofa to rearrange some flowers in a vase, plucking out the dead ones almost frantically.

'You mean about what happened to Walker? Why should you have to think anything?' Ralph asked in genuine surprise. 'It isn't on your conscience.'

'Why should I have to think anything?' an astonished Amelia repeated. 'George is my husband, Ralph. Do you know what George has

497

suffered since – since you shot this man?'

It was Ralph's turn to look astonished. 'I don't understand what you mean by *suffered*. I always thought George was rather phlegmatic – I mean that's the impression he's always given. Something happens, he deals with it, rationalizes it – and that's that. Over ball.'

'George couldn't sleep for a year. He would shout and call out in his sleep – often begging this unknown person not to shoot. Phlegmatic? Ralph – we very nearly had no marriage because of that rape incident alone.'

'I really didn't know. I suppose because he went to hospital, and we lost touch.'

'He was in hospital because of his mental state, Ralph.'

'For his *mental* state?'

'Yes, Ralph. For his mental state. He had a breakdown.'

'George! Good God. I'm so sorry. I really had no idea.'

'Yet you seem to have walked away with no more marks on you than you'd get during a game of cricket.'

'No more visible mark.' He paused. 'I shouldn't have told you.'

'No, I don't think you should,' Amelia agreed, staring at an earwig which was emerging from the yellow dahlia she was holding in her hand.

'I wonder why I did tell you?' he said, half to himself.

'I don't understand,' Amelia sighed. 'Not only why you should wonder about telling me, but why you're here.' She glanced over to him, then, as soon as she saw how intently he was staring at her, she busied herself once more with her flowers.

'But I suppose I shouldn't wonder why you're here,' she went on. 'You're George's best friend. You know you are welcome here any time. You were passing the gate—'

'But you see I wasn't passing the gate. I wasn't anywhere near here – I wasn't even in the neighbourhood.'

'I don't understand. You said you were on your way to Bath and when you saw exactly where you were—'

'It wasn't true.' Ralph stopped her, now kneeling on the sofa and facing her directly. 'I was in London. And when I heard from a mutual friend that George was up in London as well, solo – the next thing I knew I found myself down here.'

'No, Ralph,' Amelia told him quietly. 'That won't do. People don't just find themselves somewhere. You came down here. You came down here deliberately.'

Ralph tipped his head a long way back. 'All right,' he finally agreed in the way people do when they are making a compromise. 'I came down here deliberately.'

'Your motor bike could hardly drive itself down, could it?'

'All right – I drove down here deliberately.'

'Because you knew George wasn't here,' Amelia persisted.

'I don't know why!' Ralph replied in exasperation. 'Yes – all right! I *knew* George wasn't here – but that wasn't the reason I drove down!'

'It was just in answer to some blind whim, is that what you're saying?'

'It was because I had to,' Ralph said, bending forward and dramatically lowering his forehead onto the back of the sofa. 'It was as if I had no choice in the matter.'

'You came down here because you knew George was away and that I would be all alone, and because you are a womanizer.'

'George is my best friend,' Ralph muttered, with his head still bowed on the sofa. 'I am his *fidus Achates*, his best friend.'

'Then you have no right to be here,' Amelia decided, taking a deep breath. 'So if you'll excuse me I have a mass of things to attend to in the garden.'

She did not realize it but on her way out to the garden she walked right past him. He was leaning with his back to the wall, his hands clasped as if in prayer and smiling the smile of an angel. 'I love you,' he whispered to her as she passed him by. 'I have always loved you. And you will love me too.' With that he touched thumb to finger and sent a mist of stardust along the breeze after her.

Twenty-Two

Amelia could not remember when she had heard the telephone ring so frequently. Long before George returned home it seemed to jingle incessantly, keeping Amelia busy writing down the list of messages and calls which must be returned, some from people vaguely known to her, some not, and a few anonymous calls from people who refused to leave a return number. Amelia discreetly fielded all these calls in the telephone room off the hall.

'Your household seem inordinately popular all of a sudden, Mrs Rafferty,' Ralph remarked, looking up from his book as Amelia entered the room. 'I thought you were trying to eschew *société*.'

'They are all for George. He is very much the man of the moment.'

'Judging from your tone you are unhappy about this.'

'It's difficult to be happy or unhappy about something concerning which you're totally in the dark.'

'Politics are most dreadfully boring, Amelia,' Ralph said, using a Noël Coward sort of voice.

'As long as it's just politics, Ralphie,' Amelia replied as a Bright Young Thing. 'Who on earth cares a fig anyway?'

On George's return Amelia dutifully handed her husband the list of calls and messages, watching and waiting in vain for any sort of reaction. George kissed her on the cheek, folded the list in two and slipped it in the top pocket of his jacket, and took himself off to his study. An hour later he disappeared upstairs with a large whisky to run himself a hot bath, where he lay for half an hour soaking away the fatigue generated by his visit to London. When he finally reappeared downstairs he could not wait to open a bottle of champagne to celebrate Ralph's visit.

After joining in and drinking a toast to the general well-being, Amelia left them alone together to catch up, going in search of Clara to help her prepare the dinner.

'We're just about up to date,' Ralph told her when she rejoined them for drinks. 'We've done Edward and Mrs Simpson, and the abdication. Although I have to say it might have been quite fun to have had a divorcée on the throne. Might have jazzed up old Britannia no end.'

'I think George might well agree with you,' Amelia said, poker-faced. 'George was a bit of an admirer of the *Duchesse de Windsor*. Maybe still is.'

As he helped them all to more champagne George gave her a quick look, but when he saw she was teasing him he smiled and refused to take the bait.

'Actually George rather likes both the Windsors, because they think the same as he does. That Mr Hitler's not such a bad egg after all.'

'Now you've stopped being funny.'

'Really?' Amelia said, widening her big eyes. 'Didn't I hear you saying – or certainly agreeing with people – recently that Mr Hitler's not someone we have to take seriously after all? That he's really more other people's problem than ours?'

'That's over-simplifying the issue, Amelia. As well you know.'

'Then educate me, George.'

'I'd rather eat,' George replied deliberately, staring at Amelia. 'I don't know about you, Ralph, but I'm starving.'

'There I go again,' Amelia sighed, getting to her feet. 'Forgetting where a woman's place is.' As she made her way out she smiled privately at Ralph. At the same time George was looking wide-eyed to Ralph to denote his present bemusement with his wife.

'You're not really on the side of the so-called appeasers, are you, George?' Ralph asked him as they finished their drinks. 'Surely not. Not you.'

'It's not a question of sides,' George replied, putting out his cigarette. 'It's a matter of finding the correct solution.'

'Yes, but not appeasement, surely. Look what's happening—'

'I've been looking, Ralph. Quite hard.'

'The Nazis are assassinating anyone who disagrees with them—'

'You're being over-simplistic, Ralph. But then politics never was your strong point. Come on – there's the gong.'

'You don't have to be a politician to see what's happening over the water, dear boy,' Ralph sighed as they made their way to the dining room.

'Of course not,' George agreed, settling himself into his place at the table. 'Although if you're not, it's all too easy to misread the signs and start warmongering. For a long time Hitler has been maintaining that all he needs is what the Germans call *Lebensraum*. In other words—'

'In other words,' Ralph interrupted, *'plenty of brrrrown bbrrrread unt butter for their piple.'*

'In a way, yes,' George admitted. 'And they'll only get that by obtaining more farmland. Germany's a big nation, you know. It's a growing nation again, and with all the land which was taken away from her by the Treaty of Versailles—'

'She cannot grow enuff brrrrown bbrrrread unt butter for her piple.'

'I don't know why you find this a subject for such mirth,' George said, observing both Amelia and Ralph with a school-masterly frown.

'Probably because it isn't funny, George,' Amelia replied, handing him a bowl of their home grown carrots. 'Especially hearing you defending Hitler.'

'I am not defending Hitler.'

'And as for warmongering, for heaven's sake, George, according to you Winston Churchill was trying to warn everyone about the Nazis' growing power years ago.'

'The young lady's right, captain,' Ralph said, nodding. 'Things are not looking good. The Italians have invaded Abyssinia—'

'Be careful what you say about Il Duce,' Amelia interrupted once again. 'Another of George's pin-ups.'

'George admires *Mussolini*?'

'Amelia's being dreadfully funny again,' George assured Ralph.

'You said you liked Little Benito,' Amelia insisted. 'You did.'

'I said I admired some of the things he had done. *Some* of the things.'

'Not invading Abyssinia, surely?' Ralph protested. 'And what about the rest of the mess of pottage? The Spanish are fighting a civil war, the Chinese are fighting the Japs and the Poles are refusing everything, which they nearly always do. We have to face it. There's hardly *time* to look the other way until the bogeymen pass by.'

'I don't think either of you understands the position,' George said defensively. 'More than anything situations like this require foresight.'

'And if ever a government needed spectacles it's this lot.'

'You really don't know what you're talking about, Amelia.'

'I may not know as much as you do, George—'

'No, you certainly don't,' George interrupted before she could get any further. 'It's part of my job to keep my ears open. To keep a finger on the pulse.'

'I've heard sharing a bed called some pretty funny things,' Amelia said in all innocence. 'But a job?'

'And what's that supposed to mean?'

'What do you think it means?' Amelia retorted. 'Namely that you are sharing your bed with a lot of rather suspicious people.'

'The point is, George,' Ralph put in quickly, seeing the glint in Amelia's eye. 'The point is that we all realize that there *is* going to be a war, and no-one seems to be preparing us for it.'

'There is not going to be a war,' George replied.

'I think there is, George,' Ralph countered. 'Or there certainly should be. If there's a shred of decency left in this country we can't just stand by while Czechoslovakia is tamely surrendered to Hitler.'

'There is not going to be a war,' George said quietly, eyeing them both. 'Not if I have anything to do with it.'

'What are you going to do, George? Wave a magic wand and it will all disappear?'

'Ever heard of diplomacy, Amelia?'

'Is that what all this appeasement is, George?

Diplomacy? Because if it is, I would colour that sort of diplomacy yellow.'

George stroked his chin thoughtfully as he looked at his wife, the way he did on the rare occasions he was about to lose his temper.

'Have you thought about the consequences of another war, Amelia?' he asked carefully, still well in control of himself. 'You have – I take it – thought a matter like this through quite thoroughly?'

'I don't want to lose my son,' Amelia replied hotly. 'If that's what all this is about, George, of course I don't want to lose my son! No mother wants to lose her son!'

'I think all mothers should go to war *with* their sons,' Ralph said, earning an amazed look from both George and Amelia. 'I think it should be compulsory. If they were made to, if every mother was conscripted with her son, they'd soon talk governments out of fighting, believe you me. From the lowliest private to the starriest general – accompanied by their mothers, end of war. QED.'

'You're not doing this because of Peter, are you?' Amelia said, turning to George and ignoring Ralph's surreal suggestion. 'You're not taking sides with these people—'

'Which people?' George wondered deliberately. 'Who said I was taking any side? I simply argued that at times like this, diplomacy plays a very important part.'

'Diplomacy, yes, maybe,' Amelia allowed. 'But not appeasement.'

There was a silence while George considered whether or not it was worth continuing. But then, sensing both Amelia's aggression and Ralph's apparent facetiousness, he decided against it, politely excusing himself from table by reason of the amount of telephone calls he still had left to make.

'Is there any pud?' Ralph enquired after a moment. 'I think we could do with some after that.'

By the following morning all seemed forgiven and forgotten. George had slept in, Amelia had brought him breakfast in bed, and after the two men had spent most of the day walking up on White Sheet Downs, Ralph appeared to have teased George back to his normal genial self.

All this had been effected by the time Amelia came down from getting dressed for the dinner party they were due to attend that evening, which meant that she found the two men in the library drinking and talking nineteen to the dozen. She had chosen to wear the silver lamé dress she had worn so famously at Riverdean. It happened to be one of George's favourites, but he was so busy talking to Ralph he did not seem to notice either her or it.

Not that Amelia minded. She was already dreading the evening ahead of them, since at George's request on his return from London she had been forced to cancel her acceptance of the

Hanleys' invitation for dinner that evening and agree to attend a large party at the house of someone known to her by name only, Sir Cedric Wareham.

'I am not surprised, dearest girl,' Mae had said when Amelia had telephoned her to tender her regrets. 'Not in the very least surprised. A friend who has friends at court, dearest one, tells us that George is rumoured to be some sort of *éminence grise* – a power behind if not the throne itself, then the chair which *sustaineth* the seat of power.'

'I don't really know what's going on any more, Mae.'

'Then, my darling – fear not. For like all great dramas, very soon all will be revealed.'

At least two dozen people were gathered at the Wareham household for dinner, most of whom were totally unknown to Amelia except a handful who again she knew by name only.

'Are you as lost as I am?' she asked Ralph as they stood with their pre-dinner drinks in the corner of the vast drawing room. 'I don't know one person here.'

'Well, you wouldn't. They're not your sort of people.'

'It's as if they've had some of their senses removed.'

'I knew a very rich woman once,' Ralph replied, changing the subject. 'In fact I knew her pretty well. She said the richer she became, the less easy it was for her to – to make love.'

'Really?' Amelia said in surprise. 'I always thought power was meant to be some sort of aphrodisiac.'

'Power maybe. But not money. At least not to this particular lady. She said gilt creates guilt. As a consequence she was forever washing herself. She used to take at least three baths a day.'

'And did – did she always have difficulty for ever more? With – with making love?'

'No,' Ralph said, looking directly at her. 'She got better. Much better, I am happy to say. She just needed someone to rationalize it for her. Now I think we're being called to the table.'

Amelia was quite silent after that for it was really rather obvious who it might have been who had helped the lady in question to 'rationalize' her love life.

As it turned out that was the last interesting exchange Amelia had for the rest of the evening, consigned as she was to sit between two men who were both apparently high financiers, neither of whom from the outset had the slightest interest in talking to her. Ralph was well down the other end of the table between two glamorous women who were obviously well on the way to falling for his charms, while George – somewhat to Amelia's surprise – had been accorded the place of honour on the right of his hostess.

Inevitably the conversation moved to the present economic climate, first in America where according to the experts either side of Amelia the current Wall Street stock market decline signalled serious financial strife, and then in Europe, a situation which also appeared extremely bleak and led Sir Cedric to declare that this alone was the best reason why there should be no war.

'I agree,' the man on Amelia's left said, 'There is absolutely no reason for us to be at loggerheads with Nazi Germany.'

'Really?' Ralph said smoothly. 'I find that very interesting. Why is that, do you think?'

'Because we taught Fritz a good lesson in fourteen to eighteen,' the man replied. 'And one that he's not going to forget in a hurry.'

'He seems to have forgotten it already,' Ralph insisted. 'Marching into the Rhineland. Sending troops to help Franco. Building up his air force. Hardly the stuff of keeping the peace.'

'You could say the same about us, if you chose to do so,' the man replied. 'Except when we keep our troops up to number and modernize our forces we are said to be doing it for the good of the country and the Empire.'

'We don't march into other people's backyards.'

'We have done. Otherwise how would we have got an Empire?'

'The point is the Nazis are being aggressive.'

'I fail to agree.' The man on the other side of Amelia now joined in the debate. 'Economically Germany is on her knees. What Herr Hitler is doing is dangerously overstretching an already overstretched economy. Were we to allow him his overheated head for a while, when the German people found they still have little or nothing to eat they would soon remove Herr Hitler from power and return to their senses.'

'Precisely so,' their host agreed. 'My understanding of the matter is that Hitler's generals have already expressed their disapproval of his expansionist programme, believing as Sir John has just remarked that any such policy would be detrimental to the health of the country. However, Herr Hitler has let it be known for some time now that there are really only two things he wants, two objectives which I and a great many other of my colleagues in actual government view with a certain amount of sympathy. The German Chancellor—'

'Der Führer,' Ralph interrupted, earning himself a glacial look from Sir Cedric.

'The German Chancellor wants the restitution of territory taken from his country after the war,' he continued. 'I have sympathy with this because like many others I feel the Treaty of Versailles was a badly designed document, one which took no account of the bad feeling it would engender in the vanquished foe.'

Ralph put his head back to laugh incredulously, much to the private delight of Amelia. 'The vanquished foe!' he said. 'It took no account of the feelings of the vanquished foe!' He closed his eyes and fell silent, before opening them and leaning right across the table in the direction of his host.

'What about the feelings of the victors, Sir Cedric? What about the feelings of the hundreds of thousands of men who fought the war to end all wars? What about those who endured a hardship which is beyond description? Who suffered wounds the like of which had never been seen before? Who lived through all those terrors and those horrors? Not only the millions killed, but the millions of parents who sacrificed their children so that people like you can sit complacently round your laden dinner tables telling us all that we must have compassion for our vanquished foe. An enemy who's now feeling hard-done-by because someone confiscated some of his lands. What sort of man are you, I wonder, Sir Cedric? Did you fight in the last war? Or did the government find you some cosy, well-paid corner to hide in?'

'That's enough, Ralph. You've had too much wine.'

'I'm well aware of how much wine I have had, George. If ever I was in need of too much wine, it's this evening.'

'I don't know who this gentleman is,' Sir Cedric said. 'But since he came with you, George, I suppose we must tolerate such monkey manners. But for your information, sir—'

'Ralph Grace,' Amelia put in. 'Lieutenant Ralph Grace MC, Sir Cedric.'

Her host shot her a frosty glance before continuing. 'For your information, Mr Grace, you like many others of your kind are responding

513

hysterically to what you see as the Nazi threat.'

'Perhaps because I and others of my kind have not seen threat, sir, we have seen war, not Wellington's war, but modern war. We know. You do not.'

Although she knew it was a lapse of manners to argue with one's host, Amelia could not take her eyes off Ralph. He was like a terrier now, his hackles up, waiting for the rabbit to run. But the rabbit showed no such signs.

'Mr Grace,' Sir Cedric said, eyeing his antagonist carefully. 'You must understand that greater intelligence is at work here, the indication being that given the present economic state of Germany, if she is to expand at all then better by far to allow her to do so eastwards. All that agriculturally useful space there is going to waste in those thinly populated areas. Once they have sufficient food in their bellies the Nazi lions will become tabby cats once more. They simply want food and the room to grow it.'

'People live in those thinly populated areas. Sir Cedric. The Czechs. The Poles. The Hungarians.'

Her host's small dark eyes flicked back to Amelia for a moment, blinked slowly and contemptuously and then returned to watch Ralph.

'This is for the greater good, Mr Grace—' he began again.

'Mrs Dashwood had something to say, Sir Cedric.' Ralph indicated Amelia. 'Of course she's only a woman, and like all your bedfellows no doubt you believe that women are morally decadent.'

'That's quite enough, Ralph,' George warned his friend.

'Mr Grace,' his host continued, and Amelia caught the look of hurt surprise which George was giving her, as if she had somehow betrayed him.

'Excuse me, Sir Cedric,' Ralph interrupted. 'As a gentleman you should at least afford Mrs Dashwood the courtesy of an acknowledgement.'

'Before asking you to leave my table and my house, Mr Grace, I shall just make my point. What those whom you have helped elect to represent you are of a mind to do is for the future health of this country. As such their actions cannot be governed by a grateful feeling that a war was fought twenty years ago and that in the process lives were lost. That is now consigned to the past. Those of us with a mind to the future welfare of England must make sure that we do not condemn yet more soldiers to their deaths through a lack of proper understanding. To the scaremongers and the rumour merchants who run newspapers Hitler looks like the bogeyman, which is a nonsense. What he is in fact is a man intent on getting his own country back into shape, and should he fail to do this or should he overstep the mark he will be removed, either by his generals or by his people.'

'Like hell,' Ralph replied, pushing back his chair. 'This is not why I fought for years in the mud. To sit and listen to this Fascist claptrap.' He was on his feet, and seeing him about to leave Amelia stood up in her place as well.

'Wait for me.'

Ralph looked in amazement over to where she was standing. But it was George who spoke.

'Amelia – please sit down.'

'I'm sorry, George, but I can't. Really not. I agree with everything Ralph has just said – and with not one word I have heard anybody else utter. I don't believe in appeasing Hitler because to do so would mean those who fought and died in the last war did so in vain. I think anyone who thinks the way everyone here appears to think should be deeply ashamed of themselves, and if you choose to remain here, George, then so too should you. Good night, Sir Cedric. Lady Wareham.'

In the deathly silence that ensued Amelia walked to the door, hoping and praying that George would get up and follow her. But he did not. He called after her twice, but sensing he was not intending to support her Amelia ignored him. Instead it was Ralph who followed her out of the room.

'How are we to get home?' she wondered as a maid went to fetch their coats.

'We shall walk, Amelia.'

'But it's miles.'

'So what? The walk will do us good.'

*   *   *

It was ten miles and it took them the best part of three hours.

At first Amelia hoped that any moment she would hear the sound of the Bentley roaring up behind to rescue them and that George would take them both on board, laughing like the old George and apologizing for his temporary loss of humour, but no car came to their rescue, least of all her husband's.

A vicar returning home late after attending a sickly parishioner did stop and offer them a lift, as did a drunk in an Austin 10, but the first offer was going in the wrong direction and the second was from a driver who was far too inebriated for his own good let alone that of his passengers.

So they walked, and the more they walked the less Amelia remembered how far they had to go, such was the power of Ralph's conversation.

He talked mostly about his boyhood, once again asserting that he was not sure what might have happened to him without George, so utterly desperate was he by the end of his first three months in battle. Before he had enlisted he had never so much as seen a badly injured body, let alone a dead one, yet two days after landing in France he was surrounded by young boys, men, his own age, dying by the hour.

'To say that it was a nightmare would be ridiculously understating it,' he sighed as they turned off the main road into a minor one which would finally lead them to the gates of The Priory. 'There are no words to describe the real horrors of war.'

'Then maybe appeasement isn't such a bad thing after all,' Amelia ventured. 'Maybe what George believes—'

'Appeasement?' Ralph cried. '*Appeasement*? When you think of all those young men who died!'

'Very well,' Amelia said hastily, taking his arm. 'I was just trying to examine the argument.'

'There isn't one, Mrs Rafferty. There is *no* argument that makes sense of appeasement. And to hear George of all people . . .'

'It doesn't make sense, does it?'

'No sense at all.'

They walked along in thoughtful silence for a while, Ralph swishing at the dark nettles with a long branch he had pulled from the hedgerow.

'You rather hero-worship George, don't you?' Amelia asked at last.

'I certainly did. When we were in the army. When I volunteered I knew nothing. Nothing at all – and suddenly there was George, who seemed to know everything. I didn't know anything about girls, let alone women—'

'I don't think George knew very much about women either, when he joined up.'

'When I met him, he was every inch the soldier-hero. An absurdly handsome officer renowned for his courage. Someone like that had to know everything there was to know about everything. Of course I hero-worshipped him. Everyone did.'

Ralph dead-headed another dozen or so nettles

before turning sideways to glance at his companion.

'I'd only taken a girl out once by the time I joined up,' he said with a grin. 'We went to a friend's party and we danced – and I fell madly in love with her – and I didn't even kiss her. Imagine, I might have been killed without ever kissing a girl!'

'What a terrible thought!'

'I'm glad you agree. Just imagine – imagine going to your grave having never kissed someone like you.'

Ralph looked at her as they walked on, and Amelia at once averted her eyes, fixing them firmly on the long road unwinding ahead of her.

'Did you hear what I said?' Ralph asked, freeing his arm from hers and turning to walk backwards down the road ahead of her.

'Of course I heard what you said.'

'Well, can you imagine such a thing? The other way round, say – dying young before you had the chance to *be* kissed.'

'What you don't know, you don't miss.'

'That is simply not true.'

'Can we change the subject please?'

'Very well. I told George after the war – that I hero-worshipped him, you know,' Ralph continued. 'We were getting drunk together, or more correctly I was already drunk – and when I told George how – I mean *what* – I felt, he smiled, put his arms round me, and hugged me like a brother. Of course by then I felt I could tell him. I mean we were in Paris and I'd just lost my virginity – so I was a man, and we could talk man to man.'

'Now it's you who's teasing me.'

'Why should that be a tease?'

'Isn't fighting a war enough to make someone a man?' Amelia wondered. 'Or is it all down to losing your virginity?'

'Oh come on!' Ralph laughed, still walking backwards ahead of her. 'You know as well as I – it's so different for men and women. A man has to lose his virginity! Just as much as a woman has to keep hers!'

'I've often tried to puzzle that one out. If all girls have to remain virgins, then with whom is it that men lose their virginity?'

'Who do you think? *Les demoiselles de la nuit*. The ladies of the night.'

'I know perfectly well what *les demoiselles de la nuit* are, thank you.'

'I'll bet,' Ralph said, widening his eyes. 'How would you have found out about such things?'

'My parents.'

'Oh, of course.' Ralph grinned. 'I can imagine. *Darling – I think it's time you learned what a harlot is.*'

'Don't be so crude, Ralph. And don't mock.'

'I'm not mocking. Tell me something else. What did you think when you got married? Did you enjoy making love straight away? Or were you frightened? It's all right – most girls are, you know.'

Amelia glared at him, shook her hair out over the top of her high velvet collar and taking the stick from his hand began her own thrashing of the roadside nettles.

'I don't see that's any of your business.'

'Don't be silly. Making love is a fact of life, not something about which you should be embarrassed. Or worse – ashamed. How does George make love to you? Is he a good lover? A fanciful one? Or just good, plain and unvarnished?'

'You are about to go too far, and you know it—'

'Of course. That is one of the most delightful things about life, knowing you are about to go too far.'

She knew he was smiling. She could feel it, yet she refused to look at him in order to be sure. Instead she just concentrated on executing as many nettles as she could on the roadside.

'People are so shy in England nowadays about making love. Don't you find? Making love is so important – and yet so many Englishmen are virgins when they get married. It's ridiculous. My mama being half French she wanted my father to take me to a brothel when I was eighteen, which of course is the custom in France.'

'What?' Amelia turned to stare at him.

'Didn't you know? In France you send your sons to experienced women to be initiated. And what a good idea it is, too, because who else is going to teach you? Who else but a professional – or an older woman? That's what is so amazing about the

English. They treat lovemaking as if it's something you pick up as you go along. But how can you? Someone teaches you how to play poker, or whist – or tennis or golf – or to ride a horse or play the piano, but no-one in England ever speaks of learning to make love. Why ever not? It's an art!'

She continued to walk and swish at the undergrowth but her mind was racing. How did George make love? she wondered. She had simply no idea, since George was the only person who had ever kissed her, let alone made love to her – so how could she tell?

'I would love to make love to you,' Amelia now heard Ralph saying, feeling his hand take hers, two actions – his speech and his holding of her hand – which brought Amelia swiftly back to earth. 'Don't look so shocked.'

'You can't tell how I look, you idiot,' she retorted, pulling her hand away. 'It's practically pitch dark.'

Ralph laughed. 'Of course it isn't. Anyway, I can feel how you look. And there's no need.' He took her hand again and this time for some reason Amelia allowed him to keep hold of it. 'You deserve to be made love to beautifully,' he said, now transferring her left hand from his right into his left so that her arm was across his body while he slipped his right arm round her waist. 'You deserve to be made love to beautifully, Amelia,' he whispered, his face now close to hers, his lips brushing her hair, 'because you are such an utterly beautiful woman.'

'You shouldn't speak to me like that, Ralph,' she protested, although not very forcefully. 'You really should not. Anyway, you're drunk.'

'Drunk with your beauty.'

'Drunk with too much wine and champagne.'

'Not too drunk to know what I want, Amelia. And you're what I want. Please let me be your lover.'

'My lover? What are you talking about, Ralph? People like me don't have lovers!'

'Of course they do, Amelia! I have been the lover of women just like you!'

'I'm sure that you have – but that's not what I meant. I meant women who love their husbands don't take lovers. And please – please don't kiss my neck like that.'

'Like this then?'

'No. Not like that either.'

'You will have me as your lover, sooner or later, Mrs Rafferty.'

'No, Ralph. You're wrong. I won't have you as my lover.'

'You will. The moment George is no longer true to you, you will want me as your lover! And what if George was already being untrue to you? Wouldn't that change things?'

'How?' Amelia pulled herself right away from him, freeing herself and turning to face him, stopped in the middle of the road. 'How is George being untrue, Ralph? You're the one who is being untrue. You're being untrue to your best friend!'

'If he was still my best friend you'd be right. But he's not. He can't be, because he's betraying me just as he's betraying you. By what he thinks. By what he is. By what he's become.'

Amelia stared at him. 'No,' she said. 'No, that just isn't true.'

'But it is, you know it is. Otherwise he would have left with us. Otherwise we would all be driving home together in his car, laughing at all those terrible people, and making plans to fight the Nazis.'

'No, that isn't so. That simply isn't right.'

'It is, and you know it.' Ralph insisted, his eyes locked on hers. 'He's becoming one of those crypto-Fascists sitting round the table.'

'Not George. He couldn't be.'

'You saw for yourself, Amelia! You heard! You heard what that lot believe! They want to cosy up to Mr Hitler!'

And Amelia knew that it was true. George had left her. George had been leaving her for weeks, maybe months. George had left her and become another person. He had become one of the people he had once so despised.

'Dearest darling beautiful Mrs Rafferty. Let me make love to you?'

She let him kiss her because she did not know what else to do, but they heard the car just in time. So that by the time the headlights were on them they were either side of the road, walking on but now innocently turning and putting hands up to shield their eyes against the glare of the fast oncoming beams.

The car pulled to a sharp halt just past them and George leaned out of the driver's seat.

'Get in. Not that either of you deserve it.'

Conversation in the rag-topped Bentley was difficult at the best of times but tonight at the speed George drove it was utterly impossible. Amelia sat up front with her husband, burying herself in her coat and keeping as low as she could to keep warm, while Ralph sat in the back with his long legs stretched out sideways across the seat.

Once home, George parked the car and went straight inside the house, and, to judge from the lights which went on above Amelia and Ralph, straight to bed. Ralph looked at Amelia as she let herself into the house but neither said a word, Ralph planting one kiss on the end of one of his fingers to signal his feelings before disappearing across the lawns to the guest cottage.

'George?' Amelia called as she closed the bedroom door behind her. 'George – what was all that about, please?'

George appeared at the bathroom door in just his trousers, with a white towel draped around his neck.

'I think it's me who should be asking you that, Amelia – and your lipstick's smudged.'

'I must have done that in the car,' Amelia said, hurriedly removing what was left of her make-up.

'I was so cold I had my coat collar up round my face.'

George merely looked at her before disappearing back into the bathroom.

'George,' Amelia called after him, going to the open door. 'George – what is going on? Please tell me?'

He looked at her via the mirror above him and she saw his eyes were full of sadness and regret, yet still he made no reply, carrying on cleaning his teeth before dousing his face with cold water and drying off on the thick white towel.

'George,' Amelia insisted as he walked past her back into the bedroom. 'George – something is going on and I really want to know what it is.'

'I'd quite like to know what's going on as well,' George replied, sitting on the bed and undoing his shoes. 'Between you and Ralph.'

'Why should something be going on between me and Ralph?' Amelia protested, a little too much to judge from the shake of George's head. 'George – there is nothing going on between me and Ralph!'

'You left with him after dinner, Amelia. How do you think that looked?'

'I don't actually care how it *looked*, George! What I didn't care for was how you sounded! That's why I left! Anyway – why should you worry about how things appear? You were the one who was perfectly ready to take a stand against not only your background but the whole establishment, remember? You're in bed with extremists, George, you're in bed with the people who don't want freedom of speech, who believe that might is right, that power is everything – you're in bed with people who like to burn books, George! Even yours!'

George stopped unlacing his shoes and sat there, staring at the ground as if at a total loss for words. After a moment he looked up at his wife. 'You don't understand, Amelia. I'm sorry, but you don't.'

'Then help me, George,' she pleaded, coming to sit down beside him on the bed. 'Help me to understand. That's all I want. To understand what is happening to us.'

She could see that George wanted to tell her, and yet he finally just took her hand and shook his head sadly.

'I can't explain. I'm sorry, Amelia, but I can't explain.'

'If you can't tell me, then how can I trust you?' She stood up and walked away from him. 'I never thought it was possible to love somebody as much as I loved you.'

'Loved,' George said quietly, watching her slender silhouette outlined against the curtains and the light from the windows. 'What do you mean – loved?'

'You're not that man any more, George. Whatever you were like when you came back from war – that wouldn't matter now. Not in light of what's happening in Europe. The old George – the

George I loved – he'd have buckled on his sword belt and put on his armour and gone after the Fascists instead of allying himself to those toads we dined with this evening.'

She moved closer to the window, overcome with the nightmare of it all.

After a few seconds George joined her at the window, and they both stood looking out, but whereas normally he would put his arm round her, or their arms would touch, quite naturally, now they just stood side by side. And Amelia, with a sinking heart, realized that for the first time in truth she might be looking to a future without George.

While outside they watched from the yew tree, high in its branches, the Noble One standing with his hand rested against the trunk of the huge tree, and Longbeard seated on a branch and slowly swinging his legs to and fro. 'This must be painful, sir,' Longbeard sighed, winding the end of his whiskers round a finger. 'Knowing what is to come.'

'Be careful, wizard, lest I put my foot in your back . . .'

'. . . and I float into the night. Like the dust, we immortals have become. But where is he, sir? Where is he?'

'There, you old goat,' the Noble One said, pointing a finger which became a light, showing the tall figure seated on the little cottage roof. 'There, here – and everywhere!' The ray of light from the Noble One's finger traced lines in the darkness as the figure they

were watching moved from place to place, filling the deepening night with his silent laughter.

'What is it?' Amelia asked him, screwing up her courage and taking his hand suddenly. 'What's come between us?' As he said nothing she persisted. 'I'm asking you. I have a right to know. There's something wrong and I want to know what that is.'

'Everything's wrong,' George said quietly. 'Everything's going wrong.'

'I don't know what you're talking about, George – and you're frightening me. Are you afraid of another war like the last one, is that it? Is that why you've joined the appeasers? Because you're afraid of losing Peter? Because of the dream I had – because of that – that vision? If it is, George – if that's the reason for all this – then I can understand. Is that what it is? Is that what all this is about?'

To her dismay Amelia saw George close his eyes.

'I came to the conclusion long ago that in a world like this if one has a son, one risks losing that son. That is just the way it is.'

'In that case,' Amelia heard herself saying calmly, 'it must be that woman who has seduced you into thinking as she does. Deanna Astley. It is all her fault.'

'You're being ridiculous, Amelia, and you know it.'

'I am not being ridiculous, George!'

'And will you keep your voice down!'

'George – you are seen everywhere with her! The gossip columns have been full of it for weeks! Months! Everywhere she goes, you're there! There or thereabouts! Whenever you're in London you see her. And you have the nerve to say I'm being ridiculous!'

'Because you are.'

'Fine,' Amelia said, dropping her voice and looking at him steadily. 'In that case – convince me.'

'I thought we'd never have the need to explain things to each other.'

'Me too, George. But it seems times have changed.'

George sighed deeply. 'All I can say is that I have no choice.'

'Now it's you who's being ridiculous, George. We all of us have a choice in what we do!'

'That isn't what I meant.'

'Then say what you do mean! For God's sake!'

'I mean that for some reason I have no choice in this matter. And because I have no choice, I can't tell you. I can't explain.'

'Now you're talking in riddles.'

Amelia turned on her heel and walked away from the window, going to the bed and pulling her nightdress out from under her pillows.

'I'm going to sleep in the spare room.'

'Amelia,' George pleaded, getting between her and the door. 'Amelia, please. . . '

'George, I cannot go *on* like this!' Amelia insisted. 'I can't go on living with a man who won't tell me what's going on because he says he can't, then asks me to understand. And to trust him. A man who's changed beyond all recognition.'

'I haven't, Amelia. You don't understand.'

'Stop saying that!' Amelia glared at him and saw the genuine surprise and hurt in his eyes as he looked back. 'I don't know what I mean exactly – but for God's sake stop telling me that I don't understand. I *want* to understand. It's you that's stopping me.'

'I will prove to you what I mean.'

'When? When you grow bored of Deanna Astley?'

'There is nothing going on between me and Deanna Astley.'

'So for one last time what the hell *is* going on.'

For one moment George hesitated.

'He is about to tell her, sir,' Longbeard groaned.

'And let him!' the Noble One replied, descending swiftly through the branches until he stood on the ground. 'Let him speak! Let him tell her! If he does not – then she is lost to him!'

'Sir,' Longbeard protested as the two men stood on the dark lawns below the window in the house. 'Sir, we cannot weaken now or this jewel set in a silver sea will be drowned, this sceptred isle lost.'

The Noble One sighed, for he could feel the sadness in their souls. Yet he knew his sorcerer was right. He could not repair a harm done fourteen hundred years before. So he took himself away to a part of the gardens where flowers of late autumn still flourished, there to hide his face among the blooms while the tears he wept washed all the colour from them.

'You were going to tell me something, George.'

'I was?' George stood back from her, frowning deeply. 'Are you sure? Well, whatever it was has quite gone now, I'm afraid.'

'There was something.'

'No, nothing,' George replied, with a vague, tired smile. 'It's very late now, Amelia, and I really must get to bed. I have a million and one things to do in the morning and have to get up at the crack of dawn, so I'll sleep in my dressing room.'

George left her still wearing that same vague smile. As to Amelia, she went to bed and dreamed of how she had once felt, when she was loved.

Twenty-Three

'He must have left first thing,' Amelia told Ralph over breakfast. 'It was hardly dawn when I woke, but he'd already packed his things and gone. All he said was that he was getting up early. He said nothing about leaving.'

'He'd only just come home,' Ralph remarked, pouring dark strong coffee. 'Now you see him, now you don't.'

'Something to do with all those phone calls, maybe. I mean Captain Dashwood is a much wanted man.'

'But Mrs Rafferty – to go off without a word. You didn't quarrel, did you?'

'No, why?'

'I thought I heard raised voices.'

'We did not have a quarrel.'

'I must say I never thought that George would change for the worse.'

'He hasn't. Has he?'

'You know as well as I do. This is not the George who came home from the war. It certainly ain't the old George Dashwood I used to know.'

Amelia drank her coffee slowly, watching Ralph

over the top of her cup while she decided whether or not to confide in him.

'No, he's not the same,' she agreed, having finally decided in favour of disclosure. 'He seems to think – he carries on as if he's got some form of – well, destiny.'

'*Destiny*?' Ralph frowned at her in apparent disbelief. 'Next thing you know he'll be hearing voices.'

'Perhaps this is a recurrence of all that business after the war.'

'He really did say nothing about going?' Ralph wondered, putting the coffee pot back down on the table. 'It seems so odd for him to come all the way home – and then take off into the blue the very next morning.'

'Maybe something came up? Among all those telephone calls there were two from Jack Cornwall. His publisher.'

'Surely if he was just going to see his publisher . . .' Ralph began, only to stop to give the situation some more thought.

'I think he's left me, Ralph.' She looked across at him. 'I don't know why, but I suddenly have this feeling.'

'Not possible,' Ralph assured her immediately. 'He loves you far too much.'

'*Loved* me far too much,' Amelia said quietly, getting up from the table. 'But not any more.'

Quickly taking herself off into the garden, Amelia tried to calm herself. It was as if something had been randomly planted in her head, all of a sudden, out of the blue. One minute she had been talking to Ralph, albeit about the events of the previous evening and night, then the next thing she knew she heard a voice saying, *George has left you – George has left you*, just seconds after Ralph had remarked that George would be hearing voices next. *George has left you, my darling love, my own*, the voice had said – and laughed.

'Maybe I'm the one who's going crazy,' Amelia muttered to herself as she walked towards the herbaceous garden.

Try as she might, she could not believe George would leave her simply because of the argument that had taken place the night before. Besides, as she recalled, it had been a very one-sided affair. George had seemed not to take particular offence. It was she who had been upset. Furthermore, George was many things, but one thing he was most certainly not was impetuous. When George decided to do something drastic, it was only after the most careful consideration.

Yet he is gone, Amelia realized. *So there are only two conclusions which can be drawn. Either he has fallen in love with someone else, or else he quite simply does not love me any more. I accused him of having an affair with Deanna Astley and for one moment he looked as if his last hour had come.*

Which was when she saw the flowers.

She had reached the herbaceous garden, entering it from the top gate so that the bed had

535

been hidden from her until she stood on the grass pathway. The beds were full of summer colour, as well as the first flowering of plants chosen for their autumn life; deep red pompon dahlias set among the last flourishes of pink and pale blue. Amelia was glad to see how perfectly glorious the beds still appeared – all except for one patch under the south wall, which she suddenly noticed was completely colourless.

'Jethro?' Amelia called as she stood staring in bewilderment. 'Jethro – have you seen what has happened here?'

Her gardener hurried through from the Wild Garden.

'Well, I'll be . . .' he muttered, pushing his cap to the back of his head. 'I never saw that before. They was as good as new last evening. I cut some for the house if you remember, and they was all as fresh as paint.'

It was a momentary interlude, almost welcome, but as soon as she left Jethro reality began once more to kick home as she wandered back towards the house. She seemed not to have spared a thought for her children over the previous days, yet she now realized Peter was due home for his summer holidays at the end of the week and Gwendolyn at the beginning of the week after. If George was still absent she had absolutely no idea what she would say to them.

She could hardly say their father had gone away without any rhyme or reason, and although as far as she knew he was in London he could actually be in Timbuctoo with no intention of ever returning home again. What, she wondered as she trod across the velvet lawns, could George have possibly meant by going off without a word? How was she supposed to find him? Who or where should she call? Or did he simply expect her to sit and wait for him to call her in order to let her know what was going on? He must have done this quite purposely, she decided as she re-entered the house. It had to be part of George's present scheme of things. Whatever that particular scheme of things might be. She telephoned his flat but there was no answer.

As she stood in the telephone room waiting to be put through to Jack Cornwall this time, she wondered whether the man she had left finishing his breakfast on the terrace had played any part in the situation in which she now found herself?

It was strange, but ever since Ralph Grace had come into their lives everything had begun to change. And had Ralph not reappeared so dramatically on this last occasion, Amelia wondered, would she ever have confronted George the way she had the night before? Would she have allowed the situation to develop the way it had, with George going off to sleep alone in his dressing room with an argument unresolved, before leaving in the morning without a word?

The slow realization came to her that Ralph Grace was a libertine who had turned her head.

'Jack?' she asked when she heard his voice at last. 'Have you seen George? Do you know where he's staying? He's not at the flat.'

'Not a clue. Sorry, Amelia.'

'You must have some idea of where he is!'

'None. Stop worrying. Husbands always turn up, in the end. Bad luck.' He laughed and replaced the telephone.

In her desperation Amelia found that she had the courage to call both known Astley households, Riverdean and the Mayfair number. The Astleys were at home at neither address. Then she tried everyone she knew in London but drew only blank after blank until, in its turn, her telephone rang.

'Amelia?' General Dashwood's voice enquired. 'My son there?'

'I'm afraid not. He's gone to London.'

'Hmm. Where's he staying?'

Amelia hesitated, tilting her head back and closing her eyes. 'I'm not sure,' she finally replied. 'He left in a bit of a hurry.'

'You're not sure?'

'Is something the matter?'

'Most certainly. Just had the editor of *The Times* on to me. Apparently the leading letter tomorrow's a pro-appeasement job. Signed by a lot of well-to-dos – as well as by George.'

'Are you trying to get him to withdraw it? Isn't it a little late for that?'

'Not the point. Point is I want to give George a piece of my mind. Had enough, I'm afraid.

Quite enough, Amelia. Sorry. But there it is.'

'Is there anything I can do, perhaps? Anything I can say?'

'Wish there was, dear girl. You know how very fond I am of you. But this is a bridge too far, I'm afraid. If you hear from George, be so kind as to ask him to telephone me, would you?'

Amelia sat on the stone bench which overlooked the round pond and stared blindly at the big fat fish as they fed lazily on the surface, cursing her stupidity.

It's all finally going wrong, she thought, *and it's all of our faults. This is Ralph's fault, and George's, and mine – and that dreadful, immoral woman who set out to seduce George so that she and her political cronies could bend his will to theirs. We have each had a hand in wrecking the happiness that was here and, as a result of our stupidity, I think I may have lost the one person who really means something to me, the one person I truly love.*

Or the one person she had loved, which was what she had told George the night before. *Loved* – he had repeated the word as if it was the end of everything. A second later her thoughts took a U-turn. It was not she who had changed so radically, it was not she who had stayed away in London. To her way of reasoning, if George was not actually committing adultery with Deanna Astley, he was still being unfaithful because of his change of character.

Looking up, still weighed down by her thoughts and the hurt they brought her, she saw Ralph walking towards her across the lawns. She knew she must remember not to trust him, yet even so, as they walked back over the Chinese bridge, she found herself discussing her fears concerning George's sudden disappearance.

'There's nothing so idle as a rumour, nothing swifter either.'

'*They say* is half a lie. Rumours are things devised by the enemy.'

'You're just trying to reassure me, Ralph.'

'Of course I'm trying to reassure you, Amelia! What sort of friend would I be to do otherwise?'

'The sort of friend who kissed his best friend's wife last night.'

'I was tight. We both were.'

'That's the only reason you kissed me?'

'Oh, come on.' Ralph looked at her in sudden irritation. 'That's one of the things that always amazes me about your sex. In the midst of death you are in life.'

'All right – but why did you kiss me, Ralph?'

'Why the hell do you want to know that at a time like this?'

'Precisely because it's a time like this.'

'I kissed you because I love you, Mrs Rafferty, I love you that should not.'

'You can't love me, Ralph. You don't know me.'

'That's another thing women always say! When you tell them you love them, they say *No you don't!*

I love you, Amelia! I have loved you not from the moment I first saw you . . .'

'When, then?'

'From the moment I first heard you.' Ralph stared at her triumphantly. 'From the very first moment I first *heard* you,' he repeated.

'Playing the piano?'

Ralph laughed, shook his head and turned to take both her hands. 'When George and I became such friends in the army, whenever we were alone somewhere – on leave from the front, trying to recover our strength and our sanity back in whatever billet we could find, wherever we were – George would read your letters. Out loud. Only to me,' he assured her quickly, seeing the look in her eyes. 'Only to me.'

'I don't care!' Amelia retorted. 'They were written to him, not to you both! How could he? How could he read my letters out to a perfect stranger?'

'I was only a perfect stranger to you. George and I were friends. Not only that – and I know, you have a right to be indignant, of course you do – but just listen. Not only were George and I friends, but we could have been killed at any moment. George wanted to share his love for you and your love for him – he had to tell someone. In case he got killed and no-one ever knew such a love existed. That's the whole point. In everyday life, when people fall in love, everyone can see how much they love each other. But when you're stuck in a trench hundreds of miles from your home and your sweetheart, mud up to your waist, surrounded by the rotting bodies of the enemy and your comrades in arms, and you think you might die at any moment, then you want to share everything. Just so that someone else – even if it's only one other bloke – just so that someone else will know how much you loved this beautiful girl and how much she loved you.'

'I see,' Amelia said quietly. 'At least I think I do.'

She walked on away from him now over the bridge and along the path beyond.

'Then there was our pact,' Ralph said, as he caught up with her. 'Like a lot of other soldiers we made a pact. George asked me to promise that if he was killed – which after all was highly likely – I would look after you and make sure you were all right. So I promised that I would. If I was spared and George killed I promised to look after you and make sure you were happy. I won't tell you what else he said.'

'Oh yes you will. Otherwise you wouldn't have said it.'

'He said that after you'd got over the shock of losing him – he said once you were over it you'd fall in love with me, and that since I was already madly in love with you anyway the best thing would be for us to get married.'

'It's no good, Ralph,' Amelia said curtly, shaking his hand off her arm. 'Whatever you say and whatever might have happened, it's not going to make any difference. *You are not going to seduce me.'*

Ralph, who was once again walking backwards in front of her, stopped, holding up his hands as if she were approaching traffic.

'No, Amelia,' he said. 'I'm not going to seduce you. I wouldn't even try. Is that the sort of person you think I am? Someone who goes around seducing absent men's wives? All I have done is tell you how I feel about you.' Ralph sighed. 'And when someone loves someone it's only natural they want to *make* love to them.'

'And you don't call that seduction?'

'No. Seduction is one thing. People making love together because they want to is quite another.'

'You think that's what's going to happen? If you think we're going to end up making love – well you're wrong.'

Amelia ducked under his outstretched arm and began to run down the path towards the house.

Days passed. With George still mysteriously absent Amelia hid herself away in the garden while Ralph took himself off for long walks in the daylight hours, spending the evenings shut away in the cottage reading and appearing only, like a naughty child, to eat his meals in the dining room with Amelia.

Peter was due home from school at the weekend and his sister two days later. By Amelia's reckoning if she could keep Ralph at arm's length until then she would be safe. She had tried to get rid of him by sending Clara across to the cottage with a note asking him to pack his bags and leave, but five minutes later Clara returned with a note from Ralph which said he would consider her proposal only if she asked him in person, which of course she was not prepared to do.

On Friday afternoon Ralph knocked on the front door of the house and enquired of Clara if he might be permitted to see her mistress. As soon as Clara had disappeared to find Amelia, Ralph let himself in to the drawing room where he poured himself a drink, lit a cigarette and made himself comfortable while he waited. Some minutes later Amelia appeared in the doorway.

'I really only came across to tell you I was leaving,' Ralph said, sitting back down on the sofa. 'So please – there's no more need to be antagonistic.'

'Where are you thinking of going?' Amelia asked, disconcerted now by the actuality of his departure. 'Back to Paris, perhaps?'

'No. I'm going back to London, but seeing what time it is, would it be all right if I left in the morning rather than having to drive back in the dark?'

'I don't see why not. I'll go and tell Clara you're staying for dinner.'

'I have a better idea,' Ralph told her before she could leave the room. 'Why don't you let me take you out to dinner? As a peace offering?'

'We're not exactly at war, are we?'

'We're not exactly at peace either, are we?'

Amelia smiled. She could not help it. Every time Ralph looked at her with his sad spaniel eyes, a clownish expression which he deliberately exaggerated by a slight lift of his eyebrows, she found herself smiling. Considering the danger to be past, she accepted his invitation to dinner.

'Do you know of this place just outside Wells? I heard about it somewhere or other. The Lantern? It's a restaurant with a dance floor – and I hear it's meant to be quite fun.'

After they had changed, Amelia into a new brilliant red dress which she had not yet had a chance to wear and Ralph into black tie and an evening cloak lined with dark blue, they drove to the restaurant.

Of course Ralph and Amelia did not realize that as soon as they were shown to their candlelit table in a window overlooking the river, they attracted every eye. But then people who are considering becoming lovers never do. They are too wrapped up in their own feelings. Happily, though, as they arrived an excellent quartet was already playing, so that many of the customers were on the dance floor.

'Would you like to dance before we eat?' Ralph wondered, once they had placed their orders. '"Falling In Love With Love". *The* very latest.'

'Why not?' Amelia agreed, getting to her feet. 'This band sounds pretty irresistible.'

She had never danced with Ralph before. Had she done so, Amelia might well have refused. There are men who can dance, just as there are many men who cannot, but there are just a few, a mere handful of men who can make a woman feel as if she is being made love to as they dance with her. Even the way Ralph held Amelia was seductive, his right hand just a little lower than was customary on her back, and the result was that they did not go back to their table after one dance but stayed on the floor until reminded by the waiter that their food was waiting. All Amelia wanted was to go on dancing. Ralph seemed to be of the same mind. He looked at her only to find her looking at him.

'The soup will get cold,' he said.

'I don't mind cold soup. In fact I quite prefer it.'

They danced on and on until the band stopped to take a break, and the waiter returned with their reheated soup.

Halfway through the main course Amelia tried to make conversation but Ralph just smiled at her and Amelia fell back to silence. The truth was she had no clear idea in her mind where everything was leading, since she was allowing herself to live only for the moment. Even when she was not looking at him Amelia knew that Ralph was looking at her, although as the meal progressed there were fewer and fewer occasions when they were not looking directly into each other's eyes as they ate and drank.

The band returned, opening the new set with 'September Song'. Hardly had the pianist finished playing the verse before Ralph and Amelia were back on the dance floor, and so they continued until they were the only couple left in the place and the waiters had started to stare at their watches, and it was time to realize that their private party was over.

They journeyed back to The Priory not in silence but to music, the music of Ralph singing 'I Can't Get Started With You'. Second time around Amelia joined in.

'You can harmonize!' Ralph cried triumphantly. 'Wonderful!'

'Long as you hold the tune I can!'

'Fine! So let's take it from the top again!'

They took it right from the top, and then they took 'A Foggy Day in London Town' followed by 'Jeepers Creepers' and finally 'Pennies From Heaven', by which time Ralph was turning the Austin into the gateway of the house to pull up outside the private entrance of the cottage.

Amelia shook out her dark hair.

'Behold the moon,' Ralph said and then sang:

> 'The moon belongs to everyone
> The best things in life are free,
> The stars belong to everyone
> They gleam there for you and me.'

'What now?' Amelia wondered. 'Will you come in for a drink?'

'Will you?'

Amelia looked ahead towards her house, then round at the cottage beside them. 'Do you think I should?'

'No. But you will.'

'I'd rather walk round the garden with you,' she found herself saying, even though her intention had been to follow Ralph into the cottage.

'There's a fire ready to be lit, rose petals in the bed.' He eased her back towards the cottage and in through the door, refusing to turn on the light and instead lighting candles which Amelia saw were placed all around the living room. Soon the whole room glowed with soft light of old-fashioned tallow.

'You did this?'

'I don't like electric light. Not at times like this.' Handing her a glass of brandy he raised his own in a toast. 'To – whatever we both want most.' Then he took her by the hand and led her to the foot of the stairs.

Amelia hesitated. 'Aren't we going to have our brandy first?'

'First? Then you agree.'

'I don't remember agreeing to anything.'

'Aren't we going to have our brandy *first*, you said. Which supposes we are going to do something *afterwards*.'

Amelia frowned. 'Yes, it does, doesn't it?'

Still holding her hand he led her up the spiral stairs, into a room which even as she had been designing it Amelia had found exciting, a long bedroom which ran the length of the small barn with a scrubbed and polished wood floor. Along one end wall she had put a round stone rose window through which the moonlight now filtered, lighting the room with a soft blue light while the candles beneath it glowed a gentle yellow. She had meant to bring George up here to make love but she never had. She felt a rush of sudden betrayal at the thought.

'No, Ralph . . .'

'Why not?' he replied, trying to ease her close to him. 'I love you – and you love me.'

'How can I?' Amelia protested, still keeping the distance between them. 'How can I possibly love you? I love George.'

'George isn't here. Besides, there is no reason why you can't love me as well.'

'Isn't there?' she wondered weakly, finding herself closer to him than she would have wished. 'Isn't there really?'

'I love you, and I love George. There is no reason why we cannot all love each other. To my way of thinking it would be more wrong for us *not* to love each other.'

'Do some magick, wizard!' the Noble One commanded.

Longbeard sighed. 'Very well, sir, but remember, it

does not always work. Besides, I am out of tune with the cosmos.'

'Magick, wizard, or he will win again!'

'What was that?' Ralph wondered, and he looked round as the candlelight was suddenly extinguished as if a breeze had blown through. 'There's no window open – no doors . . .'

'It doesn't matter. It's for the best, you'll see. Just follow me.'

'Where are you going?' Ralph called as he saw her hurrying downstairs. 'Wait – Amelia? Wait.'

'No, *you* wait,' Amelia called back as she pushed open the front door of the cottage. 'I am going to take you to the most wonderful place you have ever been.'

'But this is wonderful.'

'I'm taking you to a place where love was born!' she called over her shoulder as she ran across the dew-soaked lawns. 'A place where love may flourish!'

'A place where you and I may find the shining of the stars – where love shall only be the love of Truth,' the Noble One and Longbeard repeated with her from the shadow of the yews.

'Where you and I may find the shining of the stars!' Amelia called as she threw open the gate leading to the mound.

Ralph ran up the flight of stone steps after her,

stopping when he got to the top as the moon suddenly hid itself behind a bank of heavy cloud, blotting out the pale blue light which had guided them safely to the place they now stood.

'I don't remember this part of the garden.'

'It's a very secret place.'

'I can hardly see, Amelia. It's got so very dark. And cold.'

'Be patient.'

They stood now by the entrance to the Kissing Garden, before she led him through the narrow entrance of ancient yew into the garden itself, which was completely aglow with a strange, infinitely pale light which seemed to emanate from no identifiable source. Ralph hesitated as soon as he set foot within the hidden place, as if reluctant to go any further, but keeping a tight hold of his hand Amelia tried to make him follow her to the centre of the lawn.

'Here it is always warm, you'll see. It is a place full of love.'

Ralph drew back shivering. 'This is no place for me.' He turned, 'You can stay here. Alone.'

Amelia did not hear him. As always, she was mesmerized by the Kissing Garden, and within seconds had sat down upon the grass, not noticing that she was, now, quite alone.

At breakfast the next morning Ralph seemed to remember nothing at all from the night before beyond kissing Amelia good night.

'Did I make a pass at you?' he wondered once Clara was safely out of earshot and he had settled himself comfortably at Amelia's breakfast table. 'I must have had far more champagne than I thought. I just hope I behaved.'

Amelia started to laugh. 'Oh dear, your face. No, you didn't make a pass, as you call it. We just got a bit tight and I took you to the Kissing Garden and you were bored and went back to the cottage and fell fast asleep.'

'Phew! I'm very glad to hear it.'

'I know, I hate not remembering anything the morning after. It means you really must have made a fool of yourself, don't you think? Oh, and you've spilt coffee in your saucer.'

While Amelia fetched him a fresh cup, Ralph pulled the copy of *The Times* towards him.

'I have to confess something . . .'

'I'm all ears.'

'Ever since I arrived here on this visit, it has been as if – as if I'd lost control of myself. In the truest sense of the word. As if – as if someone else was at the wheel.'

'Perhaps someone else was.'

'Meaning?'

'You can never tell with these old houses,' Amelia teased. 'You never know what spirits lurk on in the bushes waiting to pounce.'

'The only spirits you'll find round this place are those consumed by that gardener of yours.'

'Not a word against Jethro,' Amelia warned

him. 'You can say anything you like about anyone but Jethro.'

'Just a feeble joke, but then I'm in a feeble state, so it's only to be expected, Mrs Rafferty. Good gracious, I see they've printed the letter after all.' He fell to silence as he read George's letter in *The Times*, and Amelia noticed an item in the *Daily Mail*.

It concerned George yet again, this time coupled with the name of his father, General Sir Michael Dashwood KG, MC, DSO. It would seem that in light of his son's continued alliance with the appeasement faction and in view of the letter he understood to be carried in today's *Times*, the distinguished old soldier had disassociated himself from his son.

'Amelia?' Ralph called as she dropped the newspaper and hurried from the room. 'Amelia, have you *read* this letter?'

But Amelia was already in the telephone room.

'General? It's Amelia. I've just read the report in the *Daily Mail* . . .'

'Amelia, my dear,' her father-in-law answered. 'I tried to telephone you last evening but your maid said you were out.'

'Do you really mean this, general?'

'Think the world of you, and the littles. My grandchildren. But there you are. George has gone a little too far now, my dear. We can't have this sort of thing. First there was that book, which nearly killed his mother, and now this, siding with extremists. It won't do. Sorry, my dear, but there you have it.'

'General?' Amelia called into the receiver, but it was no use. The old soldier had hung up.

A moment later, just as Amelia was about to leave the telephone room, the bell rang again.

'That the Dashwood residence?'

'Who is this, please?'

'Having it painted – bright yellow – I shouldn't wonder?'

'Who is this, please?'

'Your husband is a disgrace,' the voice interrupted. 'A filthy blot on the honour of this country. And you, missy – to live with a man who has tarnished the heroism of those who fell in the Great War so this country could be free—'

'I'm putting the telephone down now. Goodbye.'

'You are a—'

Amelia had the telephone back in its cradle before she learned the full truth of what she might or might not be. For a moment she stood trembling with anger by the small table. But her anger was not against the crank who had just telephoned, not against old General Dashwood, but against George.

How could he?

Twenty-Four

Later that morning, after dealing with the usual domestic problems that arise from running a large house and garden, Amelia went across to the cottage in search of Ralph, only to find the place deserted. Nor was there any trace of her guest, the bedclothes having been neatly folded back and the chest of drawers and wardrobe emptied of all Ralph's belongings. But there was a note left in an envelope on the fireplace, addressed to *Mrs Rafferty*.

Dear Mrs Rafferty [it read], You have been so understanding that it breaks my heart to leave. You are without doubt unique and exceptional, and George is the luckiest man alive. So although I want you to forgive me for my emotional trespassing, I also don't want you to. I'm glad you know how much I love you. What I am not so glad about is that I should have gone about declaring it. You are George's wife and I am his best friend. How could I have done that? How I dared I shall never know. All I can say in mitigation is that I felt compelled to do so. If that sounds like a feeble excuse, so be it. But it's true. There is something about this place which takes a person over. Perhaps it's you? Perhaps you are such a magical person you charm us into this sort of wild romanticism. I have no intention of trying to explain further. Other than to say that here I was captivated and that captivation was you.

Ralph.

Amelia finished reading the letter, consigned it quickly to the fire, and then stared round the room. It was so strange. She had wanted him to go, but now he was gone she wanted him back. He had pushed the button that made her enjoy life again, he had made her laugh, they had danced and sung, but now it was as if Ralph had never been there. As if in some way he had, all along, been just a figment of her imagination. There was nothing left of him, no sign that anyone had even been in the room, other than the unmade bed and a hand towel dropped over the back of a chair. Out of habit she started to tidy the room even so, pushing open the window to air it, folding the towel, throwing dead flowers into the waste-paper basket – and then she saw it.

It was lying half hidden under the bed, where Ralph must have dropped it before falling asleep.

The ex-libris plate at the front announced

that the book belonged not to the Dashwoods but to Ralph, just as the old, faded gold letters proclaimed it to be *Avalon. By Richard de Grasse*. The story of King Arthur and his round table, the story of the eternal three, Arthur, Guinevere and Lancelot. The friendship torn apart by the love of a woman.

The inscription in the book was written in a handwriting very familiar to Amelia. It read, *To Ralph Grace from his friend George Dashwood, who, like him, fought to keep the spirit of Avalon alive.*

Settling herself in an old chair in the cottage sitting room, Amelia took the book onto her knee, pausing for a second before she began to read, almost as if she was afraid of what she was about to discover within its leather binding.

As soon as she turned back the semi-transparent sheet which protected the frontispiece and studied the beautiful engraving of a boat carrying the dying hero across a dark and magical lake she thought she might be going to understand the truth of their lives for the first time.

At first she did not read but leafed through the thick pages, looking at the illustrations and reading the captions below them. Underneath the first illustration of the boat carrying Arthur's body across the dark waters was written, *And here I shall heal me of my grievous wound and from which place one day I shall return.*

Before she began to read the book properly she stared out of the window opposite her.

Somewhere out there they had a lake, just like the one illustrated in the book. Who knew, she thought suddenly, what lay beneath its dark waters, and what was more, who might have returned there?

Twenty-Five

That weekend Amelia collected Peter from school for the start of his summer holidays. He was now a tall handsome boy of nearly sixteen years old.

'Sorry it's only me and no Papa,' Amelia said as Peter piled his luggage into his mother's little car. 'He's been called to London on business.'

'It doesn't matter,' Peter said laconically, getting into the car. 'Couldn't matter less, actually.'

'Oh, but you always like it when your father picks you up,' Amelia replied. 'I don't know what you can mean.'

'I mean – Mother – *it doesn't matter*. Now can we please get going?'

Amelia put the car into gear and started to head away from the school down the long poplar-lined driveway.

'Papa said he was sorry to miss the Fathers' Match, but—'

'It couldn't matter less, Mother? All right?' Peter interrupted, draping one long arm over the car door and tossing his mane of blond hair out of his eyes. 'It Could Not Matter Less.'

'I don't think that's very nice, Peter,' Amelia

559

remarked, glancing at her son. 'Your father wouldn't miss the Fathers' Match normally for all the tea in China. It's just that—'

'It couldn't matter less,' Peter repeated, turning round and matching her look. 'Because if he had turned up they'd have probably thrown rotten eggs at him anyway.'

'What a perfectly dreadful thing to say!'

'And don't you think you ought to look where we're meant to be going?' Peter said, grabbing the steering wheel and straightening out the car, which had been heading for the verge.

'What a perfectly dreadful thing to say,' Amelia repeated, smacking Peter on the back of his hand as she regained control. 'Why should anyone want to throw rotten eggs at your father?'

'Because he's a lily-liver. That's why.'

'I *beg* your pardon, young man?'

'I said, because he's—'

'I heard what you said, thank you. And if I were you I would unsay it pretty jolly quick.'

'What's the point?' Peter sighed. 'It's true. It's all over the newspapers – practically every day!'

'You don't know what you're talking about, Peter,' Amelia retorted angrily. 'You're far too young to understand anyway.'

'Really? So listen to this, then.' Peter glanced at her, sighed a deep sigh of dissatisfaction and shook his head. 'We had a mock debate this week. You know what a mock debate is, Mama?'

Amelia nodded. 'Two sides are picked to debate

an issue. And it doesn't matter what you really believe, you have to debate what your side is pretending to stand for. So?'

'Mr Harding, our head of history, organized it. It was all about appeasement. You know about appeasement, don't you, Mother?'

'There's no need to patronize me, young man. I know a lot more than you think.'

'Well, I was chosen to lead the debate for the anti-appeasement lobby, and Paul Holmes who is a perfect freak and I cannot abide for a moment – he was chosen to speak for the appeasers. The lily-livers as they're called. As you probably know.'

'I know. Go on,' Amelia said.

'He spoke as *Father*. Incredibly embarrassing, as you might imagine.'

'Just tell me how the argument went,' Amelia said curtly. 'In brief. Go on.'

'I maintained the government is being weak-kneed with Germany. That they're bending backwards to appease Hitler which will allow him just to march into Austria and annexe it to the Reich. And as for the way we're treating the Russians—'

Amelia raised her eyebrows.

'You've become quite an expert on current affairs, haven't you?' she said. 'I haven't quite caught up about Russia yet.'

'Russia's a big country.'

'That much I do know.'

'Yes, but the point is, Mama, modern Russia –

post-Revolution Russia – is obviously going to be quite a force to reckon with – and what I argued was, which is true, was that all the Russians want from us is for us to stand up to Germany. While all our government does is cold-shoulder them, which I considered to be asking for trouble.'

'Sounds as if you have a point.'

'Can't we talk about something else?'

'No. this concerns us all.'

'So then I went on to say that if the government go on accommodating Hitler,' Peter groaned, leaning back in his seat, 'then Russia will sulk, Herr Hitler will ride roughshod over all the bits of Europe he wants, and there'll be a war anyway – so far better to stand up to him now and see him down.'

'Meaning fight a war.'

'It won't be a long one. Couple of weeks at the most.'

'My generation has heard that said before, Peter, I wonder where or when?'

'Look – what we must do is to stand up to the Nazis. Along with France, Belgium, Poland and most of all Russia. If we make it clear that we don't allow them to put a foot out of their wretched country, that will be that.'

'I don't think it's as easy as that.'

'Don't tell me you're a lily-liver too, Mama?' Peter said, with an appalled look at his mother. 'We jolly well have to stand up to Hitler! There isn't any other way!'

'Let's hear what the other side had to say, Peter,' Amelia said, turning the car out onto the Castle Cary road.

'They just had no argument, they made no fist of it.'

'Come on – I'm interested.'

'And they lost. How anyone can think that the way to get out of this mess is to suck up to Hitler beats me.'

'You think your father's one of those, do you? One of the suck up to Hitler brigade?'

'Mama . . .' Peter sighed in despair. 'He writes about it every day in the papers! Look, it's not that my burning ambition is to be a hero like my father. As my father *once* was.'

Amelia slapped Peter hard again on the back of his hand. 'As your father is!' she snapped. 'And always shall be!'

'I was just trying to explain how I feel! It isn't about not wanting to fight, it really isn't! No-one in their right mind wants to fight a war. But a war has to be a whole lot better than England becoming a Fascist state. Which is what will happen if the lily-livers win the day.'

'They didn't win your debate,' Amelia reminded him.

'Mr Harding says that rather than face another major war, a lot of people would be only too happy to let Hitler have the land he wants in the east, which apparently doesn't amount to much.'

'People *live* in the land in the east. People who

don't want to be crushed by the jackboot.'

'Neither do I. But from the sound of it, Father wouldn't mind that much.'

'I don't think that's so,' Amelia assured him. 'I really don't.'

'I mean, what about his letter to *The Times*? It could have been from Mosley.'

'Do you really believe someone like your father is like that?'

'Does it matter what I believe? Everyone else thinks so! Everyone who thought he was a hero thinks he's a traitor and a coward and should hand back his Victoria Cross.'

'It doesn't matter what everyone else thinks, Peter,' Amelia interrupted, bringing the car to a sudden halt at the side of the road and turning round to stare at him. 'Do you *really* believe your father is capable of being a traitor and a coward?'

'No,' Peter said slowly. 'No, of course I don't.'

'Fine,' Amelia said with a nod, putting the car back into gear. 'Then in that case let's just go home and have tea and chocolate cake. Clara is waiting for us.'

Despite her spirited defence of George to his son, by the time Gwendolyn was home from school, because she had still received no word from George, even Amelia's much-vaunted belief in her husband was beginning to wear thin. Gwendolyn fortunately was relatively unaffected by the scandal surrounding her father's current political beliefs. The only real interest she seemed to show in anything was to do with exactly how many parties she and Peter could get themselves invited to in the coming holidays.

Peter too seemed to forget his private anguish and returned to being very nearly his old bright self. Amelia did her best to keep up the pretence that all was well and their father simply away in London on a prolonged business trip. Finally, unable to stand it any longer, she rang the only man besides George whom she knew she could trust completely. She rang Ralph Grace.

She could have fainted with relief just hearing his voice.

'If no-one else knows where George is, Mrs Rafferty, then why should I?' Ralph wondered, sounding as humorous and relaxed as ever.

'Why you? One – you're in London; two – you know what George looks like; three – you must know some of his old friends; and four, again, because you're in London.'

'Those are four of the very worst reasons I have ever heard,' Ralph returned with a laugh. 'And because of that I shall leave no stone unturned. The thing is to find out where the main social action is, and get myself somehow into it.'

'You really are my last hope, Ralph.'

'I thought you'd stopped worrying about what George was up to?' Ralph offered as a parting thought.

'I have. It is just that not knowing *anything* is very hard.'

Two days later Ralph was able to telephone Amelia and tell her that George must certainly be alive and well since he had dined the night before with a very well placed socialite friend. A political ally of Lord Southgate, a well-known appeaser. Ralph had managed to post himself outside the Mayfair address where the party was being held in the hope of following George home, but after a long and fruitless vigil he gave up the attempt.

The arrival of her parents at The Priory helped take Amelia's mind off her worries, although she found it difficult to keep up the pretence that all was well and George simply away on business. In deference to her feelings Clarence tried at first to steer their conversations away from politics, only giving in once he had downed a martini or two. It seemed that he could not believe that George of all people harboured the beliefs that he did. It staggered him. And he felt sorry for Peter. 'Poor chap, having to go to school and hear what the other fathers have to say about his. It doesn't bear thinking of.'

Constance, on the other hand, was far more interested in the gardens, which as always entirely captivated her, even at the most dead time of year.

'Did I tell you, by the way?' Amelia asked as they strolled round together, scarves knotted under their chins. 'Did I tell you about all the flowers in one section of the border losing their colour entirely?'

'No. *What* an extraordinary thing! Do go on.'

'Jethro thought it must be a blight, but as it transpired when we cut all the flowers off to examine them they were as healthy as their colourful neighbours.'

'*How* extraordinary.'

'It was just as if someone had poured bleach over them.'

'My mother *always* used to say that to me when I was a little girl. Don't cry near a flower, darling, she'd say, or you'll wash all their colour away. Particularly roses, for some peculiar reason. Are you *sure* I never said that to you?'

'Now you come to mention it, in a book I was just reading . . .' Amelia's words petered out.

'Yes?'

'No. Nothing more boring than someone telling you about the book they're reading. Come on,' she said, taking her mother's hand. 'I want to show you what I've done to the water gardens.'

Clarence was following on some way behind the two women, Peter and Gwendolyn keeping him company. Gwendolyn's arm was through her grandfather's, Peter's eyes were on the clear sky above them, as if already searching for the enemy.

'So you're convinced there's going to be a war, are you, young man?' Clarence asked him. 'In spite of all this last minute diplomacy?'

'I hope there is, Grandfather,' Peter replied. 'As I explained to Grandmother, not because I want to fight—'

'But because he feels he has to,' Gwendolyn finished, with a certain pride.

'I think right's on our side, you see,' Peter said.

'We thought that back in 1914 as well.'

'And wasn't it?'

'I couldn't tell you, dear boy,' Clarence sighed. 'I don't think men fight wars because of right and wrong. I think men fight because they like fighting.'

'You don't?' Gwendolyn asked in shock. 'Not really, surely, Grandfather?'

'To knock something down, if it's cocked at an arrogant angle, is a deep delight to the blood. To fight for a reason is something your true warrior despises. That's what I read somewhere or other. Don't ask me where. I can't even remember why I've gone into a room nowadays.'

'Maybe that's what it is, though,' Peter said, putting his hands deep in his pockets and looking ahead of him. 'Maybe that's exactly what it is. Germany is cocked at an arrogant angle – and we want to knock her down.'

'Even so,' Clarence sighed. 'Even so, give me peace any day.'

'You'd fight to defend your family, surely, Grandfather?'

'Put like that, who wouldn't, young man? But war can only protect. It can't create. And I happen to think creation is the most important thing of all.'

'But you have to be free to create, don't you? To create as you would want to create? Freely, that is. You have to be free to create freely.'

'Of course.' Clarence smiled at his grandson and paused in the middle of the green path. 'I just hate waste, Peter, that's all. I hate to see lives wasted. Young lives.'

'I know, Grandfather,' Peter replied with a nod. 'But they won't be wasted. Believe me. Not this time.'

Just as the family were all about to go in to dinner, the front doorbell rang, and minutes later Clara arrived with a telegram for Amelia.

'Oh, heavens,' Constance said, seeing the small brown envelope. 'Not bad news, I hope. No good news ever comes by telegram.'

'Stuff and nonsense,' Clarence replied quickly, downing the last of his martini. 'Sometimes, Connie, you can be a right old gloom pot.'

'This isn't bad news,' Amelia said with a smile, the open telegram in her hand. 'It's very good news actually.'

'May we share it with you, darling girl?'

'Of course,' Amelia agreed, folding the paper in her hand. 'George has just secured a very good deal for his new book.'

'Well, well.' Constance smiled, as if expecting something of somewhat greater import. 'How very nice for him. I'm so glad it wasn't horrid news, anyway.'

Taking her husband's arm, Constance led the party out to the dining room, leaving Amelia enough time to read the text of her telegram once more before committing it safely to the flames of the fire.

G alive and well, it read. *Am meeting him for a drink p.m. R.!*

Twenty-Six

'You're sure you weren't followed?' George asked him, shutting the door behind Ralph in the small back room of the set of offices which was the designated meeting site.

'I even changed taxicabs in the middle of Piccadilly,' Ralph assured him, looking round the book-lined room. 'Got out of one straight into the one alongside in the traffic. Where in heck are we, by the way?'

'Jack Cornwall's office,' George replied, lighting a cigarette and opening a filing cabinet. 'You know? My publisher?'

'Of course,' Ralph replied. 'Don't tell me he even keeps his whisky in his filing cabinet?'

'Jack is nothing if not traditional,' George smiled. 'When he first worked as a cub reporter on the *Yorkshire Post* I understand he even wore a green eye shade.'

'So why are we meeting here in his office? Aren't publishers famous for publishing things?'

'Jack's partly responsible for all this,' George said, handing Ralph a tumbler of Scotch. 'This cloak and dagger stuff. Jack's the one who recruited me.'

'Recruited you?' Ralph pulled a chair out from behind the small desk and sat himself down. 'Jack's an appeaser?'

'The opposite.' George put the bottle back in the filing cabinet drawer, closed it, then propped himself up between the wall and the cabinet. 'Jack also works for the War Office.'

'The War Office? I don't understand—'

'I'm glad to hear it,' George assured him. 'Because I'm certainly not going to make you any wiser. Savvy?'

'When you say so, Captain Dashwood, my mind will become a complete blank.'

'Why you're here is for one reason and one reason only,' George continued. 'If anything happens to me, you're going to have to tell Amelia everything. They won't tell her anything. If anything happens to me, they'll just wash their hands of me and I wouldn't expect them to do otherwise. But I don't want Amelia *not* to know. I don't want her having to guess, or thinking the wrong thing, or coming to the wrong conclusion.'

'Understood.'

'Thank you.' George drummed his fingers on the top of the filing cabinet as if deciding whether to continue or not, then taking a deep draught of whisky he put his glass aside and straightened himself up. 'These people with whom I've been associating.'

'The Riverdean set.'

George nodded. 'And others. My brief was to

get them to accept me completely as one of them.'

'Odd chap to choose. Famous war hero, VC and all that stuff.'

'Not when you remember the furore my first book caused. That was really what started the ball rolling. Jack published the book, even though he might not have agreed with everything I said, and after that we became pretty close friends and he started marking my card.'

'Blessed with foresight, is he?' Ralph asked lightly, taking out a pack of cigarettes from his pocket.

'There was a pretty strong faction who didn't want to fight the last war either, Ralph,' George replied, leaning over and lighting his friend's smoke. 'And not just the Kaiser's relatives. People like Jack have been monitoring them for a good while now. Anyway, the long and short of it is Jack organized a plan, and by the time my father disowned me I was well and truly welcome in the company of my newfound friends.'

'Just to play I Spy? To make out a list of offenders – except they haven't really done anything. Or have they?'

'Other than air their views in public, views which while not popular with everyone are hardly seditious. No – it's more to do with what they are *about* to do. You see, their aim is to seal a pact they have already put before their friend Hitler, an agreement which includes deposing our present monarch and putting the Duke of Windsor on the throne, and to form a government sympathetic to the Third Reich, all in return for a promise that this country will not be invaded and will retain its sovereignty.'

'No-one would hear of it. People would string 'em up from the lamp-posts.'

'They have a lot of support in very high places. They're even said to have backing within the armed services.'

'George – if this is true, then it's treason.'

George looked at him for a moment, then came and sat down opposite Ralph at the small office desk.

'It's true – and it wasn't just Jack who convinced me, Ralph,' he said, looking his friend in the eye. 'In fact it wasn't Jack at all. I convinced myself. You have to imagine what this country would be like under a Fascist government. Imagine what living under a government such as that of the Third Reich could really be like.'

By the time George had finished telling him, Ralph had smoked his way through a whole fresh cigarette and drunk a second large whisky.

'So what can you do about it? To stop it, or to help stop it?'

'I have to get hold of a certain dossier of files which contain the names of all the people involved.'

'Do you know where this dossier is?'

'It's in a safe. To be precise, it's in the Astleys' safe in their house at Riverdean.'

'Any idea how you're going to steal it?'

'Yes. I'm going to try and get Deanna Astley to give it to me.'

It was, the way George put it, as simple as that. Much as it disturbed him he had now apparently reached a point of such intimacy with Deanna Astley that he was convinced he could somehow get hold of the key to the all-important safe. If he was right, then once he had the files in his possession he had to get them post-haste to Rex Bowater, the hugely influential proprietor of United Newspapers whom Jack Cornwall had already primed concerning the supposed treachery. When the facts contained in the dossier became known by the right people, Cornwall and Bowater knew there would be an end to the sedition as well as the ruin and disgrace of a large number of very rich and important people.

Once the file was in the right hands, George's involvement would be at an end, leaving him free to return to his home and his beloved wife and family. As they finished their whiskies Ralph wished him well, while George tried to reassure him that the worst part was in fact over, it having been when he was forced to ally himself publicly with a set of people he would now gladly set adrift in a boat in the Atlantic without food or water – to say the least of it.

'So I shall take my leave of you, brave Horatio,' George smiled as he put out the light in the little office before opening the door to let them both out. 'I to steal the file, and you to keep your mouth tightly shut.'

'I never saw you, Captain Dashwood, sir,' Ralph murmured, as they eased out of the back door of the offices. 'I saw nothing, heard nothing, and know even less.'

'Good man. But remember, if I don't come back—'

'You will.'

The two old comrades in arms exchanged a last look, then, carefully shutting the door which had led them out into the alleyway at the back of the building, vanished into the night to their quite separate destinies.

George was convinced he knew where the key to the Astley safe was kept. Deanna Astley wore it attached to a slender chain which she wore around her waist. He had already been sufficiently intimate to become aware of this piece of jewellery and had once even remarked on it, having first noticed it when dancing with her and feeling what he thought to be the shape of a small key beneath her silk dress. Deanna had laughed it off as being the key to the safe where she kept her jewellery, an explanation which George might have accepted as a perfectly valid one had he not by chance one evening observed her unfastening the chain through the front of her evening gown and handing her husband a key with which he then opened a large wall safe hidden behind the panelling.

It was, of course, a long shot that the documents George needed were still in the safe at Riverdean, but it was the only one he had left to make. With the Prime Minister due to make another visit to meet the Führer in Munich, time was fast running out, for if the PM could be gulled into making a pact with Hitler it would be the very foundation stone for the coup which had been so meticulously planned by the appeasement party.

'You're awfully quiet this evening, George,' Deanna remarked, some time after George had arrived at her Mayfair address. 'You're really not being much fun, if I may say so.'

'I am sorry, Deanna,' George said, picking up his cocktail from beside him. 'Brown study time.'

'Can I pay a penny entrance fee?' she asked, coming to sit on the arm of his chair. 'And know exactly what you are thinking?'

'I was thinking what a fool I'd been,' he replied. 'What a fool for wasting so much time.'

'What sort of time, George?'

'Time spent with you, of course.'

Deanna slipped off the arm of the chair and into his lap in order to kiss him. 'Time does have a habit of marching on. And I have to go away to Germany. And you won't be able to come with me because of me being the little wifey person and my big husband person coming along.'

'Exactly,' George agreed. 'So it's high time I

stopped being such a positive old stick in the mud.'

'Is that what you are, sweetie?' Deanna smoothed his hair back and smiled at him. 'I don't think that you're a stick in the mud at all. I think you're a tiger.'

'I have a brilliant idea. Why don't we drive down to Riverdean? We can't stay the night here because your husband is in town—'

'Don't be silly. Marmy doesn't give a fig what I do.'

'I know. But knowing he's here just cramps my style.'

'And your style is *much* too good to cramp,' Deanna agreed. 'Good. I think that's a lovely idea. I adore houses when there's no-one there but me and the servants. I find them very sexy. You will love my room at Riverdean. It has a seventeenth-century four-poster. You can have such fun with four posts.'

'I intend to,' George assured her.

It was a surprisingly cold and rainy night, so when they arrived at Riverdean they sat for a while silently warming themselves up in front of the fire in the library which Deanna had ordered to be lit on their arrival. But although they said little or nothing to each other, Deanna never took her eyes off George all the time they were drinking the large brandies she had ordered the liveried footman to pour for them. She slipped her shoes off and eased her silk-stockinged feet up under her as she and George settled comfortably onto the large sofa in front of the blazing fire.

'It's lovely and warm in here now,' she said, gently easing her stockinged feet into George's lap once the servant had left them alone. 'Much, much warmer than the bedroom.'

'I can imagine,' George agreed, trying to work out his next move.

'Who needs a cold bedroom?' Deanna murmured. 'We have the sofa – and this lovely fur rug, as you can see.'

'What about this lovely fur rug?'

'You've never read about Elinor Glyn and the sin she committed on the tiger skin? Don't move,' she added with a smile. 'I'm just going to lock the door.'

Having done so she came back to stand in front of the sofa. In one easy deft movement she slipped out of her dress to stand before him wearing nothing except her black silk underwear and stockings.

'I don't mind if you take your jacket off,' she teased after a moment. 'In fact let me take it off for you.'

In between kissing him, Deanna slipped off George's jacket and tie, slowly undid his cuff links, and slipped his shirt off his shoulders.

'You have the most lovely body,' she said, kissing his neck and then his chest. 'The most lovely body I think I have ever seen.'

'You haven't ever seen my body,' George protested. 'Not all of it.'

'I am about to make good that omission,' Deanna assured him, undoing the belt of his trousers.

'And I'm not making love to you with that key around your waist,' George told her, fingering the thin chain. 'It makes you look like some sort of gaoler.'

'Wouldn't you like that, George? For me to be your gaoler? And you to be my prisoner?'

'I already am, Deanna,' George replied, feeling for the catch on the chain. 'So we won't be needing this.'

Having undone the slender chain, he placed it neatly on a side table by the sofa, still uncertain as to how exactly he was going to gain access to the safe. His somewhat rudimentary plan had been to get possession of the key, then simply overpower Deanna and shut her away perhaps in some cupboard or closet in her bedroom while he effected his burglary. Now that he found himself trapped in the same room as the safe he briefly entertained the notion of knocking her out with one of the handy fire irons, only to reject this idea as one which could possibly cause too much commotion and attract the attention of a footman. As he knew from his previous visits to the great house, a member of the household staff was never out of earshot of the reception rooms, whatever the time of day or night, so he wondered whether he would simply wrap her up in the rug and carry her upstairs to the more distant privacy of the bedroom where he could safely lock her away out of anyone's hearing? But there again, as soon as he considered the practicalities of such a move he realized that in spite of her avowed bravura Deanna would never take the risk of being seen by a member of her staff in such a way. As he held her in his arms he recognized that perhaps the only way he was going to achieve his purpose was to do what he had vowed he would not do, and that was to make love to her in the hope that in the aftermath Deanna would fall so fast asleep that it would leave him free to effect the robbery.

'Mmm,' Deanna sighed, suddenly and surprisingly yawning, an act which to judge from her expression apparently caught her also unawares. 'Heavens. Must be the fire. I suddenly feel incredibly drowsy.'

She smiled at him, at the same time blinking her eyes and frowning, as if suddenly bewildered. 'It's either the fire or the brandy. I can hardly keep awake. Here.' She slipped her arms round George's neck and kissed him once more. 'Here,' she whispered faintly. 'Quickly. Down on this lovely furry rug. So warm, so sexy.'

Looking at the beautiful woman in his arms, a pearl choker round her neck, her perfect, black silk clad body lit by the flickering of the fire, for a moment George nearly forgot the true purpose of his presence in her house.

'George,' Deanna whispered, her eyes slowly closing. 'George?'

'Yes?' George whispered in return, feeling her body suddenly heavy in his arms. 'Deanna?'

He leaned back from her to take a better look, at the same time easing his hold on her. She began slowly to slide from his arms, finally to collapse flat on her back on the white rug at his feet.

Even before he knelt down beside her to make absolutely sure, George knew she was completely unconscious. The only thing he was uncertain of was how she had come to be in this state. It was as if she had been drugged, yet he was the only other person in the room.

'Apart from the footman,' he muttered to himself as he knelt beside her, making sure of the depth of her oblivion before reaching over to the remains of the glass of brandy Deanna had been drinking. He ran the tip of his little finger round the bottom of the all but drained glass, then carefully tasted the retrieved drop of cognac.

'Aha,' he said to himself, sensing a slight but definite aftertaste. 'So the butler did it – or the footman, anyway. Or else, who?'

As to why, he knew not. What he did know was that what seemed like an intercession by Fate had provided him with exactly the opportunity he needed, so, grabbing hold of the chain and key, he stepped over the recumbent Deanna to begin his search for the hidden wall safe. After two false starts he found the panel which, far from needing pressure on some secret switch to release it, swung open as soon as George took hold of one edge to reveal the wall safe. A moment later he had the key in the door, the door open, and sight of a bundle of buff folders loosely held together with a thick black ribbon.

Having quickly checked that the dossier was indeed the one he was after, George hurriedly made for the door, only to hesitate on the threshold to wonder if the footman whom he suspected of spiking Deanna's drink was still on duty, and if he was whether he really was on his side? If he was and was also still around then it would not matter if George was seen leaving alone with a bundle of confidential documents under one arm. The man might even help him effect his escape, while on the other hand if George had read the runes wrong – as in the wrong person drinking the drugged brandy – then he could not afford to be caught *in flagrante*. So before he left the comparative safety of the library, George took a careful look through the barely opened door to check the lie of the land. Seeing an apparently deserted hallway he quickly tucked the bundle of stolen files under one arm, draped his jacket over his shoulder to conceal his booty, and ventured out into the unknown.

At first sight it appeared the inner hallway where he found himself was in fact completely deserted, allowing him time to plan his next move. Leaving by one of the main doors he considered far too risky, particularly since he seemed to remember that for security reasons they were all kept tightly locked after dark and their keys left in the charge of the staff. The best and possibly only way out was going to be via a window, although once again George found himself hesitating as he wondered which particular one he should choose. As far as he could recall all the windows in the main rooms were fitted with lockable catches, leaving him the option of trying to drop to the ground from a first-floor window, a notion he found somewhat daunting when he considered the height of the windows in question.

'You seem to be in a bit of a quandary, sir,' a soft voice said from the shadows behind him. 'Might I perhaps be of some help?'

Turning quickly in surprise George saw the footman who had attended them earlier in the library emerging from the dark recess of a doorway.

'That all depends,' George answered carefully. 'It depends on what you mean by a quandary and what you consider to be of help.'

'By a quandary, sir, I mean the fact that you need to get the information you have to Mr Cornwall as soon as possible, and by help I would consider suggesting the best means of escape.'

'Thank you,' George said with a smile, now getting the picture. 'Jack Cornwall recommended you for this position, did he?'

'Absolutely, sir,' the footman replied. 'With

instructions to keep a special eye on your good self. If you would like to follow me, Captain Dashwood.'

George did as requested, tailing the footman across the hallway then down the corridor which he remembered led to the cloakrooms.

'I would rather offer you the choice of a doorway, Captain Dashwood,' the footman said, standing to one side to admit George to the gentlemen's washroom. 'But I'm afraid the kitchens remain staffed until Mrs Astley retires, while all the main doors of the house are now securely locked. The best way out would be for you to let yourself out via the windows over the basins.'

'And the coach house?' George wondered, looking up at his proposed escape route and trying to remember the exact lie of the land.

'More or less straight in front of you once you're safely outside. Follow the path that leads from the kitchen door. You'll have to raise the coachman to get the keys for your car.'

George looked round sharply. This was something he had not considered, having lived in the hope that when the coachman had taken his car away to park it for him on their arrival he would simply have left the keys in it.

'Won't that arouse suspicion? My leaving suddenly in the small hours?'

'You've been called away urgently, Captain Dashwood. A personal matter. As long as Mrs

Astley remains oblivious, there'll be no need for questions.'

'Perhaps you can make sure of that, yes?'

'I shall do my very best, Captain. Bon voyage.'

Left to himself, and realizing that time was at a premium, George hurried across the flagstoned washroom, opened the window above the hand-basins, climbed up onto the stand and eased himself into the aperture. Looking down he saw the drop was greater than he had imagined, possibly between ten and twelve feet, which meant that rather than jump and risk spraining or even breaking an ankle he would have to drop down onto the steep bank of grass below. So, folding the papers securely inside his jacket and keeping them in place by tying the arms, he dropped the package out of the window, turned himself round while still holding on to the central stone mullion, then eased himself out into the night, hanging for a moment by his fingertips before letting himself fall silently and safely to the ground.

Making his silent way along the path to the coach-house where they always parked any overnight visitors' motors, he hoped and prayed that his ally inside the great house had been wrong and that the coachman had in fact left the keys in the ignition of the Bentley. He knew very well that his sudden and precipitous departure in the small hours of the morning was bound to arouse some suspicion. Better by far to simply climb into his car and drive away before anyone had the chance to ask any questions. But as soon as he had reached the large outbuilding which had been converted into garages his worst fears were realized, for not only had his car been safely put away but the line of sliding doors which secured the front of the garages was closed and firmly locked.

He could see his Bentley through the glass panels set high in the doors, the big car parked there with her hood up, ready for the road. But judging from the weight of the doors and the solidity of the locks there was no way he was going to be able to get at her. Even were he to break one of the glass panels and be able to reach a key in one of the locks well below the window, George imagined the heavy doors would probably be bolted on the inside as well at ground level. So there was in fact only one thing for it. He would have to raise the coachman.

Shivering with the cold from the rain but unable to put his jacket on because of what it contained, he gritted his teeth and, trying to look as nonchalant as possible, climbed the steps at the side of the coach-house to knock on the door at the top. In response to a second knock a light finally went on, and a moment later by the sleepy dressing gowned figure of Martin, the head chauffeur, appeared at the door.

'Sorry to disturb you,' George said crisply, 'but I've been called to London urgently, and I need my car.'

The chauffeur blinked at him, consulted his wristwatch and started to say something, only to be interrupted by George.

'I know it's late,' he said with practised authority. 'But I have a serious domestic emergency and have to leave now. So jump to it, man, and open up the coach-house immediately.'

'Of course, sir,' Martin said, in response to George's officer-like orders. 'I'll just go tell Mr Robins first—'

'No need for that,' George assured him firmly. 'As I said, this is an emergency.'

It was obviously enough, for a second later George heard the chauffeur clattering down the steps after him.

George was already in the driver's seat and trying to fire the engine up by the time the man had begun to roll the heavy doors along their rails so that the car could reverse out. But due to the increasing drop in the night's temperature the engine refused to start. He was just about to make one last attempt to spark it into life when he became aware of another figure standing on the driver's side of the car, the person who had in fact just flicked on the light switch.

'Is there some sort of problem, Captain Dashwood?' Robins the butler wondered, leaning so close to George that he could see the man was still wearing his pyjamas under the tailcoat he had hastily donned. 'We were given to understand you would be staying until morning, sir.'

'There is a problem,' George returned brusquely, checking out of the corner of his eye that his jacket was still safely concealing the files on the passenger seat beside him. 'I was just saying to your man here, I have to return home immediately.'

'In response to a telephone call, sir?'

'Well of course! What else, man? A carrier pigeon?'

'It's just that all calls to the house come through our own switchboard, sir, even at night. When there is no-one in official residence.'

'So?' George said, breathing an inward sigh of relief as the engine finally burst into life and preparing to back the Bentley out of the garage.

'The fact is no call came through the board tonight, sir!' the butler called over the roar of the revving engine.

'How would you know?' George shouted back, engaging the gearbox in reverse.

'Part of my duty, sir! Is Mrs Astley not travelling back with you?'

'Of course not!' George shouted. 'Now if you don't mind taking your hand off the door, I really must go.'

'Before you do, sir, I really would rather check that everything is all right with Mrs Astley!'

Sensing that the man was about to lean in and reach for the ignition key, George realized he would have to make a dash for it, knowing that the moment they woke Deanna and she saw her precious wall safe open, the game would truly be up. He therefore jammed his foot on the throttle and shot the big car straight out of the garages.

By the time he had swung the car round to head for the archway at the top of the mews, both Robins and Martin the chauffeur were in full pursuit. Ramming the Bentley's gears into first, George prinked the throttle only to hear the engine miss a beat. All he needed now was for the car to stall, but knowing that the surest way to make that happen would be to panic, George calmly slipped the gears back into neutral, revved the engine to make sure he had sufficient power, then again engaged first gear and floored the accelerator. Unfortunately the brief delay had given Martin enough time to take a flying leap onto the passenger side running-board while the slower and heavier figure of Robins was trying to get a hold somewhere on the back of the car.

As the Bentley leapt forward, its enormous tyres screeching on the cobblestoned yard, in his driving mirror George saw Robins fall to the ground as he failed to get a grip anywhere on the back of the bodywork. But Martin still had a firm hold on the passenger door, and was leaning into the car in an effort to grab hold of the steering wheel with his free hand, which he managed to do just as the car reached the archway. Too late the man realized the mistake he had made as in response the car slewed violently to the left, throwing him off balance. A second later, as the car roared safely out of the yard, George glanced quickly in his mirror to see the chauffeur flat out on the ground, with Robins, who had been fruitlessly pursuing him on foot, now nowhere in sight.

Fearing that Robins might have gone for a car of his own in which to mount a pursuit, George accelerated as hard as he could up the long drive which led out of the five hundred acre estate, past the home paddocks and lakes, until finally he crested the rise which ended in a pair of lodges either side of the heavy ornamental iron gates – gates which as they came fully into view George saw to his horror were closed.

Cursing roundly, George realized he would have to take the chance of ramming his way out, particularly when he caught sight of the beams from another car's headlights closing on him down the drive. So, with his foot still flat to the boards, George aimed the car straight at the middle of the gates, which burst open on impact, allowing the Bentley to roar out on to the open road.

From the sound of her still roaring engine and her ever-increasing acceleration George realized the car had miraculously sustained no immediate mechanical or physical damage, due no doubt to her great weight, the speed of the collision and the fact that the heavy gates were in fact only secured by a none too heavy chain. But then thanks to the relatively easy exit his pursuer's car had also escaped damage, and in his mirror

George could see it was not losing any distance.

He could only guess at what make the car behind him was, although he knew that the cars the Astleys kept were all fast and powerful. As he was leaving he had in fact noticed a brand new SS Jaguar parked beside the Bentley, and to judge from the shape of the headlights he could see getting ever closer to him in his driving mirror, his bet was that this was the car his pursuers were driving, meaning he had a race on his hands.

By the time they had both passed through the gates he still held a good hundred-yard advantage, but that was soon reduced to a lead of less than twenty thanks to the narrow twisting road which led from Riverdean to the main London road, more suited to the lighter Jaguar than the heavy Bentley. But the tortuous country lane was also to George's advantage. He held the Bentley to the crest of the narrow road and – always provided there was nothing coming in the opposite direction – he knew he could prevent his pursuers from overtaking him until they finally swung onto the London road, now only some half a mile off. Once on the broader, straighter road it was all going to be down to driving skills and sheer horsepower, a prospective contest which would probably be to the advantage of the newer and lighter model of car which was so urgently trying to find a way up alongside the Bentley.

'Luck is what we need!' George shouted aloud to his car as he swung it hard into a right hand bend, giving the wheel plenty of opposite lock as he felt the rear end begin to slide away from him. 'Good luck for us – and bad luck to the enemy!'

Yet it would seem that the lady Luck had deserted him, for as they raced towards the London road the Bentley's engine began to misfire. Dreading the thought that it might be either an airlock in the petrol line or, worse, dirt in the fuel, George pumped the throttle, but the car just spluttered all the harder while continuing to lose power. Moments later the car behind him was swarming all over his tail, as George saw when he checked his mirror.

What he also saw was that the man riding in the passenger seat, whom he assumed to be Robins, was now half standing to take better aim with the pistol he had in his hand.

Before he could fire a shot, George jammed on his brakes as hard as he could, an emergency move totally at odds with the expectations of the driver behind him, since he immediately ploughed the Jaguar into the back of the Bentley. At once there was the sound of breaking glass and the crash of metal as the cars collided, the impact knocking the still spluttering Bentley up onto the left hand verge where for a moment its rear wheel lost its grip and spun hopelessly. George quickly checked his mirror again, hoping that the crash would have knocked the would-be gunman clean out of the open-topped car, only to note that although the collision had extinguished the Jaguar's headlamps he could just make out the silhouette of Robins not only still in place but back on his feet and seemingly about to take aim once more.

Then, as quickly as it had deserted him, his luck returned. When he floored the throttle one more time in a do or die attempt to get the Bentley back motoring, the engine gave one tremendous backfire and allowed George to accelerate away. He heard what he thought was a second backfire, only to realize that it was a bullet when the shot shattered his windscreen. Unable to see for a moment, George continued to drive the Bentley one-handed, shaking the files free of his jacket and pushing them safely to the floor before rolling the garment into a ball and using it to punch out the rest of the lethally jagged glass.

If he had been cold before, driving in only his shirtsleeves with no windscreen now to protect him from the full blast of the night wind George was frozen down to the very marrow of his bones. Though he longed to slow down sufficiently to at least pull his jacket around him, one glance in the mirror told him he was not yet far enough from his pursuers to afford himself that luxury. Instead he pressed on faster and faster until there was nothing reflected in his driving mirror except the night.

Nor was there anything on the London road. In fact it was not until he was well past Reading that he saw any traffic at all, and that was just a handful of trade vehicles making an early entrance into the town. After that George had the road more or less to himself, arriving outside Jack Cornwall's flat in Ebury Street shortly after two o'clock.

'You look as though you could do with something nourishing,' Jack said after he had let him into his apartment, peering at him through his thick-lensed spectacles. 'Looks as though you've had a bit of a night of it.'

Summoning his half-awake wife to fetch George some warm blankets and make them all some hot toddies, Jack took the files from George and began carefully to scrutinize each and every folder, while Miranda returned to wrap George up in two heavy wool blankets and sit him by the gas fire, where they both sipped their hot whiskies in complete silence as Jack finished his reading.

'Jolly good,' he said finally, closing the last of the buff folders. 'We have everything we need here and more. I'd better go and call Rex now. He's waiting to hear from me.'

'How did you do it, George?' Miranda wondered while Jack went out to the hall to make his telephone call. 'Did you have to do the dreaded deed you poor chap?' she teased.

'No,' George replied. 'Thank God. I'd rather lie down with a cobra as a bed companion.'

'Not what most men would say about Deanna Astley. So how in hell did you get the files? What did you do – hypnotize her?'

'Blast!' George gave a boyish grin. 'Now my secret is out. Blast.'

'Jacko had his doubts, you know,' Miranda told him, lighting up a black-papered cigarette. 'For Jacko, he was a worried man.'

'Jack's permanently worried, Miranda.'

'He was *really* worried. I can always tell when he's *really* worried. Because he whistles. And for the last twenty-four hours Jacko has done little else but whistle.'

'He'd taken precautions, Miranda. He'd installed one of his – what does he call them? He'd installed one of his *bogeys* there.'

'Only as a failsafe. No-one could get into the actual safe except you, he knew that.'

'Rex is sending his car over at once,' Jack said, coming back in and picking up the matches to light his pipe. 'He wants you to take the papers over to him. All right with you?'

'What does he intend to do? Now you've franked them?'

'You mean is he going to publish them? You tell me.' Jack shrugged, tapping his pipe against the side of an ashtray. 'A lot of this unsavoury lot have friends in very high places. Might be difficult.'

'Surely you're not going to just smack them on their wrists and tell them not to be so silly again?' Miranda protested. 'In the good old bad old days, people like them went to the Tower, and off with their blasted heads.'

'More than one way to skin a cat, precious,' Jack muttered, lighting his pipe. 'We don't chop off their heads nowadays. We chop off their

596

assets. Fate worse than death department.'

'Do be a little more specific,' Miranda sighed. 'You are dealing with a bear of very little brain, beloved.'

'There are other ways of immobilizing people without putting them in jug, ducky. Like recommending they go and find somewhere else far away to play their games. Funny thing, you know. But even to traitors, there's no place like home.'

George opened his eyes very wide and looked at Miranda. 'Now you see why it's best not to mess with old foureyes here,' he said. 'If you're not careful, Mrs Cornwall, you could end up eking out your old age in exile in Bognor.'

Deciding it was still too early to ring Amelia to tell her all was well and he would be home later that day, George had just enough time for a quick wash and shave before a chauffeur-driven Rolls Royce arrived to take him round to Rex Bowater's penthouse apartment in Park Lane. Once there he was served a perfectly cooked breakfast by the Bowaters' butler and maid while the proprietor of United Newspapers and the all-powerful editor of one of the nation's favourite daily newspapers stood reading the documents that George had brought him standing up at a large lectern he used especially for such purposes.

While he read George leafed through the early editions of his papers. His reading was finally interrupted by a firm squeeze on his shoulder.

'Cornwall said you were one hell of a fellah,' Bowater growled. 'He was right.'

'Thank you,' George said, putting down his napkin. 'But in this instance, Mr Bowater—'

'Rex. Please.'

'While honoured by your comment, Rex, as they say, I just did my bit.'

'Nonsense, man. This could and damn well will turn the tide of anti-war propaganda in our favour. This is just the proof we needed to defeat the appeasers. Doing your bit isn't the half of it.'

'Then I'm glad to have been of service.'

'You really can have no idea of what this means, George. I dare say none of us can.'

'At a guess I would say what it means is war.'

'There are wars and there are wars, George. And this is a war we have to fight. Don't you agree?'

'I'm afraid so.'

'You wouldn't have done what you did otherwise. You'd never have risked your all, damn it, unless you believed what must be believed. That the Nazis have to be stopped.'

'After the last war, Rex,' George said, getting up from the table and going to stand at the big picture window that overlooked Park Lane, 'after we'd finished fighting the last war I vowed never again. The sheer waste of life. The complete folly of it all. And yet now I can't see any alternative.'

'You have to stand up to the bully boys, George. Wrong causes wars – and so Right has to get up and go fight 'em.'

'I have a son,' George said, looking up at the blue skies above London.

'So do I, George,' Rex said, coming to his side and lighting a large cigar. 'And if your kid is anything like mine, he can't wait to get at 'em.'

'Odd, isn't it, though? The older our civilization gets, the more destruction and havoc we wreak.'

'Not so, George,' Rex said with a sigh. 'I'm afraid that war's as old as the hills. It's only peace that's a new-fangled concept. We have to fight this one. There's no saying what the Nazis will do if we don't.'

'There's no saying what they're going to do anyway, Rex.'

'Sure. But we just don't want 'em doing it here, right, George?'

'No, that's the very last thing we want.'

'It'll all fall into shape one day, George, and make good sense,' Rex assured him, his arm round his shoulder. 'And don't worry, my friend. I'll make sure what you did doesn't go unnoticed.'

'I'd rather you didn't, if you don't mind.'

'What?'

'There's only one thing I want, Rex, believe me,' George said, taking a last look at the skies above him, skies he now saw full of fighter planes and bombers. 'And that's to go home to my wife.'

'Of course, old man. Only natural. Go to!'

Twenty-Seven

Amelia put out her hand and he took it in his.

'I'm sorry I left without warning,' he whispered. 'I couldn't explain.'

'It's all right,' she whispered back. 'You don't have to explain anything. And you don't have to be sorry. If anyone's sorry it's me. I was the one who lost trust. For a moment I thought you really had changed.'

'Maybe I'm not such a bad actor after all.'

She squeezed his hand more tightly. 'Archie and Mae would be proud of you. As long as you can forgive me for not trusting you?'

'There's nothing to forgive.'

'Maybe you'll be able to make it up with your father now,' she said. 'Now we know what it was all about.'

George turned on his side and looked her in the eyes.

'There's nothing to make up,' he told her. 'That was all his idea. The so-called estrangement between us. He knew it would help what I was doing. Give me the credibility I needed.'

'Couldn't you have let me in on it?' Amelia asked, suddenly once again bewildered and a little hurt.

'We discussed that – but in the end he advised against it. He said the less you knew, the less danger you'd be in.'

'So there's nothing to be made up, then?'

'Nothing at all, Amelia – except for lost time.'

He made love to her then, and for Amelia it was as if the sun had suddenly broken through a forest of trees in which she had been lost for many months.

'Do you know how much I love you, George?'

'No, I don't. And I hope I never live to find out. Just as much as I hope you never live to find out how much I love you.'

'Why? Why don't you want me to know?'

'Because I don't know myself. How can you understand infinity? The way I love you – it's eternal. For ever. I can't possibly begin to quantify it. But if you want some idea of how I feel – look up at the sky at night. That's where you'll see how much I love you. Because that's what lights the stars.'

That night she did as he said and looked out through the window of their bedroom on to the shadowy gardens below, hearing a nightjar call and making out the flight of owls as they flew silently through the dark. She looked then above the shapes of the mysterious old yews up to the deep blue-black of the heavens, night skies decorated with an infinity of tiny stars, and in their eternity and their mysterious beauty it seemed to Amelia that at last she had begun to understand the nature of love.

Part Four
1945

'To where beyond these voices there is peace.'

The Idylls of the King Tennyson

Twenty-Eight

He appeared out of the smoke as if by magic, stopping to stand quite still by the locomotive which had drawn the train of carriages into the station. Jennifer felt her mother's hand tighten on her arm, as if making ready to stop her from running to him before it was proper to do so, but she need not have worried because it was clear that he was neither aware of Jennifer nor indeed it seemed even looking for her. He just stood by the stationary locomotive as if still somewhere else, his gaze fixed far above their heads.

'Peter?'

Jennifer heard his mother call out from the group hurrying to greet him just ahead of her own family, and watched as Lady Dashwood detached herself to hurry to be the first at her son's side.

'Peter! You're home!' Jennifer heard her cry before taking his hands in hers. 'Peter – you're back home at last! At long, long last!'

With her own mother still holding her back, Jennifer continued to watch as Amelia stood on the tips of her toes to kiss her son on the cheek. She knew why her mother was restraining her – it was because she considered it was not Jennifer's place to be the first to welcome Peter home. They had discussed the matter endlessly on their journey to Castle Cary, much as if they were discussing who should sit where at the dinner table rather than the safe return of a man now loved by two families. In the end Jennifer knew that her mother was right, because although she had accepted Peter Dashwood's proposal of marriage on his last leave home, they were still only engaged since on his return to his squadron he had been shot down over Germany.

'Welcome home, Group Captain.'

Sir George Dashwood stepped forward and saluted his son affectionately.

'Papa.'

When his son had returned the salute George smiled at him, then took his boy in his arms to embrace him. Jennifer's mother eased her grip on her arm and began to move forward alongside her daughter.

'Something's the matter,' Jennifer said, suddenly coming to a standstill. 'I can see from Lady Dashwood's face.'

She looked anxiously at Peter as she began to move towards him again. He seemed still to be staring at the sky above him from over his father's shoulder, rather than at any of those who had gathered there to welcome him home.

'Peter?' she heard his mother saying once more, this time with a definite note of anxiety in her voice, a tone which prompted Jennifer to take a longer and even more careful look at her returning hero.

'Peter, darling?' Amelia prompted him again. 'Look – Jennifer's here. Jennifer and her family have come to welcome you home as well.'

But in spite of his mother's prompting, Peter continued to pay no apparent attention to his whereabouts, prompting his father to come over to where Jennifer and her family now stood.

'Look here,' George said quietly, his back turned to Peter. 'I'm afraid this might be proving just a little too much for him. Which in a way is hardly surprising. Seeing what he's been through.'

'Perhaps if I went and said hello close to?' Jennifer suggested.

'Of course,' George agreed. 'But go easy. This sort of thing can be quite difficult.'

'Peter?' Jennifer called as she approached him, reaching out one hand and placing it on his arm. 'Hello, Peter – it's me.'

'Jennifer,' Peter said, looking down at her with a sudden frown, as if he had just worked out who she was. 'Jenny-wren, how good to see you. Do forgive me, will you? It's been a hell of a journey.'

'Hasn't touched down yet, I imagine,' Jennifer's father, who had been a First World War pilot himself, remarked to George. 'Still looking for his landfall.'

'Absolutely,' George agreed, the clock turning back what seemed now like a lifetime. 'I'm

sure he's very happy to see us all. It's all just a bit
– overwhelming.'

As planned they all returned to The Priory for tea,
which Clara had laid out beneath the shade of the
old yew trees. For a while George and Peter sat
apart talking together, although it was apparent to
anyone watching that it was George who was
doing the talking, while Peter sat in almost total
silence, holding his officer's cap on his knees, as if
he was afraid to let it go, as if in some way it held
more reality for him than anything that was going
on around him.

Jennifer hesitated before taking his father's
place beside her fiancé but at an encouraging nod
from Amelia she did so.

'I expect you'd rather not talk at all, just sit and
soak it all up,' she said, determined to be matter of
fact while inside she was struggling not to fling her
arms around his poor old head and hug him to
her for ever.

'That would be best. You talk. I'll listen.'

'I – er – we all er – have missed you so
dreadfully.'

He nodded, still not looking at her. Still clasping
his officer's cap just as he must have clasped his
schoolboy's cap while waiting for his parents to
collect him.

'You know I escaped, don't you, Jenny? From
the first place, but not the second,' he said

608

suddenly. 'I did get away from the first place, but not – not the second.'

'You *escaped*?'

'Didn't I tell you? Didn't they tell you? I'm sure I told them. Perhaps I didn't.'

He lapsed back into silence, still staring around, silent, wordless before saying again, abruptly, 'I think I'll go for a walk, look at the garden. Can't really take in anything yet.'

Jennifer watched Peter cross the lawns of his family home and go through the gate which led to the Wild Garden.

'I should go after him, if I were you,' Amelia told Jennifer, joining her future daughter-in-law by the ancient trees.

'Actually, I think he'd rather be alone, Lady Dashwood.'

'You think so, but believe me, he wouldn't. I know,' she added firmly, as she saw the younger woman still hesitating. 'Really, I do know. Go on, you'll catch him if you hurry.' She turned back as Jennifer started to hurry after her son. 'Oh and by the way, Jenny, be sure to make him take you to what we call the Kissing Garden. It's a little garden surrounded by high hedges near the Wild Garden.'

'Is it special to Peter?'

The question came floating back to Amelia, but since the questioner had long disappeared from sight, Amelia did not bother to answer, only thinking to herself, that if it was not now, it soon would be. After which she gave a thankful sigh and went to find George.

'Forgive me, sir,' Longbeard protested as the Noble One pulled on his sleeve. 'I understood our services were no longer required here.'

'Our services, as you call them, wizard, shall always be required in this place. We have a duty to this place.'

'I fail to see why, sir, now we have put the dangerous one to flight and all is now calm,' Longbeard grumbled as his companion settled himself comfortably on the thickest branch of the tree he could find. 'We have bestowed favour after favour on this place.'

'And in return they have bestowed favours upon us,' the Noble One reminded him. 'And none more than the man they call George, who you may recall was ready to sacrifice his happiness for all that matters to us!'

'So what is it I must do now, sir?' Longbeard moaned. 'I have but few dazzles remaining. You know I have still to make my journey of replenishment.'

'If you do not adopt a more cheerful countenance, you wretch,' the Noble One warned him, 'I may push you from this tree. Now see the young people who enter our ground? They need no great dazzle – just a simple kiss of magick. So touch them if you will with a spell that will assuage this young man's disarray.'

Longbeard smiled for the first time in perhaps a century, and then, shaking his head at his own obstinacy, from his belt he undid his favoured leather purse to take from within a tiny heart-shaped jewel which

610

shone with yet another new colour of his own invention.
'I was saving this, sir, for a special occasion.'

'And do you not think this such a moment?'

'Of course, my liege. I see this moment is exactly that.' Longbeard pressed the tiny gemstone against his sovereign's heart and let go his hold of it. For a moment the jewel remained where it was before spinning off into the sky where, visible only to those who had spelt its magick, it burst into a million tiny radiant beams which fell in a gentle healing shower on the lovers in the Kissing Garden beneath.

From that day in the Kissing Garden

Fell not hail, or rain, or any snow,
Nor ever wind blew loudly; but it lies
Deep-meadow'd, happy, fair with orchard lawns
And bowery hollows crown'd with summer seas.

THE END

LOVE SONG
by Charlotte Bingham

'A perfect example of the new, darker romantic fiction . . . a true 24-carat love story'
Sunday Times

Hope Merriott has always thought of herself as truly blessed with her three daughters, Melinda, Rose and Claire, until, that is, the arrival of a fourth daughter, Letty. Loved though she will be, the baby's birth co-incides with the failure of her husband Alexander's newest business venture.

Nevertheless, life at West Dean Avenue continues on its usual cheerful – if improvident – course, until Alexander's Great Aunt Rosabel comes to stay for Christmas. Unaware that a considerable inheritance was dependent upon her fourth child being a boy, Hope is full of seemingly unreasonable forboding when the old lady offers to gift Alexander her large, elegant house, Hatcombe, in Wiltshire.

Overnight, Alexander moves the family from what Hope sees as their cosy life to the loneliness and isolation of Wiltshire's rolling acres. Indeed, once at Hatcombe, many of Hope's premonitions seem about to be realized when Jack Tomm, a neighbour, comes to call on her. Although they intend only to introduce their teenage children to each other, all too soon Jack and Hope fall passionately in love . . .

Award-winning novelist Charlotte Bingham has dazzled readers with an array of spellbinding best-sellers, including the highly acclaimed *To Hear a Nightingale*, *Debutantes* and *Grand Affair*. In *Love Song* she presents an irresistible and heart-rending tale that once more demonstrates her unique storytelling gift.

A Bantam Paperback

0 553 50501 7

A SELECTED LIST OF FINE NOVELS
AVAILABLE FROM BANTAM BOOKS

50329 4	DANGER ZONES	Sally Beauman	£5.99
50630 7	DARK ANGEL	Sally Beauman	£6.99
50631 5	DESTINY	Sally Beauman	£6.99
40727 9	LOVERS AND LIARS	Sally Beauman	£5.99
50326 X	SEXTET	Sally Beauman	£5.99
40803 8	SACRED AND PROFANE	Marcelle Bernstein	£5.99
50469 X	SAINTS AND SINNERS	Marcelle Bernstein	£5.99
40429 6	AT HOME	Charlotte Bingham	£3.99
40432 6	BY INVITATION	Charlotte Bingham	£3.99
40497 0	CHANGE OF HEART	Charlotte Bingham	£5.99
40890 9	DEBUTANTES	Charlotte Bingham	£5.99
40296 X	IN SUNSHINE OR IN SHADOW	Charlotte Bingham	£5.99
40469 2	NANNY	Charlotte Bingham	£5.99
40171 8	STARDUST	Charlotte Bingham	£5.99
40163 7	THE BUSINESS	Charlotte Bingham	£5.99
40895 X	THE NIGHTINGALE SINGS	Charlotte Bingham	£5.99
17635 8	TO HEAR A NIGHTINGALE	Charlotte Bingham	£5.99
50500 9	GRAND AFFAIR	Charlotte Bingham	£5.99
50501 7	LOVE SONG	Charlotte Bingham	£5.99
50717 6	THE KISSING GARDEN	Charlotte Bingham	£5.99
40615 9	PASSIONATE TIMES	Emma Blair	£5.99
40614 0	THE DAFFODIL SEA	Emma Blair	£5.99
40373 7	THE SWEETEST THING	Emma Blair	£5.99
40372 9	THE WATER MEADOWS	Emma Blair	£5.99
40973 5	A CRACK IN FOREVER	Jeannie Brewer	£5.99
50691 9	FOR THE SAKE OF THE CHILDREN		
		June Francis	£5.99
50580 7	SOMEBODY'S GIRL	June Francis	£5.99
40730 9	LOVERS	Judith Krantz	£5.99
40731 7	SPRING COLLECTION	Judith Krantz	£5.99
81290 4	FINISHING TOUCHES	Patricia Scanlan	£5.99
81286 6	FOREIGN AFFAIRS	Patricia Scanlan	£5.99
81288 2	PROMISES, PROMISES	Patricia Scanlan	£5.99
40962 X	MIRROR, MIRROR	Patricia Scanlan	£5.99
81287 4	APARTMENT 3B	Patricia Scanlan	£5.99
40943 3	CITY GIRL	Patricia Scanlan	£5.99